Laura

'Be Thou My Vision'

To Margaret
God bless!
Jo-Anne Berthelsen
Happy 80th!!

JO-ANNE BERTHELSEN

Ark House Press
PO Box 163, North Sydney, NSW, 2059 Australia
Telephone: +61 2 9007 5376
PO Box 47212, Ponsonby, Auckland New Zealand
Telephone: +64 800 534 620
www.arkhousepress.com

Cataloguing in Publication Data:
Berthelsen, Jo-Anne
Laura / Jo-Anne Berthelsen
978-1-921589-09-6 (pbk.)
Fiction

Printed and bound in Australia
Cover design and layout by BBD Agency
www.bbdagency.com

For Heather Field
an inspiring friend
who sees so much
and in loving memory
of
Angela Faith Rice
1973-2009

Acknowledgments

I would like to thank the following people and groups who put time aside to answer my many questions about vision impairment, thereby enabling me to write this novel with as much accuracy and understanding as possible:

General information about vision impairment:
Andrew Head, student, Pacific Hills Christian School, Sydney, NSW
Jo-Anne Green, Royal Institute for Deaf and Blind Children NSW, School Support Service
Ken Martin, Greenacre Church of Christ, Sydney, NSW
Mike Corrigan, Access Technology Consultant, RIDBC NSW

Education issues:
Rosemary Mammino, Information Officer (History), Library Services, Queensland Department of Education and Arts
Christine Douglas, Hon Historian, Brisbane School of Distance Education, Queensland
Leona Kitson, Education and Special Requests Section, Queensland Braille Writing Association
Narbethong State Special School for the Vision Impaired, Brisbane, Queensland

Medical matters:
Edith Trefry, Taylor and Trefry Artificial Eyes, Sydney, NSW
Jim Stewart, ocularist, Royal Brisbane Hospital, Queensland
Trevor Dorahy, artificial (prosthetic) eye specialist, Brisbane, Queensland
Dora Newson, Sydney Eye Hospital Library, NSW
Roy Millar, retired eye specialist, Lower Blue Mountains Church of Christ, NSW
The Royal Australian & New Zealand College of Ophthalmologists, Sydney, NSW

Above all, I wish to acknowledge the debt I owe to my friend Heather Field, now residing in Nashville, Tennessee, USA, for teaching me so much about vision impairment, both directly and indirectly. This story would definitely not have been written unless our lives had intersected as they did under God's hand.

chapter one

Margaret Harding had sensed for weeks that something was wrong. Now, glancing out of the window at Laura and the boys playing in the nearby paddock, she was sure of it. Icy fingers of fear gripped her deep inside. She gasped, as Laura again tripped over and fell flat on her face, in the midst of a valiant effort to keep up with her brothers.

Soon the little girl was on her feet, slightly shocked, but apparently none the worse for wear. She struggled on a few more steps, before stumbling yet again over some obstacle hidden from view in the grass. This time she let out a despairing howl of rage and stayed put, rubbing her eyes hard with her small fists.

Now Jamie had stopped and come back for her, bless him. He could never resist her plaintive cries. Margaret watched him brush his little sister down carefully, take her hand and determinedly begin leading her towards the house.

'Mum! Mum! Laura's gone and fallen over *again*! She's so clumsy—she *never* looks where she's going.'

Margaret picked her daughter up and comforted her. Yet it was more in an attempt to comfort herself, she knew, that she held her close and patted her.

Having safely delivered Laura into his mother's care, Jamie shot off to rejoin

laura

his brothers in their latest escapade. Margaret had no worries about the boys – they were sensible and could look after themselves. It was her daughter, now held tightly in her arms, who caused her to lie awake at nights, tense with anxiety, trying to tell herself that everything was fine, yet knowing in her heart it was not. Not at all.

Laura's sobs had begun to subside. Now she was content to lie quietly against her mother. Margaret gently stroked her hair, remembering how Laura had begun to walk unaided long before her first birthday even, determined to join in with the boys as soon as possible. She had had her share of tumbles, just like any toddler, but it was not long before she was following her brothers everywhere, attempting to copy everything they did. Usually they let her tag along, often piggybacking her around whenever she got tired. But lately, she had become so accident-prone that their patience had begun to wear thin – just like it had today.

'She's a big nuisance!' Greg complained, whenever Laura wanted to go anywhere with them these days. He was almost eight and always the first to voice his unhappiness if things did not go his way, with the result that the family, even Margaret, usually ignored his objections.

'Yeah, she is so too!' Ian could be counted on to add, echoing his older brother's opinion.

Ian knew instinctively, even at five, that he had to stay on the right side of Greg. Jamie would always look after him, but Greg – well, he was just Greg, sometimes sticking up for you, at other times acting like you weren't even there. Ian reckoned he needed all the help he could get, being new at school and quite small for his age. Besides, he wore glasses – and at their school that was asking for trouble. Already he'd learnt it didn't pay to be different.

Margaret would normally have taken little notice of the two younger boys' complaints, but when ten-year-old Jamie reinforced their view as he just had, she knew she could no longer ignore the situation. He loved Laura dearly – in fact, he had doted on her from the very beginning, when they had first placed her in his arms at the small local hospital. It pained her now that even he did not want his little sister around so much.

Perhaps there was more to it than that. Jamie was into the roughest games with his friends and brothers and could give as good as he got, but he was also a sensitive, intelligent kid. He could tell a mile off when she herself was tired or upset.

'Don't wowwy, Mummy! Everythink will be okay,' he had often said to her from an early age, stroking her face gently, when things had occasionally become too difficult for her.

Now Margaret wondered how much of her concern over Laura he was picking up – how much his impatience masked his own worry over both his mother and sister. The night before, when he thought no one was looking, she had noticed him staring intently at Laura's eyes, before holding out a favourite toy to her, his own eyes almost begging her to take it. She had not responded at all. Eventually, he had placed the toy directly in front of her, where it was quickly grabbed up and cuddled. Margaret had watched helplessly, the lump in her throat almost choking her, as, without a word, he had quietly got up and announced he was going to bed.

'But it's early yet, Jamie,' Greg had howled.

They slept in the same room, but Greg was definitely not keen on going there one minute sooner than he needed to.

'Mum, I don't have to go to bed yet, do I? Jamie's a big spoilsport!'

'I'm a bit tired,' Jamie had mumbled rather red-faced, eyes suspiciously bright. 'I'll read for a while – you can come later.'

Margaret had wanted with all her heart to follow him to his room and assure him things would be all right, but her own fears had held her back. Now, as she cuddled Laura and stroked her small blonde head, she came to a decision. She would talk about it again with Ken when he came home – that is, if she could stay awake that long.

Soon Laura's body relaxed and her breathing became deeper. Margaret continued to hold her, telling herself there was plenty of time before she needed to start preparing dinner. It was unusual Laura would want to sleep at this time, she thought to herself – especially after she had already had an afternoon nap. But then she remembered how disturbed Laura's nights had been recently, how she had heard her tossing and turning and moaning softly a number of times. She herself had lain awake for what seemed like hours, after getting up to check on her and straighten the covers yet again. It would be great when Ken could get around to finishing off enclosing part of the side veranda, she thought for the hundredth time, yawning as she did. Then Laura could have her own room, rather than share theirs. Not that that really worried Ken. Nothing disturbed him these days, once he finally came to bed.

Gradually the slanting rays of the late afternoon sun began to form long, wavering patterns on the worn carpet at Margaret's feet. She shifted her weight a little, trying to ease the small, inert body on her lap into a more comfortable position. Laura whimpered, then closed her eyes again, content to stay put. In the distance, Margaret could hear the boys' voices as they shouted excitedly to one another in the midst of an energetic game of Cowboys and Indians. She was proud of them, the way they played so well together – at least most of the time. She loved all four of her children. And she was sure, come Christmas, there'd be

Laura

a fifth. Not that she'd told anyone yet – not even Ken.

Drifting on the edge of sleep herself, her mind played games with her, traversing the years back to the day she and Ken had met. It had been at a church social – he was in the band invited to provide the entertainment. She was new to the area, having recently been appointed to teach at a small primary school nearby. She was aware his parents owned a large store in the town – she'd even caught sight of him there a few times, but his interests had seemed to lie elsewhere. Besides, she'd always been in a hurry, preoccupied with getting home to prepare the next day's lessons. Everything had been so new to her then, so different and challenging. She was living away from home for the first time. She was teaching a class of her own for the first time. She was slowly but surely beginning to find her feet in a small country community.

And soon she was in love for the first time.

By the end of that year, they were engaged. Even now, years later, a smile played around her mouth as she remembered those heady, romantic days. Ken was warm and friendly, a good musician and an energetic member of various local community groups. He had not enjoyed study very much, he told her, so after a brief stint at university, had given it up in favour of helping out in the family business. By the time they met, his parents had retired and moved closer to their only daughter down in Brisbane, who was trying to raise three children on her own. Ken was left in charge of the store, a task he tackled with great gusto but minimal business acumen, as soon became apparent to most of the other storeowners in town at least. However, he was popular, and the business had managed to keep functioning largely on the strength of the family name – that is, until the end of their second year of marriage. By that time, Margaret was expecting their first child and knew she would soon have to give up teaching. She remembered now how she had faced the prospect with considerable reluctance, not only because she loved her pupils and they loved her back, but also because it was obvious by then the family business was in serious financial difficulties.

Suddenly, the same reluctance and uncertainty that had haunted her then was there again in the pit of her stomach, evoking memories she would rather forget – memories of the day, a month after Jamie was born, when the liquidators had arrived and the shop doors closed. Now she felt again the panic that had engulfed her when Ken broke the news. Soon after, they had moved to an old house on several acres of mediocre farmland a few kilometres out of town, renting it from Ken's uncle at a nominal rate. The plan was for Ken to work the farm as best he could, supplementing their income with odd jobs, as well as occasional gigs with his band. By then, his days of entertaining church groups were a thing of the past and he had become well known at several of the local pubs – not only because of his music, but also the extended periods he spent drinking there. Deep emotion stirred in Margaret, as she remembered the heated discussions that had regularly taken place between them in those days.

Eventually, Ken had listened and tried hard to reform. Things had improved, but Margaret was painfully aware he had never quite succeeded in shaking the habit. Not even the arrival of two more sons in the years ahead had served to wean him away from his drinking mates completely, despite the fact that he loved his boys and was immensely proud of them. He spent time with all three whenever he could, yet often, after they were safely in bed, he would find some pressing reason to catch up with one or other of his friends at the pub.

'Got to sort out our next gig, Marg,' was the most common excuse. 'You know how we need the money. The guys and I have to work out some new songs.'

All that had changed markedly, however, when Laura was born. Now, even as she half dozed herself, her arms around their daughter, Margaret remembered Ken's reaction when Laura had first made her appearance. He had been speechless at first, but then had not tried to hide his delight.

'Wow, a girl! She's so gorgeous, Marg – just like her mother,' he had burst out.

Looking down at Laura in her lap now, she could still see the broad smile on his face, as he held his daughter for the first time. From that moment on, Laura had enchanted him. More than that, she had won his heart completely.

'I'll be such a good Dad to you,' he had whispered softly, tears in his eyes, as he gently stroked her cheek.

Mostly, he had kept his word. He had tried to make more of a go of the farm, clearing and ploughing paddocks that had long been neglected and tending the old fruit trees his uncle had planted years earlier. He had taken the boys with him as much as he could while doing these jobs, in order to help her out with the baby. And by and large, he had stayed away from the pubs. If the band needed to get together, they met in an old hall not far away, where they could practise without disturbing anyone. And when their gigs were on, Ken was usually the first to pack up and leave afterwards. Better not to hang around drinking away any of the profits, he had told the others straight up.

In the evenings as he relaxed after a hard day, he had loved to hold Laura in his arms and look down at her perfect little features – especially her big blue eyes, so like his own. Then, as she had grown, he was in his element playing all sorts of pretend games with her, or reading her first books to her, while she sat snuggled up close to him on his lap. Margaret loved to hear them laughing together, enjoying each other's company.

But lately, there had been much less laughter from Laura. She was not

Laura

sleeping well at nights and had been clingy and irritable during the day – and her clumsiness had become so marked, that, against Ken's wishes, Margaret had finally taken her to their local doctor.

'Marg, she's probably dreaming a lot or something and just gets clumsy when she's tired,' Ken had said irritably. 'She'll be right – don't waste the doctor's time!'

Margaret knew he was worried, but could not face the dreaded thought that something was actually wrong with his beautiful little princess. He had always preferred to stick his head in the sand and pretend everything was all right – like when they had lost the family business. That was the way he coped.

Looking down again at the sleeping bundle in her arms, Margaret remembered how she had listened to the doctor's verdict with a mixture of relief and disquiet. It was obvious to her that day that he was tired of seeing too many patients with trivial problems and that he was of the opinion Laura was another one.

'I can't find anything wrong with her, Mrs Harding. Whatever's troubling her, she'll get over it in no time, I'm sure. You should know that after three active boys – don't worry so much!' was his very peremptory diagnosis.

Margaret left, but the next day quietly took herself off to the new doctor in town. This time Laura had been examined a little more carefully, but no clear diagnosis had been forthcoming. Still not fully satisfied, on a rare visit to Brisbane to see her mother, she had taken Laura to her own old family doctor. While he could find nothing specifically wrong, he knew Margaret well enough to sense she would not fuss unnecessarily.

'If you want a further opinion, I can refer you to a paediatrician in the city,' he had offered, 'but unfortunately he doesn't come cheap.'

Margaret had taken the referral letter and made the appointment. That was the easy part. Telling Ken was much more difficult.

'No, Marg, she doesn't need a specialist!' he had responded angrily. 'It's not only the money – it's just that I'm sure you're making too big a deal out of it. Let her be for a while – she'll come good, you'll see.'

Beneath the anger, Margaret could hear panic in his voice. She gave in, knowing it was useless to argue, and cancelled the appointment.

Laura had not improved, however much Ken liked to pretend otherwise over the next weeks. She cried more and could not tell them exactly what was wrong, except that her eyes hurt. She rubbed them a lot and was constantly falling over things, just as she had with the boys only an hour or so earlier. She had been much more lethargic too.

Suddenly Laura stirred in her arms and whimpered, her little hands rubbing her eyes once again.

'Hurting, Mummy,' she cried, still half asleep. 'Make it better!'

Brought back to reality with a jolt, Margaret kissed her softly and smoothed the fine, slightly damp curls off her forehead.

'What say we give you a nice warm bath? Daddy will be home soon and then we'll have some dinner. It's one of your favourites too – sausages. Yum!'

Ken was tired. He had been fixing fences along their western boundary most of the day, not even bothering to return home for lunch. It was late afternoon now – time to finish off and clean up before dinner. Momentarily, he toyed with the idea of heading into town for one quick drink with his mates. After all, he hadn't seen them for ages – it felt like he'd been stuck on the damn farm working for months.

The thought no sooner came, however, than he dismissed it, although not without a struggle. Normally he loved this part of the day – but lately he had begun to dread it. Not that he didn't like being with Marg and the kids. Sure, the boys were always rowdy, climbing over him and fighting for his attention, but he could handle that. It was just that he found it hard to see his Laura so unhappy and obviously not herself. It worried him too much.

Better make an effort to talk to Marg tonight about it, he decided, as he packed up his gear and slowly headed home.

Margaret greeted him with a quick smile and a kiss, but he could see she was pale, with dark rings under her eyes. She was trying to balance a tearful Laura on her hip, while she finished getting dinner.

'How're my big girl and my little girl doing? Not so well?' he asked lightly, more for something to say than anything. 'Just give me time to clean myself up a bit and I'll be right back to help out.'

Laura whimpered louder and reached out for him, but he had already disappeared in the direction of the shower. Finally Jamie came to the rescue, distracting her with her favourite dolls. Soon dinner was on the table and food took priority over everything else. Laura was quiet for a while, content to chew on her pieces of sausage, as she tried hard to make the peas stay on her spoon. Margaret ate hurriedly, in between helping Ian with his food. She knew the lull would not last for long.

She was right. Soon Laura grew restless and wanted to sit on her father's lap. Margaret let her climb out of the old high chair, taking her time cleaning her up in order to let Ken finish his dinner. He must be hungry – and besides, she wanted to give him some breathing space.

Eventually, Ken took Laura and sat her on his knee, while he helped Ian with the rest of his dinner. Margaret quickly ate the remains of her own meal, then served a simple dessert of jelly and ice cream, which all four children greeted with

13

Laura

whoops of delight. Ken helped Laura eat hers where she was on his lap, while he talked to the boys.

'So what did you guys get up to after school today?' he asked. 'No fights, I hope.'

'We played Cowboys and Indians in the bush up the hill, Dad,' Jamie explained. 'Ian and I were cowboys and Greg and Laura were Indians, but then I had to bring Laura inside, so after that we made a cubby up there.'

'Yeah, Dad, we were having a good game, until Laura spoilt it all. She kept falling over and when she cried, Jamie and Ian could find us real easy,' Greg complained.

'We would've found you anyway, so stop whingeing!' Jamie promptly responded.

'Would not have either.'

'Would so too.'

'Yeah, we would so, Greg,' Ian added, joining in the argument as he usually did by supporting whoever seemed to be winning at that strategic moment.

'That's enough, boys!' Ken cut in sternly. 'I guess she couldn't help it, after all.'

'I know she can't, Dad – but she does spoil things for us a bit right now,' Jamie said then.

It was not his usual way to complain about his sister. Reluctantly, Ken enquired further.

'How's that, Jamie? She's not even three yet.'

'I know – but lately you and Mum never have much time to play with us at nights or read to us, because you're so busy looking after Laura, when she's crying because her eyes are sore. I wish someone could fix them up.'

To Jamie's horror, his voice wobbled on the last few words. Ken could not help noticing the tears that began to well up in his son's eyes, but made no comment. Quickly, Jamie jumped up from the table.

'I'll go and wash the dishes,' he muttered, grabbing his own plates and making a dash for the kitchen – but not before Margaret saw him lift the front of his old T-shirt and surreptitiously wipe his eyes with it.

'Come on, Greg,' Margaret intervened, 'clear the table and take the dishes in to Jamie! You know that's your job. Ian, I think the bin needs emptying. Maybe, if you hurry, we can all play a game of hide and seek.'

Ken could hear them continuing to squabble in the kitchen, until Margaret silenced them with the threat of early bedtime. He sighed, as he moved to his favourite old lounge chair. Laura still clung to him, so he manoeuvred both of them into a reasonably comfortable position, before closing his eyes and leaning his head back. I could sure do with a beer, he thought to himself – but he knew Marg hated him drinking with the boys around and he didn't want to disappoint her. She had enough on her mind right now. They all did.

The boys managed to squeeze in their game of hide and seek before bedtime, although it was not without incident. Laura naturally wanted to join in, but in trying to hide alongside Jamie, had fallen over a chair that had been left jutting out from the table and crashed to the floor. Margaret quickly picked her up and carried her onto the veranda. Maybe the cool evening breeze would soothe her.

'You stay with the boys!' she yelled to Ken above the din. 'They want you to keep playing – I'll look after her.'

Somehow none of them had the heart for it after that and the game soon ended on a rather lame note. Laura's cries could still be heard outside, as Ken read one last book to Ian before bed.

'Daddy, do you think Laura will be all right soon?' he asked in a sleepy voice, as Ken tucked him in.

'Sure she will, mate,' Ken replied confidently. 'Don't you remember how you used to fall over lots when you were little?'

'Well, sort of, but I was just a baby then – and I didn't do it as much as she does, anyway.'

Ken agreed, but didn't let on, as he kissed his youngest son.

''Night, Ian – sleep tight!'

He did not fare much better with the two older boys, as he went to say good night to them. At first they were unusually quiet, until Greg suddenly spoke up.

'Go on, Jamie – ask him! You said you would.'

'Ask me what, Jamie?'

Jamie hesitated, but finally the words came tumbling out.

'Dad, if we gave you our pocket money, could you and Mum find a doctor in Brisbane who might know how to fix Laura? Her eyes always hurt and she keeps falling over – '

' – and we don't like it,' Greg chimed in then. 'If she was better, we could have a lot more fun.'

Ken was now the one who had difficulty finding his voice. Greg's motives were no doubt mixed, but he could tell by the look on Jamie's face that he had Laura's best interests at heart, as always. In fact, now Jamie had buried his face in his pillow and Ken could see his shoulders shaking with the effort of trying to cry quietly. Without a word, he ruffled his eldest son's hair and let his hand rest on his shoulder, before moving to Greg's bed to do the same.

'Thanks, guys! I'll talk to Mum about it,' was all he said in the end, as he turned out the light.

Laura

Laura had cried herself to sleep, as Margaret had walked around outside with her. Now Ken sat in the dark on their front veranda, waiting while she was put to bed and thinking about what he needed to say next. He was not the best at apologies, but he knew that had to be part of it.

Eventually, Margaret came and sat down in the old wicker chair next to him with a deep sigh.

Slowly, he reached his hand across the space between them.

'Marg, I've been thinking – and so have the boys. I reckon I made a mistake when I told you we didn't need to take Laura to that specialist in Brisbane – a *big* one. And I'm sorry. Now Jamie, Greg and I all want to find the best doctor possible to look at Laura and see what can be done.'

Ken recounted what had just happened. Margaret could not hold back the tears and soon Ken was holding her close, his own eyes moist.

'I feel so relieved! Something *has* to be done – for Laura's sake, as well as ours. And I'm so proud of the boys – they've tried really hard to look after their sister.'

She lapsed into silence for a few moments, before taking a deep breath and plunging on.

'Ken, I'm not sure how you'll feel about this, but ... Ken, I think I'm pregnant again! So there'll be another one around to care for soon. It'll be hard going for a while, but we'll manage. I've always wanted a big family, as you know, so I'm really happy about it. Laura will love having a baby brother or sister around. I won't know for sure until I go to the doctor this week, but I'll get him to give me another referral for Laura while I'm there.'

She was babbling now, unable to look at him. For what seemed forever, he said nothing. Then, to her relief, he hugged her tight.

'Poor Marg – no wonder you've looked so tired, what with Laura's troubles and now this new baby coming. That's wonderful news – and of course I'm happy about it! But that's all the more reason we need to see what can be done for Laura right away. Somehow – *without* the boys' offer of help – we'll find the money we need.'

That week, Margaret's pregnancy was confirmed, but they decided not to tell the boys straight away. Now that Ken requested it as well, their family doctor begrudgingly agreed to refer Laura to an old paediatrician friend of his in Brisbane.

'He'll probably think I've gone crazy referring you to him, but I'll do it if you really want another opinion,' he said gruffly, still sure the problem was simple childish clumsiness.

The paediatrician in Brisbane had been somewhat brusque and non-committal after examining Laura, but concerned enough to refer them to an eye specialist at the Children's Hospital for tests. When Margaret finally managed to get an appointment and arrange to make the trip once again, she was hopeful there would be some sort of breakthrough at last. Laura had days when she seemed somewhat better, but even with the medication the paediatrician had prescribed, she had shown little real improvement.

This time they stayed with Margaret's mother in her small unit not far from the hospital, for the three days it took to complete the tests the new specialist had ordered. For Margaret, these were anxious days, not only at the hospital but also at home. She knew her mother wanted to be helpful, but Margaret found it hard to relax around her, particularly with Laura so unsettled. Jean fussed so much and seemed to take it as a personal affront whenever Laura refused to be comforted by her, preferring her mother.

'There's got to be something really wrong,' Jean would say many times over, until Margaret almost wanted to scream. 'Children *always* stop crying for me.'

They could not believe it then, when the ophthalmologist, a courteous, quietly spoken younger man, explained that nothing untoward had been discovered in any of the tests they had conducted.

'If nothing's shown up, then there really is very little we can do – I'm sure you understand that. Bring her back in a couple of months' time, if you're still worried, but I have a feeling things will settle down. She's not much over two and a half, is she? Sometimes children that age are a little difficult to manage – as my wife and I are finding out ourselves right now. Perhaps it's your little girl's way of getting attention in a noisy, busy family. Three boys and a girl must be quite a handful.'

Margaret felt a surge of anger rise up that threatened to overwhelm her, but she tried to respond as calmly as possible.

'Doctor, I think I know how young children behave – and I assure you Laura isn't falling over on purpose, nor is she only *pretending* to have sore eyes. Are there any further tests or X-rays that can be done, just to make sure?'

The doctor tried to answer politely enough, but could not help a slightly patronising and impatient tone creeping into his voice. He had noticed Margaret was not dressed in the latest fashion, to put it mildly. Probably poorly educated too, he decided – so why bother to try to explain things to her further? Besides, he was tired and extremely overworked – and he'd had his fill of overanxious mothers for the day. His words came out shorter than he meant them to and he regretted them the moment they left his lips – but by then it was too late. He had lost Margaret's confidence forever.

'Mrs Harding, please don't waste my time any further! I have other children

laura

to see to who really *are* very ill. If you want to spend hours waiting around in doctor's surgeries and having more unnecessary tests, then that's your business, but it's not what I'd suggest. As I said – she'll grow out of it.'

With as much dignity as she could muster, Margaret quickly rose, clutching Laura in her arms. The tears began spilling over as she made to leave the room. Hastily, the young doctor sprang to his feet.

'Mrs Harding, please forgive me – I'm so sorry! It's just that we're so overworked here...'

But Margaret turned away, brushing unseeingly past nurses and patients alike as she hurried out of the building.

Later, she had almost no memory of the long, tiring drive home from Brisbane that day. Fortunately, Laura slept most of the way, as Margaret fought to gain control of her whirling thoughts and emotions. There *was* something wrong with Laura – she was convinced of that. But what could she do, in the face of the lack of medical evidence to support her claims? Only hope and pray, she supposed now – but it had been a long time since she or Ken had prayed about anything. And right now God seemed very, very far away – certainly not at all interested in their little girl.

Ken did not say much when he was told the news.

'She'll be right, Marg,' he mumbled awkwardly, trying to comfort her. 'Anyway, nothing we can do about it right now, I guess. If it doesn't settle down though, like the doctor said, we could ask to be referred to someone else – no harm in a second opinion.'

'But he was already the fourth doctor we've seen,' she responded tearfully. 'How many more won't believe us when we tell them something's wrong with her?'

Two months passed – months that were difficult for the whole family. Laura was seen by the local doctor several more times before he reluctantly referred them to another paediatrician in Brisbane. After examining Laura carefully and studying the previous test results, he also refused to believe anything was radically wrong with her. Appointments with a local naturopath followed, who suggested a complete change in Laura's diet, but after some weeks of trying to get her to eat things that were unfamiliar to her, and with no great improvement resulting from the new regimen, Margaret gave up persevering along that route.

Laura seemed to settle a little more the following week, but was still listless during the day. Now she rarely tried to follow her brothers around when they played in the bushes above the paddocks or fossicked along the nearby creek bed. Any confidence she had developed in earlier months to run here and there with them seemed to have deserted her. And she definitely walked more slowly and cautiously these days, Margaret noticed, taking her time to look where she put her feet. She seemed happiest playing nearby on the floor with her favourite toys, or curled up in Margaret's lap watching TV. But that lap was fast disappearing with the coming of the new baby and any energy Margaret had was stretched to the limit, as Laura clung to her more and more. Whenever she sat mending the boys' clothes or peeling vegetables, Laura would want to be held. Often Margaret thought she noticed her feeling around on the table in front of her until she found the thimble or cotton reel or saucepan lid she wanted to play with. Was it that she was just tired—or could she really not see them?

Finally, a comment from Ken one night galvanised Margaret into further action. He and Laura were reading a bedtime book together after dinner, while Margaret supervised the boys as they finished their various jobs. She sat down to rest for a minute, closing her eyes and stretching her tired limbs, but as she opened them again, she found Ken's eyes on her, a look of uncertainty – almost of fear – in them.

'Marg,' he said quietly. 'I hate to say this, but I think Laura might be having real trouble seeing these pictures or even knowing which one I'm pointing to. Have you noticed that? She likes to listen to the stories and cuddle up close to me, but she doesn't seem so interested in what's on the pages. And her eyes don't look right to me either – the pupils seem really big. Is that normal?'

Margaret turned Laura's face gently towards her and examined her eyes closely. Not that she needed to – she knew what she would see. Then together they watched Laura turn her head at an awkward angle and move closer to the book she was holding, until her nose almost touched the paper. Her eyes were screwed up and her little pink tongue was poking out of her mouth, as she concentrated fully on the task in hand. Then she suddenly gave up and leant back against her father, whimpering and rubbing her eyes and putting her thumb in her mouth. She'd been doing that more and more, Margaret had noticed – as if she needed extra comfort that none of them could give her.

'I don't know, Ken,' was all Margaret could say, the lump in her throat too huge.

Ken's face was white and his hand stroking Laura's hair shook a little.

'What'll we do, Marg? There must be *something* more ... the doctors must be able to help *somehow*.'

They sat staring miserably at each other, until Margaret finally made up her mind.

'I'm driving to Brisbane again tomorrow, Ken,' she announced, desperation clear in her voice. 'I'm going straight to the hospital – and I'm going to sit there until they give us some answers. Surely *someone* there will help us this time.'

Laura

She and Laura left home before sunrise, while the boys were still asleep. They were among the first of the outpatients to arrive at the busy Children's Hospital and spent all day moving from one waiting room to the next, traversing long corridors between medical departments. They sat for hours, as one specialist after another asked endless questions and repeatedly examined Laura, until she clung sobbing to her mother and refused to let them touch her. All the way, Margaret had to remain firm and unyielding, determined not to leave until she had received some answers.

Exhausted, she and Laura stayed overnight at her mother's, returning to the hospital the following morning for further consultations. They passed through the hands of the lowliest of interns, then on further, step by step, right up to the most experienced of paediatricians, neurologists and ophthalmologists. Margaret would not take no for an answer – and they seemed to recognise that.

Finally, after more hours of waiting, as the various specialists compared notes and checked X-rays and test results once more, Margaret was called in to consult with two of the most senior staff members.

One of them, a tall, thin man with a kindly face, began to talk gently to her.

'Mrs Harding, my name's John Brandon – I'm head of ophthalmology here. And this is Dr Vincent, one of our surgeons. Perhaps it's best if I get straight to the point. I'm afraid I've got some bad news for you. You were right in thinking Laura's eyesight has been getting worse – unfortunately we've found tumours growing in both her eyes. The tumour in the right eye has possibly been there since before birth even, but doesn't seem to have caused any trouble until recently. I'm afraid there's no gentle way to say this, but it would be best if my colleague here operated as soon as possible, to remove both of Laura's eyes. You see, if we don't, there's a strong possibility the cancer will spread through the optic nerve into her brain, or maybe to other parts of her body through the bloodstream – and then she wouldn't have long to live at all. Even if we don't remove her eyes, she'd be blind soon anyway – so it would be far better to try to save her life, rather than hold onto what sight she now has. Perhaps if we had seen her even a couple of months ago, we might have been able to save the sight in her left eye at least – but I doubt it. Who knows? Now I'm afraid it's too late for that. I'm extremely sorry, Mrs Harding. This must be so difficult for you!'

chapter two

It was just as well Margaret was holding on tightly to Laura at that point, trying to comfort her. Now she crushed her daughter to her, cradling her face against her chest, with her hand over her little ear, as if to shield her from hearing the awful words the doctor had uttered. Having to hold Laura also helped her fight the shakiness she could feel in her arms and legs and the strange, weak sensation that seemed to be sweeping over her.

'Oh no – no! That can't be right!' she heard herself say in a trembling voice, as if from a long way off. 'She can't lose her eyes – she's not even three yet! She *has* to have her eyes – how will she manage otherwise?'

Dr Brandon had by now moved to sit next to Margaret. He felt great pity for her, but knew he had to speak firmly and keep things as professional as possible.

'Mrs Harding, as I said, Laura *will* lose her sight, whether we operate or not. But she'll most certainly lose her life as well, if we don't. There's really no choice, you know. And no time to lose, since this cancer is particularly malignant. A pity we couldn't have seen her weeks ago.'

'But I tried – no one would take any notice of me! Then, when we did finally get to a specialist, nothing showed up in the tests they ran. Oh, I can't believe this! Why didn't the doctors pick it up earlier?'

Laura

'I can't say for sure,' Dr Brandon responded slowly, 'but I think the main reason could be that usually this type of condition is hereditary – yet neither you nor your husband has had any problems with your eyes. So it's really quite an unusual case. Also, you told me your three boys have had no problems either, so there'd be no obvious reason to think along those lines – although I'd like to check their eyes as soon as we can, just to make doubly sure they're fine. Then sometimes it's not until further tests are conducted that the real problem emerges, as it has now. Undoubtedly, too, the tumours have grown very fast in the past few weeks – they may not have been large enough to show up at all on x-rays until now. And finally ... I hate to say this, but doctors are just people, after all, Mrs Harding. Sometimes they do make mistakes and misdiagnose. Of course, even now you may prefer to get a second opinion – but I warn you, the longer we wait, the more difficult the operation will be. If we're able to do a few more tests tomorrow, we could perhaps even fit her in before the end of the week.'

'I ... I don't know what to say – I can't seem to think clearly at all. Do you want an answer straight away? Or can we go home first? I ... I really need to talk to my husband before deciding anything,' Margaret managed to gasp out, before great, shuddering sobs began to rack her body.

Dr Brandon gently tried to lift Laura from Margaret's lap, but she hung on tightly, determined to stay where she was. Alarmed by her mother's sobs, her own wails soon increased in volume. A nurse was summoned to help, but her gentle, cajoling efforts to entice Laura away were completely ignored. Even her attempts to prise Laura's arms free from where they were locked firmly around her mother's neck met with no success whatsoever. Helpless, Dr Brandon patted Margaret awkwardly on the shoulder, before instructing the nurse to remain with her, as he made to leave.

'Dr Vincent and I need to check on several of our other patients now, but I'll come back in about half an hour. We'll decide then what to do next.'

It was fortunate that Dr Brandon took longer than he had intended. By the time he returned, Laura was still in her mother's arms, but fast asleep, exhausted by all the emotion of the day. Margaret was more composed, but very pale and shaken. And she had come to a decision. Before the doctor was able even to open his mouth, she began speaking.

'Dr Brandon, I know you said you want to operate as soon as possible – but I *have* to take Laura home first. The nurse has already phoned my husband for me and told him we'll be there later tonight. I have to talk about it with him – and I can't do that without seeing him face to face. Besides, if the operation goes ahead – and I know in my heart it has to – I want Laura to see her father and her brothers and her home just once more before .... I mean, I know she's not even three yet, but perhaps she'll remember ...'

Her voice faltered, as the horror of what lay ahead for Laura swept over her once more. Her eyes filled with tears and, as she looked directly at Dr Brandon, he found he could not find it within himself to resist their unspoken plea for understanding and compassion. He was silent for some time, before clearing his throat and answering her rather gruffly.

'Well ... Laura's case is extremely urgent, as I've explained already – but I can understand why you feel you need to do this for her and for your family. ... I tell you what – let's compromise here! Phone your husband and tell him you won't be home tonight after all. Stay here in Brisbane and bring Laura here tomorrow so we can run final tests on her. Then go home, but be sure to bring her back again before dinner, say, on Sunday evening. We'll operate on Monday. We have to, Mrs Harding.'

Margaret knew she had no alternative. All she could do was nod and whisper a few words to him.

'We'll be here, Dr Brandon – thank you!'

In the end, she asked the nurse to phone Ken the second time. She knew she would be unable to speak without breaking down – and she did not want that to happen. He had enough troubles trying to care for the rest of the family while she was in Brisbane, as well as doing everything around the farm. She left quickly, carrying a still sleeping Laura to the car and gently placing her in her seat.

It was painful explaining the situation to her mother and then enduring her endless questions and constant fussing. She meant to be kind, Margaret knew – but what she craved right then was quietness, to try to still the whirring in her head and come to grips with the situation. She went to bed early, but lay awake for hours, her mind filled with the horror of it all and the awful prospect of having to tell Ken.

The next day, she and Laura were at the hospital before eight, ready for the necessary tests to be done. Dr Brandon had scheduled them as early as possible, at Margaret's request. She wanted to be home soon after lunch, in order to talk to Ken without the boys around.

As she finally drove in their gate, she was relieved to see Ken's old ute still parked near the back shed. He must have waited for them to arrive before heading back out to finish fixing the fences. Then he was at the door to greet them, lifting Laura out of the car and hugging her tight.

'How's my girl?' he asked, kissing her all over her face. 'All better?'

Laura smiled and hugged him back, trying to plant big kisses on his face in return. She seemed refreshed this morning, after a reasonably good night's sleep and a further nap during the drive home.

Laura

Was it all a bad dream, Margaret asked herself, as she watched the two of them together? Yet she knew the answer to that in her heart already – and she knew too that the moment would not last.

Soon Ken put Laura down to kiss Margaret and help her with their cases, while Laura made her way to the pen behind the nearby shed to check on her precious chickens. The next minute she was face down in the dirt, having stumbled over Ian's bike left in the middle of the yard. She sat up, wailing loudly, streaks of dirt on her cheeks now where her little hands had rubbed her eyes.

In that same moment, as Margaret still stood encircled in Ken's arms, looking up at him, she noticed his bloodshot eyes and the dark rings under them. Her heart turned over. He'd been drinking again, she was sure.

Silently, she went to pick up Laura and they moved inside. She watched Ken carefully over Laura's head, but said nothing. In the end, he brought it up himself.

'I'm sure glad you two are home. It's been tough trying to juggle everything and look after the boys. And I'm afraid I drank a bit much last night, so I'm not feeling the best today – sorry Marg! It was okay – it was after the boys were in bed, but I know you don't like it. Now you're back though, things will be fine again.'

Margaret took a deep breath and tried to swallow the lump in her throat. Better to tell him immediately, she decided. Anyway, she needed his support, just as she knew he'd need hers.

Now Ken was talking again.

'I have to get going and fix the fences up in the back paddock – I meant to do them this morning, but I wasn't really up to it. But time for a coffee first, I reckon. Think I need a strong one – and you look as if you do too. What did the doctors say? Do you have to take Laura back again, or is this the end of it for a while?'

Margaret forced herself to frame the words she hated to have to say, as she continued to hold Laura close.

'Ken … this is awful news, but I have to take Laura back to the hospital again by Sunday night, so the doctors can operate on Monday. They only let me bring her home because I insisted I wanted her to see you and the boys before they did anything. Ken … she has cancer in both eyes – the tumours were probably there before she was even born. She … she has to have her eyes removed, Ken – as soon as possible!'

Ken stared at Margaret, horror gradually dawning on his face, as he took in what she had said. Then he began to shake his head, at the same time moving to sit beside her, lifting Laura onto his own lap to hold her close against him.

'But why? What happened? Why didn't the other doctors pick this up before now? Surely *someone* would have noticed it?'

Margaret simply looked at him, unable to answer.

'Oh my God ... are you *sure*, Marg? Did you see the x-rays? What if this doctor's wrong? The others didn't find the problem – why would this doctor find something when they didn't? ... Marg, this *can't* be right!' Ken continued desperately.

Tears were rolling down Margaret's cheeks now and her shoulders shook with sobs.

'Ken, I asked all the same questions – there's no doubt Dr Brandon's found what the problem is. It all makes so much sense and explains the changes we've noticed in Laura's eyes – why her sight seemed to be getting worse and why she's been rubbing her eyes so much and crying. Of course I hate the thought of saying yes to this operation – but I think we have to. If we don't, then Laura will only get worse and – Ken, he says she'll die otherwise!'

Now Margaret cried as if her heart would break. Ken shifted Laura a little on his lap, so he could put his free arm around his wife and hold her against him as well, her head on his shoulder. Yet he knew he could in no way comfort her – he was too shocked himself to do anything more than make this almost involuntary movement towards her. They sat silent, locked together in their misery.

Eventually Laura herself broke the silence.

'Mummy, I hungry!'

Without a word, Ken got up and went to find some milk and a biscuit for her. When he returned, Margaret was a little more composed. There were various things they needed to talk about now, before the boys came home.

'Ken, I know you're still trying to take it all in, but we have to decide a few things together,' she managed. 'Firstly, are you agreed that we have to go ahead with the op? If you are, then perhaps we can try to make these next couple of days really special for Laura. I'd want her to remember as much as she could – all our faces, what the flowers and trees look like – and her chickens and the other animals. Maybe the ocean and the beach too. Perhaps we could all go out to the coast and have a swim ...'

Margaret was weeping as she spoke, the words coming out in short bursts. Ken was crying too – big tears that seemed to spring out of some deep dark well inside him. Laura, obviously sensing something was wrong, clutched her father's shirt, her head leaning against his heart as she munched on her biscuit.

'It's okay, Marg. We'll get through this – you'll see. My little girl's a fighter, aren't you dear?' Ken managed to say, stroking Laura's hair.

Even as he spoke, the difficulties ahead for her and for them all began to hit home. Yet he tried to collect himself and banish such thoughts from his mind.

Laura

Better just to take one step at a time and let the future look after itself. They'd manage somehow. They'd have to. Yet he had to ask at least one question at this stage.

'I ... I don't suppose there's any other way of getting rid of these tumours is there, Marg, other than removing her eyes? Or even if they could remove just *one* eye she'd still at least be able to see. Did you ask him about that?'

'I didn't have to – Dr Brandon told me straight up there's nothing else we can do. And he said it was a pity we didn't bring her to him earlier – when I tried so hard and took her to doctor after doctor, but no one would listen.'

'Shh – it's okay, Marg! You did your best – you did all you could. Don't upset yourself about what might have been. If anyone's to blame, it's me. I was the one who didn't want you to go to the specialist in Brisbane in the first place.'

They sat silent, lost in their grief and misery. Eventually, Ken spoke again, his voice tentative and tinged with horror.

'Marg, what do they do when they operate? Do they just take out her eyes... and then that's that? I mean ... what's she going to *look* like?'

'I don't know, Ken – I don't even want to think about it. Dr Brandon didn't say – there was no time. I probably wouldn't have taken it in anyway.'

'Well, I guess if that's what has to be done to save her, then we'll have to go ahead – but Marg, when you see this doctor next, ask him again if there's any way that one eye at least can be saved – just to make doubly sure. We have to fight to the last for her sake. Will they let you stay at the hospital with her?'

'I'm not sure – I hope so, but I guess I'll have to go by what they say. I don't want to be away for long though, Ken – I don't want you trying to manage everything. I wish your parents could help, but I know they can't let your sister down. And my mother would never cope. Anyway, I know she can't get time off right now. I'm sure the boys will try to help as much as they can – but they're only kids, after all.'

By now Laura was getting restless and demanding their attention. Ken tried to quieten her, but she wriggled off his lap and headed for the door, falling over his old work boots left untidily nearby in the process. He picked her up, patting her tenderly but rather mechanically, his mind still numbed by the horror of what lay ahead for her. How would she cope growing up and going through life blind? How many more falls like this would she have? Would she always need someone beside her, guiding her, caring for her? How would they manage things for her? So many questions tumbling through his brain – a brain that today, of all days, could not cope with such an onslaught. He knew he had to get out, to be by himself and work out his frustration and confusion on postholes and fencing. Unceremoniously handing Laura over to Margaret, he mumbled his excuses and turned to leave.

'Ken ... wait! We have to work out what we're going to do. What will we tell the boys? And what do you think ...'

Margaret was frantically calling out after him now, as he strode across the yard, willing him to stay and share their grief, but soon she fell silent, knowing her pleas were falling on deaf ears. Wearily, she moved back inside, clutching a now crying Laura.

It was not long before the boys arrived home, running into the house and talking over the top of one another in their excitement.

'Hi, Mum! Hi, Laura! It's great you're home again,' Jamie yelled enthusiastically. 'Dad was good, but you cook better than he does.'

'Yeah, Mum – I hate Dad's cooking! I'm glad you're home,' Greg grumbled, unable nevertheless to hide his delight.

'Me too,' Ian added, not wanting to be left out.

Laura brightened momentarily when she heard her brothers' voices. As Margaret sat watching them, she wondered with a pang how many more such occasions she would witness. How would the boys manage to play with a little sister who was totally blind? Already they were finding it hard. And would Laura remember her brothers' faces? Tears began to well up in her eyes, but she quickly brushed them away, hoping the boys would not notice her distress. This was not the time to tell them about the operation, she decided. Better to wait until Ken came home.

But Jamie had noticed. Carefully avoiding her eyes, he began talking softly to his sister.

'Laura, how about you come with me and we'll feed the chickens together? Then I'll take you for a ride on my bike around the yard, if you like.'

As he had known she would, Laura sat back and clapped gleefully at the prospect. He took her by the hand and they headed down the steps and across the yard. At first, she tried to keep up with him as best she could, but eventually he swung her up and piggybacked her the rest of the way. Soon Greg and Ian followed, as Jamie had secretly hoped they might. He knew when his Mum needed to be alone. Something was really worrying her today, he could tell. And they hadn't even asked her how Laura had got on at the doctor's. Maybe it was something to do with that – he'd find out later at teatime, when Dad was home.

Teatime came and went, however, with no sign of Ken. At one stage, Margaret thought she heard the ute being driven along the fire trail that followed the back fence line until it joined a rough track that eventually led to the main road into town. A deep foreboding engulfed her. Perhaps Ken had been unable to face coming home and had headed into town instead. Yet she did not want to let the

Laura

children see her fear – and she had no time to dwell on it anyway.

'Let's eat, everyone!' she announced brightly, after waiting half an hour past their usual dinnertime. 'Something must have held Dad up. He'll get here when he can.'

For once, Margaret was glad of the boys' constant chatter and minor squabbles around the table, as she helped Laura with her food. It kept her mind off things – and for a moment, she could pretend everything was still normal in their little family. But not for long. Soon Jamie remembered the question he had forgotten to ask earlier.

'Mum, how did Laura go at the hospital? Did the specialist find out what's wrong?'

'Can he make her better now?' Greg added.

'Whoa – one question at a time!' Margaret forced herself to say with a smile, in order to give herself time to think how to respond.

Eventually, with three pairs of eyes looking enquiringly at her across the table, she realised she could not put the moment off much longer. If only Ken would come home! Perhaps he would in the next few minutes – then they could explain things together.

'Let's deal with the dishes first, boys,' she said eventually and as firmly as possible. 'Then when your jobs are done and when you've had your baths, we'll sit down and I'll tell you what's happening for Laura. Maybe we can play a game too. I'm sure Dad will be here long before then too.'

To her relief, the boys co-operated reasonably well that night. Even Greg cleared the table and stacked the dishes without much complaining. They also managed their own baths quite well, but Margaret found it difficult to bend down and help a squirming Laura, who wanted to play with her yellow ducks and bright pink sponge fish even longer than usual. Yet she did not have the heart to stop her. Come Monday, she suddenly realised with a pang, Laura would never be able to catch a glimmer of their bright colours again. Perhaps even now it was more their shape and texture that interested her and captured her imagination. She dried and dressed her, looking intently into her big blue eyes again as she did – eyes the exact replicas of Ken's.

Where was he, she asked herself for the tenth time, all the while knowing the answer in her heart.

Now three pairs of enquiring eyes were looking at her once again, as she sat with Laura in her lap, the boys sprawled on the carpet nearby.

'It's not good news, boys, I'm afraid,' she began, trying vainly to swallow the big lump in her throat. 'Laura's specialist is a very nice man and he knows lots, because he's one of the main doctors at the hospital. He says there are some tumours growing in her eyes, so that's why she hasn't been able to see properly lately. And they've been making her eyes hurt – that's why she's been crying a lot.'

Jamie immediately looked relieved.

'That's good, isn't it, that we know what's wrong with her now? Can he give her some new medicine that will make her better?'

'Well …' Margaret could think of no way of softening the blow, so decided she had to press on. 'Actually he can't, Jamie. I have to take her back to the hospital on Sunday afternoon, so the other doctor who works with him can operate on her.'

'Does that mean they'll put her to sleep and take the tumour things out?' Ian asked, his eyes like saucers at the thought.

'Course, silly!' Greg said scornfully. 'She won't feel a thing.'

Jamie was silent. His questioning eyes met Margaret's, but she looked away, not wanting to see his pain when she told them the rest of her terrible news. Looking down at Laura's head nestled against her, she took a deep breath and made herself go on.

'Well … actually, the doctor can't just take the tumours out. Instead, he has to remove Laura's eyes completely, I'm afraid. You see, the tumours are getting bigger and soon she'd be blind anyway. It will be a very serious operation, but you're right, Greg – Laura won't feel any pain while it's happening.'

All three of them were staring at her, trying to take in what she had said. Jamie had gone as white as a sheet, while Greg's mouth hung open in disbelief. Ian, uncertain what to do, began crying.

'But … but Mummy, she won't be able to see at *all* then! How will she play any of our games with us and feed the chickens and everything, if she doesn't have any eyes? She won't be able to see the board at school either, Mummy – and no one will want to play with her.'

'Course they'll play with her!' Greg covered his grief in scorn at his little brother again. 'She'll still be able to talk and listen to things and …' but here his ideas ran out.

Margaret looked at Jamie and saw his eyes were bright with tears. They were close to the surface for her too, but she willed herself to stay calm for everyone's sake. She opened her mouth to explain further, but Jamie suddenly scrambled up from the carpet and made a dive for his bedroom, closing the door with a slam. Greg and Ian crowded around Margaret and Laura, patting their sister, seeking comfort for themselves.

'She'll be okay, boys,' Margaret whispered, swallowing the big lump in her throat once again and trying to put her arms around them both. 'It'll take a while for her to get better after the operation, but we'll all help her, won't we? How

Laura

about you two look after her for a bit and play with her, while I go and talk to Jamie?'

For once, Greg did not complain.

Margaret sat Laura down on the carpet near the boys and straightened up with an effort. Quietly, she opened the door of Jamie's room, unsure how she would comfort him. He had burrowed down under the covers, but even with the pillow over his head, she could still hear his sobs – big painful ones that shook his whole body. Even when she patted his back through the blankets, he did not stop.

Eventually, she pulled the covers off his head and spoke firmly to him.

'Jamie, shush – please stop! I know you're really sad for Laura – we all are. Sure it's okay to cry when we need to, but it's not going to help her manage any better. And I need you now to help me with the others. You're so good with Laura – and Greg and Ian always take notice of you, even though they might pretend not to. Come on, Jamie – Laura will get through this. We'll all do our best to help her with everything.'

Gradually his sobs lessened. At last he sat up and turned a blotched, but fiercely determined face towards his mother.

'I'll be the best brother to her ever! I'll always look after her, Mum – you'll see! Only ... Mum, do you think she'll remember our faces? And what the chickens look like? And the flowers she used to like to pick and ...'

But here he stopped, overcome by fresh sobbing. Margaret held him close, rubbing his short blonde hair, so similar in colour to Laura's.

'We'll try our best to make sure she does, Jamie, in these next couple of days – okay?'

Back in the lounge, she read each of them a favourite book – first Laura, the boys crowding round trying to point out everything on each page to her. Margaret did not have the heart to stop them, even though she sensed Laura could see very little of what they were trying to show her. By the time they had finished Ian's book, Laura was asleep on her mother's lap. After a gentle kiss from each of her brothers, Margaret carried her to bed, certain that at any moment they would hear the ute driving into the yard. But the only sounds were the boys' voices and the occasional bark of a dog. With a sigh, she leaned her tired body against the bedroom door for a moment, before returning to the boys. They needed her, she knew, just as she too needed comfort that night of all nights.

It was around ten-thirty when Ken eventually came home. She had sat up for as long as she could, but it had been such a physically and emotionally tiring day that she finally had to give in and go to bed. She dozed fitfully, until she heard the ute drive in the yard. A few minutes later, she became aware of Ken's figure in the doorway, followed by the sound of the shower running. Then at last he was in bed beside her, the smell of beer very evident on his breath, but he took her hand and held it tight.

'Marg, I'm sorry – I'm really sorry! I just couldn't handle it. I love you, Marg. Let's sort it out tomorrow. 'Night!'

The next morning there was little time to talk privately. Ken avoided his wife's eyes, but was eager to help however he could.

'Marg, how about I take care of the kids this morning? I've got work to do first off, up the back paddock again, but Laura and the boys can come with me. I know you've got washing to do and cooking and stuff. Then after lunch we could all head to the coast for a swim and maybe fish and chips on the beach. Does that sound all right?'

Margaret waved them off, Jamie holding Laura tight in the cabin, while the others bounced around in the back of the ute. Normally he would have wanted to join them there, but today he had other priorities. Today he wanted to make sure this was the best day his sister ever had.

After lunch, the whole family headed out to their favourite spot on the coast, where the beach was not too crowded. Ken carried Laura into the water, where she happily rode on his shoulders and sat on his back as he swam underwater, splashing her hands hard on the surface so that the spray flew up in her face. Then, when she had had enough, the whole family worked hard to build a huge sandcastle. Eventually, Margaret took Laura to find some shells.

'Wow, Laura, here's a pretty one! It has such lovely colours inside it – purples and pinks and all so shiny. Feel how smooth it is underneath, but kind of crinkly on the top! And this one's all speckled – it's a funny shape, isn't it, fat at the top and pointy at the other end? Put them in your bucket and we'll take them back for the castle.'

But even as she said these things, her heart was almost breaking. It was obvious that it was the shape and surface feel of the shells rather than the colours or patterns on them that captured Laura's attention. Margaret knew this, but she still competed with the others, all that afternoon, in trying to draw Laura's attention to the sights around them – the deep blue of the ocean, the wide, white curve of the beach, the green grass of the nearby headland. Yet how much of this beauty and colour would Laura manage to remember? And how much of what they were showing her could she even see at this point? In the midst of her pain, Margaret could not begin to imagine other ways of appreciating the beauty around them – ways she herself had lost or overlooked, in her own dependence on sight.

Later, as they all sat together on the warm sand, munching chips straight out of the paper wrapping, the boys tried to draw Laura's attention to the white

laura

feathers, red beaks and bright button eyes of the seagulls flocking around them, eager for leftovers. Yet soon they too began to realise that the squawking of the birds and the flapping of their wings were much more interesting for Laura than their appearance. Jamie found a seagull's feather and began to show Laura how smooth the fronds were as they brushed their fingertips gently one way along its length, but how prickly and pokey they were when they ran their fingers the opposite way. Yet despite his best efforts to amuse her, she tired easily, rubbing her eyes and whimpering at times. They headed home, Laura soon falling asleep on the way. Then there was silence in the car, each one of them locked in their misery and grief.

That night Ken and Margaret talked. Not much, because both of them were so sad and confused – but enough to decide the way ahead, for the moment at least.

'Marg, sorry again I let you down last night. I just felt I had to get right away – it won't happen again. It must have been really tough to have to tell the boys by yourself. How did they take it?'

'Shocked and sad, like us – Jamie especially. I know they'll try to help out as best they can, but after all, they're only kids. Ken, I have to be with Laura of course, but I'll come home as often as possible. I'll ask my Mum to be at the hospital when I can't, or maybe your Mum could fill in at a pinch. I know Laura will be scared – she won't be able to see anything at all or really understand what's going on.'

The thought was too much for both of them. Margaret was crying openly and Ken swallowing hard. At that moment, he became aware of a deep anger rising up in him – a huge frustration that he was unable to make everything right for his Laura. He felt like smashing something – he felt like a drink.

He could do neither.

He got up, pacing around like a caged lion, one part of him trying to think what to do and how to help, the other trying to block it all out, to pretend things would be fine. They would have to be.

Margaret watched him through her tears, fear and uncertainty gripping her. Ken would try his best, she knew – he truly loved them all. But would it be enough? Could she trust him while she was in Brisbane? He needed her around – he needed her love, and the stability she gave him. But Laura needed her even more right now. She sighed, wiping away the tears. There was nothing to be done. She could not be in two places at once – she could not do the impossible.

On her final morning at home, Laura was fussed over by everyone. It was as if they all wanted to get as close to her as possible, to try to implant their features on her brain, to make her remember their eyes, their hair, every expression on their faces. Then it was time to go, as Laura sat in the car clutching the little posy of her favourite 'lellow' dandelions that Ian had carefully picked for her. One by one, Ken and the boys poked their heads in her window, kissing her once more, with eyes suspiciously bright.

'Bye, Laura! See you when you come home.'

She was still waving as the car turned onto the road, her innocence about what lay ahead like a knife in Ken's heart.

Margaret drove straight to the hospital. She knew she did not have the strength to deal with her mother's fussing. Once there, things moved ahead in a swift and businesslike manner. She felt the cold, impersonal nature of it all, but at the same time was glad of it, since it enabled her to hold herself together – at least until Dr Vincent came that night to explain the next day's operation. At first, for Laura's sake, she had been determined to understand exactly what was about to take place, but as the surgeon talked, a strange sense of unreality began to creep over her. She felt as if she were floating somewhere above Laura's bed, observing what was happening and listening impartially to his words.

'... and I'll remove the right eye first, Mrs Harding, cutting the optic nerve as far back as I can. Then I'll put an implant in place, to make sure the socket keeps its shape, as well as a special plastic disc called a conformer, so the eye area won't shrink and the tissue and bone will grow as normally as ...'.

She was aware his voice had stopped, but she could not work out why – until she saw herself by the bed, face in hands, shoulders shaking with sobs and heard her own voice crying loudly for him to stop. By now Laura was crying in earnest too. Then suddenly Margaret was back in her own body, holding Laura tightly to her.

'Please, please ... don't tell me any more! I can't bear it! I know it's a very serious operation – and I know she'll take some time to recover. We just want her *well* – we just want our lovely little girl back!'

'Mrs Harding,' Dr Vincent said finally, after giving her time to calm herself a little, 'I'm very hopeful that Laura *will* be well again soon – but you need to prepare yourselves for the fact that she'll never be the same little girl. It will take a few weeks for her to recover, but she won't be able to have proper artificial eyes fitted for a while at least – not until everything's healed well and her facial bones and muscles are a little more fully developed. We'll do our best, but, apart from being blind, she'll *look* a bit different for quite a while – and that will be hard for you all. She'll have to have the conformers replaced quite often at first, then every three months or so after that, until it's time to get her new eyes. But it's all very necessary, I'm afraid, if we're going to save her life.'

'I know,' she whispered – but the tears would not stop falling.

Laura

Eventually the doctor arranged for a nurse to sit with her, talking calmly until Laura fell asleep in her mother's arms. Together, they placed her gently in her bed.

'Go home, Mrs Harding, and try to get some rest,' the nurse told Margaret softly then. 'We'll look after her when she wakes up – it's best that way. By the time you see her again, it will be all over.'

Margaret would never forget the sight of Laura the next afternoon, her little head immobilised and swathed in bandages, lying still and apparently lifeless in intensive care. Later, Dr Brandon called by.

'Dr Vincent tells me the op went well, Mrs Harding – I'm glad. We'll need to keep her sedated for the time being, so why don't you go home to your family for a few days? There's nothing you can do here – and I'm sure your boys need you, not to mention your husband. We'll phone when it's time for you to come back.'

Margaret hated to leave Laura, but she saw the sense in what Dr Brandon said. Better to be at home while she could be – for all concerned.

She decided to set out then and there that evening, to give Ken firsthand news of the operation. It was late when she pulled in their yard, but the lights were still on in the lounge. She lifted her bag from the car and walked to the door. Strange Ken hadn't come out to greet her. She put the key in the lock and turned it, expecting to hear his cheery voice at any moment.

All was silent.

She walked towards the lounge-room door and looked in, knowing in her heart what she would see. And there he was, asleep in his old armchair, several empty beer bottles on the floor beside him.

Some days later, she received the long-awaited call from the hospital. Laura was conscious again and wanting her mother.

Margaret returned with mixed feelings. Ken's promises were still ringing in her ears, but, while she found it hard to believe them completely, she knew she had no choice. She forgot everything, however, at the sight of Laura, eyes still covered and so restless, constantly crying for her and screaming whenever the nurses or doctors touched her.

After some time, Margaret finally managed to soothe her to sleep, Laura's little hand clinging tightly to hers. Later still, she managed to extricate herself at last from Laura's grasp without waking her and headed home exhausted. The next morning, however, the nurses told her Laura had apparently woken again soon after she had left – and then no one could console her. Margaret offered to stay at nights, but there was no provision for parents at the hospital.

'Besides,' Dr Brandon said when he next came on his rounds, 'you need your rest too, Mrs Harding. You have your new baby to consider, let alone your husband and other children. Let's see what happens the next few nights after you leave here. If she doesn't settle, then it might be best if you came only occasionally to see her. That way she'll be less upset and her recovery might well be quicker.'

In the end, Laura did not settle – and even Margaret could see that such hysterical crying was not good for her.

'But she's so frightened!' she pleaded, when the nurses supported Dr Brandon's suggestion wholeheartedly. 'Can you imagine what it must be like, not to be able to see anything, not to know what's really happening? Couldn't I please sleep somewhere here?'

But the hospital was adamant. It was against their policy and no exception could be made in her case.

'Go home, Mrs Harding – please!' Dr Brandon urged her. 'We'll take good care of her. Come when you can, but the sooner she settles, the sooner she'll be back home.'

Weeks went by, punctuated by painful visits to the hospital by Margaret. Ken did not want to come, she discovered. He had an irrational fear of hospitals, and, she suspected, a dread of seeing his Laura so upset and, despite the hospital's best efforts, still in pain.

She had been very glad he was not with her the day she arrived to find the last coverings removed from her daughter's face. In vain Laura had tried to pull them off, no doubt thinking that was why she could not see at all. Now she seemed dazed and even more confused, attempting to peer around at any sound she heard, still unable to see what was happening or who was nearby. Margaret had been told what to expect, but no words had prepared her for the reality of the moment. Gone were the beautiful, sparkling blue eyes so like Ken's that had smiled into her own over the last three years. Now, in contrast, her face had a blank, shuttered look that pierced Margaret to the core.

She held Laura on her lap, pressing her poor little face close to her own heart, soothing her, crooning to her as she rocked her to sleep. O God, she cried silently, how could this happen? I don't really believe you hear me or are interested – but what's to become of this poor little one of ours? How on earth will she manage?

chapter three

Laura came home at last on a gusty November day, when winds howled around the old farmhouse and the skies were grey and threatening. She had been in hospital for almost two months, her father and brothers visiting her only once in that time. Margaret of course had seen her more often, but each time she had left, Laura was inconsolable. She had needed her mother desperately and had longed so much to be held and comforted by someone familiar – yet instead she had been deprived of everybody and everything she had always known. While the nurses did not let on a great deal, Margaret gathered that, despite their best efforts, Laura had often cried piteously for hours on end. The more they had tried to get near her, the more terrified she became, screaming for her mother at the top of her lungs and fighting their every effort to soothe her. Lost in a strange, new world, fear and uncertainty had held frightening sway.

Jamie had been the one who had pestered his father the most to be allowed to visit his sister. Yet when they had, he had been so affected at his first sight of her that Margaret was almost sorry she had agreed to it. He had approached Laura's bed so excitedly, running ahead in his eagerness to see her again.

'Laura! Laura! Are you feeling better? I've missed you lots, Laura.'

She was sitting up, playing idly with an old teddy. At the sound of his voice,

laura

she had quickly turned her head in his direction, listening intently. Then, as she realised who it was, a huge smile had lit up her face and she quickly scrambled to her feet.

'Damie!'

He hugged and kissed her over the side of her bed as best he could – and then she would not let go, her little arms locking firmly around his neck.

Eventually, when the rest of the family began to crowd around, she slackened her hold a little and brought her face close to his, as if trying to distinguish his familiar features.

'Damie ... can't see Damie.'

'It's okay, Laura,' he had managed to get out. 'We can still play lots of games and feed the chickens and stuff.'

Then he had turned away, his eyes brimming with tears. His Dad had taken over, lifting Laura up and hugging her tight, hoping the others could not see the tears in his own eyes, as she put her face close and tried to see him. He had chatted brightly with her for a while, before abruptly handing her over to Margaret.

'I'll take care of Jamie – we'll both go for a walk,' he had muttered, with a look that pleaded for understanding.

Greg and Ian had kissed and patted their sister lovingly too, as she clung tenaciously to Margaret, but could not help staring at her poor little face and the conformers that had replaced her beautiful blue eyes. Eventually Margaret had tried to set her down on the floor to play with them. They each held her hands and talked to her for a while, awkward and confused, and soon Laura had retreated again to her mother's lap, happier to relate to them from a place of comfort and safety.

On the evening of her homecoming, when all the children were finally in bed, Ken and Margaret sat together in the lounge, too spent at first even to talk. Laura had taken a lot of coaxing to stay in her own bed and Margaret sensed there would be a disturbed night ahead. She leant back and closed her eyes, trying to ease her tired body into a more comfortable position. Not long now until their next little one would be born – less than three weeks, if all went as expected. How would she manage, she wondered, trying to help Laura find her feet, taking her back and forth for further check-ups and treatment, as well as caring for the new baby?

One thing was certain – Ken would have to be home more in the evenings than he was now.

At that point, she was pulled back from the edge of sleep by Ken himself, speaking as if from a distance.

'Marg, come on – time we were in bed. You look exhausted. We'll talk more another time, but there are two things I want to say now. Firstly, I plan to be here for you every night in this next little while, believe me. I know we have to pull together as a family and I know I've been trying to avoid things again a bit lately. Secondly, I've been thinking lots about how we'll manage, ever since that day the boys and I saw Laura at the hospital. Marg, of course we need to take good care of her and give her the best opportunity to grow up and learn like the others, but we can't spend our lives rescuing her and coddling her either. You'll wear yourself out – and I think the other kids might suffer too. From the beginning, let's agree to treat her the same as the rest of them! Let her grow up as normally as possible – in the end, it might be the best way to help her make something of her life.'

Margaret swallowed hard, her eyes enormous with fear as she looked at Ken. His last words had sounded so heartless – how could they behave that way towards a small, defenceless child? Yet deep down, she knew he was right. Deep down, she knew it was the only way for all of them to survive. She had thought about it herself over and over during her trips back and forth to the hospital and had discussed it with Dr Brandon as well.

'Mrs Harding,' he had said, kindly but firmly, 'you must be determined to teach her to look after herself. She's a fighter – we can see that by the way she's resisted the nurses! She'll survive – but will *you*?'

Now, as she answered Ken, her voice was filled with tired resignation.

'I know you're right. I'll find it hard, but I'll try. And Ken – I'm relieved to hear you'll be around more. I'm realistic enough to know I'll need plenty of help.'

Ken had held her then and the two of them had wept together. It would be a hard road ahead – but not nearly as hard as the one their little girl would have to walk.

Laura's third birthday took place a few days later, with all her favourite food, plus a big chocolate cake with three pink candles on it.

'But Mum, she can't see where the candles are to blow them out,' Greg had said, half scornful, half secretly worried that Laura would miss out on a special part of her celebrations.

'We can help her – don't worry!' Margaret had said calmly.

Ken had held her in his lap, letting her feel the edge of the plate and guiding her hand to touch the icing lightly in one spot. All three boys had crowded around, each eager to help.

But Laura had not needed any assistance. She heard the candles being lit and then, without needing to be told, took a big breath and blew with all her might in the right direction.

'Wow, Laura, you did it! You blew them all out in one go,' Jamie said proudly.

Laura

Greg and Ian both drew back, somewhat disappointed. They had been leaning across the table, lips pursed, ready to help out with generous blows of their own. As Margaret removed the candles, she took a moment to let Laura feel their shape, explaining how the wax had melted down the sides.

Laura had definitely not required any help to devour a generous wedge of her delicious cake either, although Ken tried, as she remained sitting on his knee. In a very short space of time, her clothes and his as well were smeared with dark, sticky fingerprints, and the floor liberally covered with crumbs. Laura sat stuffing large chunks into her mouth, blissfully unaware of the resultant mess. She was laughing for the first time in months – and no one had the heart to scold her.

A fortnight later, Laura's little sister entered the world. In the end, Margaret only just made it to the local hospital in time.

Laura must have sensed something was happening that day, since she had been particularly demanding, not wanting to leave Margaret's side for a moment. Ken, busy with a casual labouring job on a neighbour's farm, was working late in an effort to finish what had to be done. Margaret gave Laura and the boys their dinner, despite the pains coming more and more frequently, and, as soon as Ken drove in the yard, told him there was no time to waste.

'Let them come for the drive, Ken,' she had managed to instruct him, between contractions. 'I don't want to leave the boys home alone and you'd have to bring Laura anyway. She's upset enough as it is.'

He did not argue, but sprang into action immediately.

When they reached the hospital, Margaret told Ken not to wait around and hurriedly said goodbye to them all.

'I'll be fine, Ken – you go. But please look after Laura!'

They were not home long, before the phone rang and Ken was able to announce to them all that their little sister, Elisabeth Rose, had arrived.

'Dad, are her eyes okay?' was Jamie's first hesitant question.

'I'm sure they are, but we'll ask the doctor to check them thoroughly,' Ken replied, holding tightly to Laura. 'We'll all go and see her tomorrow.'

'Are her eyes all right?' had been Margaret's first breathless question to the midwife assisting with the birth.

'I think they're fine – but she doesn't seem too keen to open them right now.'

Margaret nodded, oddly relieved and comforted, despite the fact that she knew the question was illogical. After all, Laura's eyes had seemed perfect too when she was born. She would be sure to have this little one's eyes checked every time she took Laura to her specialist, or even more regularly.

'Well, Elisabeth Rose, eh,' their family doctor had commented, when he finally arrived to check on her. 'I'm sure she'll be a special playmate for Laura – but you'll have your hands full for a while, my dear.'

Both statements turned out to be very true. At first, Margaret's hands were more than full, trying to manage both Laura and Elisabeth. In a valiant effort to help, not long after Elisabeth's birth, Ken had taken Laura to Brisbane himself for her first follow-up appointment, along with the boys, in order to have their eyes checked as well, but it was not the happiest experience for any of them. Laura had been fractious from the beginning, hating to leave her mother and new little sister. As soon as she realised Ken was taking her back to the hospital, she had been frantic, resisting anyone and everyone – even Jamie – until the doctor had had to sedate her. And she had been sick on the way home, crying endlessly for her Mum, with the result that Ken had never been more relieved in his life when he finally drove into their yard. Reunited with Margaret, Laura had clung even more tightly, inconsolable whenever her mother was not close by.

'Shush, dear! It's okay,' Margaret would call to her, from wherever she was in the house, trying to comfort her. 'I'm here. Shush – you'll wake the baby! You're such a brave girl to go to the hospital with Daddy and the boys. Next time, Mummy and Elisabeth will come with you and you can show the nurses your new baby sister.'

There was no doubt Laura was very proud of her special little sister. Nothing delighted her more than to be allowed to sit and nurse her 'Libbeth', or to stand in the circle of her mother's arm at feed time and hold the baby's tiny hand, feeling each little finger carefully, one after the other, or each tiny toe. She would kiss her all over, rubbing her cheek against the soft baby flesh and smiling delightedly.

'Lovely and soft, Mummy,' she would often giggle. 'Weally squishy!'

After the boys' initial caution in relating to a little sister who now could not see at all, they had quickly invented games that made her laugh and tempted her to leave her mother's side. In particular, it soon became a matter of pride and no little competition to see what words they could teach Laura that would help her understand exactly how things looked and felt. 'Squishy', they had decided, was a very useful word, since it was equally applicable to the jelly she loved to eat for dessert or the pink foam fish she played with in the bath, as it was to baby Elisabeth's little arms and legs – hence it soon became a favourite. Then her brothers would tease her by gently squeezing her own chubby limbs as they said the word, until she giggled in delight.

Yet being children – and boys at that – such games inevitably became rougher as time went by and Laura's energy began to return, resulting in her initial cries of delight sometimes turning into a squeal of anguish. At first Margaret sprang to her defence, indignantly putting a stop to whatever was happening.

Laura

'Leave her alone, boys! Don't be so rough with her! You should know better. You're supposed to care for your sister – not hurt her. You know she can't see – and apart from that, she's littler than you.'

'We didn't mean to hurt her, Mum,' Jamie would say, looking upset. 'We were only having fun.'

'Yeah, she just yells for no reason sometimes,' Greg would complain. 'Then *we* get into trouble.'

'Yeah, it's not fair!' Ian would invariably echo.

And it wasn't fair, Margaret realised, even before Ken pointed it out to her.

'Marg, don't you think you're overreacting a bit as far as the boys and Laura are concerned? They're only kids – and they *are* trying to help. They can't be expected to be completely gentle with her *all* the time. Of course I want them to look after her, the same as you do, but if we're too tough on them, they mightn't want to play with her at all. We don't want them to resent her and feel she's the favourite because she can't see.'

'I know, I know. It's just that I'm tired from looking after Elisabeth, as well as trying to work out ways to help Laura learn how to do things herself and find what she wants. I don't want to discourage the boys – Jamie in particular is so good with her most of the time.'

'We have to stick to what we said, love, and not mollycoddle her. She's only little now, but the sooner she learns to be independent, the better it'll be for her in the long run, I reckon. You can't fight all her battles for her, Marg – especially when she starts mixing with other kids and goes to school and all that.'

It didn't take much these days to reduce Margaret to tears. Ken took her in his arms and tried to comfort her.

'She'll be right, Marg, you'll see. She's a bright little one – she'll work things out. Remember what the doctor said – she's a fighter!'

'She'll have to be. I've decided though that I'll start learning Braille as soon as Elisabeth gets a bit bigger. Dr Brandon told me there are books sighted people can get to learn it – and the Blind Society or the folk at Braille House will help. But he also said that later on, we'll have to let her board at the School for the Blind – or otherwise move to Brisbane. Anyway, whatever we do, I'd still want to learn Braille.'

Yet such talk about Laura's future, Margaret soon discovered, always met with strong opposition from Ken.

'There's no way I'd agree to sending her off to boarding school, Marg! She'd miss us too much. Anyway, I think it's much better if she can learn to do things like any other kid does. As to moving – what would I do in the city? Our little town here is the only place I've known really, apart from my time at uni – what there was of it! I'm happier doing outdoor stuff anyway – you know that. Besides, I'd miss the guys too much – not that the band gets much time to practise now. Let's wait and see – plenty of time yet.'

Margaret almost always bit off the sharp comments she wanted to make whenever he said such things. Ken would usually take off before she could say much anyway, a troubled look in his eye. He loved Laura dearly, she knew, and would do anything for her, but moving to Brisbane was definitely too much for him to contemplate – yet, at least. And for now, the boys were happy on the farm, spending hours those holidays playing all sorts of imaginary games in the bush beyond their paddocks and down by the nearby creek. She was particularly glad they had been able to occupy themselves so well in those early weeks after Laura came home and the new baby arrived.

It was a big decision for her, however, the day Jamie suggested he take Laura with them on one of their adventures.

'Mum, she'll be fine,' he pleaded. 'I'll pull her up the hill in the old cart Dad made for us and then I can carry her on my back the last bit, if it's too hard for her to climb. We've made a good cubby in the bushes there – I think Laura would like to see it.'

The family had come to a tacit agreement by that stage that they would not avoid the word 'see' when it came to Laura. Early on after she had come home from hospital, Ian had used it as he played with her, much to his initial embarrassment.

'Laura, come and see me ride my bike! I don't even need my trainer wheels now,' he had called out excitedly from the front yard.

Greg had soon put him in his place.

'Silly – she *can't* see you. You're an idiot!'

Ian had gone almost purple in the face when he realised his mistake, dumped his bike and run to the far end of the yard in tears. Fortunately, Jamie had come to the rescue.

'It's okay, Ian. Anyway, she *can* sort of see, Greg – just in a different way! She can hear things and feel things – she can work out what's happening, without seeing it with her eyes. Watch!'

Jamie had quickly gone with Laura down the stairs and across the yard, picked up Ian's bike and instructed him what to do next.

'Here, Ian, hop on your bike and let Laura feel how you ride off. Then ride back past us and she'll hear you coming. ... There, Laura, this is the tyre on Ian's bike – can you feel it moving a bit now? He's riding it all by himself. See how high the handlebars are – a lot higher than your old trike, aren't they? Now stand back ... off you go, Ian! Now ride back past us ... can you hear him coming, Laura? Go

43

Laura

round again, Ian! That's really good. Laura, when I'm a bit bigger, I'll get Dad to make a little seat for the back of my bike and you can sit in it and ride with me … okay? Then, when you're older, you might even be able to ride all by yourself.'

Margaret had watched it all from their bedroom window where she had been feeding the baby. Later that night, as she told Ken about it, he was delighted.

'Good on him, Marg! Jamie's got a good head on his shoulders. Let her do more things with the boys, love – she's bound to hurt herself and get a few bruises, but she'll learn. She won't feel so left out then either. Let her have a go at everything! She'll work out what she can and can't do.'

Now, faced with whether to allow her to go with Jamie and the others, Margaret gave in to the pleading look in her oldest son's eyes.

'All right, Jamie – but take good care of her! And don't be too long!'

She watched with mixed feelings as Jamie trundled Laura across the yard, down the bumpy laneway and up the hill. When she had called out goodbye to them, Laura had waved in the direction of her voice and continued on chattering away to Jamie. Laura seemed to have fewer qualms now about not having her close by, Margaret realised, with a momentary feeling of sadness. On the other hand, she was greatly relieved that the frightened child she had brought home from hospital was beginning to shed her fears and not cling so tightly.

A couple of hours later, she heard them coming back down the hill, laughing together and singing nursery rhymes at the tops of their voices, Laura joining in when she could. Then they were in the yard and Jamie was lifting her out of the cart and dusting some grass and dirt off her.

'Did you have a good time, all of you?' Margaret asked, as Laura followed the sound of her voice and climbed the front steps towards her, along with the others.

She noticed with pride that, while Laura was naturally slower than the boys, she nevertheless managed it by herself, Jamie holding her hand for just the last few steps. She also saw that Laura was holding some rather wilted flowers – her favourite 'lellow' dandelions and some small purple wildflowers.

'Look, Mummy!' she said proudly. 'For you!'

'Wow! They're beautiful – thank you so much!'

'She picked them all by herself, Mum,' Jamie added proudly.

'How …'

'I took her to where there were lots growing and she felt their shapes and picked them. It was fun, wasn't it, Laura? We found a ladybird too – I put it on your hand and it tickled you, didn't it?'

'Tickled!' Laura repeated, giggling.

'She climbed right up the rocks into our cubby – and we didn't even help her much,' Ian added, as he bounced up the stairs.

'We had to help her one time when she fell down and clean her up a bit,' contradicted Greg, 'but she didn't cry – well not much, anyway.'

Margaret looked at Laura's dirty hands and scratched knees.

'Oh dear – we'd better get you tidied up before dinner and before Daddy comes home.'

But Margaret knew that, much as Laura was precious to Ken, he would have applauded the fact that she was doing whatever the boys did, learning to manage like other 'normal' children. That night, when Laura told him about it as best she could, the boys interpreting where necessary, he had hugged her tight.

'I'm so proud of you, Laura! You're getting very grown up. Soon you'll be able to do almost everything the boys do.'

Laura's brothers taught her lots of things those holidays – how to dogpaddle a short way at least in the nearby waterhole, how to hide and wait until they found her, how to look for them as they called out softly to her, how to roll her ball and knock over her plastic skittles in the hallway so they fell over with a clatter, how to turn on the TV and change channels. Jamie was particularly patient with her, helping her dress her dolls and sit them up beside her on the carpet, or make 'cakes' for them with Margaret's homemade play-dough, or spread out her tea-set, complete with tiny spoons and forks, so her dolls could have a 'burfday party'. At first, Laura would become frustrated and lose interest, when she kept knocking over the little cups as she tried to put them on their saucers. But soon, with Margaret's and Jamie's patient help, she learnt to touch things lightly and to move her hands more slowly and carefully, holding each cup and searching with both hands close together, until she found an empty saucer where she could put it.

Jamie also liked helping her find special treasures to put in her plastic handbag with the zipper that she loved opening and closing, and always tried hard to ensure she knew exactly what each precious item was. Initially, he was at a loss, as were Ken and Margaret, to describe things to her in a way she would understand and to know how to help her identify the various items, when colour meant little to her. Yet Margaret was determined to learn such things as quickly as possible, reading whatever she could lay her hands on, despite her busyness. Gradually, with her help, Jamie and the others began to learn what things to point out to Laura, as they added treasures to her bag.

'Laura, feel this one! It's a squishy plastic clown – you can bend his legs and arms all sorts of ways. He's got a funny smiley face and big baggy pants and a silly hat. This is a shiny, brown stone from the creek – can you feel how smooth and round it is? You know what these ones are – your own little pink brush and comb to make your hair look pretty. And here's some money I found. It's only

laura

five cents – you can keep it, if you like.'

If she were sitting feeding Elisabeth nearby, Margaret would often add to their comments.

'The five cents has a little rough edge all around it, Laura – show her, Jamie! And if you hold Jamie's special stone up against your cheek, I think it will feel nice and cool, as well as smooth. Lovely, isn't it?'

Jamie often tried to read her favourite books to her too. He would put his arm round her and she would nestle close to him, looking down intently at each page, as if she could see every picture. But Jamie was her eyes – and he took great pains to describe each illustration at length, not wanting her to miss out on anything.

The time soon came, however, for the boys to head back to school. At first, the days dragged for Laura. She became Margaret's shadow again, holding onto her skirt or leg wherever she went, from kitchen to bedroom and outside to hang the washing, feed the chickens and do the occasional gardening task. Margaret did her best to play with her and teach her things, in between caring for the baby and tackling the seemingly endless list of jobs waiting to be done. Laura learnt fast, constantly amazing Margaret with how much she remembered and how quickly her little fingers would feel the surface of objects to identify what it was or where she was. She loved helping with the washing up, standing on a chair at the sink, while Margaret worked nearby. Elisabeth's bath time was also a special part of her day, as she learnt how to squeeze the soft sponge onto her sister's fat tummy and heard the splashes as her little legs kicked in delight. Often Margaret let her put her dolls in the bath afterwards, showing her how to dry them properly and helping her choose new clothes for them. Laura liked to choose clothes for herself too, emptying out her dress-up box almost daily in search of just the right 'swirly skirts' and necklaces and big shoes to 'clomp' down the hallway in and make as much noise as possible.

Soon she was able to find her own way around the house and come looking for her mother, even when Margaret did not keep guiding her by the sound of her voice. And once, when Margaret thought Laura was having her afternoon rest and had briefly gone down to the garden to pick some vegetables for dinner, she suddenly turned around to see her making her own way down the front steps. Margaret held her breath – she knew Laura could climb *up* them by herself, but coming *down* was quite another matter. She forced herself to stay where she was, however, hearing in her mind Ken's voice urging her to let Laura try things for herself. And eventually Laura did arrive safely at ground level and made her way towards the spot where she heard her mother working.

This was the first of many such adventures, as it turned out. As the weeks and months passed, she became more and more independent, always averse to being shown things a second time.

'I can do it mysipe!' she would often say crossly, as Margaret went to do up her shoes, or brush her blonde curls, or help her wash her hands.

And invariably there were accidents. Laura discovered to her pain, as her brothers had before her, that it was not a good idea to turn the hot tap on too hard, or to climb on the kitchen table, stand up and jump off.

'How could I let these things happen to her?' Margaret sobbed, after the second or third such escapade. 'As if she's not injured enough!'

'Marg, she'll never learn otherwise. Remember what the other kids did at her age – they got into trouble just the same as she is,' Ken had responded. 'It might seem hard, but I'm sure she'll thank us for it one day.'

Margaret never forgot the time she found Laura with a chair pulled up to the kitchen bench and the lids off all the canisters, as she proceeded to investigate their contents, taking handfuls out to smell and touch and taste. She had put a bit of each in a bowl and was stirring it with a big wooden spoon, spraying the mess all over the bench and floor and herself in the process. Or the day Laura managed to climb right to the top of a large old wardrobe they kept in the hallway. Just as Margaret walked past, Laura had poked her head over the edge and yelled out 'Boo!', giving her the fright of her life. Laura had laughed delightedly at first, but was soon chastened by the scolding she received. As Margaret tried to explain to Ken later, there was often a fine line between letting Laura learn by her mistakes and preventing her from doing foolhardy things where she was oblivious to the dangers involved.

Yet there were even more difficult and painful moments for her where Laura was concerned at times. Moments when she literally felt as if a knife were being thrust into her heart – like whenever she had to take Laura back to the specialist in Brisbane to have her 'eyes' attended to, or when Laura would knock something over and simply sit crying with frustration.

Margaret hated too to see Laura miss out completely on some of the special things the rest of the family enjoyed – certain action cartoons the boys loved, a beautiful pink sunset sky, baby Elisabeth smiling up at her, with eyes alight with love. Yet, as Ken pointed out so logically and as she recognised herself, this was not so much Laura's problem as her own.

'Marg, *you're* more upset about it than Laura ever will be. She'll find other things she enjoys just as much. Anyway, she can tell Elisabeth loves her by the happy little noises she hears when she holds her or plays with her.'

But even Ken could not deny he found it hard when Laura woke up at night screaming, fear and panic overwhelming her, her little hands tearing at her hair, as if to pull off imaginary bandages. At first she would fight even their loving arms,

Laura

until she was fully enough awake to realise these were not the arms of strangers and they would never hurt her. On these occasions, neither parent had the heart to leave her to sleep alone in the small enclosed section of the veranda Ken had at last managed to fashion into a bedroom for her. They would carry her back to their own bed and hold her close until she eventually calmed down and slept.

But Margaret's worst moments of all occurred when other children stared at Laura or made comments – like the day she overheard a slightly older girl's loud questions at the supermarket checkout.

'Mummy, look at that little girl! What's the matter with her eyes?'

'I don't know – but don't stare at her!'

'Why Mummy? She looks a bit weird – I don't think she has any proper eyes at all.'

Or when a former teaching colleague called in with her own two children, who had promptly refused to play with Laura and clung shyly to their mother.

'Her eyes look funny, Mummy. Why has she got those sunglasses on?'

'I don't want to play with her – I want to go *now*!'

These incidents were few and far between, but each time, anger and grief would almost overwhelm Margaret. She would turn away, choking back a biting response, and hope Laura had not understood what was happening.

'Marg, we can't control other people's reactions,' Ken had said, when told. 'It's bound to happen – kids can be so cruel. Perhaps the sooner she gets used to such things the better. All we can do is give her as normal a life as possible and help her find things she can do well – or maybe even better than anyone else. Maybe she'll be good at music – I reckon she might. She loves singing – she picks up a lot just listening to me practising.'

Ken was good for her, Margaret knew, with his practical, down-to-earth mind and 'she'll be right' attitude. His focus was definitely on living in the now, as opposed to worrying about the future. Often this had its down side – but for now it did help her cope. He'd stayed true to his word too and been home much more often at nights – so far at least.

Ken still played and sang with the band from time to time, but group practices were few and far between. Often in the evenings, after the children were in bed, he would sit on the veranda near Laura's little sleep-out bedroom, strumming his guitar and trying to remember all his songs. Laura loved listening to him and singing along when she could. Sometimes when he stopped playing, she would object.

'Don't dop yet, Daddy! I like your singing,' her plaintive little voice would float out onto the veranda.

'You should be asleep,' he would growl back.

She would giggle loudly, sometimes creeping out to lie on the bare floorboards as he sang, her head resting on his foot and moving up and down as he tapped in time with the song. Then she would giggle even louder, until he eventually shooed her back to bed. But the spank he gave her on her bottom as he did was always gentle and the kiss on her forehead full of love for his special girl, his Laura.

By the time Laura was four, life at home with Margaret and Elisabeth was filled with varied activities. She continued to enjoy the children's TV programs she had watched before her operation, singing along with the music and copying whatever the presenters were doing. 'Play School' and 'Humphrey' were firm favourites. Initially Margaret was surprised at how much Laura took in, smiling when she observed her trying to act out something from a show, often with Elisabeth as her real life 'baby' or patient, as required. She was also amazed Laura remembered all the instructions on how to make the various 'pretend' objects featured in the programs and how determined she was to create her own. By lunch time each day, the lounge room floor would often be littered with whatever was needed for Laura's 'projects' – old cartons Margaret found for her, or cardboard cylinders, or paper plates to use as 'wheels' for a pretend bus or train. Having assembled her vehicle with Margaret's help and made it comfortable with cushions and blankets, as well as food for the journey, Laura would then take Elisabeth and her dolls or toy animals for a long, noisy ride to Brisbane, or to the beach, or even 'to faiwyland'.

And she *did* love music, as Ken had predicted she might, soon developing favourites from old tapes of children's songs Margaret had kept from her teaching days. It did not take long before Laura knew all the words and even, to Margaret's amazement, the order of the songs, often beginning to sing the next as soon as the last was finished. But it was her ability to remember her father's songs that astounded them the most. At odd times during the day, Margaret would often hear her singing snippets from a melancholy country ballad or one of Ken's favourite pop songs. For Laura's fourth birthday, her father built her a swing in the corner of the yard, which soon became her own singing spot. Sometimes in the afternoons before the boys came home, she would swing the whole time Elisabeth was asleep, while Margaret watched from the veranda or listened from the kitchen. She would sing at the top of her voice, one song after another, moving from nursery rhyme to sentimental love song and back again, according to whatever came to mind next.

Little Bo-Peep has lost her sheep, an' duddn't know where to find them
Leave them alone and they'll come home dwagging their tails behind them

laura

It's so lonely without you
I'm so sad, I'm so blue
When will I get over you?
Oh when will I get over you?

If she ever heard a car coming or someone walking nearby, she would stop, embarrassed, and wait until she was alone again. On the swing, Laura was in her own private little world of dreams and imagination, where she was queen – and where nothing was impossible.

And every day there was the ritual of caring for her special pets – Cobber, the black and white kelpie cross, who had taken to shadowing Laura most of the time unless put to work by Ken elsewhere on the farm, her pet lamb Lucy, who had limped from the day she was born, and her very own chickens, which were kept in a little pen Ken specially built for them. Laura loved them all, hardly needing any reminder to make sure their water or feed bowls were kept full. She would take ages over it all, talking to each one, especially poor Lucy, who would always greet her with copious, pitiful baaing and eat from her hand, as Laura stroked her and assured her her foot would soon be 'all better'.

Before long it was time to decide about Laura's schooling – whether she should wait an extra year until she turned six, or start after the Christmas holidays. In every spare moment Margaret had managed to find since Laura's operation, she had taught herself Braille. In turn, she had started to teach Laura the basics also, using beginner texts provided by the School for the Blind in Brisbane. From the outset, Laura had loved it all, grasping the concepts in no time.

'She's like a dry sponge, soaking up every little drop of information,' was Ken's comment, as he came in early one day from working around the farm. 'Beats me how they'll keep up with her at the boys' school. I hope she's not too much for them.'

But Laura was too much for them even from the outset, when Margaret tried to talk with the principal. At first he had wanted to help, but when the infants' teacher pointed out in no uncertain terms the difficulties she already had to contend with, without having to cope with a blind child, he soon became less enthusiastic about accommodating Laura.

'Our school isn't large, as you know, Mrs Harding,' he explained. 'Next year, with fewer enrolments, it looks like we'll have to form a composite class of beginners and some of the younger ones in their second year. So Miss Fletcher will definitely have her hands full, even without a handicapped child in the class.'

Margaret hated the word 'handicapped'. It jarred on her, causing her to respond in a less friendly manner than she would otherwise have used.

'My daughter will be extremely quick to learn, despite being 'handicapped', as you put it. And I think we could explain to Laura that she'll have to sit quietly and listen, while the others are learning to write or drawing or whatever. She could write in Braille on her own slate anyway and I'd check it when she came home. If Miss Fletcher could write out an outline of what the class had done each day, I'd make sure Laura understood everything and kept up with the others. She wouldn't be any trouble.'

'But what about outside the classroom, Mrs Harding? How would she find her way around? How would she go to the toilet herself, for example? She'd need others to help – some older girls maybe – at recess and lunch time.'

'Mr Brown, if you were to show Laura once – or twice at the most – she'd remember exactly where to go. Besides, Ian would watch out for her as much as he could.'

'I really don't think it would work. My suggestion to you is to move to Brisbane, where Laura could go to the School for the Blind. Or if you can't or don't want to consider that, then the only other options at present are to let her board with a family in Brisbane, while she attends the school, or to keep her at home and teach her yourself. I did hear some talk that the Department might be setting up a special unit for children who need extra help at smaller schools like ours. If that happens, then maybe we could consider having her – but not right now, I'm afraid.'

Margaret knew she was beaten, but gave it one last try.

'What if ... what if I offered to sit in the classroom some mornings and help with Laura myself? I'd have to bring Elisabeth, but she'd play quietly, I'm sure. Could you please suggest that to Miss Fletcher?'

But Miss Fletcher was more unwilling than ever, when the principal put it to her.

'The last person I want in my classroom is another teacher checking up on what I do all the time! Add to that a blind child *and* her little sister – well, I'm afraid you're asking the impossible! We don't even have a teacher aide to help me with the children we have already, let alone someone who's blind.'

'I understand ... you do have a point. I'll let Mrs Harding know.'

'They don't want to give it a go even,' Margaret told Ken in a disappointed voice, the day she received the call. 'The teacher's got too much on her hands already. The only other option would be to send Laura to the Blind School in Brisbane – apparently students from the country board with families now rather than at the school. Or of course, we could move there ourselves.'

Margaret knew what Ken's response would be before he opened his mouth.

'Well, let's wait until next year and give it another go, Marg. After all, she's

Laura

only just turned five. She'll probably do even better then... You know already what I think about the Brisbane idea – and there's certainly no way I'd ever want another family looking after Laura.'

chapter four

Margaret had continued to take Laura to Brisbane regularly to have her eyes checked and her conformers enlarged. Each time she set out, she hoped this would be the visit when Dr Brandon would say Laura was old enough for her new eyes, but his answer was always the same.

'Better leave it a little longer, Mrs Harding. Her face has a bit more growing to do yet. If we act too soon, then her new eyes won't fit well for very long and she might have more problems. When she does get them, she'll need several new pairs over the next few years anyway, plus some work on them in between to keep them fitting well, so you'll be back and forth enough then. It makes sense to wait, if she's managing well enough as she is. Perhaps next time, eh?'

Dr Brandon was always kind, but firm. He sympathised with all his patients – especially this little girl sitting so alert and still beside her mother. But he knew it would be foolish to rush things.

But now Laura had turned five – and Margaret felt sure the moment had come. Laura had got by so far, but Dr Brandon, of all people, would know how important it was for any child starting school to look the same as all the others.

As usual, he greeted them warmly.

'Goodness, Laura, you *have* grown quite a few inches since I saw you last,

laura

haven't you? Now, let's see what's happening in this eye area of yours. .... Hmmm – it looks hopeful, I think. Quite hopeful, in fact.'

He completed his examination in silence and then sat down at his desk to make a few notes. Finally, he looked up and cleared his throat.

'Yes, I think we can do it now, Mrs Harding. I'll speak to the folk who provide the prosthetic eyes and see if we can make a time for an initial consultation as soon as possible. They'll need to measure Laura's eye sockets carefully and will probably try several different standard shapes and sizes, so they can make her own special ones that will fit perfectly. I'll phone through to them straight away for you. Perhaps you could even stay overnight and see them tomorrow. Let's hope so!'

Before Margaret and Laura had time to recover, it was all arranged. As they stood to leave, Dr Brandon patted them both on the shoulder.

'Well, it's taken a while, but I'm sure Laura's new eyes will look wonderful – she should have quite a bit of movement in them, because the nerves and muscles around that area are still in good condition. All the best, Laura! You're very pretty now, but you'll look even prettier with your new eyes. Come back and see me soon, won't you – don't leave it any longer than a year!'

Laura skipped along, as they headed for the car. She understood enough to know that this was an important moment.

'Mummy, Dr Brandon told me I'm really pretty,' she said, in a very satisfied tone, as they drove off. 'I like Dr Brandon, don't you? And he said I'll be more prettier when I get my new eyes.'

When Margaret phoned Ken to tell him the news, she could hear how pleased and relieved he was.

'That's fantastic! Everything's fine here – don't worry! But Marg ... could you see if ... do you think they could make Laura's eyes the same colour blue as mine?'

Next morning, Margaret and Laura arrived early for their appointment, both a little nervous, but also excited. Their prosthetist, Andrew, turned out to be a large, friendly man in his thirties, with a firm handshake and a hearty laugh – Margaret warmed to him immediately. He soon managed to put them at ease, especially when he told them his own daughter had an artificial eye.

'Does ... does it look all right? Just like the other one?'

'Sure – most people don't even know. Unfortunately she was running down a hill a few years ago and fell over on something very sharp – as a result, she lost her right eye. We were lucky not to lose her altogether, actually. She had to be careful for a while, but she's okay now.'

Andrew chatted on to Margaret in order to keep Laura relaxed, as he examined her.

'I was working as an optometrist when the accident happened, but after that, I became very interested in this whole business of making prosthetic eyes. We've spent the last few years in the States – I studied some of the latest techniques being pioneered there and worked in a very modern lab with some excellent ocularists, as they call them. Of course, this all benefited our daughter too, since she was able to have a really good eye made especially for her – just like we're going to make for you, Laura,' he said, focusing on her again and tapping her playfully on the nose. 'Only you'll be doubly lucky, because we'll make *two* for you.'

'My Dad's got blue eyes,' Laura said very definitely then.

'Has he indeed! Well, I guess you want blue ones too then, do you?' Andrew said, reading between the lines. 'In a little while, I'll get Mummy to look at some of the colours we have to choose from and she can pick just the right one – okay?'

The whole process took some time, but Andrew worked deftly, measuring Laura's eye size and trying for the best possible fit as quickly as he could.

'This is a bit of a business, Laura – but it'll be worth it. You're very lucky you've had Dr Brandon looking after you. He's made sure your eye area has kept growing and stayed healthy – and that certainly makes it easier for me. ... There you are – I've finished for now. When you come back again, I'll have your eyes polished up really smoothly so they feel good and don't give you any trouble. Then all we'll have to do will be a final fit and maybe a few adjustments – and you'll be as right as rain!'

Andrew's prediction turned out to be exactly right. With only minimal changes, Laura's eyes fitted perfectly. She soon felt comfortable, opening and closing them so often that Andrew accused her of flirting with him.

'Now, young lady, don't go batting your eyelids at me!' he joked. 'After all, I'm a married man. I *would* like to see you again, even so – say in a month's time? That way, we can make sure everything's going fine. Then in about a year we'll check again to see how much you've grown and decide whether you need replacements. Don't go breaking too many hearts between now and then, my young friend!'

Laura returned home very excited, but determined not to show it. Elisabeth had made the trip with them and several times during the journey home, Margaret heard Laura explaining to her how she had new eyes and asking her if she liked them. Thankfully, Elisabeth's response each time was a resounding 'Yeth', which seemed to satisfy her sister.

Eventually, Margaret drove in the yard and barely had time to turn off the engine, before Ian came bounding down the steps.

Laura

'We've been waiting for you for *ages*! ... Wow, Laura, you look *really good*! Wow! Wait till Jamie and Greg see you. *Jamie! Greg!*'

He raced back upstairs, yelling for the others. They emerged rather sheepishly, unsure how to handle the situation.

In the end, Laura simply walked to where she could tell they were standing, opened her eyes wide and looked straight at them.

'Do you like my new eyes? I'm pretty, aren't I?'

'You look great!' Jamie and Greg chorused together.

That was all they said – Greg was never one to go on much about anything, while Jamie was at that awkward, tongue-tied, early teenage stage. Margaret noticed, however, how they would look across occasionally at Laura that first afternoon with delighted grins on their faces and then quickly turn away. Jamie was particularly proud, she could tell – proud and relieved. He was still Laura's 'hero', always protective of her, hating the thought that her eyes might not look good and that she might be stared at. Now Margaret could hardly wait until Ken saw Laura. He would be over the moon, she was sure.

He came in from the farm work early that night, eager to see her, but quite apprehensive too. He hoped she really would look all right – he didn't want to have to lie to her.

Laura heard him coming up the steps and scrambled up from where she had been sitting watching TV with the others.

'Daddy! Hi, Daddy – I've got my new eyes! I look just like you now, Mummy says.'

'Yep, Laura, you sure do,' was all Ken could say, a lump in his throat.

But he hugged her for a long time and she knew he was happy for her.

'I wish ...' Laura said after a while.

'Wish what?' Ken asked, when she stopped in mid-sentence.

'Well, I want to see them myself.'

Already Margaret could tell how the family's positive reaction had made Laura feel proud and special. It was such a relief to know that this hurdle at least was now over. She dared to hope there were brighter days ahead for Laura, when she would be readily accepted, the same as any other child, and when no unnecessary barriers would be put in her way.

After the holidays had ended and Laura again had only Elisabeth for company for most of the day, Margaret wondered if they had made the right decision not to worry about school as yet for her. She seemed so ready to learn, always full of questions about whatever Margaret was doing, and always eager to try everything. Margaret continued to teach her Braille and to become more adept at it herself, as time permitted. She also read whatever she could find about how to encourage blind children to reach their full potential. But she wished with all her heart she could do more for her.

'If I had more time to read to her and explain things, I'm sure she'd love it,' she said to Ken one night. 'But I can't neglect Elisabeth – and the boys alone keep me busy enough. I only hope they can take her at school next year.'

But when Margaret tried again to enrol Laura, the same reasons were given as to why it would not work – except they sounded even weaker now. Yet the principal did try to be as helpful as he could.

'Mrs Harding, unfortunately Miss Fletcher will have to manage a combined class again this coming year – so I really don't think it would work. If sending Laura to Brisbane is out of the question, she could possibly travel each day with Jamie when he goes to high school in Nanto. The primary school near there is quite a bit bigger, but again, I'm not sure how much help she'd get – and it *is* a fair way for her to travel each day. Of course, the government would pay for it, but I think she'd get pretty tired. The other option would be ...'

He hesitated a while, before continuing.

'Had you thought of the Correspondence School, Mrs Harding? I probably shouldn't be suggesting this, since I believe Laura would be better off in Brisbane, but it might work for you – especially since you're a teacher.'

Neither Margaret nor Ken liked the idea of sending Laura with Jamie each day to the nearby town. They liked it even less when they discovered how big her class would be and also that there was no funding to provide extra help in the lower grades.

'Looks like the Correspondence School's the best option for now,' Ken finally conceded. 'That means you'll be even busier, Marg, but I'll try to help more round the place. We'll manage, love. Laura's a bright little thing – she'll learn fast.'

So Laura stayed on at home, exceeding even her father's expectations. In no time she had a good relationship with her correspondence school teacher, Miss Charlton, as they communicated by mail and sometimes phone, as well as occasional visits when the Hardings were in Brisbane. With the help of volunteers at Braille House, who willingly provided any material that was not already available through the Blind School, Laura soon forged ahead with her reading and writing in particular. Ken usually picked up the mail whenever he was in town and Laura's 'big brown bundles' of books and schoolwork always caused great excitement, whenever they arrived. As time passed, she also came to look forward to some of the extras the school offered, such as their 'On Parade' radio program. On one occasion, she even featured in one of the 'Mailbag' segments, with Margaret's help.

And when, at the end of that first year, Margaret consulted with Mr Brown

Laura

again, together with Miss Charlton and the guidance officer for their area, they decided it was best to stick with the current arrangement for the time being.

'We'll keep reassessing things, although of course, Laura does need to mix with children her own age more, as soon as possible – especially other blind children,' the guidance officer commented. 'She should be at the School for the Blind. Still, she seems to be doing extremely well, all things considered.'

Ken snorted when Margaret told him about it all, as she knew he would.

'Of course she'll do well, Marg, wherever she is! And when she does get to school, I bet she'll be miles ahead of all the others.'

Margaret had a feeling she would too, judging by the speed with which she completed her work each day. She was glad Laura seemed happy enough to play with Elisabeth in the afternoons or was usually able to occupy herself in some other way until the boys came home. She loved playing with 'her' Cobber and helping Margaret with the cooking in particular. The swing remained a special spot, but gradually the big old mulberry tree near the front door became almost her own private sanctuary. Soon she was exploring every inch of the gnarled old trunk and the sturdy branches that fanned outward and upward in all directions. She was not afraid at all to climb it by herself – and Margaret let her do it, knowing Laura could easily tell where she was by the width and slope of the branches and the thickness of the leaves around her. When the fruit appeared, Laura would sometimes emerge covered in purple stains from head to foot, a few squashed mulberries hidden away in her pocket for Elisabeth to enjoy as well.

But the small keyboard the family now owned provided her with her most interesting challenge. She played by ear, patiently picking out the melody lines of her favourite songs and somehow remembering all the notes. Then, when she turned seven, Ken gave her a little ukulele, which instantly became a treasured possession. Eventually, after he had shown her some simple chords, she would try to play along with him each evening, sitting cross-legged on the floor as he practised, a frown on her face and little fingers stretched to the limit, while she hunted for the right spots to press on the strings.

'She'll have to do something musical, Marg, no doubt about that,' Ken often commented, a pleased smile on his face. 'She's a natural!'

Jamie, fifteen by then and almost as tall as his father, was impressed as well.

'Laura will run rings round all the other kids, even though she can't see,' he scoffed. 'She will when she gets to high school too. I wish she could go to a better one than ours though. It's all right for Greg and me, but we don't have any good music teachers and I don't think she'd like it much. She needs to go to a bigger high school in Brisbane – somewhere where there'd be lots of subjects to choose from and the kids would treat her the same as anybody else and not even worry about her being blind.'

'We'll see, Jamie,' Margaret answered quietly. 'I'll talk about it with Dad again.'

But invariably such talks were put off.

'Plenty of time, Marg,' Ken, never one to plan ahead, would always maintain. 'She's got years of primary school yet – don't let's cross our bridges before we come to them. Maybe when Jamie finishes, we'll need to think about things again – or when Greg does. Let's wait and see.'

Ken was a strange mixture of contradictions, Margaret often reflected. Part of him wanted every opportunity for Laura. He had been the one who had pushed for her to do everything the boys did – and still encouraged her to do so. He dearly wanted her to develop her musical abilities, patiently helping her almost every evening, as they sat together on the veranda or in the lounge. Yet he wanted to protect her from the outside world, from putting her in situations where she might be hurt or rejected. On occasions when he witnessed this happen, Margaret always knew what his response would be.

'They treat her like she's got no brains as well as no eyes!' he had exploded one night, after they had arrived home from a family celebration in Brisbane. 'You'd think my parents would know better. As for my sister's kids ...'

That night he had gone out, slamming the door after him and driving off to join his mates at one of the pubs in town. It was the same on the rare occasions Margaret's mother visited them, or when they made the trip to see her.

'Oh my goodness – the poor little thing!' Jean would say over and over, until Ken wanted to yell at her. She would watch with pity in her eyes, as Laura tried to play with the others, or read her Braille book, or carefully feel her way around her grandmother's unfamiliar house – and she would also quickly straighten up anything Laura managed to displace.

But it was her look of disgust, despite her attempts to hide it, whenever she watched Laura eat, that most offended Ken. Seeing a child feeling the food gently and manoeuvring it carefully onto spoon or fork with her fingers was too much for Jean's sensibilities. Yet, as Ken later fumed to Margaret after Laura was in bed, how else did she expect her to eat? Laura was very neat the way she ate her food anyway. Wasn't she allowed to enjoy choosing what she would put in her mouth next, the same as anyone else? Then off he would go, out the door, to deal with his anger in the way he believed worked best.

Yet it never did. Not for any of them. On those nights, Jamie would be particularly gentle and caring with his Mum.

'Don't worry, Mum!' he would say, making her some tea and awkwardly patting her shoulder. 'Laura will be fine – it'll work out.'

Laura

But Margaret wondered if it ever really would, when, as Laura's eighth birthday approached, she enquired again about her starting school with Elisabeth, only to discover once more that it was considered unworkable.

'I hoped we'd have some help for handicapped students such as Laura by now, as well as others with different learning difficulties, but it looks like that won't happen for another year or two, unfortunately,' Mr Brown informed her.

'We don't consider her 'handicapped' in the same way as you obviously do, Mr Brown — and she certainly doesn't have learning difficulties!' Margaret had retorted angrily, stung by his comments.

Ken had responded even more strongly when told.

'If that's what he thinks, Marg, then we don't want her there. Let's keep on as we are for another couple of years. Something might change in that time, who knows?'

'Of course she doesn't have learning difficulties!' the guidance officer had said, when Margaret managed to speak with him. 'In fact, judging from Miss Charlton's comments and Laura's last school report, I think she might well be too *advanced* for her year. If you're still unwilling to send her to the Blind School or possibly to the school in Nanto each day with her brothers, although nothing's really changed there, then I'd suggest you stick with your present arrangement, Mrs Harding.'

So it was that Elisabeth headed off to the local school the following year very tentatively and in tears, while Laura did not. It was ironic, Margaret thought, how Laura, who was fearless when compared to Elisabeth, was the one who had to stay at home.

Laura was definitely unafraid to try new things. While she enjoyed doing her lessons on the whole, her favourite time of the day was when her brothers arrived home. Then she knew there would no doubt be some adventure to be had. Usually, she could talk Elisabeth into tagging along, until things became too daring or dangerous. Then Elisabeth would bow out — but not Laura. That was unheard of.

The boys never held back from what they wanted to do because Laura happened to be with them. On weekends she would often join them on excursions up one of the steep hills nearby, clinging onto rocks as tenaciously as they did — and sometimes even more fearlessly, since she could not see the dangers clearly visible to them. On other occasions, they would hold competitions to see who could walk along the top rails of the paddock fence the furthest before falling off, or push a big old drum up a nearby grassy slope and stand on top of it, turning it with their feet, as it rolled down the steep incline, quickly gaining momentum. Often, if Elisabeth were nearby, she would scream in fright, but Laura seemed fearless, trusting Jamie or Greg to tell her when to jump, before they crashed into the fence at the bottom.

In summer, they swam in a big waterhole in the creek that ran through the neighbouring property, taking turns to see who could swing the highest on the thick rope Ken had tied over the branch of a big gum tree. Laura loved the feeling of total freedom, as she flew through the air, letting go exactly when Jamie said to, then the shock of the sudden splash into the cool water below. But Elisabeth could see what Laura could not see – she would always watch from the safety of the bank, her heart in her mouth.

'Jamie, don't let her! I … I'll tell Mum!'

'Scaredy cat! Scaredy cat!' Greg, and sometimes even Laura herself, would yell back. 'Come on – it's great fun!'

And yet the two sisters remained firm friends, despite Elisabeth's more cautious nature. They now shared the small veranda bedroom Ken had built, hands easily touching across the space between their beds, as they lay talking before they fell asleep each night. Often during those years when Laura did her lessons at home with Margaret, their conversations followed a similar pattern.

'What did you do at school today?'

'Nothing much – just sums and spelling. Then we went to the library and looked at some pictures of Australian animals. We have to do a project about one for next week. Then we did reading and I had to read out loud – but I made some mistakes. And then we had to write something about our family.'

'Did you write about me?'

'Yes, silly!'

'What did you say?'

'Oh, just how we go climbing and swimming at the waterhole and stuff. Miss Anderson says you must be very brave.'

'She doesn't know anything.'

'She does so too – she's my teacher!'

Silence for a bit – then Laura would start up again rather sleepily, a wistful tone creeping into her voice.

'It must be fun to look things up in the library.'

'It's okay – Miss Anderson helps us. My project's going to be about wombats.'

'I read about the wombat the other day with Mum. I could help you.'

'Okay.'

Then finally silence, interspersed with the sound of gentle breathing. Laura had grown used to the fact that sleep came less readily to her than to her sister, but it did not bother her. As she lay there, she thought about so many things and

Laura

listened to all the sounds she could hear outside – the wind rustling the leaves of the bushes near their window, the screech of flying foxes in the fruit trees down by the fence, a chorus of frogs croaking in the creek across the paddocks, a dog howling in the distance.

And whenever she woke up screaming and clawing frantically at her head, as still happened sometimes, Elisabeth would reach over and try to calm her, tears running down her own face from fright, but also from a deep sadness that she did not fully understand.

'It's okay, Laura! It's Elisabeth – I love you, Laura!'

Then their mother or father would come – and Laura would settle after a while and feel safe again. Or she would be carried to her parents' bed and Elisabeth would eventually fall asleep again, her own pillow wet with tears.

When Laura was nine, the Hardings found themselves with new neighbours. For some time, the farm adjacent to theirs had been up for sale. Ken had talked with his uncle about it at length.

'Uncle Bill, you know the farm isn't going so well,' he reasoned. 'If you could see your way clear to making an offer on the next door place, then we could fatten a few more cattle there. We'd have room to grow more fodder too – perhaps we could even try planting a few avocado trees or some macadamia. They'd do well on those slopes near the creek, I reckon. Greg says he wants to leave school next year – maybe he'd like to work on the farm for a bit with me. Jamie could do a few odd jobs around the place in his uni holidays. What do you think?'

But Uncle Bill had thought very little of Ken's idea. He was not keen to throw good money after bad and in reality had not seen any great financial return for the years Ken had worked his farm. Give it a couple more years, he thought to himself, and I'll sell up too – but he did not say that to Ken. He wanted to help the family for as long as he could – for the little blind girl's sake as much as anything.

Now some southerners from Melbourne had bought the neighbouring farm – nice enough folk, it seemed to Ken, when he first met them as they were moving in. Not long after, Margaret invited them over for a meal.

'We should be neighbourly, Ken. After all, they don't know anyone up here.'

'Let's hope their kids treat Laura okay,' Ken had growled, ever protective of her.

He need not have worried. There were two girls in the Thomas family, both older than Laura. The meal had gone well, except for when the visitors had bowed their heads for a moment before eating. Ken had looked at Margaret, but did not comment. Later, Barry Thomas explained a little more about the reason for their move.

'Actually, it's true we've moved here to get away from the rat-race, but more importantly, we want to set up a community farm to help people struggling with drugs or alcohol. The group we've been part of in Melbourne is supporting us financially until we can get on our feet. I come from a farming family, but moved to the city to study and later work – Rachel's city born and bred. We'll have a lot to learn, but I believe we're doing what God wants us to do. Do you folk attend a church in town?'

Margaret had looked across at Ken, rather embarrassed, but Ken answered Barry honestly and directly.

'Haven't been in a church since we were married – except for a couple of weddings and one or two funerals. Marg and I met years ago at a church function – but a lot of water has flowed under the bridge since then. Not sure I even believe in God any more, as a matter of fact – seems God gets a few things mixed up sometimes.'

He had glanced briefly at Laura as he finished speaking. The girls were chatting amongst themselves, so had not overheard the conversation. Barry and Rachel both caught his meaning immediately, but Margaret was relieved to see they did not seem offended at all.

'Yes …yes, I can understand why you might feel like that,' Barry responded. 'Rachel and I went through quite a lot of questioning after our son died three years ago – but gradually we came back to a place of firm faith in God again. There's a lot we don't understand, but I guess we feel God's in charge and can bring some good out of these terrible things.'

Ken looked sceptical and Margaret could see the light of battle beginning to dawn in his eye. Hastily she intervened with a question of her own.

'Your son … what happened?' she asked gently.

'He was knocked off his bike by a drunk driver,' Rachel answered quietly. 'He had severe head injuries and spent months in hospital before we could bring him home, but he was permanently brain-damaged. We knew he didn't have long to live, but we wanted to care for him at home. The girls were wonderful, talking to him and playing with him, when he was well enough. It was certainly a very hard, testing time, but God got us through it.'

'Why did it have to happen at all though – that's *my* question,' Ken commented. 'I don't expect you to answer that – I probably wouldn't be convinced, whatever you said! But I respect your beliefs and I hope it works out for you here.'

'We won't be looking for a church to attend in town, by the way,' Barry added. 'Our community meets in members' homes on Sundays for worship and some teaching from the Bible – and then we share a meal together. At first there'll be just us, of course, but some others from Melbourne will join us soon – another

Laura

couple to help us run the place, plus one or two who've been battling drug problems. When they get here, perhaps you'd like to join us one Sunday?'

Ken's answer was deliberately non-committal, clearly conveying the fact that he had no intention of taking up the invitation.

'Perhaps – we'll see.'

He had no defence, however, against their girls' complete acceptance of Laura that evening, or the special friendship that quickly sprang up between them in the following weeks.

'I guess they understand from their experience with their brother,' Margaret commented, after the visitors had left. 'They certainly have different ways of doing things, but they all seem nice, don't they?'

'I suppose so, but they'll definitely have some challenges ahead. A bit too religious for me – but I liked how they treated Laura.'

Margaret had no qualms after that in welcoming the girls, when they asked to come over and play the following week. It was the beginning of many visits back and forth, Laura soon managing to make her way to their place easily by herself. As Margaret listened to them laughing and talking together ninety to the dozen whenever they visited, she felt as if a healing ointment were being placed on some wound deep in her heart. She noticed how much happier and more relaxed Laura seemed afterwards too, now that she had special friends of her own who accepted her without question. She would quote endlessly things that either Sarah or Anne had said – things, Margaret soon realised, that increased her confidence so much in mixing with girls her own age.

'Anne says I'm pretty and have really nice skin and hair. She says she wishes she had my colour hair. Is Anne pretty, Mum?'

Margaret swallowed hard, unsure how to describe Anne's sturdy build and rather large, round face framed by straight brown hair pulled back tightly in two long, old-fashioned plaits.

'Well ... she has a kind, friendly face – and her hair's lovely and long and thick. I'm not sure if people would call her pretty – but she's so nice it doesn't matter, does it?'

'I guess not – she's pretty on the inside anyway. I know her hair's long – she lets me play with it. She likes people doing her hair. She says she wants to try putting on makeup, but her parents won't let her wear any yet. I'm going to wear makeup – but you'll have to show me how to put it on properly. It might be a bit hard at first.'

Margaret was glad Laura could not see the tears in her eyes.

'I'm sure you'll work it out, love – look at all the other things you've managed to do! Anyway, you're pretty just as you are, like Anne said.'

It was definitely time Laura went to school, Margaret decided, after that particular conversation. She needed to mix more with others, whatever difficulties that might present to the local school.

Not long after, she asked the principal once again.

And this time he reluctantly agreed to try it – at least for that coming year.

'We'll put Laura in Grade Five, but it remains to be seen if she really is up to that standard,' he commented rather sceptically. 'She seems to have done well enough with her correspondence work, judging by her reports – but we'll soon see. The teacher taking Laura's class next year will be new to the school. In fact, she's new to teaching, so she won't have any time to prepare special material for your daughter, but I know she'll be fine about having a blind child in the class. She used to be a student of mine years ago. Also I've been told someone from the new special education unit for isolated children might be able to visit and advise Laura's teacher, if she needs extra help. Let's hope it goes well, anyway – for all concerned.'

So for the first time, Laura set off for school that January, nonchalantly climbing up behind Elisabeth into the old bus that stopped at their corner, as if she had done it for years. At least, that was the impression she hoped she conveyed. She had resisted with all her might Margaret's suggestion that she drive them to school on her first day.

'Mum, I *don't* want you fussing over me! I can look after myself – I've been to the school enough times with you and Ian and Elisabeth. Anyway, Elisabeth will show me where everything is. I wish Anne and Sarah went to our school though – then we could all go on the bus together. Why do their parents want to teach them at home?'

'It's something to do with their church, Laura. They used to go to school in Melbourne, I think, but they wanted to try home-schooling here. They have material provided for them, just like you did with your correspondence lessons.'

As the bus jolted along the winding road into town, Laura squared her shoulders and sat up straighter. Yes, it would have been nice to have someone older beside her, especially someone kind like Anne. But she could do it – with a bit of help from Elisabeth at first, of course. Anyway, she'd soon find her way around herself – and she could ask questions if she had to. But not too many. She'd just have to learn to listen extra carefully and try hard to remember every single thing she heard. She'd show them she could do it – all the teachers who hadn't wanted her before now and all the kids as well.

That morning, it was a very determined Laura who carefully stepped off the bus with her younger sister at the school gate.

She needed to be in the weeks ahead. That first day largely set the pattern

laura

for what life would be like for her at primary school – days filled with a mixture of boredom, challenge and confusion, as well as an increasing sense of isolation and of not fitting in. From that first morning, when Elisabeth had guided her to where the Grade Five class was lining up at assembly, Laura sensed things were going to be much more difficult than she had ever imagined. That only made her more determined to prove she could survive in such a situation, where everything and everyone was largely new to her – except for her sister. But Elisabeth, with a hurried 'Bye – see you at recess!' and a quick explanation to the girl standing behind Laura in line, had had to run to find her own class.

The school bell rang nearby with a resounding clang. Then, after what seemed an interminable time of waiting in the sun while names were called out and classrooms allocated, Laura found herself jostled and pushed from behind up a particularly long flight of stairs. All she needed were a few moments to gauge the height of each step, but there was no time for that. She stumbled on and up, somehow managing it, and stood confused at the top, until her teacher spotted her.

'Oh, you must be Laura – I was told about you, but I'd forgotten. I'm sorry – I'm still trying to find my way around myself. Here, we'll give you the first peg near the door for your bag and hat, so it will be easy for you. Just take out your books or whatever you'll need in the classroom and I'll show you where you can sit. … Yes, perhaps here would be best – right on the end of this row at the front, so you can get in and out easily. … Class, my name is Miss Stephens. I look forward to learning your names and getting to know all of you much better. Now, please stand around the walls and we'll do this in an orderly fashion. Rather than allocate you your seats, I'd like to let you choose for yourselves where you want to sit first off. Then after a couple of weeks, we'll see how it's worked out. Perhaps if the girls go first – boys, stand back, that's right – there'll be plenty of spots left for you. Now, how about someone sit next to Laura here? She's new like me and she can't see, so she'll need some help.'

Laura heard a quick rush of bodies to various areas of the room. Then, with a sinking feeling, she realised that the seat beside her and others in front and behind were still empty.

'Now, come on, girls, you need to spread out better than that! Look, there's lots of space down the front near Laura. You girls there – what are your names? Christine, Annette and Sandra? Okay, Christine and Annette, why not sit here? Then Sandra can sit in front of you and beside Laura. That way you'll still be near one another.'

'But we wanted to sit in the same row! We don't want to be split up.'

'It's not fair! Everyone else got to choose.'

'Laura didn't — and I think one of you should at least be kind enough to sit next to her. Why not take it in turns? ... Come on girls, this is dragging on far too long! Sandra, you sit next to Laura for now, please. As I said, we'll see in a couple of weeks how you've all gone sitting where you are, so things will probably change anyway. No need to grumble or cry about it. Boys, you can sort yourselves out now. Hurry up!'

It did not work — certainly not for Laura, or for Miss Stephens either. Sandra sniffed and sulked beside Laura all that day, and it was no better the next, when Christine swapped places with Sandra. The three friends giggled and chatted amongst themselves, deliberately leaving Laura out of the conversation, helping her only when she was holding them up in any way, or when Miss Stephens asked them to. In fact, the whole class chatted amongst themselves, it seemed to Laura, while Miss Stephens vainly tried to maintain some semblance of order.

Laura sat by herself at recess and lunch, except when Elisabeth came to check on her and guide her to the toilets. Miss Stephens had asked the other girls in her class to help her, but they inevitably 'forgot'. Laura quickly vowed she would not rely on them for anything — ever. After Elisabeth had shown her several times, she took herself there when most of her classmates would be eating their lunch or playing. Then often after she had eaten, she would make her own way the library, where she would sit alone, doing homework or writing whatever she felt like.

When, after the first two chaotic weeks in Miss Stephens' classroom, seats were eventually reallocated, Laura found herself in a corner at the back, the only girl in a row of boys, with more boys seated in front of her.

'There'll be more room for your special books here, Laura, and you can do your own work without getting in anyone's way,' Miss Stephens explained, in her almost permanently harassed voice. 'And the boys will be gentlemen and help, won't you?'

They were in fact more help, Laura quickly discovered, than the girls. At least they were never catty and mean, talking about her under their breath in a way she could easily hear, since she was so attuned to picking up every sound. The boys were awkward but uncomplicated and in the end, she was grateful for their presence — grateful she did not have to relate too closely with the girls, especially Christine, Annette and Sandra. She would never fit in with them, she knew that. She couldn't make snide comments behind her hand about how others looked. She couldn't see to giggle when Miss Stephens smiled at one of the young male teachers as he walked past their windows. She couldn't write secret little notes and pass them quickly along the row, undetected by Miss Stephens. She could never be the best at netball, or the fastest at running, or even the neatest at craftwork.

Laura

But there *were* things she was much better at than anyone, both in and outside the classroom. Many things. Except that these did not endear her to her classmates – and especially not to the girls. She loved being in the school choir, often catching the early bus to school by herself, to be there in time for extra practices. She was a favourite with the choir conductor, since she never talked instead of listening and always knew the words by heart. She loved the recorder group that met on Wednesdays after school, remembering perfectly every new tune they learnt. In Miss Stephens' class, she retained much of what she heard and almost everything she read from her Braille textbooks. She soaked up information, often answering questions put to the class before most of the others had worked out what Miss Stephens was even asking. She could do sums in her head before the class had time to write them down and she could spell better than any of them. Eager to please at first – and even more eager to outsmart the others – she would often call out answers, forgetting to put up her hand, thus greatly frustrating an already overwhelmed Miss Stephens.

'Laura, please don't call out the answers so quickly! We *know* you know them. Give the others a chance! If you don't stop, I'm going to have to send you to work by yourself in the library.'

And sometimes, in her boredom, she would distract Miss Stephens with difficult questions or argue about something she was teaching the class, until the others would begin talking amongst themselves. Then Miss Stephens would lose her temper and take it out on the whole class.

'Oh, you're such a difficult lot! Why can't you have some manners?' she would storm. 'Perhaps you'll learn a few by staying behind for an extra ten minutes at lunch time.'

'Miss smarty pants!' Laura would often hear hissed at her on these occasions, as she eventually ate her solitary lunch. 'You always think you're so clever.'

As well, she would sometimes hear comments that were not meant for her ears. She tried to wipe them from her mind, but they stuck like glue, embedding themselves somewhere deep in her psyche. She was only ten – and she did not know what to do with them. Eventually this showed itself in aggression towards, or alternatively, withdrawal from those around her at school. Sometimes she would give as good as she got – or even more. When she overheard an unkind remark, she would fire up, hurtling equally cutting comments as loudly as possible in the direction of her unseen enemies.

'You don't know *anything*! You're so *dumb*! You just *think* you're smart. I *know* I'm smart – I *know* I can do things. I'll show *you*!'

With that, she would often lash out at her opponents with her hands or feet or with whatever was nearby. Then she would put her head down on the desk, so that nobody, least of all Miss Stephens, could reason with her. She became deaf to any pleas or orders directed towards her, only moving when the bell rang and marching out of the classroom without a word, her little figure as erect as possible. A silent bus ride home would follow – but when Laura finally reached the safety of the Harding's kitchen and felt the warmth of her mother's arms around her, she would hold on tight, wordlessly asking for acceptance and reassurance, until the tears came.

But she never ever spoke about the things she overheard, or the names they called her that hurt so much. They were locked deep inside her, too upsetting to share with anyone.

Laura

chapter five

At the end of that year, it did not come as a complete surprise, therefore, when the principal and the area guidance officer, having consulted at length with Miss Stephens, informed Margaret that, in their opinion, it would be better if Laura completed her schooling elsewhere.

'Mrs Harding, there's no doubt your daughter's very bright,' Mr Brown began. 'She has an excellent memory and, apart from that, has obviously read so much more than the other children, despite her handicap. You've taught her well – *too* well really, I think, for her to fit in, either academically or socially, with the other children in her year. It seems she's been quite bored with some of the work, but unfortunately we can't put her up a year, as that's not department policy. Then she's been asking questions and making comments that Miss Stephens finds difficult to handle in front of the class, which in turn causes the other students to become disruptive. The special education teacher from the isolated children's unit did try to help, particularly in the Maths area, but Miss Stephens simply didn't have time to put her suggestions in place for Laura – and, as you know, we don't have any resource teachers available for such tasks. Miss Stephens will be taking that same class again next year, so we think it would be better all round if Laura

laura

were not part of it.'

'You've done a great job with Laura, Mrs Harding,' the guidance officer added, 'and I understand the Correspondence School would be happy to enrol her again. Or perhaps you might consider the Blind School in Brisbane, now that she's older?'

But Margaret was determined to fight the decision.

'Do you realise Laura's waited for years to go to school the same as anyone else? I know she's been difficult for Miss Stephens on occasions in the classroom and I'm sorry about that, but surely there's *something* more we can do? Would it help if I came and sat with her next year – would Miss Stephens mind?'

'I don't think that's the answer, Mrs Harding,' the principal responded firmly. 'Miss Stephens has enough on her hands, without having to consider Laura's special needs all the time. Remember, we did say it might only be for a year. I'm sure this will work out best for Laura in the long run – and for Miss Stephens too. Perhaps her class will be able to function more normally next year then.'

By this time Margaret was extremely angry.

'Mr Brown, it's my opinion Miss Stephens' classes will never be anything *like* 'normal' whether Laura's there or not, from what I hear. It sounds to me as if things are pretty disorganised and chaotic most of the time. Laura hasn't said much about the other children, but apparently they've often gone out of their way to make her feel different and unwelcome. To be honest, they seem to have resented her – no doubt because she's more intelligent. I don't want to cause trouble for anyone and I'm sure Laura wouldn't want to be where she's not welcome either, so she'll definitely go back to learning at home with me. However, I do have one request. Her favourite activities at school have been the choir and the recorder group – and she can't do *them* by correspondence! Would there be any reason she couldn't continue to take part in both these activities? Surely you could see your way clear to letting her do that at least!'

The principal, acutely uncomfortable, and also very aware that Margaret spoke the truth as far as Miss Stephens' classroom management was concerned, wished with all his heart to end the painful interview.

'Well … it hasn't been done before, but … well, I don't see any real reason why not – as long as Laura arrives on time and leaves straight after. Yes, perhaps that *is* a good suggestion, Mrs Harding. We'll look forward to seeing Laura then for these activities at least next year.'

On Laura's last day in Miss Stephens' class, she did her best to finish well, deliberately waiting for others to answer questions before she put her hand up. Then just before the bell rang that afternoon, Miss Stephens announced that Laura would not be coming back the following year.

At first there was silence – and then Laura heard a few quickly muffled claps coming from Christine, Annette and Sandra's direction, followed by some stifled giggling.

Miss Stephens heard it too. She began speaking again quickly, feeling inadequate to deal with such a situation.

'Laura and her family have decided to have her learn at home by correspondence, until she starts high school. She'll still be coming here for choir and recorder group, however, so we won't lose her altogether. Three cheers now for Laura, everyone!'

The class managed some hasty cheers, before scrambling for the door and freedom. A few moments later, as the three girls pushed past her on the veranda, the words 'good riddance', followed by more giggles, easily reached Laura's ears.

The following year, Laura applied herself to her schoolwork with even more determination, but Margaret detected a driven-ness in the way she pored over her Braille notes and books – and it worried her. She was glad to see how much Laura enjoyed her twice-weekly visits to the school for choir and recorder group, but even then, there was an intense look about her, as if she felt she had to justify her inclusion in such activities. Margaret tried to think of a variety of ways to make her daughter's days a little more relaxed, to make learning more fun. For eleven-year-old Laura, life was becoming too much of a serious business all round.

Whenever Sarah and Anne came over to visit, however, Laura's face would light up. Margaret always felt her spirits lift at the sounds of laughter that would invariably emerge from Laura and Elisabeth's room, as the girls chatted, played board games or whatever took their fancy, or practised their recorders together.

It was Anne who eventually thought of a way to spend even more time together.

'Mrs Harding, can I ask Mum if Laura would be able to come over some afternoons and do schoolwork with me? Now Sarah goes to high school, it sometimes gets a bit lonely doing lessons by myself. Next term our friends from Melbourne will probably be here living with us and they have kids our age, but right now there's just me. If it's okay with you, I could ask Mum tonight. *Please* say I can!'

Margaret was a little cautious. Anne's schooling was different from Laura's, she knew that much – and not just because Laura needed to use Braille and listen to tapes. Barry and Rachel viewed things from a distinctly Christian perspective and taught the girls to do the same. She was not sure if she herself, let alone Ken, who had even less time for God these days than she did, wanted such input for Laura or any of their children.

Yet, when Rachel came over later that evening to discuss the idea and answer any of their questions, their fears were soon put at rest. As they talked, it became obvious to them that it was the right thing to do.

Eventually, Ken had come straight to the point.

'As you and Barry know, we're not church-type people – at least Marg and I used to be, but we haven't even thought about it for years now. Especially since Laura's eye trouble. We've been so busy – and anyway, I definitely have reservations about a God who lets little kids go blind before they're three. But if, as you say, Anne and Laura will just be doing normal lessons and school stuff together, then that's okay with me. Laura always gets on well with your girls. Right from the beginning, they accepted her – and I like that.'

Ken's voice had gone a bit gruff, so Margaret hastily intervened.

'Let's see how it goes anyway – for both girls. We don't want to hold Anne back at all, since she's a year ahead of Laura – but I know Laura will be very quick to catch onto anything new you teach her.'

'I really hope it works well,' Rachel responded. 'It's only two afternoons a week and usually Anne has done all her formal schoolwork by lunchtime anyway. I thought maybe Anne could read to Laura sometimes, or they could listen to different types of music together, or do some cooking, or go for walks. I'm sure Laura knows lots of things Anne knows nothing about – and vice versa. That will leave you free to do whatever you want, Margaret, and me too, for that matter. And it will be good for both of them, I think.'

It worked even better than any of them could have predicted. On the days she was due at Anne's, Laura would quickly gobble down her lunch and make her own way over to her house, often accompanied by her faithful Cobber. The two girls loved the same sort of books and had the same sense of humour, often laughing together at the strangest things. When it came to music, Laura taught Anne to play simple chords on the guitar and introduced her to the country ballads and current pop songs her Dad sang with his band. In turn, for the first time in her life, Laura listened to some of the well-known old hymn tunes that were part of Anne's heritage, as well as a few more contemporary Christian songs, with catchy melodies and upbeat rhythms. But the words and concepts were foreign to her – and besides, she knew her Dad wouldn't approve of her learning anything too religious.

She and Anne went for long walks beside the creek and into the nearby bushland, often with Cobber tagging along. Not adventurous expeditions such as Laura and her brothers had undertaken in the past and that she and Ian still sometimes did, but slower, more meandering strolls, chatting as they went and stopping whenever the fancy took them. Often Anne would find different leaves and wildflowers and interesting stones and carefully show them to Laura, letting her explore their shape and texture with her light butterfly touch. Then Anne would try her best to describe the appearance of each one with painstaking exactness.

'Oh, Laura, look at this leaf! It's so smooth and glossy. Can you feel its really neat serrated edges? They're so perfectly even! You know, I think God's so clever to have made all these different beautiful things.'

It was not that Laura's own family did not take time to describe things to her or explain how this or that worked. Jamie in particular had taught her so much, before he had left to study in Brisbane, and her Mum was always careful to give her as accurate a picture of things as possible. Elisabeth tried hard as well, even though she was younger, and her Dad did too when he was around. But here was someone right outside her family who cared enough to share so much with her – and who did not think she was odd, or a misfit.

It was a healing experience for Laura. She was so grateful to her friend – and her heart melted.

Their most exciting discovery in those months together was the sheer magic of C S Lewis's *Chronicles of Narnia*. Anne was already reasonably familiar with the books, since Sarah had read them some years earlier, but she had been a little too young to really appreciate the language and symbolism in them. Now, as she read them aloud to Laura, she drank it all in afresh, revelling in particular in their mutual favourite, *The Lion, The Witch and the Wardrobe*.

'Ooooh, I don't like the White Witch, do you?' Laura said one day, shivering excitedly, despite being curled up in front of a cosy fire with Anne. 'She feels so cold and hard, and – well, sort of evil and creepy. Edmund's just stupid and greedy, but she knows exactly how to tempt him and trick him. I *love* Aslan though. I know *exactly* what he looks like – he's so strong and beautiful!'

Both girls were in floods of tears by the time they reached the account of his death, just like the sisters Susan and Lucy in the story.

'Oh, keep reading, keep reading! What happens? This *can't* be the end!' Laura wailed, as the witch prepared to plunge her knife into Aslan's body.

Anne tried valiantly to read on. Laura was so relieved and delighted when Susan and Lucy found the stone table broken in two and heard a great roar behind them.

'Oh, that's so good! He came alive again. I *knew* he would!'

'Just like Jesus,' Anne commented softly, tears still in her eyes.

'What do you mean?'

'Just like Jesus. He's called 'The Lion of Judah' in the Bible – did you know that? And he came alive again after he was killed, just like Aslan did.'

'Well – I knew he came alive again, but I didn't know he was called "The Lion

Laura

of Judah".'

'And Aslan's really good and wise and kind and strong and powerful – all the things Jesus is too.'

Laura was silent for a while and then there was some hesitancy in her voice when she finally replied.

'I don't know – I don't know if Jesus is like that or not, Anne. I don't think Dad believes he is anyway. ... but it would be wonderful if it really *was* true.'

'You ... you mean wonderful if *Jesus* was true and he really was good and kind and everything else, or if the story of Aslan was true?'

'Both, I guess – but anyway, I'd better go home now. It's late.'

Anne sighed. She wished Laura could believe Jesus truly was all those things she had just said, but she knew how hard it would be for her. She gave Laura an especially warm hug as she said goodbye.

'I love you, Laura – and I'm going to pray that one day you'll know Jesus really *is* just like Aslan. See you Thursday!'

One evening in October, the primary school held a special fundraising concert, featuring the choir and the recorder group. There was much excitement in the Harding household, since both Laura and Elisabeth were in the choir. It was to be held in the old School of Arts – the only venue in the town large enough. But best of all, Sarah and Anne were coming with them.

Everything went well at first. The choir sang its first bracket and then Laura's recorder group performed excellently. There were various solo items, as well as a sterling effort from the small school orchestra. Some folk dancing from the younger classes followed and then it was time for the final item – the second bracket of songs from the choir.

But Laura was missing from the stage.

Margaret and Anne finally found her waiting for them near the main hall door. Laura never told them the whole story, but from what little she did say, they gathered she had overheard Christine, Annette and Sandra whispering loudly and laughing at her. Then, because she was upset and lost concentration, she had missed following the others onto the platform and been unable to find her way there by herself, since she was in an unfamiliar place.

'They were just talking about me as usual, like they did when we were in the same class – things like I walk a bit differently and my eyes don't look *that* real and I always think I'm smart and why would anyone want to be my friend – and that I'd never be pretty without proper eyes. But I don't want to talk about it. Anyway, I showed *them*! They probably thought I'd stand there like a big cry-baby until they came off the stage, but I just went back the way I came in and walked along the wall outside. And by the time I heard the clapping, I was nearly at the front door, so I decided to wait there for you.'

The journey home was completed almost in silence, except when Margaret dropped Sarah and Anne off at their gate. Then Anne leant across to where Laura was sitting huddled in the corner of the back seat and put her arms around her as best she could.

'I love you, Laura – *I* want to be your friend. And you *are* pretty too!'

It took a few days before Laura was prepared to say anything more about it and then she seemed to want to laugh it off, as if it were no big deal. But Margaret knew it was and that it still hurt, so chose her words carefully.

'I'm sorry your special night was spoilt, Laura. Those girls don't deserve you as a friend – they don't deserve to be listened to at all. Anne was right – you certainly *are* pretty. And in the next few months, I think you'll get even prettier as you mature and your body changes. Soon you'll have a lovely grown-up figure and you'll be almost as tall as I am. So don't worry about anything those girls said – ever! You've shown them you can do so much better than they can in just about everything anyway.'

Margaret spoke so fiercely and with such conviction, that Laura finally laughed and hugged her tight.

'Oh Mum – you're the best! That's what Jamie always says.'

'Well, there you are,' Margaret said smiling, in an endeavour to lighten the conversation. 'It must be right, if Jamie says so. At least, I know *you* think that.'

They joked together a little longer, but underneath, Margaret's heart was heavy and her mind in turmoil. She had suspected Laura had always heard more than she let on and now that had been confirmed. Anger welled up in her at the ignorance and cruelty that had caused such hurt and also the injustice of it all. Worry for her daughter as she approached puberty also fuelled her anger. Things were hard enough for any girl at that time, let alone someone who couldn't see.

Laura's comment about Jamie had brought a further concern bubbling to the surface. It seemed that living with his grandmother in Brisbane while he studied at uni was definitely not proving to be ideal for a nineteen-year-old. She was so particular – he never felt free to invite his friends there. As a result, he often came home on weekends. He seemed lonely to her – and there was something else wrong too, she felt, but she couldn't put her finger on it.

She squared her shoulders and resolutely put such gloomy thoughts from her mind. Jamie was a dear and such a support to her – especially when Ken stayed out drinking with his mates on Saturday nights. Recently the band had re-formed, with regular gigs in a local pub each weekend. Ken loved it all, but while it did help the family finances, the farm work suffered as a result. And it certainly did not make for good relationships all round on weekends. No, Margaret would not

Laura

like to do without Jamie coming home as often as he did, whatever the reason. But she knew she sometimes depended too much on him – and that was possibly unhelpful to them both.

That night, Margaret talked at length with Ken again.

'We *have* to begin making some decisions about the future, Ken,' Margaret began firmly. 'We said we'd think about moving to Brisbane when Jamie finished school, or maybe when Greg did. Well, school will be over for Greg in a couple of months. And the year after next, Laura will be ready for high school – she's ready now, academically. But some of the kids here have been really cruel to her, Ken – and I feel it's wrong she should have to battle on through high school with those same kids. Then there's the problem of her having only a pretty narrow choice of subjects as well. Maybe we should consider sending her to the Blind School now – but if you still don't want her going away to live with another family, then we'll have to move down there ourselves.'

'We've been over this before, Marg,' Ken responded wearily. 'I know what you think – and you may be right. Of course I want the best for Laura – but really it's out of the question for us to move. The band's going well and all my friends are here. I'd be letting Uncle Ken down too. Anyway, what would I do in the city? I don't have a head for business and I enjoy working outdoors and being my own boss. What would you suggest I do down there?'

'I don't know exactly. But you'd find something – and I could always go back to teaching. I know I'd have to do a refresher course, but I'd manage that. It would give Laura such a wonderful new start. She'd love to have singing lessons, or maybe even learn the piano – but where can she do that here? Couldn't we take the plunge, Ken, and tell your uncle we need to move? He'd understand – especially since it's for Laura's sake.'

'It's not as simple as that, Marg,' Ken sighed exasperatedly. 'Anyway – I don't want you back teaching. You'll still have enough to do at home, even when Laura goes to high school. She'll be right – Ian will be there if she needs any support and I'm sure they'll have enough subjects to keep her interested.'

'We don't even know for sure yet what the principal thinks about enrolling her, or whether she'll be any better off than she was at the primary school. The discussions I've had with him so far haven't been encouraging.'

Margaret's voice contained a hopeless, despairing note that Ken for once did not miss. He knew he'd let her down a lot lately. In his heart, he didn't want to. He truly loved her – and all his kids. Especially Laura. With a sigh, he reached out for her hand.

'I'm sorry, Marg – I know I haven't been as helpful as I could've been the last little while. I think you've done a great job, spending so many hours each day with Laura. It's really hard to know what's the best thing to do about it all. Especially when the band's just coming good again …'

In the end, the issue was decided for them. Since the discussion about purchasing the neighbouring property, Ken's uncle had kept a stricter eye on business matters relating to his own farm. It had continued to struggle under his nephew's management, consistently losing money. In the past, Bill had had long phone conversations with Ken over it all, especially when tax time came around, but Ken had always been able to talk him into giving it a go for just one more year. Bill knew his nephew was a charmer, but somehow he always ended up agreeing to Ken's latest proposal and wondering later why he had. Part of the reason, he knew, was young Laura. He remembered how much she'd been looking forward to going to the local school when he last visited the farm.

Yet during a phone conversation with Margaret one night when Ken was out, he discovered that things had not turned out so smoothly for Laura at school after all.

'So does that mean, Margaret, that she'll be able to go to the same high school as the boys when the time comes?' he had asked.

Margaret had responded rather cautiously.

'Well – we hope so. I've had some initial discussions with the school, but they're a bit doubtful about how she'll go. As well, I think they believe she'll be too much of a liability in the classroom. Anyway, I'm not so sure it's the best place for her really. I'd like her to have more choice of subjects – and I'd especially like her to be able to learn piano or singing.'

'But … that's the only high school in the area, isn't it?'

'It really is – anywhere further away would be pretty impractical.'

'Sounds like she needs to go to a school down here – maybe the School for the Blind, Marg.'

'As far as I know, it doesn't cater for high school age kids, but I understand there *are* Special Units for visually impaired students at a couple of the high schools in Brisbane now. I'm not sure if Ken would be keen on that though, just as he's always hated the idea of her going to the School for the Blind itself. He's always wanted her to go to a normal school with other sighted kids – and I must admit I agree with him on that. I'd love her to be able to go to a big school in Brisbane – somewhere with a good music department and a high academic standard. Laura's done really well at the Correspondence School and I've seen myself how quickly she catches onto new ideas and remembers so much. But no point in dreaming. Ken likes it here and wants to stay put, as you know.'

'Hasn't he told you about our plans yet? He might want to stay put, but Dot and I aren't getting any younger and we'd like to retire and buy a place in the

Laura

mountains behind the Gold Coast. Unfortunately that means we'll have to sell the farm – I did warn Ken about that possibility last time we talked. We certainly don't want to inconvenience you folk, but sounds like it might be the right time for you to move anyway.'

Margaret could not respond at first, shocked at what he had told her, but also relieved. There seemed something inevitable about this turn of events – as if things were meant to happen this way.

Eventually she found her voice again.

'Yes, Uncle Bill – you could be right. Ken hadn't mentioned your plans – he's been very busy, so I guess that's why. I'll tell him you called and want to speak to him. He should be home tomorrow night – I'll get him to phone you then.'

'Fine. And Marg – I'm glad we've had this conversation. I trust our news hasn't taken you too much by surprise. The only way you could stay where you are would be if you folk bought us out – but I don't think that's likely, do you?'

'No, not at all!' she had laughed. 'Don't worry about us – and I'm glad I got to talk to you too. I hope everything works out well with your retirement plans. Bye for now!'

Margaret sat deep in thought for a long time. In the end she decided not to wait up until Ken came home – who knew when that would be anyway? She'd tackle him the next night instead, before he phoned Uncle Bill.

The following morning, she made several calls of her own – to the area high school, the Correspondence School, the School for the Blind and finally the Education Department itself. She was determined to discover exactly what schools Laura was eligible to attend and what support the Department could be relied on to provide. It took most of the morning, but Margaret came away from these conversations with a much clearer idea of their options. Providing Ken would agree.

That night, he was late for dinner. Margaret was not overly surprised – she knew he had planned to take care of some banking in town that afternoon, since it was Friday.

'He's probably met up with some mates for a drink and forgotten the time,' she said to Jamie in a resigned voice, when he arrived home for the weekend around their normal dinnertime.

By the time Ken drove in the yard, the dishes were cleaned up, Jamie had started work on an overdue assignment, the girls were in their room and Greg and Ian were watching TV.

'Sorry I'm late,' he mumbled, as he kissed Margaret on the cheek.

He turned away quickly, heading into the kitchen to retrieve his dinner – but not before Margaret smelt the alcohol on his breath. She made no comment, however. Better to keep the peace, this night of all nights. But she'd have to speak to him about the phone call – Uncle Bill was expecting him to ring.

Ken finished his meal and headed for the veranda, beer in hand, to practise a few songs. Margaret followed him, deciding to come straight to the point.

'Ken, I've been waiting to tell you that Uncle Bill phoned last night. I said you'd call him back tonight, but before he hung up, we talked a bit. ... Ken, why didn't you tell me about their plans to retire soon? It certainly changes the picture for us – it makes it ...'

Ken interrupted her then, angrily putting his guitar down with a lot less care than usual, so that it clattered to the floor.

'Marg, what right do you have to talk to Uncle Bill behind my back? How dare you? He's *my* uncle!'

'I didn't deliberately talk behind your back! All I did was answer the phone and tell him you weren't around. *He* was the one who wanted to talk to *me*!'

'I find that hard to believe – he's no great shakes on the phone and he's only ever wanted to talk to *me* in the past. *I* run the farm – not *you*!'

'But why didn't you tell me about his plans? Especially when you know how I feel about moving.'

'Marg, I don't want to discuss this. And I'll tell him when I phone that he had no right to talk about anything to do with the financial side of the farm with you. That's my concern – so keep your nose out of it, do you hear me?'

'I most certainly do!' Marg responded angrily, stung by his tone. 'I'm sure the whole *family* can hear you! Uncle Bill didn't talk about business matters with me – he merely explained how they want to retire soon. I even covered for the fact that you hadn't told me – I said you've been very busy, which is true.'

'You're damned right I've been busy! I've tried to make a go of this farm – it's not *my* fault it hasn't made much profit these past few years. The soil's poor and there's not enough water – I tried to tell Uncle Bill he should buy the property next door. Then we could've had access to the creek. But he didn't listen – and now he wants to sell up. You should've told him he *can't* do that, if you're so keen to talk to him. ... Ah, *I* get it ... you're probably in cahoots with him! You probably worked all this out between the two of you – *I* know how keen you are to move to Brisbane. How many other times have you discussed our business with him?'

He was shouting even louder now. Suddenly, Jamie was there beside Margaret, concern on his face.

'Dad ... belt up! Stop yelling at Mum!' he said firmly, glaring at his father. 'The others can hear you – and it's not true what you're saying anyway. Mum's been the most loyal person ever to you – she's the best Mum anyone could have.

laura

Sit down and get your head straight! I'll go and make you some coffee – but don't even think of yelling at Mum again!'

The shock of Jamie's arrival sobered Ken immediately. Jamie had never spoken to him like that – but then Ken was sure he himself had never spoken to Marg like he just had either. He slumped in his chair, picked his guitar up and cradled it between his knees. Jamie brought the coffee and left again without saying a word. Ken took a few sips and then realised Margaret was still standing nearby.

'Marg ... I'm really sorry! I didn't mean to bite your head off. I know you wouldn't hatch up plans with Uncle Bill. You're right – I should've told you about how they plan to sell this place and retire. I guess I wanted to put it off – it made me feel such a failure all over again. If I'd been able to make a real go of the farm – and I know I would've, if Uncle Bill had bought next door – then they could've kept it and retired on the profits and we'd be staying here. Makes me look great, doesn't it? First the family business goes bust and now I can't even make a success of the farm for my uncle – or for us.'

Margaret sat down beside him.

'You tried your best, Ken. Anyway, don't worry about it now – let's leave any more talking till tomorrow. Drink your coffee – there's still time to call Uncle Bill.'

She spoke calmly, but her eyes were suspiciously bright and she could feel anger inside her – and embarrassment that the kids had no doubt heard everything their father had said, as Jamie had pointed out. Better to leave Ken to himself for a bit and make sure the others were settled. She got up and moved inside, first checking the lounge, where Greg and Ian were watching TV. They each gave her a quick, curious look, but, after she had signalled that everything was okay, merely shrugged their shoulders and returned to watching their movie. They hadn't heard exactly what Ken had said because of the noise of the TV – only his shouting. Things must be fine though, if Mum said they were.

As Margaret moved to the girls' bedroom, she heard Ken on the phone to Uncle Bill. The conversation seemed quite amicable, but she deliberately refrained from listening. Better to let Ken tell her about it. She passed Jamie's room on the way, and he poked his head out.

'Okay, Mum?'

'Okay, Jamie – thanks for your support, love! Dad didn't really mean it. He's just a bit discouraged – and he's obviously had a bit much to drink.'

Jamie took note of her heightened colour and the unshed tears in her eyes. He put his arms round her and gave her a long hug.

'I love you, Mum,' was all he said.

She knocked on the girls' door. They were quiet, but she knew they would not be asleep.

'Can I come in – or is there something secret going on?'

She opened the door and Elisabeth turned to stare at her with big, round eyes.

'Mum – are we really moving to Brisbane soon?' she asked a little apprehensively.

'Well, that's quite likely, according to what Uncle Bill said – obviously you heard what Dad and I were talking about on the veranda. But not until the end of the year.'

'Well, I like it here, because I can have my pony and the chickens. Plus there's lots of space to play and a mulberry tree so we can have leaves for my silkworms – but I wouldn't mind living in Brisbane either. Then I could go to the shops more and the movies and see Grandma. I'd miss all my friends – but it'd be fun moving to a new house. I hope it's really big. Will we have our own rooms?'

All the while that Elisabeth rattled on, Laura did not say a word. Suddenly her muffled voice came from under the bedcovers, which she had pulled over her head.

'Elisabeth, I hate you! You only *ever* think about yourself. You never even bothered to ask Mum if she was okay!'

Margaret heard the fear in her voice and tried to turn the bedclothes back, but Laura held them fast. Instead, she patted her shoulders through the blankets.

'I'm fine, Laura. Dad's just tired – and he got angry because he thought Uncle Bill was telling me things I didn't have to know. But we've sorted it out, so don't worry!'

'Yes, but I know I'm the reason you were arguing.'

'That's nonsense – I'm sure you heard what Dad said. It was nothing to do with you!'

'But you wouldn't even think of moving to Brisbane, if it wasn't for me.'

'That's not true, Laura – we have to move anyway, because Uncle Bill wants to sell the farm.'

'Dad doesn't want to go to Brisbane, I know – I've heard you talking about it before. You could just move somewhere else nearby, if it wasn't for me.'

'Laura, Dad will be fine. He'll get a job easily, you'll see. Besides, I think it will be better all round – maybe Jamie can even live with us again.'

Suddenly Laura flung the covers back and threw her arms around her mother's neck – but not before Margaret noticed the tears on her blotched cheeks.

'We'll have a great time in Brisbane next year, Mum – I know it. And I'll work really hard at high school when I get there. I'll make you and Dad so proud of me! I'll show them *all* I can do it.'

Laura

As if by tacit agreement, all five of the Harding children disappeared in various directions the following morning, leaving Ken and Margaret alone. Greg, with a strong interest in all things mechanical, had promised to help his friend fix his prized new possession – an old Ford Cortina, purchased for a few hundred dollars.

'It'll take all day, Mum, it's such a rust-bucket,' he informed Margaret briefly, as he set off on his bike. 'I'll be home after tea some time.'

Greg badly wanted his own car, Margaret knew. He was going to try to get an apprenticeship next year and save hard. He had wanted to leave school for some time, but Ken and Margaret had encouraged him to stay on. She hoped they'd done the right thing – he'd been very uncommunicative of late.

Ian had tennis every Saturday morning and today was going on to a friend's birthday barbecue afterwards. Ian was popular and easygoing – he'd miss all his friends when they left, Margaret reflected, but she was sure he'd easily make more.

Jamie, bless his heart, had decided to take the girls to the coast for the day. They had pestered him the previous night, but in the end it hadn't taken him long to give in. He could rarely deny Laura anything, even though it now meant he'd have to work hard on Sunday to get his assignment finished.

Margaret left Ken to sleep late, while she did her various Saturday jobs. He woke around ten and when he had surfaced enough, they talked.

'Well, Uncle Bill certainly sounded pretty definite. He says his decision's final – no going back now. He'll put the farm on the market soon, but will stipulate that we are to stay until the end of the school year. Not that that's too far away anyway. At least it's decided things for us,' Ken said gloomily, as he munched his toast.

'Uncle Bill's been very fair to us over the years, Ken. And we knew he'd retire some day. I know how much you don't want to move, but really this is the best year to do it, if we're going to, with Greg finishing. He'll have more chance of getting a good apprenticeship in Brisbane. And Ian's quite easygoing and adaptable – he'll make new friends quick enough, the same as Elisabeth. It might be best for Laura to continue at the Correspondence School for her last year of primary school though, I think, rather than try to get into the same school as Elisabeth. I know you're not keen for her to go to the School for the Blind – but maybe she could visit there occasionally at least.'

'Oh Marg, trust *you* to look on the positive side of it all! What about my mates in the band – not to mention the small matter of a job for me?'

'Ken, there'll be all sorts of possibilities for you in Brisbane. We can start looking in the papers next month. Maybe there'll be more opportunities in the music field for you there as well. Perhaps you could even start up another band – who knows?'

'Actually, I've met a couple of guys already who might be interested – Andy's brother and a mate of his. I was introduced to them the other night. So you never know. As for a job – well, I'm not sure what I'd even want to look for yet. I'd still prefer outdoor work – I'd hate to be cooped up in an office all day, like I was when we had the family business. And I'd want to be my own boss too.'

'Something will turn up, Ken, I'm sure of it. Not that I want to minimise how hard the move will be for you. But I think it's something we really *have* to do for Laura, quite apart from anything else. Yesterday I phoned the boys' high school, to see if they'd made any decision about having Laura there the year after next. They hadn't – but it didn't sound very positive. Then I phoned the Correspondence School to see what they thought and also the Blind School – and then finally the Education Department. I had to hang on for a long time and talk to different people, but at least I found out what seems to be the best option for Laura. Apparently there are two high schools in Brisbane with Special Units for students with disabilities, including visual impairment. The idea is that these kids are mostly integrated into normal classes, but they can go to their own resource room when the others are doing subjects like phys ed or art. And they have specially trained staff there to give them any extra help they might need. That's worth considering, don't you think?'

'Marg, you *know* my thoughts about that. I don't want Laura labelled as 'handicapped' or 'disabled', or treated differently from anyone else. Imagine how the 'normal' kids would laugh at the ones from the Special Unit – they'd probably treat them like idiots. Anyway, let's leave it until we see where we end up finding a place to rent. It's going to have to be somewhere not too expensive, that's for sure. Perhaps Andy's brother can give us a bit of an idea about that – he works for a real estate agent.'

Ken had got up then and wandered out to the veranda, picked up his guitar and begun strumming. Margaret wanted to tell him that the government would pay for a taxi for Laura to get to school, wherever they lived in Brisbane, but she knew there'd be no more talking that morning at least.

Laura

chapter six

Things moved quickly after that. A week later, a 'For Sale' sign went up on the Harding's front fence and in less than a month, a further sign was plastered across it – 'SOLD'.

In reality, the property was sold almost before it went on the market, since, as soon as the Harding's neighbours heard about it, they were quick to express their interest. One evening, Barry came to discuss it with Ken and Margaret.

'We'd planned by now to have another home built on our property for our friends from Melbourne, but the council keeps knocking our application back. So when Laura told Rachel this afternoon that your uncle's selling up, she made sure I heard about it as well. If we could combine the two properties, that would be wonderful! I think with the added acreage and easier access to creek water for this place, we could make a go of it. We're very sorry to hear you're leaving – the girls are particularly sad – but it would be a wonderful provision from God if our friends were able to buy it. Of course, they'd need help from the rest of our supporters in Melbourne, but we'll pray it will all come together.'

'Well, you'd better pray for things to work out for us in Brisbane, while you're at it,' Ken responded in a joking tone, but with a noticeable touch of cynicism. 'What with no house and no job, plus having to find good schools for Ian and

Elisabeth, as well as for Laura eventually, that should keep God busy. We could do with all the help we can get – and I'm not choosy where it comes from.'

Laura, sitting quietly nearby while the adults talked, felt embarrassed at her father's tone. She still hadn't made up her mind completely about the things she heard at the Thomas's to do with God and Jesus, but deep down she felt there was something good and right in what they believed. To them God was a friend they loved and trusted – and she would never ever laugh at anyone for wanting that.

Fortunately, Anne's Dad had not seemed offended.

'We'll do that for sure, Ken. I think God's up to the challenge!'

When the offer was put to Uncle Bill, he did not think about it for too long. He knew the farm was unlikely to attract much interest in its current unprofitable state and it was true, as Ken had maintained, that more acreage was required to make a go of things. Besides, he and Dot had already found their retirement home and needed the extra funds to close the sale. He had quickly instructed the agent to accept the offer and now it seemed everything was going ahead smoothly.

The last few weeks sped by for the Hardings in a mixture of excitement, apprehension and sadness. Ken was particularly touchy – he felt their leaving deeply, since he had been born and bred in the area. Besides, he had no job prospects and was definitely not looking forward to the endless interviews ahead. Uncle Bill had generously offered to pay their first month's rent in Brisbane, but Ken did not want to presume on his kindness any longer than he had to. He felt a big enough failure already.

Laura could sense his sadness as he sat on the veranda at nights, strumming his guitar and singing some of the slower, melancholy country ballads he liked. She knew all the words by heart and would often harmonise with him. Most were sentimental tales of lost love – Ken would secretly smile in the dark to hear Laura's sweet young voice singing so earnestly about such things. Yet with a pang he realised too that she did know something already of the loneliness and rejection these songs expressed, even though she could not fully understand these emotions. In the dark, when they came to the final bar of a song, he would often ruffle her hair and let his hand rest on her shoulder, as she sat on the floor nearby.

'Well done, Laura – that's my girl! You can be in my band any day. Wait till you get to that high school in Brisbane – you'll run rings round everyone.'

To some degree, Laura shared her father's reluctance to move. She hated the thought of leaving the farm and, in particular, of losing Anne's close friendship. On the other hand, at times she found it hard to contain her excitement about moving to Brisbane at last, especially since that would mean they could see more of Jamie. Laura loved each of her brothers for different reasons. Greg had a gruff exterior and could be hard to get on with, often rubbing his father up the wrong way, but he was honest and straightforward and could always be relied on to do what he said he would. Ian was everybody's friend, warm and easygoing, sometimes dreamy and forgetful, but always apologetic afterwards. But Jamie – well, Jamie was her champion, her protector. And now there was even a possibility he might move back home.

Anne's family came to say goodbye on the Hardings' final night. But before it was time for hugs and handshakes all round, Anne and Laura ran off to spend a few brief moments together.

'Laura, I didn't know what you'd like best for a present, so I bought you a couple of different things. Open this one first!'

'I love unwrapping presents, don't you? It's fun trying to guess what's inside,' Laura commented, determined to be cheerful.

She took her time examining the shape of the gift Anne placed in her lap and carefully felt for the opening in the tissue paper.

Anne sat quietly, knowing her friend well enough not to offer to help.

She had chosen well. Laura smelt the lavender and rose-scented potpourri long before her fingers finished exploring the round glass container, with its silver latticework lid decorated with tiny flowers. Soon she found the small catch holding the lid in place and opened it eagerly, gently feeling the dried petals inside. She buried her nose in them, trying to hide her emotion.

'It's wonderful, Anne! The perfume will always remind me of you. I can feel little shapes on the lid – are they flowers and leaves? I thought they would be. I'll carry it all the way in the car myself, so it won't get broken.'

The second gift was small and rectangular. Laura knew it was a tape as soon as she felt it and shook it gently. Anne anticipated her next question.

'I hope you like it – it's got some of my favourite Christian music on it. I know your Dad probably won't like it, but I thought maybe you could play it in your room sometimes. And when you do, it might help you remember the good times you and I had together and the things you heard about God and Jesus at our place as well. I'm always going to pray for you, Laura – every night, before I go to sleep!'

Laura could feel the tears coming again, but tried to hold them back, as she reached behind her for her present to Anne.

'I found one part of this when Mum and I looked through a little antique shop on our way home from Brisbane last time. I hope you don't mind – I love the smell of old stuff. The man in the shop wanted to show me everything, but as soon as I found this, I really liked it. I hope you do too.'

Anne opened it quickly. It was a beautiful old carved rosewood photo frame, smooth and oval-shaped. And in the frame was a photo of herself and Laura, heads together reading their favourite Narnia story. Laura's Mum had caught them both smiling happily, as they looked up at her from their book.

'I wish I could see the photo – Mum said it's a good one of us both. Do you like it? Do I look okay? Is my hair tidy?'

The anxious questions came tumbling out, one after the other. Now Anne could not stop the tears from falling.

'Oh, Laura, it's a fantastic present – I love it! The frame's so beautiful and I'll really treasure our special photo. Don't worry – your hair looks great and you have such a cute, cheeky smile on your face!'

They laughed in the middle of their tears. There was only time for one more hug, before Anne had to leave.

'Bye for now! Make sure you let me know your new address!'

And then she was gone.

During their first week in Brisbane, the family was divided between Margaret's mother's small unit and Ken's parents' place on the opposite side of the city. It was difficult enough for Jean to have Jamie boarding, let alone Margaret and Laura there as well. In the end, Jamie stayed at a friend's place for the week, but things were still awkward. Ken did not fare any better, since relations between him and his parents had been strained for some time. They were disappointed in him, Ken knew – all the more reason to be determined not to be obliged to them in any way.

Laura's parents soon discovered that, for the amount of rent they could afford, they could not be too choosy about where they wanted to live. Uncle Bill was still willing to pay the first month's rent, but it was up to them after that – and Ken still had no permanent work prospects. Eventually they leased an old weatherboard house in South Brisbane large enough to fit all six of them, plus Jamie, if he chose to move back in with them.

'Uncle Bill says the high school just up the road has always had an excellent reputation. Only the brightest kids go there, apparently – so I reckon Laura will love it next year,' Ken told Margaret, hoping to lift her spirits, as they stood gazing at the peeling paintwork of their new home and its small, untidy yard.

'I hope so, Ken – but we'll have to see if they'll take her first. I hope we get used to this traffic noise too.'

Margaret found it hard to keep her voice from sounding doleful. Ken heaved a sigh. He was hot and tired, not to mention discouraged. The morning's job interviews had not gone well.

'Well, *you* were the one who was so keen to move to Brisbane, remember. *I* would have been happy to stay where we were, either in town or somewhere nearby. Too late now though.'

Margaret bit off a sharp rejoinder. She knew he was worried about finding work – better not to say anything.

They moved in a few days later. Ken busied himself looking for work, but by the time the holidays were over, he still did not have a permanent job.

Greg was more fortunate. He left the house early each morning, scouring the various garages and car repair places in the nearby suburbs, and then headed south along the railway line, until he finally obtained an apprenticeship as a mechanic. He was determined – and Margaret was very proud of him.

But it did not go down well with Ken.

'How do you think I feel, with my son getting work before *I* do!' he growled to her one night, after he had spent the afternoon drinking with Andy's brother Jeff and his friend whom he had met back home. 'You know what, Marg? Think I'll start up my own lawn-mowing business. The guys said they'd help me get it off the ground. Jeff works in a printing company, so he could get some flyers done. And we think we'll start up another band – Andy knows some pubs where he could get us a gig, if we're good enough.'

Laura knew her mother was worried. She was sometimes absentminded, as she helped her get started on her Correspondence lessons and come to grips with the harder maths she had to do. Laura's new teacher, Miss Glasson, tried to help, but was not quite as resourceful as Miss Charlton had been.

'Don't worry, Mum!' Laura said gently to her one afternoon. 'Jamie can explain it next time he comes. You've got enough to do, organising things here.'

Jamie came to visit a few nights later. Then he moved back altogether the following week, into the little room at the end of the side veranda. He hated to see his mother stressed in any way. At home, he could keep an eye on her and give Laura any help she needed with her schoolwork. If he paid board, as he had at his grandmother's, it might help make ends meet too. He wanted to continue at uni, but at least his part-time job at the restaurant brought in something. If he and Greg both boarded at home, then things should be okay.

Greg was not keen on the idea, but acquiesced in the end. He wanted a car badly and was trying to save hard for one.

'I'll help while Dad doesn't have a fulltime job,' he told Jamie, 'but if he starts wasting his money, or doesn't make a go of this new business, then I'm off.'

Ken did try hard. He took out an ad in the local paper and he and Ian walked the nearby streets distributing flyers. But most of their neighbours had no yards to mow, nor could they afford to pay someone even if they had. He canvassed further afield, but soon ran into stiff competition from other gardeners already established in these areas. Yet his greatest difficulty was the same one that

Laura

had emerged both at the family store and on the farm. Ken was simply not a businessman. He had no head for figures and little interest in financial matters.

'We'll be okay, Marg,' he said often during those early months in Brisbane. 'It takes time to build up businesses – let's keep going for a bit longer. Besides, I like the outdoor work. And I get on well with most of my customers.'

For the moment, there was nothing more Margaret could do. Ken still did not want her to look for paid work, so, apart from generally caring for the family, she funnelled her energy into making Laura's final year of correspondence schooling as pleasant as possible. She sensed how much Laura missed Anne, so redoubled her efforts to find interesting books to read to her, regularly raiding the children's and young adults' sections of the local library for new material. Laura almost devoured books, often enlisting the help of the volunteers at Braille House in her quest for more material to read herself. As well, audio material and even more reading matter arrived regularly from the Blind Society and whatever other sources Margaret could discover. Soon Laura became used to getting her mind around books and poetry aimed at much more mature readers. Her vocabulary quickly grew and Margaret was kept busy explaining the meaning of a wide variety of complex words and phrases to her. Together they devised a Braille card system to help Laura keep track of quotes and interesting words she came across. She was a naturally gifted student, Margaret felt, her determination and ability to focus on the task in hand only serving to enhance this giftedness.

Laura's tastes in music also widened, as the two of them attended as many free concerts as Margaret could find – lunch hour orchestral programs in the City Hall, organ recitals in the Cathedral, occasional brass and pipe bands, jazz by the river. Then one Saturday, Laura auditioned for a junior choir at the nearby Conservatorium, standing shakily beside the grand piano while the rather awe-inspiring Director told her what to sing.

'First, I'll play a few notes and then I'll ask you to sing them for me. Ready? ... Good! Now these – very good. Next, can you sing me the National Anthem? Hmm ... excellent! Let me see –what if I play this note, which is Middle C, and then a higher one. Can you tell me what it would be?'

Laura quickly sang the notes in between in her head and hesitated only a fraction before responding.

'I ... I think it would be 'A'.'

'Excellent again – perfect pitch all round,' the Director commented in a rather pleased tone. 'That's all for now – we'll be in contact.'

She made it through, to everyone's great delight. At first, Margaret or Jamie accompanied Laura to the Saturday morning practices, but soon she insisted on going by herself.

'I want to, Mum – please let me! It's not far to walk – and I can always ask someone, if I need help. I want to be just like all the other kids in the choir. Anyway, it's good practice for next year – Ian and I can maybe walk to school together, but I'm sure he won't want to come home with me every afternoon as well.'

'Perhaps we should think about getting you a white cane from the Blind Foundation – I'm sure they'd help you learn how to use it. It's a bit different in the city from back home. I know Dad doesn't like the idea, but ...'

Margaret did not get any further with her suggestion, as she suspected she might not.

'No, Mum ... no! I'm *never* going to use one of them – I don't care *who* asks me! I'd feel so stupid and hopeless, using a stick like that. Besides, I'd probably poke someone or trip them up or something.'

Margaret knew there was no point in arguing. She was well aware that when Laura set her mind to do something, or *not* to do something, it was a brave person who would try to dissuade her.

And sometimes they visited the Blind School, despite Ken's antipathy towards the place. The principal usually let them sit in the oldest class, but it soon became obvious that Laura was far more advanced than the other students.

'You'd be very frustrated here, Laura,' the principal, a kindly woman in her fifties, had told them honestly after their first visit. 'But you're welcome to borrow anything you need from our library. I predict, my dear, that when you get to high school, you'll be a match for everyone else – even the most perfectly sighted student.'

Margaret felt a twinge of apprehension on Laura's behalf, however, after one of their visits.

'Mum, I'm not sure I want to be in a class again,' she had commented. 'I'm always waiting for everyone else – it's so boring! And you all have to do the same stuff – even things I'm not really interested in. I hope high school won't be like that all the time.'

'Laura, you'll have to get along with all sorts of kids at high school, just as you wanted the kids at primary school to get along with you, remember? And you'll have to do what the teachers say, or you'll soon get a bad reputation. Perhaps I should start being stricter with you and *make* you do lots of boring sums – even more than Miss Glasson says you have to. How would that be, eh?'

'I'm not sure you *could* – but you wouldn't anyway, I know. You're too nice – but I love you just the way you are, Mum! I can't wait to get to high school, but I'll miss our times together. I'm going to make you so proud of me – you watch! I'm not sure what I want to be yet, but one day I'll repay you for all the hours you've

Laura

put into helping me with my work and reading to me and taking me places.'

That year, Laura also channelled her energies into two challenging projects that were to have lifelong repercussions for her. The first began almost by accident, not long after their move to South Brisbane. One afternoon as she was leaning on the front gate, waiting for Ian and Elisabeth to get home from school, she met the boy next door. He was nine years old, a cheeky young imp with little to do, she soon discovered.

'Hi, you girl! Why aren't you at school?'

'Why aren't *you* at school?'

'I asked *you* first.'

'I don't go to a school – I learn at home by correspondence.'

'Why?'

'Because I'm blind – I get lessons in Braille and my Mum helps me.'

'I wish I didn't have to go to school – ever. What's Braille?'

Laura ignored his question for the moment.

'Why aren't *you* at school today?'

'Because I didn't want to go – and Miss Morton told Mr Daly she didn't want me in her class anyway. Mum's at work – but she thinks I'm at school. You won't tell, will you?'

'Why don't you like school?'

'Because the other kids laugh at me.'

'Why do they laugh at you?'

'Because I can't read properly. I like Maths though. Maths is easy. Miss Morton says I'll have to repeat next year, but I've already repeated once. Mum says she'd help me if she could but ...'

'Why can't she?'

'Well ... don't tell her I told you, will you? She can't read either. Sometimes she works at the boot factory when they need extra help – she'll be home soon.'

'Can't your Dad help you? Do you have any brothers or sisters?'

He was quiet for a while then. All Laura could hear was the creaking of the next-door gate, as he swung back and forth on it. Finally he mumbled an answer.

'There's just Mum and me. ... What's Braille?'

'Like me to show you some?'

'Okay. Can I come over for a while?'

Kevin was fascinated with Laura's Braille books and how she remembered which lots of dots meant what.

'You must be real clever – that's a lot harder than just learning ordinary letters and words. Miss Morton says I'm dumb because I can't remember all the words, but I don't care – I *hate* reading.'

Laura could feel the fear in Kevin and hear the defensiveness in his voice.

'If you didn't have trouble understanding the words, don't you think you'd like it? You'd get to read lots of interesting things and adventure stories and stuff. Tell you what! I'll ask Mum if I can help you learn to read – how would that be?'

At first, Kevin was doubtful.

'But ... you're blind! How would you see the letters?'

Kevin's words made Laura even more determined.

'We'll work something out. *You're* the one who has to see them anyway – you can spell the words out to me or sound out the letters. And Kevin – I went to a normal school for a bit back home and I hated it most of the time. The kids didn't like me much – but I'm going to show *them*! And you can too. Let's make a deal – let's decide to show that Miss Morton and the kids in your class that you *aren't* dumb at all. I promise to help you, if you promise not to wag school again. If we both try hard, I bet you'll be reading in no time.'

Kevin was still doubtful, but something about Laura's determination spurred him on.

'Well, I guess if you can learn to read dots like that, then maybe I can read good too. Just don't tell mum I wagged today – and don't let on you know she can't read!'

They shook hands on it. Many afternoons after that, when Kevin's mum was working, and with her permission, Kevin sat with Laura and tried his hardest. And from the beginning, even without Laura saying anything, Margaret knew to stay out of it. This was Laura's project. She'd work out a way to do it – and do it well.

And she did. Occasionally Margaret would listen in from nearby – and marvel. Laura's patience was endless. Time and time again she would have Kevin repeat various sounds and letter combinations, until he recognised them with ease. At first he stumbled through sentences, but Laura seemed to know intuitively when to offer help and when to hold off. She was firm and thorough – an exacting taskmaster – but Kevin rose to the challenge and tried his best to carry out every instruction he was given. He was only nine, but with Laura, something inside his head and heart seemed to click into place. If Laura could manage things, then so could he. It was as simple as that.

They held a party the day Kevin brought home his report card for the year. In the middle of it, his mother arrived.

'Mum, Mum, guess what? I don't have to repeat! And Miss Morton and Mr Daly have both written really good things on my card. Here – I'll read it out. '*Kevin's reading has greatly improved these past three months. He now has a reading age of above average for his class. Well done, Kevin!*' And the headmaster wrote

Laura

this, Mum. *'Con ... congratulations! Keep up the good work, Kevin!'*

'Wow – I'm so proud of you! You worked very hard, I know – but Laura did too. Thank you so much for all your time and effort, Laura!'

'It was fun – it really was. Because I love reading so much myself, I really wanted Kevin to as well. When I finish uni, I want to help other kids like him. But that's a long way off yet.'

Laura's second project was quite different – something she had dreamed of doing ever since as a little child she'd been unable to see the pictures in her favourite books. Her family had always described what was on each page, but it was not the same as discovering things for herself. She could still remember times before her operation when she would sit on her father's knee, as he pointed out what was on each page. She had often tried to say the words after him, even though she was only two.

After her operation, Margaret and the boys had managed to work out ways to make up interesting fun activities for Laura. A favourite game had been collecting things that Laura could feel and smell, like leaves, nuts, pinecones, flowers, even strawberries from the garden or beans or little tomatoes, as well as objects like smooth stones, buttons, bobby pins and thimbles. They would place them all on a tray and challenge Laura and Elisabeth to try to remember every item. Sometimes the boys would take one away and the girls would have to work out which one was missing. On other occasions, Margaret would line up the herbs and spices in the kitchen for Laura to work out which was which. Or she would get cotton balls and put a drop of liquid on each – vanilla, peppermint, various sauces, Ken's shaving cream, cleaning products, perfume, or nail polish. Sometimes they would blindfold the boys and make them guess as well – but Laura was always the clear winner.

Now Laura tried to explain her latest project to them all and enlist their help.

'I'd like to make a book for blind kids – especially those who can't get to school. I want to have a page for every letter of the alphabet and find *something* beginning with that letter to stick on each page that they can touch or smell or hear. Remember the games you used to make up, Mum, collecting things we could feel and smell and making us work out what they were? I'm going to use those ideas in a book. Do you think it would work?'

'Nice try, Laura,' Jamie laughed good-naturedly, 'but count me out! I don't have much spare time at the moment. Perhaps I could get some cardboard and special paper from the art supplies shop at uni for you to use though. My mate Alan works there – he might get it cheaper for us.'

He was true to his word and soon Laura had embarked on her special project. In fact, soon the whole family was drawn into finding the bits and pieces she needed.

'Any of you – next time you buy lollies with wrappers, save them for me! I want to make pretend lollies for the 'l' page. And I want a paddle-pop stick to glue on the 'S' page. Or do you think a little shell would be better? Or perhaps some cotton wool balls for pretend snow? No – that might be too hard to understand. … Wait a minute – *sandpaper* would be even better. They'd love to feel that. Oh, and Mum, I need some really nice buttons for the 'B' page, like those little ducks I used to have on my cardigan when I was little. Or what about the ones on your dress, Elisabeth, with the raised up flowers in the middle? Wait – maybe a bell would be better, so they could hear it. You know, like the ones you get on Christmas decorations. Thinking of Christmas, I could put tinsel on the 'T' page, couldn't I? That'd work really well.'

Laura's enthusiasm was infectious. Even Ken was roped in to provide a guitar pick for the 'G' page, as well as a piece of guitar string.

'But the pick has to be a really nice colour, Dad – and one that the kids will know is special when they feel it.'

To Margaret's surprise, Ken thought about it long and hard. Finally he came up with what Laura felt was one of the best things in the whole book – a smooth tortoiseshell pick with the name 'Elvis' engraved on it. As he handed it to her, she sensed his pride in finding something just right. She gave him a warm hug – the warmest they'd had for some time.

'Thanks, Dad!' she managed to say huskily. 'I don't know which page I like best yet, but this one's bound to rate pretty high.'

In the end, the book turned out to be quite a large volume, as more and more interesting items were added, some flatter than others. Even Greg contributed, after some pestering from Laura, by cutting a small piece out of an old rubber tyre for the 'R' page.

'Might make your book smell a bit,' he mumbled, when he finally gave it to her, but she could tell he was pleased she still wanted to include it.

'Oh, that's exactly what I wanted – the boys will probably like this page best of all!'

Ian, the neatest and most artistic in the family, drew a large outline of each letter on the relevant page and Elisabeth carefully painted them different colours.

'You choose,' Laura had said in a rather offhand way to her sister, when asked what colour she wanted each letter. 'I don't care.'

But Elisabeth thought Laura really did care.

'I've got gold and silver glitter, Laura – perhaps I can use that on the 'L' page and the 'E' page, because they're our special initials. Which do you want – gold or silver?'

Laura

'You choose,' Laura said again – but Elisabeth could tell she was pleased.

Alongside each letter, Margaret helped Laura put its Braille name clearly.

At last, when Laura was reasonably satisfied with her creation, Jamie attached the pages firmly together.

'Now you can't change your mind any more, Miss Perfectionist,' he teased her. 'That's enough bright ideas!'

Eventually, although Laura felt some qualms about it, she was able to distance herself enough from her labour of love to donate it to the School for the Blind. At first, the principal was reluctant to accept it, however.

'Laura – this is so beautiful! It must have taken you hours and hours to make. Are you *sure* you want to part with it? Because you're not likely to get it back, once our little people know it's here.'

'Yes, I want to give it to the school. I've been really lucky to have a Mum who's a teacher, plus a family who've all helped me learn things, so I hope my book can help some of the kids here now.'

'Thank you so much, Laura! All the best for high school next year – I know you'll do brilliantly.'

In November, something occurred on Laura's birthday that Margaret, Jamie and Elisabeth deliberately dismissed from their minds. Laura's own conscious memory of it was almost lost too in the excitement of holidays and Christmas and getting ready for high school – but not quite. Anne had phoned, as she always did for Laura's birthday, and, after wishing her a special day, was eager to tell her about a meeting in the old picture theatre just a few blocks from Laura's place.

'I think you'd enjoy it, Laura. The music should be really good and I'm sure lots of people will be there. The main speaker's a friend of ours. We call him Uncle Brian – my Mum and Dad have known him for ages. He's funny too – not boring at all. He says lots of good stuff about God and he's really easy to understand. Please ask your Mum and Dad to take you, Laura! It's so close to where you live – ple-e-e-ease!! I'm going to pray *so hard* that you'll be able to go.'

'Well ... I'll ask ... but I can't promise anything. I'd like to hear him, Anne, but it depends if anyone wants to come with me. I'll see what I can do.'

Laura was curious. And, because it was her birthday, Ken gave in and let her go.

'No way I'm going with you though, Laura. Besides, I promised Ron I'd meet him at the pub. You girls will be right – but how about you walk down with them, Greg?'

Greg had simply snorted at the idea and informed them he was heading out with his mates.

'What about you, Jamie – do you have time to go with your mother and the girls?' Ken persisted, feeling somewhat guilty.

'Yeah, Jamie – please come with us!'

Jamie always found it hard to resist any request from Laura, let alone one put to him on her birthday, and eventually gave in. Then after Laura had walked arm in arm with him to the theatre, she begged him to stay.

'You've got this far, Jamie – might as well come in for a bit at least.'

But Laura soon forgot his existence, as she listened to the bright music and excellent singing. Then Anne's 'Uncle Brian' spoke – and as he did, she began to feel something stirring deep inside her. It was as if everything she'd heard or read about God and Jesus suddenly fitted together and made perfect sense. It was as if God were speaking just to her – as if somehow God really knew her and cared about her.

She sat very still, drinking it all in. Eventually the speaker finished by asking anyone who wanted to know more about Jesus to come to the front of the theatre. He would pray, he explained, and then someone would come and talk more with them.

Laura felt an intense, almost overwhelming longing to join those around her she could hear moving to the front. She wanted desperately to find out more, to respond to those strings that seemed to be tugging at her heart. She leaned forward and turned towards Jamie sitting beside her, but before she could say anything, she found herself being hustled out of the theatre.

'Come on, Laura – it's late! Let's move quickly, before we get caught in the crowd.'

'But ... but I ...'

Laura was unable to put into words how she felt – how much she longed to have whatever it was the speaker had been offering.

'Get going, Laura!'

Jamie's voice behind her was stern – even a little angry. She had rarely heard him speak like that, but she obeyed immediately. She had no choice anyway, as she shuffled along the row wedged between her mother and him and was hustled out of the theatre.

Outside, she tried to work out what the others were feeling.

'Mum, what did you think of it? I really liked what the man said – I wanted to stay for a bit ...'

She felt a little tearful, for some reason. It was as if something precious had been snatched out of her grasp, just as she had managed to get hold of it. Margaret could hear the longing in her voice and was sorry to upset her – especially on her birthday – but felt she had to remain firm.

'I think he was sincere, Laura, but I know Dad wouldn't have liked you to stay

Laura

behind and talk to them. You know how he feels about church and stuff. Maybe when you're older you can make up your own mind …'

It was the only way Margaret could think to respond. She had warmed to what had been said that night too, but as things were at home just then, she knew it would be unwise to stir up unnecessary trouble. Ken was particularly touchy, working hard to keep the lawn-mowing business afloat, as well as trying to form a new band. He'd allowed them to go tonight, but any further talk about God would not be warmly welcomed, she knew.

They headed home in silence. Laura was particularly aware of Jamie beside her, breathing heavily as he walked, as if still angry about something.

'I guess I'm with Dad in this,' he finally burst out. 'I don't get it! How can anyone believe in a loving God – a God who *really* cares about us? What about your eyes, Laura? What about the Thomas's son? How can they explain the bad stuff that happens to people who've tried to do the right thing all their lives? It's just not fair! Besides, I think God expects too much when …'

He stopped abruptly then. Laura could sense he felt he had gone too far. At the same time, she was taken a little aback by the passion and vehemence of his words. Jamie was her champion and her hero – how could she think of believing things he felt were so very wrong? And she certainly didn't want to upset her Dad either. Yet she knew she hadn't imagined those invisible strings tugging at her heart back in the theatre. The speaker's words had rung so true – for a few moments at least, she had felt that, despite everything, there truly might be a God who loved her and would protect her. But what did she know? She'd only just turned thirteen. No doubt Jamie was right. She sighed, putting her arm through his as they walked along together.

'It's okay, Jamie – don't worry! I don't want to have any arguments on my birthday. Anyway, there's lots of time yet to think about what the man said. And maybe I'll even find out some answers to your questions one day. But it would've been nice …'

Laura's voice trailed off on a wistful note that was not lost on Jamie.

'I'm sorry, Laura. I get pretty steamed up over things sometimes – and I guess I'm just a bit confused myself at present. I'm glad you enjoyed the meeting – and I know you'll sort things out for yourself as you get older. Besides, I'll always be around to argue with you and set you straight!'

That night, as Laura lay in bed, she carefully felt for her new watch, still strapped firmly on her wrist and gave a satisfied sigh. It had been a special birthday present from all the family, chosen with care at the Blind Foundation. It felt good knowing that when she went to high school, she wouldn't have to keep asking the time. It was very late, but she found it hard to sleep. She kept remembering all the things she had heard at the meeting and how she had felt. And she was worried about Jamie – he'd seemed a bit irritable lately. Then tonight he had admitted he felt pretty confused. Eventually, as she drifted on the edge of sleep, she found herself thinking about Anne's phone call. Anne would pray right now, she thought to herself. I know she would – but I don't really know how. If I did, I'd ask you, God, to help Jamie sort things out – and to help me work out if you're really there and if you care about us at all.

Laura

chapter seven

Before the Christmas holidays began, Margaret checked at Ian's school to ensure Laura would in fact be accepted there. At first, the principal argued Laura would be better off at one of the schools with a Special Unit that catered for visually impaired students.

'These students are integrated into normal classes as much as possible, Mrs Harding, so she'd soon find lots of sighted friends, as well as others the same as herself. Are you *sure* you're making the right decision? Of course, this school is handier, but the government will pay for a taxi to the other school and back each day. Anyway, it's not all that far by bus, if she wanted to travel with her friends. I know you want Laura to go to the same school as your son, but I'm almost certain she'll have difficulty keeping up with the workload. This school has a high academic standard. Most of our students go on to university, so our teachers expect everyone to work hard.'

'I'm sure Laura will work as hard as any of them – she's a very determined young lady', Margaret said to the principal 'And she's certainly bright enough, if her results from the Correspondence School are anything to go by. Besides, we're still very keen to have her attend a normal high school and be treated the same as

laura

any other young person.'

'I understand that, but whether it's possible is another matter. I'm not sure our headmistress would think it is – and she's in charge of all our female students, so the final say rests with her. Unfortunately, you can't meet her at this point though – she's overseas. All I can suggest is that Laura begin the year with us and see how she goes. Don't buy her uniforms until you know for sure – she can wear her normal clothes until we see if it works out.'

'I'm coming here, Mum,' was all Laura said, as they left the school grounds. 'I'm going to show them I can do as well as any of them. And I'm not going to wear ordinary clothes either, like the principal suggested. Imagine how all the other kids would look at me! They'd all want to know why I didn't have the proper uniform. They'd probably think we're too poor to buy it – or that I can't tell the difference between one lot of clothes and another.'

Fortunately for Margaret, help arrived from an unexpected source. That afternoon, Ian brought his best mate home, so they could complete an assignment together. Over dinner, Brendan mentioned how his sister had just finished at their school.

'She couldn't wait to pack up her old uniforms and she's about the same size as Laura. They're still sitting in our lounge, waiting for Mum to get rid of them. She was going to send them to the school clothing pool, but I'm sure she wouldn't mind if you had them instead.'

When Margaret drove him home later that night, she returned with Laura's uniforms.

'They're a bit threadbare, especially the tie, and the hat's pretty scruffy, but perhaps they'll do for a while. Especially since Brendan's Mum wouldn't accept anything for them. When we know for sure you're staying, we can buy you a new hat and tie.'

After that, the holidays could not end quickly enough for Laura. A brief visit from Anne and her family, on their way through to Melbourne for Christmas, shifted her focus for a few days, but soon she was champing at the bit again, begging whoever was available to read to her from the pile of second-hand Grade Eight textbooks Ian had managed to get in the school bookshop. She tried to avoid asking her mother, however – she'd need lots of help from her once school started. Besides, over the holidays Margaret had taken on some shifts at the boot factory where Kevin's mum worked. They had needed casuals, since January was their busiest month, with the usual demand for school shoes. Ken hated her doing it, but money was tight – very tight.

Jamie was working hard too over the uni holidays, taking on as many hours as he could at the restaurant. He was glad of the extra work. He planned to pay more board in the coming year to help the family out of its current tight spot. Apart from that, being busy gave him less time to sit around – and less time to think about Alan, away overseas. He missed his friend a lot – but it was not something he could talk about with his family. He hardly understood his feelings himself, but he knew that after Alan returned, they'd have to have a serious talk. Their honours work at uni threw them too close together not to sort out where they stood with each other.

Usually Ian stayed home with Laura and Elisabeth when Margaret had to work, but from time to time he was needed to help Ken mow lawns or clean up someone's garden. Over Christmas and New Year, Ken's hours at the pub drinking with his mates increased, making it hard for him to complete the amount of work necessary to stay afloat. Hangovers did not mix well at all with outdoor work in the sticky Brisbane heat. Ian hated mowing – especially when his Dad was like a bear with a sore head – but he put up with it as best he could. He wanted to help out – and besides, he was saving up to buy an electric guitar. He was pretty good on Ken's old acoustic, but he and Brendan had ideas of forming a rock band that year with a few mates – perhaps even playing at the school dance. The girls would like them even more then, they figured.

Laura was more aware of the undercurrents in her family than most girls her age would have been – and certainly more than her mother realised. She loved her father and the evenings spent with him as he practised his music, but it angered her that he seemed unable to help himself and provide better for them. She knew her mother felt pressured as a result to be there for everyone as they needed her to be. She sensed the turmoil that Jamie, her knight in shining armour, was going through and, although she could not understand it, she grieved for him. And she admired Greg for standing on his own two feet and making his own decisions, even though they were unwise at times. Already he'd had some brushes with the law, which she knew had caused her parents much pain. And lately he'd been talking about moving out to share a place with his mates. She knew that worried her parents – but he was almost nineteen now. Sometimes she would lie awake at nights, thinking about them all, wishing she were not such a burden on her mother in particular. But then her determination to succeed and the natural optimism of youth would come to the fore, despite all the difficulties surrounding her. God, if you're there, she would sometimes pray as she lay half asleep, please take care of us all! Help me to be popular at school like Ian is and good at my work – as well as pretty like Elisabeth!

Elisabeth was indeed very pretty. Laura could tell that, from the spontaneous comments people made about her. Also, she often let Laura brush her lovely thick black hair that curved under her chin, framing her oval face, with its soft skin

Laura

and perfect little nose. Laura knew too that Elisabeth's eyes were only a slightly lighter shade of blue than her father's – but she always tried to put that out of her mind.

'Your hair feels lovely, Elisabeth – so soft and smooth. Not like my curly mess. I'm going to grow mine long this year. Mum says I can, but I'll have to tie it back for school. When you get to high school, I bet you'll have lots of boyfriends. I bet you get married a long time before I do too. I'm not going to get married for ages – I want to go to uni first and teach kids and sing in Dad's band and maybe even go overseas.'

Elisabeth believed Laura implicitly, like she believed most people. Laura was the one who would take the lead in any escapade and own up later, if caught. Elisabeth was a follower, soft and compliant, ready to fall in with whatever was planned. And Laura was right. All Elisabeth wanted to do was to grow up and get married. But Laura – well, Laura wanted to try everything, to scale the heights, to make her mark. And in her imagination, that was exactly what she did. In her dreams, she was unstoppable.

But reality turned out to be a different matter. And reality struck with great force not long after first term started, in the form of the school headmistress, Miss Mellingham. From the beginning, she had been vocal in expressing her doubts about accepting someone with a disability such as Laura's.

'What? She can't see at *all*? Hmmm. Unfortunate, but I really don't think she'll be able to cope here,' were the terse words she uttered, when first informed about Laura's enrolment.

Miss Mellingham did not have the reputation of changing her mind easily. Yet something within her stirred, despite herself, when she saw Laura standing at the door of her office in her slightly baggy uniform, gripping her brother Ian's arm so tightly that the knuckles of her hand showed white. Ian introduced Laura respectfully, but rather self-consciously. Miss Mellingham caused even his usual easygoing manner to desert him for a moment, with her peremptory response to his knock and the glare she gave him over the top of the rimless glasses perched on her nose as they entered. Suddenly, he found himself feeling glad Laura could not see her.

'Miss Mellingham, this is my sister, Laura. She's enrolled for Grade Eight, but we were told to bring her straight to your office. She's blind, so she'll need someone to show her where to go ...'

'I'm quite aware, young man, that your sister will need help. I was expecting her. Now run along to your own classes – we'll take care of her. Go on – do as you're told! I don't have all day.'

With a muttered 'See you at the front gate this afternoon, Laura!' Ian hastily disappeared. Miss Mellingham did not tolerate fools gladly and was also highly suspicious of any representative of the male species. She had a theory, put firmly into practice at the school, that it was folly for teenage girls to mix with boys and vice versa. Most classes were therefore segregated, with certain areas of the school grounds set aside for girls or boys only, such rules being enforced firmly by staff members. It was unusual to have a male student accompany a girl – even his sister – to the sacred precincts of Miss Mellingham's office.

'Now good morning, Laura! Welcome to our school – but I remind you at the outset, it remains to be seen whether you'll be able to continue here. Nevertheless, during the next two weeks, we'll try our best to help you settle in and see if you can manage the work. You'll be in Grade 8.1 – I'll ask one of the prefects to show you your home room and also to collect you at recess and show you where the toilets are and so on. I'm sure once you get to know others in your class, they'll look after you. Now, I'm a very busy person, but if you aren't coping, please ask to be brought straight to me. I'll be teaching you History and English – we'll meet in those lessons anyway. At the end of two weeks, I'll personally test you, to see if you've managed to keep up with everyone else and understood the lessons. If not, then I'm afraid we'll have to ask your parents to send you elsewhere. You'll only be unhappy if you can't do the work – and we don't want that. Do you understand me, Laura?'

Miss Mellingham, while trying to be kind, had sounded quite abrupt and stern. She had also spoken loudly and slowly, making Laura squirm inside. She would like to have pointed out she was neither deaf nor stupid, but instead, responded with a simple 'yes' in her meekest voice.

'Yes, Miss Mellingham is the correct response, Laura. And by the way, it's a rule here that girls must wear their gloves while travelling to and from school. I noticed you were carrying yours when you arrived. Did you wear them on the way? Good! If you remember the standard of behaviour acceptable here, as well as everything you learn in class, then we'll get along well. I think things will be difficult for you, Laura – but let's hope for the best.'

She patted Laura on the shoulder then, in an awkward attempt to display some warmth. She wanted to help the poor child – but really, she had too many other important things to do than spend time catering for handicapped students. What on earth had the principal been *thinking* of to offer to accommodate a blind girl at the school? Well, she'd try – but the girl would be better off somewhere else.

Over the next two weeks, Laura survived well – in all but Miss Mellingham's History and English lessons. Most of her classmates were friendly and helpful, taking her from one room to another until she got her bearings and guiding her to a spare seat. Laura took notes with her slate and stylus, carefully recording,

Laura

if nothing else, the page numbers of the textbooks studied in class and catching up after school with her mother, or whoever was available. Sometimes the other girls whispered explanations to her, while on other occasions, her teachers offered individual help when they could. Laura began to relax – except in Miss Mellingham's classes. These she quickly came to dread, knowing that by the end of them she would be wishing the floor would open and swallow her up. The problem was that Miss Mellingham had obviously decided she needed to move at a snail's pace, if Laura were to have any hope of keeping up, and seemed determined to inflict this same slow progress on the entire class. Each lesson her voice would drone on, every sentence spoken slowly and clearly, her pronunciation meticulously exact. Occasionally she would punctuate her words with the query 'Have you got that, Laura?' until Laura found it hard to respond civilly. What she taught was interesting – but oh so slow! Not only that, each day, Miss Mellingham seemed to feel she needed to repeat most of what they had covered the previous day, until Laura could clearly hear the exasperated sighs of the other girls and feel their boredom. They knew it was not Laura's fault – but they were bright students and it was hard for them to contain their frustration.

Each time Miss Mellingham walked in the room for their History lessons in particular, Laura could feel a slow flush begin to mount up her cheeks. She kept her head down, praying Miss Mellingham would forget she was there, but that was a vain hope, since she paced up and down the rows continually as she talked, making sure the girls took down her notes *exactly* as she dictated. No variants were allowed.

'I have taught for many years,' she explained, in a voice that would brook no interference. 'My methods work. They produce results – so please do exactly as you're asked!'

She could not check Laura's notes, however. Even Miss Mellingham was unable to read the baffling collection of dots that appeared on the back of the paper Laura used in her slate, as her hand quickly moved from right to left across it.

Towards the end of the trial fortnight, Laura was given oral tests in History and English. To her teacher's barely concealed surprise, she easily answered questions on the poetry they had studied and also the play they were reading aloud in class. But she did not fare so well in History – at least according to Miss Mellingham's standards. Laura already knew lots about early Australian history – her mother had fostered her special interest in it by borrowing a wide variety of books from the local library and the Blind Society. But she had taken little notice of how Miss Mellingham wanted the facts she explained in class recorded and organised, since she knew she would have to set things out differently in Braille. Now she found she could not list off the five facts she was asked about the First Fleet exactly how Miss Mellingham had taught them, or the six points about the explorers who had first crossed the Blue Mountains, or three key statements describing the first colony in South Australia. She could have written pages about each one, but was unable to feed back the information exactly as required.

'No, Laura – you're not actually answering my question. All I want are the simple facts we talked about and that you were to summarise and learn. I don't need to be told all that irrelevant detail. See, this will be the problem, if you can't set out your notes in class as I tell you to. You have to be able to list all the facts, otherwise you won't pass the exams I set for the class. You must have noticed how much I slowed down for your benefit these past two weeks. I certainly can't keep doing that, or we won't get through the syllabus – and it doesn't seem to have helped you greatly anyway. I'm sorry, Laura, but I don't think it will work. Ask your mother to come and see me tomorrow. We'll talk to the principal – but unfortunately, I can't recommend you continue on here.'

Laura could not bring herself to return the next day. She buried her head under the covers when Margaret called her and refused to budge.

'I don't want to go, Mum. I liked the girls in my class and some of the other teachers, but Miss Mellingham just doesn't want me in her school. I'm too much trouble – she can't be bothered with me. Besides, I hate her old History and English classes! I know it all anyway – it's really boring. She makes me feel embarrassed too.'

Margaret was determined to keep the appointment and fight on her daughter's behalf. But she had met her match in Miss Mellingham, who was equally determined to run her classes the way she wanted. She was unwilling or unable to accommodate anyone who could not toe the line, Margaret soon realised, as they both talked with Mr Wallace, the Principal.

'I can't hold back the other students for the sake of one child, Mrs Harding,' Miss Mellingham stated firmly. 'I'm sure you'd agree with that, wouldn't you, Mr Wallace? This school's renowned for its high academic standard and we want to keep attracting the brighter students – but this won't happen if we constantly have to teach at a much slower rate to accommodate handicapped students. I know Mr Wallace will encourage you, as I most certainly do, to enrol Laura at a school where there is a Special Unit to help students like her. She'll be much happier – and that will be weight off your mind, I'm sure. I don't mean to be unkind – I feel very sorry for Laura. But this is simply not the right school for her – is it, Mr Wallace?'

After a slight pause, the principal agreed, albeit a little unhappily. Margaret noticed he would not meet her eyes and his face had taken on a distinctly reddish

Laura

hue. In the midst of her own swirling anger, she began to feel a little sorry for him. He could hardly gainsay his headmistress in public and was obliged to defer to her view on the matter, as he had intimated to Margaret at the very beginning. Taking a deep breath, Margaret steadied herself before responding.

'Well, I'm sorry you see it this way. I believe you're wrong, but thank you for at least trying to accommodate her. Obviously I'm very disappointed, as is my husband. In fact, we considered changing our son Ian to another school as well, but because this is his second high school already and close to home, we've decided he can stay. As far as Laura's concerned, however, why try to make her go somewhere where she knows she's not wanted? One day, Miss Mellingham, you'll see what an excellent student you missed out on having the pleasure of teaching. Laura will excel in English and History and go on to study at university and teach one day herself. And she'll definitely know from experience how to make allowances for those who don't fit into the mould, or who need that extra bit of time and understanding to achieve and be all they were meant to be. Goodbye to you both!'

She could not remember walking the few blocks home. Fortunately, she had calmed down considerably by the time she climbed the steps to their front door. She found Laura sitting in the lounge trying to read, but with a blank, faraway look on her face. On the table nearby were her school uniforms, neatly stacked in a pile.

'Oh Laura, please don't take it to heart so much!' Margaret burst out, before she could stop herself. 'Miss Mellingham tried her best, according to what she believes is the right way to teach. She just didn't understand what you really needed, love – it wasn't that she didn't like you. It's a shame, as the school's so close and it does have a good reputation, but don't worry – we'll just try somewhere else. You can be sure I left them in no doubt as to what we thought about it all though, Laura. I told Miss Mellingham she'd be sorry one day. Well, I didn't say those words *exactly* – but that was the general idea.'

Laura managed a rather watery smile, but inside she was unsure whether to laugh or cry. The pain of past rejections ran deep, with each new one taking on far greater significance than was warranted. But she was too young to realise that – too young and too vulnerable, Margaret thought, the knife twisting in her heart as it did many times when she looked at her daughter. Yet Laura often surprised her with her maturity and insights. Now, as Margaret watched, she saw her square her small shoulders and sit bolt upright.

'Okay, Mum, let's do it! Let's go to this school with the Special Unit. I don't like the idea, the same as Dad doesn't – but maybe it's the best way to go, after all. It can't be that hard for me to get to – I know I'm entitled to catch a taxi, but I'd rather go by bus like the other kids. If you phone them today, maybe I can start next week. But I feel bad you'll have to pay out money for more uniforms.'

'Let's worry about that later. Perhaps you could wear the uniforms you have for a bit. They won't mind, I'm sure.'

'Yes, but *I* would. I have to look right, Mum – I have to be the same as the others!'

Margaret could hear the panic in Laura's voice. She understood her dread of looking different, but money was tight and she had to be firm.

'Perhaps there'll be a clothing pool where we can get some cheap uniforms – let's wait and see, Laura. I'll phone now, before I go to work. You'll have to be here by yourself for a bit, but Jamie said he'd be home early and cook dinner for us tonight.'

It was soon arranged. Margaret was asked to take Laura to the new school for an interview and assessment the following Monday. They had of course already sorted out their classes and had their quota of special needs students. Fortunately for Laura, however, someone had dropped out, so there most likely would be room for her, they were told.

'Over the weekend, we'll work out how to get there,' Margaret had time to say, before heading out. 'I'm sure it'll be easy – there's bound to be a bus right to the school.'

Margaret sighed, as she walked the considerable distance to work. The family car had ground to a halt a few weeks earlier. Greg had shaken his head when he looked at it, quickly declaring it beyond repair. Not that they had the money to fix it anyway – and certainly not enough to buy a new car. Ken needed their old ute for his mowing business, so Margaret could hardly rely on using that to drive anywhere. She sighed again, as she hurried along. She'd soon have to take on more shifts at the factory or look for extra work, with money so tight. Perhaps next year she could do a refresher course and go back to teaching …

That day, Laura spent several hours pounding away at the Perkins Brailler the family had managed to get her for Christmas. She had wanted one of her own ever since her first visit to the Blind School. After some initial lessons, she had practised whenever she could borrow one of their Braillers, rapidly gaining speed. Now, over the holidays, her own 'Mr Perkins' had become like a good friend to her, as she summarised her folders of notes and sorted out quotes from books and tapes. Today she attacked the keys particularly fiercely, unconsciously attempting to relieve some of her pent up emotions.

Jamie heard her working hard as he bounded up the stairs later that afternoon.

'How's school going, Laura? Lots of homework, eh?'

laura

'Not exactly.'

Then out came the story.

'... and anyway, I don't want to go to their old school. It's too boring! But I'm sorry Mum and Dad have to buy more uniforms for me, just because Miss Mellingham didn't want me there. *She* should pay for them, I reckon.'

'Calm down, Laura! No point in getting all upset over it. Besides ...'

Jamie stopped then.

'Well ... I'd like to help out with your high school stuff,' he finally continued in a rather gruff voice. 'I've earned a bit more doing extra shifts over the holidays – I'll tell Mum tonight. It won't matter what you wear on Monday, Laura, because you're only being interviewed. Mum can probably buy uniforms there and you'll be right for the next day. It'll work out – trust me! I have a good feeling about it.'

Jamie often said such things. And Laura did trust him – with all her heart. Jamie would never let her down, she was convinced.

It worked out exactly as he had predicted. The interview with the deputy principal went relatively smoothly, despite Laura's somewhat curt responses to the occasional questions put to her. Margaret held her breath, hastily intervening to smooth things over. She knew how anxious Laura was and how little she trusted school authorities, with good reason – but this was not the time to show it. Fortunately, things improved somewhat when they were conducted to the Special Unit for Laura to be assessed. There they were greeted warmly by the teacher-in-charge, Carolyn Burns.

'Hi Laura! I was told this morning to expect you. I'm Miss Burns. Welcome to our place! How do you feel about coming here?'

Margaret breathed a sigh of relief. Tackling things head on, but in such a friendly way, was exactly what Laura would like.

'Not very excited, to be honest. I don't mean to be rude, but it's just ... it's just that I've always wanted to go to a normal high school like my brothers.'

'Well, I hope you'll find the best of both worlds here. Of course, you'll do most of your classes with the sighted students – but we're here to make sure you don't miss out on anything and get any help you need. So if you look on our Special Unit as the icing on the cake, then we should get along fine.'

Laura began to relax, Margaret noticed. Carolyn Burns had just the right touch with her. There was something about her that was very engaging – a genuine warmth and a complete acceptance of Laura that put her at her ease. Margaret could not understand why, but she reminded her for a fleeting moment of Sarah and Anne.

The assessment tasks did not take long and Miss Burns was suitably impressed.

Neither did she miss the little satisfied smile of pride on her new student's face, when Laura realised she had done well. An interesting one for sure, Carolyn thought to herself. No doubt quite a challenge – but well worth the effort. Her first impressions were not usually wrong, but this time, for some reason, she particularly hoped she was right. There was something about Laura that touched her quite profoundly. Later, when she thought about it, she was unsure whether it had been the determined tilt of her chin or the rather desperate note in her voice, as she answered the questions put to her. There was no doubt Laura wanted to succeed and would hold nothing back in her attempt to do so.

'It looks like we'll be seeing a lot more of each other, Laura,' the deputy commented, when he was shown her test results. 'Well done! Now, Mrs Harding, if you'll please fill out some forms with the office secretary, then she'll explain about books and uniforms and show you more of the school. See you tomorrow, Laura – go straight to the Special Unit when you arrive!'

Then he was gone. The secretary fussed over them, making sure Laura knew the way to the Special Unit and eventually conducting them to a room behind the canteen, where one of the parents was sorting out uniforms. Margaret had been warned by Jamie in no uncertain terms the previous night not to settle for anything shoddy.

'Mum, I want you to take this and get a couple of nice new uniforms for Laura. I think it's pretty important she looks and feels good. ... No, Mum, don't worry! And don't argue! I want to do it. But promise not to tell Dad I paid for them!'

In the end, Margaret had taken the money. But she had held Jamie close for a long time and he could feel her tears through his thin T-shirt.

'Thanks, Jamie!' she had whispered huskily. 'I'm sorry things aren't going too well financially – but we'll come good. Your father does try, Jamie – he really does.'

'Yeah, sure, Mum. It's okay!'

Margaret had detected a bitterness in his tone that had disturbed her, but she left it at that. The most important thing was to get Laura settled at school – it was worth swallowing her pride and accepting Jamie's offer for that.

It was worth it too, watching Laura that night, as she paraded around proudly in her new uniform.

'Perhaps if I'm careful, Mum, you won't need to wash my skirt and blouse every day. I really love the 'new material' smell and how crisp and firm it feels. Do I look good, Dad? What do you think?'

'I think my little Laura's growing up too fast – that's what *I* think! *And* getting too smart along with it. Go take all your finery off and come and sing a couple of songs with me on the veranda!'

laura

Laura could hear the pride in his voice as he teased her and felt good. She hurried to get changed. They hadn't sung together much lately and she could hear him tuning his guitar already. But before she did, she made sure she had a word with Jamie, who had disappeared to his room.

'Jamie …'

'Yep?'

'Mum told me.'

'Told you what?'

'*You* know what I'm talking about – don't pretend you don't! Thanks, Jamie – thank you *soooooo* much! You're the best!'

'Okay, okay – I believe you. Don't strangle me!'

Laura had her arms around his neck, hugging him tight.

'Sorry you had to spend it on me and not on a car or whatever, Jamie.'

'Plenty of time to get a car – you need your uniforms *now*. Just see that you run rings around all those other kids for me, do you hear? Now, will you let me go? I've got work to do, even if you haven't.'

Laura knew he was only pretending to be exasperated with her. He was still her Jamie and her champion, whatever else was happening in his life.

With a sigh of contentment, she joined her father on the veranda. Ken loved the country ballads that had become popular in recent years – songs by Jim Reeve, Johnny Cash, Marty Robbins, Glenn Campbell and others – and Laura did her best to harmonise along with him. Occasionally he would stop and let her sing a verse on her own, especially when it came to songs by female artists like Tammy Wynette, or certain ones that were Laura's favourites – 'Bridge Over Troubled Water', 'Close To You', even a couple of gospel songs. Laura loved it all really. Her voice was not over strong, but very sweet and true and her pitch was perfect, as the Conservatorium director had said.

When they had finished most of their usual repertoire, they lapsed into silence. Ken could not help feeling a twinge of guilt, as he realised again how much Laura enjoyed being with him. And she wasn't a bad little singer – not bad at all. He should give Marg a break and spend more time with Laura, but often he felt he just needed to get away from it all and be with his mates instead. Sometimes seeing his special girl struggling to be accepted as normal and persevering so hard at things, despite her disability, was just too much for him. Now she was holding his guitar and idly picking out some chords he had taught her.

'Dad, do you know that gospel song 'He Touched Me'? I heard it on the radio the other night.'

She began singing it softly, stopping from time to time to find the right chords, which she worked out by ear as she went along.

'No, love – can't say I go for those gospel songs, or see why *you* like them so much either.'

'I don't know exactly myself. Maybe it's that they make me feel kind of peaceful inside. And they remind me of Anne and Sarah. I wish Anne could be here. I wish she was going to my new school too.'

'You'll be right – I reckon there'll be lots of girls who want to be your friends. Especially when they find out how fast you learn new stuff and how good you are at music. Just make sure you do your old Dad proud – and make sure they treat you the same as everyone else. None of that kid glove treatment for us Hardings!'

Laura did not need any such encouragement from her father. She was determined to stand on her own two feet from the very beginning, even with regard to getting to and from school. After Margaret came with her several times and showed her how to change buses at the 'Gabba, she insisted on going by herself.

'I'll be okay, Mum – I can always ask someone. And the bus driver will know where I have to get off. Anyway, I'll soon meet up with other girls from school who'll help.'

She was right. But Miss Burns made sure she did have others around her, not only on the afternoon bus, but also whenever she needed to find her way from the Special Unit to other parts of the school. She quickly realised, however, that once Laura had been shown where to find this or that, she did not relish any further assistance or instructions. She would answer politely, when help was offered, but with a note of finality in her voice that teachers and friends alike soon learnt to recognise. At first, Miss Burns would watch from a distance, or quietly move obstacles out of Laura's way where possible, but soon she saw that such precautions were mostly unnecessary. If she got into difficulty, Laura would either work things out herself, or politely ask someone nearby for help.

The school principal did not know that, however. It was several weeks before Laura crossed Mr Williams' path, but then it happened quite literally – and in a rather unfortunate way. Laura was walking back from a music class, a little in front of several sighted students, when she rounded a corner and cannoned into him.

'Here, young lady, watch where you're going! What do you think you're doing? You can't take up all the space on these verandas like that! People need to go the opposite direction as well. What's your name?'

'Laura … Laura Harding, sir.'

'You're in Grade Eight, are you? Didn't think I'd seen you around before. Well, Laura, please take more care moving around the school! Where are you

Laura

heading now?'

Laura was quiet for a moment before answering.

'To the Special Unit, sir,' she eventually said in a small voice.

'You ... you mean to tell me you can't see properly? Then what is Miss Burns *thinking* to let you find your own way around like this? And why don't you have a white stick?'

'I ... I can't see at all, sir – but I'm perfectly able to find my way around by myself, because Miss Burns showed me where everything is. I don't *need* a white stick.'

Laura did not mean to sound rude, but the slightly defiant tone in her voice did not go down well. The students behind her giggled, but were soon quietened by a flustered and annoyed Mr Williams.

'Go to your classes, you others! Laura, please come with me and we'll talk this over with Miss Burns. Here, watch out – these steps are steep! You'd better let me hold onto your arm.'

'I'm fine, thank you! I don't need any help.'

Laura shook his arm off, extremely embarrassed. Mr Williams did not respond, but followed her down the long flight of stairs and on to the Special Unit. Laura made herself walk calmly and carefully all the way and not hurry. She could not afford to make any mistakes – not with Mr Williams almost breathing down her neck.

To her relief, they had no trouble locating Miss Burns. As Laura stood stiffly beside Mr Williams, listening to his opinions, she felt decidedly small and stupid – and definitely an unwelcome interruption to his busy schedule. Something about his manner made her squirm. At times, she even wondered if he had forgotten she was there, or if he thought she was deaf as well as blind, or perhaps intellectually disabled.

When the conversation became a little too heated, Miss Burns turned to her and quietly suggested she go to the next room. Laura left, but could still hear them.

'I understand your concern,' Miss Burns was saying firmly, 'but I think as a community here we have to consider our special students' needs, rather than make *them* consider *us* more. They have enough hurdles to overcome, without our adding to them. This is certainly true in Laura's case. She's already had a bad experience at two schools, so right now I believe it's important to build up her trust in us all. She's a very bright student, Mr Williams – I'm sure you won't regret having her here in the long run.'

Mr Williams knew when he was beaten at least. He had applied for this particular school principal position because he had wanted a promotion and because of the boost to his career the Special Unit would bring. But he definitely felt the disabled students were a nuisance and seriously drained the school's already stretched resources. He could override Miss Burns – yet he had to admit she was a gifted teacher and a popular staff member, whom he had no wish to alienate. Much better to be seen in a good light by both the Department and his staff.

'Well, I hope you're right – for everyone's sake,' he reluctantly conceded then, hating to back down at all. 'But perhaps it wouldn't hurt to explain to Laura about the need for a little more respect towards the staff. She might be blind, but that's no excuse for rudeness.'

Laura

chapter eight

As time went on, it distinctly looked like Miss Burns would be proved right. Laura thrived in the accepting atmosphere of the Special Unit, sometimes taxing to the limit the energies and abilities not only of Miss Burns, but also the teacher aides. Her mind was so quick, and she was so eager to prove she was as able as any of the sighted students that she needed constant reminding there were others in the Unit besides her wanting support. Margaret helped her at nights when she could, sorting out her notes, reading aloud from her textbooks and generally helping her with homework or assignments. She constantly marvelled at the way Laura could retain so much information, despite sometimes hearing it only once, and then store it away in that small head of hers for future reference. Maths was definitely a problem area, however, largely because it did not interest Laura, but she persevered, often enlisting Jamie or Ian's help to grasp new concepts.

Yet while Laura's academic abilities gave her a distinct advantage over many of her fellow students, they also caused some relationship difficulties. She was not used to the classroom environment and had little experience in getting along with students of differing abilities, not to mention those less committed to working hard. At home, her family had often played games together. Her brothers were older and were usually a good match for her – and she had never had any trouble

laura

making allowances for Elisabeth, since she was two years younger. Yet whenever Miss Burns would test their group orally on material they had all covered in class, Laura would often heave a sigh when a wrong answer was given, or make an exasperated comment clearly audible to everyone.

'No, silly! That *couldn't* be right.'

'What? How could you *not* know *that*?'

'We did that just *yesterday*! Don't you remember?'

Eventually, Miss Burns took her aside.

'Laura, do you realise how you sometimes come across in class, when you get annoyed that others don't remember things?'

Laura could feel her face going red.

'Well ... some of them are so *slow*! They never remember anything – they mustn't do any homework.'

'Maybe they don't have a Mum who can help them, or a brother like your Jamie, who'll always do what he can for you, it seems to me,' Miss Burns explained gently. 'And Laura, they might not be as bright as you, but that's not *their* fault. We all have different gifts and abilities – so do you think you could be a little more tolerant? Remember how you sometimes have trouble in your Maths class and how you feel if you don't understand something? That's how the ones here who exasperate you feel *most* of the time at school.'

Laura swallowed hard and tried to think of something to say in her own defence. She never cried easily, but now she could feel tears coming. She owed Miss Burns a lot and hated to disappoint her – and she felt she'd let herself and her family down too.

In the end, sensing how upset she was, Miss Burns patted her gently on the shoulder and did her best to encourage her.

'I didn't mean to hurt you – I'm sorry! But I felt it wasn't fair to you not to say anything. You see, I happen to have a very high opinion of you, Laura, and I really want the other students and teachers to like you too. I often need to think twice before I open my mouth myself, so I'll pray you'll learn to as well. Now I have a suggestion to make. I think you need some extra interests to keep you busy and out of my hair. It's almost the end of the year, but over the holidays, why don't you think about what activities you'd like to be involved in next year? I know you're already in a choir, but you could join our school choir as well. And I think you'd be very good at debating – Grade Nine students are allowed to join in that. Then there's the school magazine committee – I could see if they need extra help, if you're interested. Or maybe ...'

And here she hesitated a moment before continuing.

'Maybe you'd even be interested in the Christian group. It meets each

Thursday at lunchtime. It's up to you of course, Laura – I don't want to push you into anything. You've settled in wonderfully here this year – I'm so pleased to have you in our Special Unit. But I'd love to see you do some new things next year and make lots more friends. Is it a deal?'

Laura gave her a rather watery smile, but inside, her heart was nearly bursting. Somehow, even in the process of rebuking her for her critical attitude, Miss Burns had managed to make her feel warm and special. Miss Burns believed in her – she really wanted her to be happy at school, to try out for things, to succeed and to get on better with everyone in the process. Interesting she should suggest the Christian group, she reflected – perhaps I *could* try going along next year, if I have time. Anne would be really happy if I did.

At last she nodded, in response to Miss Burns' question.

'It's a deal!'

By March the following year, Laura had begun to explore a number of the possibilities Miss Burns had suggested. She joined the school choir. She became the youngest ever representative on the School Magazine committee. And it was not long either before she made her presence felt in the debating arena. Yet she was a little slower to visit the Christian group, largely because her friends laughed at the idea when she first mentioned it.

'What? The *Christian* group? Why on earth would you want to spend the lunch hour cooped up with *that* bunch of losers?'

'*You* can go, Laura – I'm sure not! I'd rather sit in the library the whole lunch hour.'

'Wonder what they do? Probably pray a lot and read the Bible and boring things like that. Sounds great!'

Still curious, Laura eventually went one day when there was nothing better to do. The group was quite small, but surprisingly, several older girls there were popular enough to have been voted in as school prefects by their peers. They were all warm and welcoming and to top it off, seated at the back, keeping an eye on things as the students ran the group, was Miss Burns. To start the meeting, someone played the guitar, while most of the others joined in singing songs Laura had never heard before. Then Bibles were handed round – not that that helped her at all. But someone read some verses out loud and Laura found the discussion that followed quite interesting, until she heard stifled giggles from a nearby window. Soon she recognised the voices of some of her friends, determined to tease her, their giggles interspersed with soft chanting.

'Look at Laura, loser Laura, Bible basher Laura!'

Miss Burns noticed the dull red flush mounting Laura's face. Silently she moved nearer the window, until the girls, catching sight of her, ran off. But the

Laura

damage had been done, as far as Laura was concerned.

It was her first and last visit to the group, despite several of the girls inviting her to come again. Miss Burns, much as she regretted Laura's decision, could not make her change her mind. She suspected that for Laura, the horror of being labelled 'different' had scarred her spirit far too much in the past to want to venture anywhere near that path deliberately ever again.

All Laura knew was that she did not want to lose her friends. It just did not seem worth it, despite Miss Burns obviously having a strong Christian commitment. But Miss Burns was a teacher – and she was only a student who couldn't see, who needed to prove herself and even perhaps become a bit popular amongst her peers – especially the sighted ones. The price was simply too high.

All the same, Laura was aware of a strange longing deep down to know what caused those other girls to give up a lunch hour to meet together and not mind being known as Christians. It was as if they had discovered some secret she did not share – like they had found a safe place from which to face the world. She thought of Anne and the things they had talked about in the past to do with God. But then she remembered her own parents' views on such matters, especially her dad's, and also the big questions Jamie had. No – it wasn't worth it. Maybe she'd think about it all again when she was older. There were too many other things occupying her mind right now.

Certainly being included in the Junior Debating Team was one of them. She made it that year and the next, by which time she had acquired an enviable reputation in the school and beyond, as having one of the sharpest minds on the team. Laura relished the challenge of pulling a good argument together, of researching her facts, with the faithful help of her family, especially Margaret. Jamie was not at home so much now in the evenings and Greg – well, Greg was always happy to argue, but never prepared to do any serious research. Likewise Ken – but most nights he headed down to the pub after dinner anyway. And Ian was in his final year of school and busy with his studies. He was determined to make it into medicine at uni, so Laura never liked to bother him.

Things were changing in the Harding household – she could feel it.

By the second last year of high school, Laura was well entrenched in the many activities on offer and generally admired for her academic ability, as well as her musical gifting. Yet the road was still rugged for her at times, with occasional violent skirmishes along the way. It was fortunate Miss Burns was still on hand to deal with the resultant fallout from these. She had the ability to smooth any ruffled feathers – Laura's included.

One such incident occurred when Laura decided to try out for the school musical. She loved the bright melodies and clever lyrics of the Gilbert and Sullivan operetta the music master had chosen that year, so was determined to get at least a minor role in the production. She sang well at the auditions, she thought, but was told she would have to wait a few days until a final decision was made.

'Jen, can you please check the noticeboard outside the music room for me? The names of the people for the different roles must be up there soon.'

Every day for about a week, Laura asked her best friend the same question. Jen was always relieved when she found nothing – she had a horrible feeling in the pit of her stomach that, when the list finally went up, Laura's name would not be there.

Eventually, her fears were realised. There was no escape – all she could do was tell her friend straight out.

'Laura, I'm really sorry – the list's up, but your name's not on it. There's only a few lead roles in the musical anyway, so lots of people must have missed out.'

Laura was quiet for a long time. When she did speak, it was in a very flat, disappointed voice.

'I know that, Jen – but I'm sure I could have done one of the minor parts really well. Probably they didn't want me because I'm blind and it would have been too much trouble.'

'You don't *know* that for certain, Laura. But if you really want to find out, why don't you go and ask Mr Lang straight out?'

Laura needed no encouragement. Jen went with her as far as the door of his room and then disappeared.

'Yes, what do you want?'

'Sir, I just wanted to know if there was any specific reason I didn't get a part in the musical. I know I can sing as well as any of the other girls, so it must have been something else that made you turn me down.'

Mr Lang was caught unprepared. He hated to be put at a disadvantage and replied more testily than he otherwise would have.

'My dear girl – we don't have to explain our decisions to every student who was unsuccessful at the auditions. Anyway, you can all be in the chorus – we need as many as possible.'

'Yes, I know, but I wondered if I was turned down because I'm blind.'

'Well ...'

That moment of hesitation, followed by a rather uncomfortable silence, was enough for Laura. Before she could stop herself, she had lashed out with her tongue.

'Oh, it's all right, Mr Lang. Of course you wouldn't want any *disabled* students possibly messing up your precious musical! I could easily have managed one of the roles – you'd only have to explain to me once how and where to move. And

Laura

I'd remember the words a lot quicker than any of the others. Thanks all the same, but I don't want to be in the chorus – I've got better things to do with my time!'

'Look here, I don't accept that sort of response from any student – even ...' but here fortunately Mr Lang stopped, before incriminating himself even further in Laura's books. 'You've been extremely rude, young lady. I'll be talking to the Deputy and Miss Burns about it – don't think this is the end of the matter!'

Neither would it have been, except for Miss Burns' calming influence and promise to deal with it, when Mr Lang told her what had happened.

'I'm sorry Laura spoke to you like that. Please leave it to me – I'll undertake to talk to her about it. I understand why she reacts like this on occasions. It's not acceptable and I know she'll see that by the time we've finished.'

Miss Burns was right again.

'I know I over-reacted,' Laura tearfully admitted, when confronted by a concerned and obviously disappointed Miss Burns. 'I guess I'll apologise – especially if *you* think I should. It's just that sometimes I feel so angry inside, I can't manage to keep a lid on it. I hate any sort of discrimination, especially because of some so-called 'disability', or because a person doesn't happen to come from the right background. I know what it feels like. The other girls in the choir I was in on Saturdays used to judge me because I didn't wear the latest fashions, or my shoes were a bit scuffed. They all came from rich families and I used to hear them whispering about me and laughing. I could sing as well as any of them, but I don't care – I was too busy to keep going to their old choir anyway.'

'But Laura, you can't go through life reacting to situations out of the pain and hurt of other past experiences you've had,' Miss Burns tried to point out. 'It's not fair really – and I know how much you value giving someone a fair go. You don't see things clearly then – you might well judge people for something they don't really mean, or haven't actually done to you. Do you understand what I'm saying?'

'Yes, I guess so ...' Laura admitted eventually, 'but I'm sure Mr Lang really *does* think I can't do it because I'm blind.'

'That might be true – but we don't know for certain. Even if he does believe that though, then the best way forward, I think, is for you to try to forgive him. I know we have to fight injustices, Laura, but when we don't know all the facts, as in this case, all we can do is let it go and move on. If you keep holding a grudge against him or anyone else, then the person who suffers the most is *you*, not *them*!'

Laura was quiet, as she reflected on what Miss Burns had said. In her heart, she sensed there was something very wise and right about it, but she wanted to keep on fighting – to *make* him treat her the same as anyone else and give her a part in the musical. Yet even as she thought that, she knew it was impossible – she would only make herself unpopular with her teachers and maybe the other students as well. She sighed deeply – and Miss Burns' heart went out to her.

'One day, Laura, I believe you'll see that what I say is true – but I know how hard it is for you. Now can I suggest something else? No doubt you've heard about the competition for a new school song. Why not try your hand at that, instead of traipsing off to lots of boring practices for the musical? I'm sure you could come up with at least one excellent submission for the judging panel. Of course, that panel will include Mr Lang – but this could be a great way of showing him what you're made of!'

Laura could not help laughing. Miss Burns had the happy knack of confronting her about serious matters, but always with a touch of humour, as well as love and respect. If she ever became a teacher, Laura decided, she'd definitely want to be like her. Each week almost, she changed her mind about what she wanted to be – but all that was a long way off yet. Right now, the idea of writing an excellent school song was beginning to take root in her mind, exactly as Miss Burns had hoped and prayed it would.

Laura tried writing the lyrics first. Many nights she lay awake, with different ideas and word combinations running round and round in her brain, until she fell into an exhausted sleep. In the morning, she would quickly type out her latest version, only to change her mind again that night. But at last she felt she had done her best and had produced something at least passably good. She had enjoyed it all so much – the nightly tussle with words and phrases, the final capturing of an image that had eluded her, the sudden inward 'aha', as lines flowed and the song began to take shape. It had not been easy, but she felt an amazing sense of exhilaration at creating something out of nothing – something that was uniquely hers.

But writing the music was even more challenging. Again, scraps of melody seemed to float in her head at nights, just out of reach. In the morning, she would endeavour to remember them and sing them to Margaret or Ian, or try them out on the keyboard. Then in the evenings, she would often perform what she had written for Ken, who did his best, feeling this was an area in which he could truly help his Laura. Her creation went through several major overhauls before she was reasonably happy with the result, but this stage was not reached without many heated discussions along the way. Sometimes Ken insisted on giving the song a decidedly 'country' feel, with his own brand of guitar accompaniment. And despite herself, Laura always ended up laughing.

'We *can't* sing it like that, Dad – but thanks for your help!'

Laura

It was good to feel closer to him again. Lately, she'd missed the times they used to spend together singing their favourite songs. It hadn't been entirely his fault either, she realised, even though he'd been out so much – she'd been busy too. Maybe in the holidays she could take him up on his offer to sing with the band some nights – perhaps they could even write some more songs together, if this first effort of hers was successful.

Margaret hoped and prayed Laura would not be too disappointed, if her song did not win.

'Laura, you set your heart on things too much – you make it so hard for yourself!'

Laura realised she had in fact banked very heavily on winning, as she sat in the crowded school hall at the final term assembly, waiting for the all-important announcement. Her palms were sweaty and her stomach was churning, but outwardly she tried to appear calm. A few rows behind her, Miss Burns noticed the way Laura was sitting, her back very straight and her chin jutting out a little defiantly. Oh Lord, she prayed silently, please protect her! She's so vulnerable – so in need of you and your love. And if she doesn't win today, please give me the right words to say to comfort her!

Now Mr Lang, at the principal's invitation, had risen to his feet and was peering over his glasses at them all. He cleared his throat and finally began speaking.

'We had a surprising number of entries in this competition, with most being of a very high calibre. So those of you who haven't won shouldn't feel you've failed at all. We narrowed down the final choice to three – those submitted by Jane Burbridge and William Steer, both in Grade Twelve, and Laura Harding, from Grade Eleven. The judges and I had great difficulty in reaching a final verdict, but in the end we decided that the winner would be ... Laura Harding. Congratulations, Laura!'

Laura could not believe her ears. Her friends began hugging her and everyone clapped and cheered so loudly that she almost missed Mr Lang's final words.

'The school choir will learn Laura's song in the next few weeks, then teach it to the rest of you. Now, Laura, would you please come forward and receive your prize?'

Jen offered to go with her, but Laura was determined to do it on her own. She was trembling all over, as she made her way onto the platform to accept her twenty-dollar cheque from the principal. Mr Lang shook her hand too, although neither, she could tell, would willingly have chosen her for the honour. In fact, earlier that year, she had crossed swords once again with Mr Williams, this time over her decision not to do Maths.

'All students at this school are expected to study Maths,' he had declared emphatically. 'If you don't, your choices at university may well be much more narrow. Besides, it's a very useful subject in itself.'

'It's not useful to me, sir,' Laura had argued. 'Anyway, I already know what I want to study at university – and I don't need Maths for it either!'

Again, Miss Burns had intervened on her behalf – but it had been touch and go this time and had definitely not served to strengthen Laura's tenuous relationship with Mr Williams. Yet here she was now being congratulated publicly by both him and Mr Lang. As Laura made her way back to her seat, this time with a little help from Jen, she could not suppress a rather self-satisfied smirk, which did not go unnoticed by Miss Burns. Yet even she had to admit to feeling more than a little elated at the turn of events.

The next day, Laura was asked to sing her song for the choir, before they began learning it – and again the ensuing applause from her peers felt so gratifying. Later, she remembered to thank Miss Burns.

'I owe all this to you, Miss Burns. You were the one who encouraged me to write the song in the first place. And I know it was really to stop me getting too mad about not being in the musical. So thank you so much – maybe we should share the prize.'

But Miss Burns would not entertain the idea.

'No, Laura – you won it fair and square. I'm sure you and your family can put the money to good use.'

She was right about that. Recently, Ken's mowing business had collapsed, leaving even more of a hole in the family coffers. Margaret had seen it coming and in the end, accepted the news with resignation. Ken always set off in the ute with the mower and other equipment on board, but she had suspected for some time that he mowed only one or two lawns each day at the most.

'It really wasn't a goer from the beginning in this area – I should have seen that back then,' Ken said, in an effort to explain things. 'But don't worry – last night, the owner of the pub where we did our gig offered me a job as a barman. It's only temporary – the usual guy hurt his back, so has to be off work for a while – but at least the money would be regular. What do you think, Marg?'

'Ken, you know how I feel about your being at the pub so much. It's just too tempting – you know that yourself. I suppose I could get more shifts at the factory, but the best thing by far would be for me to go back to teaching.'

'Well, let's see about that next year, eh? I know you want to, but it'd mean no money coming in from you while you did your retraining – and you'd have to find time to study, as well as do everything else. Leave it a bit longer, Marg. We'll get by.'

His answer was always the same. The real reason, Margaret was sure, was his

Laura

own feelings of inferiority. On a teacher's wage, she'd definitely be earning much more than he would. She sighed deeply. Ken desperately needed to change his perspective on such things – but she was getting very tired of waiting for that to happen.

At the end of the year, Greg finally moved out, after a disastrous argument with Ken one weekend. All Laura knew was that the police had called, looking for Greg. They had informed her parents he was suspected of being involved in a car parts stealing racket and of doing up old models and selling them without the proper papers. Ken had gone out that night and drunk even more than usual, with the result that he was not in the best of moods when he and Greg finally got to talk the next day. Even now, Laura hated to think about the argument that had followed. She could not help overhearing – and neither could the neighbours, as Margaret had tried to point out.

But Greg had had enough.

'That's it – I'm moving out! There's a spare room where my mates live. Anyway, it'll be closer to work – I won't have to get up so early. I'm sick of paying board here, when all you do is sit in the pub and drink, Dad, and waste your time with your precious band trying to make it big. I didn't do anything wrong – but you don't believe me, so why should I stay? Some of my mates might do a few shady things at times – but I'm not going to dob on them, am I? I know how to keep my nose clean – I can look after myself. You'll see – one day I'll have my own garage and then you'll come to *me* for a loan. I know how to work hard – unlike *some* people!'

He had gone straight to his room then and begun packing his belongings. Not long after, Laura heard him roar off in his hotted-up Holden, his pride and joy that he had spent hours working on. By Sunday night, he had moved out completely – without even a proper goodbye to her.

Christmas Day was quiet that year, although Greg eventually turned up rather sheepishly for dinner, with presents for them all. Laura could feel the tension in the air, but both he and Ken managed to speak civilly enough to each other, for which she was thankful. She could argue a point vehemently when it came to debating at school, but she hated family disagreements with a passion. And whatever Greg's faults, Laura knew he was aware of that and was trying hard – not only for her sake, but for their mother's too.

Then, early in the New Year, both Jamie and Margaret took matters into their own hands as well, making important decisions that impacted Laura greatly. Jamie, now finished at uni – at least for the time being – and soon to graduate with honours in psychology, accepted a position as an adolescent counsellor on the far side of town.

'This means I'll be moving out too, I'm afraid,' he informed them, his eyes lowered. 'Sometimes I'll have to be on duty overnight at the detention centre where I'll be doing most of my counselling. Anyway, it's too far to travel each day, especially since I don't have a car. I'm sorry – I know you really need my board money, but there's not much I can do about it, I'm afraid. Unfortunately, jobs in my field are few and far between at the moment – if I don't take this one, who knows how long I'll have to wait?'

'We'll get by,' Ken had said rather hastily. 'Don't worry about us, son!'

He hated to be reminded that he was not earning enough to keep the family afloat.

'Actually ...' Margaret began, and then seemed about to change her mind, before taking a deep breath and ploughing on.

'Actually, this might be as good a time as any to tell you about my own plans. At the end of last year, I applied to do a retraining course in teaching. I heard yesterday that I've been accepted, so looks like it'll be back to study for me for a while. But it's okay, Ken – the course only goes for a couple of months. I reckon I can still do some afternoon shifts at the factory during that time, if I have to.'

'You're damned right you might have to, Marg! You could've told me you'd applied to do the course. Too late now though, when it's all signed and sealed. Well, looks like me and the boys will have to line up a few more gigs to pay the bills, doesn't it? Only trouble is, Ron wants to take a break for a few months, while he renovates his house. Maybe we'll have to send *you* out to work next, eh, Elisabeth – you're just about old enough. Or perhaps your sister could fill in for Ron – what do you say to that, Laura?'

For once, Laura was lost for words. All this change was too much in one go. It was enough for her that Jamie, her knight in shining armour, was moving out, let alone that her Mum was going back to study and would be even busier than she already was. She felt something akin to panic rising up in her and knew tears were not far away.

'I ... I don't know – I can't think right now. Maybe I could – a bit anyway – but this is my final year of school, so I'll have lots to do. I *have* to do well, otherwise I won't get into uni – and that would be awful.'

Jamie always knew how she was feeling. Now, unwilling to let her down even more than he had by his news, he tried to take charge of the situation.

'I don't think there's much chance you won't do well, Laura – judging by how you went last year. And even if I'm not available as much to help you with your schoolwork, or Mum either at first, Ian and Elisabeth will still be here. Anyway, once Mum's done her retraining, she'll be home about the same time as you and Elisabeth every day – plus she'll have all the school holidays off, which will be

Laura

great!'

He was trying to cheer her up, Laura knew. Later, he came to her room to talk.

'Laura, I know you don't want me to go – but I have to. I can't explain everything right now – one day you'll understand. And this job really does look great – it'll be a good opportunity for me to get some hands-on practice as well as earn a bit more money at last. More than my waiter's job pays, anyway. But promise me that if you're ever worried about Mum and Dad – or anything for that matter – you'll let me know. Do you hear me?'

Laura heard. But she also heard a kind of desperation in his voice that made her a little uneasy, for some reason. She sighed and hugged him for a long time, as he stood uncertainly in the doorway.

'It's okay, Jamie – I understand. At least, I *think* I do. And yes, I promise to phone if I'm ever really worried about anything. But you'll come back and see us lots, won't you? It's not as if you're moving to the ends of the earth.'

'No ... no I'm not, Laura – but I'll be working long hours and also I'll be sharing a house with Alan. So we'll need to take care of the place and all that. I'll try to get my licence and buy a car as soon as I can, but it'll take some time – and until I do, it won't be so easy to get here all that often.'

Now, even to Jamie's ears, it sounded as if he were making excuses. Again, an uneasy feeling came over Laura and a strange suspicion that he was keeping something from her. She had met his friend Alan once or twice, but he had not been a frequent visitor to their home. He'd seemed nice enough – and she knew he and Jamie had worked together on their research at uni. She was at a loss to know what to say, so merely held him tight again.

'I'll miss you such a lot, Jamie – but as Dad often says, we'll get by. You're a great brother – I love you so much!'

That was all she could get out, before the tears came.

'Don't worry, Laura! Whatever happens, I'll still be the best brother ever to you.'

Not long after Jamie left, school began again. Soon Laura was back in the thick of things, busy with the magazine committee, of which she was now chairperson, singing in the choir, and debating – the only female in the senior team, which represented the school in interschool competition. And although the male team members refused to admit it at first, Laura ran rings round them in many ways. They were soon in awe of her ability to think on her feet and to file things away in her memory, ready to be retrieved at a moment's notice. She was adept at summarising her opponents' arguments, pointing out any flaws with her razor-sharp mind and responding in a way that often left them floundering, grasping at straws to try to sound even remotely convincing. She did not need notes, this in itself often unnerving her opponents.

Eventually, her male team-mates acknowledged openly that she was the best and elected her captain of the team. Beneath the banter and friendly rivalry that went on between them and Laura was an obvious deep respect and admiration. She was fair, she was open and honest, and she was always happy to help them formulate their arguments when necessary. In short, she was one of them. Laura thrived on their complete acceptance and friendship, treating them as she would her brothers, more at ease with them than with many of the girls at school.

The fact that she got on so well with her male team members and the boys in general in her classes gradually began to cause difficulty with some of the girls, however.

'It's funny, but I find the boys so much easier to get on with,' Laura shared with Miss Burns one day. 'I often hear girls who are supposed to be my friends whispering behind my back when they don't think I can hear, but boys aren't like that. They'll tell me things straight to my face instead. At least that way we can argue about it and deal with it. I'm just one of their mates – nothing to be jealous about!'

Miss Burns knew what Laura meant. She had observed her easygoing manner with the boys and the envious looks and snide remarks from some of the female students. Recently, Laura had missed out on being elected as a prefect by the other girls, which had hurt her deeply. She was convinced her ability to get on well with the boys was at least partly to blame. Miss Burns could not help but agree – she wished she could make it all right for Laura, but knew that was impossible. But she could at least talk with her and try to help her understand and accept the outcome.

'Laura, I'm sorry you missed out on being a prefect. I think there probably was some jealousy involved, but it won't help to tell anyone that. Just be gracious in defeat – and ask yourself what positive thing can come out of this disappointment. Maybe too you could try to appreciate how insecure and unattractive many of the girls feel around the boys and how they wish they could be cool, calm and collected like you! And be thankful you have brothers – wonderful ones, by the sound of it.'

Laura tried not to bother her Mum too much these days. Margaret was so busy balancing work and study, as well as managing things at home. Laura could tell by the sound of her voice how tired she was. But Jamie was not around to talk to – and anyway, right now she needed her Mum. As Laura told her what had happened, she could not stop a rather bitter tone creeping into her voice.

'Strange, isn't it, Mum, that they'd be jealous of a blind kid like me, who can't

131

Laura

even see what she looks like in the mirror.'

Margaret held her close, at a loss to know how to comfort her. It was not often that Laura spoke like this, but when she did, it cut her to the heart.

A month later, Margaret was appointed to a primary school within walking distance of home. At first, being unused to the daily grind of lessons, she spent hours preparing and marking, but gradually this eased and she was able to enjoy her work and the children in her class, as well as spend more time with Laura and help her with her work. It was wonderful too, to be free of immediate financial worries and able to relax a little, with a good wage coming into the household each week.

During the time when money was particularly tight, Laura, true to her word, did fill in for her father's friend Ron in his band as best she could. In reality, she brought more work their way – it was not long before she became the drawcard, the 'novelty' that tempted the patrons in the door of the pubs where the boys played. At first, Ken was delighted to have her 'on board', as he put it.

'You're a good little singer, m' dear – I can always rely on you to come up with a great harmony every time. Besides, you look a heck of a lot prettier than Ron!'

But all the same, he was reluctant to call on her too often and was glad when Ron could come back. He was proud of Laura, but he still squirmed at some of the comments he overheard from the patrons and the pitying looks she received on occasions. He was sure she was aware of some of the things that were said. And he could not help the old anger welling up inside him whenever he noticed a slight uncertainty in her about where to look as she sang, or how to move, or where to put her feet in the midst of microphone leads and guitars. She would have been a stunning little performer, he found himself thinking with bitterness – especially with her big blue eyes shining with laughter or tears, depending on the mood of the song. He wanted to protect her, not put her on display like this. Better take her home, he would think to himself, as he reached for one last drink before packing up.

Yet Laura enjoyed the gigs. She was used to the spotlight now, as a result of her debating experience, and she had learnt to hold her head high and to act as if she had no trouble at all doing the same things as all the other students. That year at school, she went from strength to strength, from one achievement to another. Several of her poems were published in the school magazine. Her school song had gained wide acceptance and was often sung at assembly and interschool events. Academically too, she was finding her niche, putting maximum effort into her favourite subjects – History, English, and Music.

Then at their school speech night, with the whole family – even Greg – in proud attendance, Laura Harding was named dux of the school, the best overall student from across the entire body of sighted and visually impaired students.

That was not the end of it. Just before Christmas, when the results of the final year high school exams were made public, Laura discovered that as well as gaining high marks in all subjects, she had actually topped the state in Modern History. For a few satisfied moments, she could not resist thinking of Miss Mellingham and wondering what she would say now.

That night as she lay in bed, she felt her heart almost bursting with thankfulness and the sense of achievement that welled up inside her. Over and over in her mind, she replayed her father's response, when he had been told the news over dinner. He had put down his knife and fork with a clatter and had immediately moved to hug her warmly. She could hear the delight in his voice as he congratulated her, yet the tears were there too, Laura could tell – tears of pride in his girl.

'Oh well done! That's my Laura – I always knew you'd show'em!'

Laura

chapter nine

Laura floated in a sea of euphoria for days afterwards. Friends phoned, including Anne, back home from Melbourne for the holidays.

'Wow, Laura – I'm so happy for you! Congratulations! And to think I used to do my lessons with you! Now I can tell everyone I've studied with the famous Laura Harding. I'm sure God's watching over you in a special way, like I've been praying. Are you going on to uni?'

They chatted for a long time, their friendship as warm as ever, despite not having seen each other for around four years.

'I want to become a teacher eventually, so yes, I'm planning to go to uni,' Laura told her. 'I always thought I'd end up doing an Arts degree, probably majoring in English and History. But now I've discovered how much I love writing and debating and public speaking and all that, I've changed my mind. I've found out you can do an entire degree in Communications now, so I hope to enrol in that. Some of it might be a bit hard, because I can't see, but we'll work it out.'

'That's the sort of thing your Dad would say, Laura – and I'm sure you'll work it out too. I'll talk to you again before I go back to Melbourne, but have a wonderful Christmas – all of you! Are you planning on going to church anywhere for Christmas?'

laura

'I'm not sure. I'd kind of like to, you know – to say a really huge thank you for my results and all. But I don't know if anyone else will want to go with me – Mum probably wouldn't have time, with the cooking and everything.'

'Perhaps you could just walk up to that old church on the corner near your place, Laura. I don't know what it's like, but there's one way to find out. You can thank God right where you are though, you know – it doesn't matter so much about buildings and all that. Anyway, I hope you have a really special Christmas – you deserve it!'

When Laura broached the subject of church with the rest of the family, no one was the least bit keen. Eventually, Margaret came up with a suggestion.

'Laura, why don't you and Elisabeth go by yourselves? It's only up the road. Someone's bound to tell you where to sit and everything. We can check the times of the services on the board outside the church – I'm sure I've seen them there.'

At seven-thirty on Christmas morning, Laura wondered whether her idea had been such a good one after all. Elisabeth echoed the same thought half an hour later, as they tentatively made their way into the rather gloomy interior of the old stone church, having been handed two smallish books and a leaflet at the door.

'I think we'd better sit near the back, Laura. Then I can watch what everyone else does. One of these books looks like a hymnbook and the other one has prayers and stuff in it – and the paper's a welcoming letter thing. I don't *feel* all that welcome though.'

At that point, a man in a white robe and clerical collar walked down the aisle and greeted them.

'Hello! I don't think I've seen you two girls before – welcome! I'm the minister here. Are your parents coming today too?'

'No – we only live down the road and just wanted to come to a Christmas service,' Laura answered politely.

'Well, I hope you enjoy it. We're using a special order of service today, but we'll tell you what page it's on in the prayer book, so don't worry!'

Laura was about to tell him she couldn't see, but thought better of it. His mind would be on the service – and anyway, he must have a lot of other people to greet. As it turned out, he quickly moved on before she had time to say anything.

The next hour or so was like nothing Laura had ever experienced before. Most of the people around her seemed to know what to do – when to stand, when to kneel, when to respond to what the minister half sang and half spoke. At one stage Elisabeth started giggling, after she tried to put the long wooden kneeler down that was attached to the pew in front of them and it fell with a resounding thud. Laura could not work out what was happening, but, in reaching out her hand to stop Elisabeth giggling, knocked the books they had been given to the floor as well. Fortunately, she could not see the mixture of sympathetic smiles and pitying looks that were directed their way – but Elisabeth did and relayed it all later to the whole family with much mirth.

Yet despite everything, Laura had found the service strangely moving. The sound of the pipe organ and the singing of the old familiar carols touched her – but beyond that, there had been something more, something intangible. A sense of holiness or awe – maybe even the presence of God. Again that vague longing swept over her that she remembered experiencing all those years ago when they had gone to hear Anne's friend speak. It was not as strong this time, yet she felt it – especially when she heard people moving around her and Elisabeth explained they were all filing to the front to receive the bread and wine. They had stayed where they were, however – Laura listening carefully, taking it all in, and Elisabeth restless, wishing it were all over.

Finally it was time for the last hymn. Then they were at the door, shaking hands with the minister. Again, Laura felt she would have liked to say something to him, but she could tell by the tone of his voice and his half-hearted handshake, that he was not particularly interested in her. Anyway, she knew Elisabeth wanted to get home.

'Come *on*, Laura!' she was whispering, almost pulling her down the steps and out into the hot sun. 'Mum will want us to help with everything – let's go!'

In recent years the Hardings had fallen into the routine of having their own family celebration in the middle of the day, when Margaret's mother would join them. Jean was getting noticeably frailer and had never really managed to be at ease around Laura, but the fact that Jamie and Greg were able to join them all for lunch helped the situation, as they joked with everyone and teased their sisters mercilessly. Afterwards, when everyone exchanged presents, Laura discovered that Ian had chipped in with his two older brothers to buy her a new briefcase for uni. Laura felt the beautiful soft leather all over and buried her nose deep inside.

'Thanks, guys!' she managed to say, as she emerged again, quite overcome by such an expensive gift. 'I love the feel and smell of real leather – I'll try to look after it carefully and not lose it or get it wet. What colour is it?'

'It's a nice rich reddish-brown,' Jamie answered gently. 'I thought you'd like that better than something plain and boring.'

That was why Jamie was still her knight in shining armour, Laura suddenly realised. Only he and her mother truly understood how important it was for her to own beautiful things, even though she couldn't see them. And only they, and perhaps Elisabeth, knew her dread of looking shoddy or old-fashioned. Laura was touched that her other gifts also reflected that knowledge – two new dresses from

Laura

her parents, which Margaret had somehow found time to make from material Laura had chosen some weeks earlier, and a pretty bracelet from Elisabeth.

For once, Laura was looking forward to joining her father's side of the family that evening for the obligatory Christmas dinner with them. She had never felt fully accepted by her aunt and two female cousins. Whenever they talked to her, they still spoke slowly and loudly, as if she were incapable of hearing and understanding. But she had shown them! Now they knew how well she'd done in her exams, they'd have to treat her differently.

She was completely unprepared for the comments she overheard then, as she and Jamie sat on their side veranda in the cool after dinner.

'She must be bright – but then again, if you're blind, I guess you don't have much else to do except study.'

'They probably marked her easier too, because she's blind. Wonder how she'll get on at uni? I can't imagine her having too many friends – you'd never have any fun, always having to look after her.'

Jamie reached out his hand and held Laura's tightly. When she had stopped shaking, he pulled her to her feet and together they walked out into the garden, where no one could hear them.

'Laura, listen! They don't know what they're talking about. They're ignorant idiots – and jealous that you've managed to do so well. It's not worth arguing with people like that – don't stoop to their level!'

'I know you're right, Jamie,' she said after a while, 'but something in me wants to slap them for their stupidity and set them straight. How could anyone think I'd be marked easier, when it was a public exam and I dictated my answers? Whoever marked my papers would have no idea I'm blind!'

'Don't worry! No one's going to listen to them.'

'But Jamie – what if I *don't* end up with any friends at uni? And what if my friends now think I'm a nuisance and wish I wasn't around?'

'You'll always have friends, Laura, because you're a good friend yourself. As for not having any fun – I dare you to go back in there now and be the life of the party! Come on, let's prove 'em wrong!'

Later, when Jamie and Greg had gone their separate ways and the rest of the family were driving home, Laura found they were all quite positive about the visit.

'At least it was bearable this year – especially when you and Jamie started that crazy game, Laura.'

Margaret was a little more perceptive.

'What made you and Jamie do that, Laura? It looked to me like you'd had enough of their boring conversation and the patronising way they always treat you.'

Laura eventually told them the story. Ken, after firing off his usual tirade about his family, summed it up for them all.

'You'll show *them*, Laura! You go on and get your degree in fine style, love – and invite them to meet all your friends at the end! You'll knock the socks off the other students – and have a lot of fun doing it, I reckon!'

'I intend to, don't you worry,' came Laura's small determined voice from the back seat of the car.

But the first hurdle to achieving her dreams almost caused her to stumble before uni even began. At the end of January, she received a call informing her she would not be accepted into the degree program in Communication, because she was blind. The secretary making the call could not explain the exact nature of the difficulties, but encouraged her to enrol in another course as soon as possible.

'The places are filling up fast, so, if I were you, I'd change my enrolment straight away.'

'But I don't *want* to change! Is there anyone in charge I can come and talk to?' Laura quickly countered.

'Well, I can find out if the Head of our Department would be available this afternoon – but I doubt he'll change his mind. The places in this course are very limited, so there's strong competition for them.'

'I *thrive* on competition! What time would you like me there?'

It was soon arranged. That hot January afternoon, Laura dragged an unwilling Elisabeth with her all the way by bus and ferry to the main uni campus. When the Professor finally called her in, after a lengthy waiting period, he was confronted by a small, determined girl with head held high and eyes that seemed to look straight through him.

'Now, Miss Harding, my secretary informs me you're unhappy about not being allowed to study for our degree in Communication. I'm sorry you've put yourself to the trouble of coming here, because all the first year places have now definitely been allocated. Anyway, we couldn't accept you, because of your vision problems. You don't have any sight at all, is that right?'

'I've been completely blind since I was almost three,' Laura responded in a rather hollow voice.

'Then, my dear, this course is definitely not for you. I've no doubt your oral and written communication is extremely good, judging by your exam results, but there's no way we could exempt you from the visual components of the course, since they're quite a large percentage of it. How would you manage, for example, in the areas of filmmaking, video and television production, and photography? Even drama would present some problems, I imagine. You must have known

Laura

these were part of the course when you enrolled – or did you not get to read the handbook?'

'Of course I know what the handbook says, but surely I could be offered alternative subjects? Couldn't I specialise in the oral and written aspects of communication? Anyway, I think I *could* manage some of the areas you mentioned. It would merely involve working our way around the difficulties and finding a few creative solutions to them, rather than just saying it won't work.'

As Laura said these words, she realised she was quoting her faithful Miss Burns, who had stood by her all through her high school years, always finding alternate ways to do things and assess her work. But now Laura was in a different world, standing in the wings of a much bigger stage, where there was no Miss Burns to fight for her and where competition was too fierce to allow for any bending of the rules for her sake.

By now, Laura could tell the Professor was quite amused, judging by the rather patronising tone in his voice as he stood to end the interview.

'Miss Harding – go and enrol in an Arts degree! That would be my advice to you. There are many subjects available under that umbrella – even some in the area of Communication. I admire your courage, but my answer is no.'

Laura knew there was no more point in fighting. She turned to leave, quietly asking the way to the Admissions Building as she did so. In the end, his secretary took pity on her and went with them, along covered walkways, across a large grassy quadrangle area and through another building, all of which were soon to become very familiar to Laura.

So against her will and very much as a second choice, she enrolled in an Arts degree, choosing to study English and History subjects, as well as Psychology and Journalism.

That same week, she paid a final visit to her old school and spent the afternoon in the Special Unit, helping some of the students. After classes were over, Miss Burns took her out for coffee.

'Like real friends, rather than teacher and student,' Laura commented, enjoying the feeling of being treated as an adult on equal footing with a staff member.

They discussed many things, not least of which was Laura's change of enrolment at uni. To her surprise and slight disappointment, Miss Burns seemed delighted.

'Laura, I believe God's hand's in this – I'm sure it will work out much better for you in the end. This will open up such a broad field of study for you, with all sorts of possibilities. It's very exciting – who knows what new discoveries you'll make along the way?'

'Yes … but the Communication degree sounded so interesting – and it would have been great to be the first blind student in that course,' Laura responded, her regret obvious. 'I want to do *different* really interesting things, Miss Burns – I certainly don't plan on having a boring, ordinary old life.'

'I'm sure you don't – and I do understand. That's why I chose specialist teaching and ended up in charge of the first Visually Impaired Unit attached to a high school. And also ...' but here Miss Burns hesitated a little, '... no one else knows this yet, so keep it quiet, but I'll be finishing up at the Unit at the end of this year. I'm doing some part-time study at Bible College at the moment, but I believe God wants me to take the plunge and study full-time for the next couple of years. Then I hope to head to Africa to work with disadvantaged children. So you see, Laura, you might think you have your life worked out, but sometimes God leads in quite a different direction. Actually ...' and here again she hesitated for a fraction, '... I believe God's got great things for you to do too, Laura, that you don't see at present – and the first step in finding out what these might be is trusting God with your whole life and your whole self. That's certainly a pretty radical thing to do, isn't it? But I know you'll never regret it.'

'You sound like my friend Anne – she and her family lived next door to us before we came to Brisbane,' Laura laughed, but then quickly became serious again. 'I think that'd be a very big step for me to trust God that much, but a few times in my life I've kind of felt I wanted to. Like once when we went to hear a speaker who sounded like he knew God as a real person. I remember I wanted to find out more, but Mum said we had to go. Even before that, when Anne and I used to read the Narnia stories, I loved Aslan best of all the characters – and Anne told me that Aslan was like Jesus. I loved some of the songs about God too that I used to hear at her place – she gave me a tape of them when we left. And ... and just this Christmas, Elisabeth and I went to a church near our place, because I wanted to. We didn't understand much, but it felt kind of good in the service – like God really was there. Then I've always listened to the things you've said about God too, Miss Burns. I never did go back to the Christian group at school, because – well, mainly because of my friends. I actually wouldn't have minded finding out more about the Bible and all that, but I didn't want to be unpopular either. I'm a bit mixed up about it all really. Sometimes I *feel* like there's a God who loves me and watches over me, like my friend Anne always says she prays for me, but then at other times I'm not sure. I think there are a lot of things about God that are really hard to understand. My family thinks so too – especially my Dad.'

Miss Burns waited a moment, but then felt she had to pursue the subject.

'I could probably guess – but what sort of things are the hardest?'

'Oh, things like little kids suffering – and so many bad things happening to

Laura

good people. My Dad used to argue with our neighbours about that. I know he's always blamed God for what happened to me – none of the doctors believed anything was wrong with my eyes until it was too late. Then our neighbours told us their little boy was killed by a drunk driver – yet they still manage to believe in God and Jesus and all that. Mum and Dad used to go to church before they had us, but now they only go to weddings and funerals and things like that. I don't think Dad believes there's a God at all – and I think my oldest brother Jamie might agree with him now. Certainly my next brother Greg does. I want to make up my own mind though – I want to find out for *myself*. Sometimes I think I'd like to really believe in God like Anne and her family do and some of the kids in the Christian group – and you too, Miss Burns. It'd be good to know there was someone strong and loving you could talk to who really understood you and had the power to answer your prayers, when things get a bit hard.'

As Laura finished speaking, she was surprised at the deep, almost overwhelming sense of longing she felt. She knew the tears were not far off and quickly looked down. But Miss Burns had noticed and put her hand gently over Laura's.

'I think what you might be looking for, Laura, is a firm rock under your feet – a secure place where you could stand and face the world, knowing God's there to protect you. Then when things change and your world seems to be falling apart, you can be at peace and know you're still safe, whatever happens.'

'Yes, that's it, I guess.'

Laura found it hard to add anything more.

'You could have that today, you know,' Miss Burns continued. 'You could step onto that safe, firm rock right now – and I know God would hold you there safely. I think God's been calling you for a long time in different ways and loves you so much. Do you think you *could* truly believe that?'

'I ... I'm not sure – maybe not quite yet,' Laura said hesitantly in the end. 'It's just that I need to think about it a bit more first – and perhaps read the Bible myself and talk it over with a few other people. I don't mean to offend you though. You've helped me so much by the way you always believed in me and watched out for me all through high school. And I honestly do admire you for being prepared to give up everything and go to Africa, all because that's what you believe God wants you to do.'

'One day not far off, you'll find that rock you're looking for, Laura, I'm sure of it. And I'll be praying for you, like your friend Anne does. In fact, could I pray for you right now? Then I have something to give you.'

Laura felt she could hardly say no.

'Lord, thank you that you've been here with us today – and thanks so much for Laura! Please continue to show her who you really are and help her to understand. Watch over her as she starts uni – and please give her friends who'll be able to support her, as she seeks to know you more. Lord, you promised that when we seek you with all our heart, we will find you – may that be so for Laura soon! Amen.'

Before Laura could say anything, Miss Burns reached down into her bag and brought out a neatly wrapped parcel.

'I've wanted to give you this for a while – today seems just the right time. It's one of my favourite books of the Bible in Braille – the Gospel of Luke. A friend got it for me, especially for you. I hope you can find time to read it, in the middle of all the new things you'll be doing at uni. I've really enjoyed talking with you today, Laura – no doubt we'll both be very busy this year, but hopefully we can fit in another coffee together some time. Let me know when you want to.'

Laura stammered her thanks, sincerely touched by such a thoughtful gift. Miss Burns drove her home and then, with a final quick hug, was gone.

'God bless, Laura!' she called out, as she drove off. 'Don't forget to read my present!'

Miss Burns had been right about how quickly other things would push any thought of God to the back of her mind, Laura realised a few weeks later. As she tackled the whole new world that university was for her, she found she needed all the energy she could muster to overcome the obstacles involved and make the huge mental and physical adjustments required of her. After a while she was able to find her own way to uni, forming friendships with other students who travelled across the Brisbane River each day on the same ferry. Eventually too, she worked out how to get from lecture room to lecture room under her own steam, as well as the library, refectory and student common room. Usually there was no shortage of people ready to offer assistance, but she invariably refused it, wanting as always to be independent and to prove she could manage the same as everyone else.

Yet it was not long before Laura discovered what a far cry uni was from the shelter of the high school Special Unit. Here there was no Miss Burns to act on her behalf and watch over her. Soon she realised that, if she did not accept at least some of the help available, especially that to which she was officially entitled, then she could easily jeopardise her chances of success. She therefore gritted her teeth and gradually learnt to accept with grace any assistance offered and gently explain her needs. And soon she began to value highly the support of her faithful Disability Services assistant, Barbara, as well as others who helped by recording material, or transcribing textbooks and notes into Braille. She kept her helpers on their toes, however, her quick mind still often frustrated by any slowness or lack of understanding, but, when their hard work paid off and she began achieving good results, she was genuinely grateful to them and lavish with her praise.

Laura was maturing fast, learning daily how to get on in the academic world and in life in general. Yet she was thankful too for both the emotional and practical support she still received at home from her mother. Often she would enlist Margaret's help as well to type out her many assignments, dictating them to her at nights or on weekends – occasionally even into the early hours of the morning. Or sometimes Laura would ask her for help in organising her notes so that she could easily find them again herself. She tried hard not to overload her mother, however. After all, she was often busy with her own preparation and marking, as well as running the household.

Yet despite the enormous amount of time and energy that lectures and assignments demanded, Laura was determined to enjoy student life to the full and try at least some of the many student activities on offer. Early in the piece, she joined the Musical Society, keen to sing in the choir and become part of the musical world in general on campus, with its wide variety of groups, bands and ensembles. Then as the year unfolded, her giftedness in clever harmonisation and also song writing began to emerge – so much so that soon she found herself in demand to help produce original student musicals and revues. It was heady stuff for a university 'fresher', but Laura revelled in the company of the interesting, creative personalities with whom she collaborated, thriving on their ready acceptance of her and also the recognition and respect her efforts brought. Many of them had quite a bohemian approach to life that appealed to her – money and possessions were far less important than expressing their creativity in all sorts of original and innovative ways. Laura felt accepted by them for who she was, with her own unique contributions to their artistic projects. It did not seem to matter to them whether she could see or not – and she loved that.

But the Debating Club soon drew her as well. It was one of the more 'prestigious' groups on campus, attracting some ambitious government and law students, as well as the usual smattering of philosophers and anti-establishment 'stirrers'. At first she sat quietly in the meetings, listening carefully to the more experienced debaters, but soon she could not resist putting her name down for in-house competitions and 'fresher' rounds. And she was good. She was not tempted to rely on notes and, as at school, her excellent memory and quick mind, combined with thorough preparation and research, soon brought success to the teams in which she was included. She always particularly enjoyed being the final speaker, summing up the team's main points succinctly and with great aplomb. There was a certain air about her, she was told – an assurance that seemed to command respect, convincing others to take her arguments seriously.

It was in the Debating Club that she first met Steve. He was a third year Law student and one of its key members, always vocal in meetings, always ready to discuss whatever topic was up for debate. At first, Laura avoided him – he was far too gregarious for her liking. She distinctly preferred people who listened well, who were not always waiting for the first opportunity to voice their own opinion. Yet he seemed good-hearted, always willing to coach new members and help with any research. And it was in this context that they first crossed paths.

'Laura, would you like to take part in the next debate against the Uni of New England students?' the teams' organiser asked one afternoon, her voice a little harassed. 'I know you're still a fresher, but most of our more experienced debaters are unavailable – and anyway, we think you'd do a really good job.'

Laura was flattered, but also a little hesitant. She had several assignments due and wanted to do well in them.

'I'd love to … but I'm not sure if I'll have time to prepare. It depends on the topic too.'

'It's on public versus private education – but Steve's team captain, so he'll help you with any research. You'll be fine.'

Steve was full of ideas, many of which were aired when the team met over coffee later that day. Soon it was all arranged. He would research the facts and figures Laura needed to strengthen her arguments and talk with her again as soon as possible.

'So … I reckon that should give you enough ammunition,' he said after they had met the following afternoon. 'I think I've explained everything. If I give you these notes, is there someone who can transcribe them into Braille for you?'

'Of course!' Laura responded a little shortly, feeling somewhat patronised.

'Well, I have to head off now – I'm involved in the Student Christian Union and we have a special speaker today. Better still, would you like to come? Are you interested in God and stuff like that? … Hey, I just realised! You might know someone I know – she used to teach at a special unit for the blind, or something like that. Do you know Carolyn Burns? She belongs to the church I go to. You do? Wow, that's amazing – she's a great person! So … did you go to the Christian group at high school? I know she had something to do with leading that.'

He barely waited for Laura to respond before beginning again.

'Our group on campus is going really well. There should be a good crowd there today – I think you'd like it. Come on – there's one way to find out. I can introduce you round, but probably you'll already know lots of people, as there are quite a few first year Arts students who come. We can get something to eat on the way – how about it? You can do your assignments later – after all, you have to eat lunch *some* time.'

Laura eventually gave in. She did not like being bulldozed into making any decisions, much less one that involved attending a meeting she was unsure about.

Laura

They quickly purchased their lunch and headed off to one of the larger lecture theatres.

As it turned out, the speaker *was* good, tackling the thorny topic of the authority of the Bible in an interesting way and handling with ease some hostile questions thrown at him by a group of very sceptical philosophy students. But she was glad when she could eventually slip out and retreat to the quietness of the library. Her head was whirling – what she needed was time to think about all she'd heard, before talking to Steve again. Time to consider whether she really wanted the pressure right now of deciding what she believed in and where God fitted into her life – if at all. Things seemed to be moving at such a fast pace for her – half the year had gone already. She had faced so many challenges and overcome them, achieving good results in her assignments and receiving encouraging feedback from most of her tutors. She aimed to keep this high standard up – but she also wanted to continue her involvement with the Music Society and pursue the friendships she had there. And of course the same went for the Debating Club, where she knew she could gain recognition and make her mark on campus. Life was busy and exciting, filled with new experiences and challenges – and the more she thought about it, the less keen she was to try to work out where God fitted into it all.

Actually, she could not even think about it one minute longer, she realised, if she hoped to finish the assignment due later that week.

But Steve was not one to let the grass grow under his feet. He liked challenges – and he liked tackling them head on, any resistance making him even more determined. He truly loved God, and his desire to share his faith with any who would listen was sincere and well meaning. However, he had yet to learn the wisdom of closing his mouth at times, of listening more than talking, of letting God rather than he himself do the persuading. Often his enthusiasm caused him to rush in where angels feared to tread – and this was definitely the case with Laura. In the days and weeks that followed, she became one of his prime targets – a stray sheep needing to be shown the door of the fold, whether she wanted to or not.

Eventually things came to a head one afternoon, when Steve cornered her in the refectory. She was enjoying a quick coffee, having just come from a lively Music Society meeting where she and her friends had pooled ideas for a prospective music festival.

'So, Laura – have you decided yet whose side you're on?'

She stiffened, deciding to play for time.

'What do you mean exactly?'

'I mean, have you decided where you stand with God yet? Have you had time to read the Bible verses I mentioned the other day? Jesus loves you, Laura – he truly wants the best for you. When are you going to take the step of giving your life to him? Come on, Laura – why spend your time hanging around those guys in the Music Society when you could …'

But by now Laura had had enough. She put down her coffee cup with a clatter, her annoyance obvious, even to Steve.

'Look, I know you mean well and I respect your views and your faith in God,' she began in a clear, determined voice, 'but I *hate* being told what to do and when to do it – just ask my family! And I *especially* hate being told what to believe in, before I've had time to think it through for myself. I *do* think there might be a God who loves me, Steve. I like the idea that there might be someone wise and powerful to turn to when I'm not sure what to do – but I don't think I can quite believe it all totally as yet. Miss Burns and I have talked about that. She gave me Luke's Gospel in Braille – I've started reading it, but I want to think about it a bit more, when I don't have so many other things happening in my life. So can you please leave me alone? I'm happy to discuss debating stuff with you, Steve – but I honestly don't want to talk about God any more.'

Steve was immediately contrite.

'Hey Laura, I'm really sorry if I've hassled you too much. I know I do that sometimes – I get impatient with people and want them to make up their minds and stop sitting on the fence. But anyway …'

His voice petered out then. For the first time Laura could remember, he seemed a little unsure of himself. She did not want to encourage him any further, however, so stayed silent.

'Anyway,' he eventually continued, 'I just want to say I truly admire you, Laura. I know I'm not the most sensitive of guys, but at least I've noticed how hard you try and how you tackle everything full on – debating, your studies, even the music stuff you're involved in. I'd have liked to get to know you better – I mean, I'd like us to have been really close friends, because I think you're a special girl. I guess now's not the time to mention that though. I hope we can at least talk to each other at Debating Club – providing I don't mention God at all.'

He was obviously shaken – and even sounded disappointed. Laura sighed, relenting a little.

'I'm sorry, Steve – I know I tell people off too quickly at times. For me, believing in a God who's loving and powerful would be a huge step, given what happened with my eyes and all. But I'm not throwing out the whole idea, as I've already explained. Besides, my friend Anne from back home and also Miss Burns always pray for me, that God will watch over me and that one day I'll take that step and believe for myself. And one day I might, Steve – but not right now.'

Laura

'I think I understand ...' Steve responded, 'but don't put it off too long, will you, Laura? Don't leave it until it's too late!'

They parted friends, but Laura went home heavyhearted nonetheless. Steve's final words stayed with her for a long while. What had he meant? Why would it ever be too late? And he'd seemed genuinely concerned for her as a person. Had he *really* said he thought she was special? Had he wanted them to be boyfriend and girlfriend – is *that* what he'd meant about being really close friends? She'd never had anyone interested in being more than just friends with her before. Now it was too late – she had snuffed out that possibility in no uncertain terms even before it began. She felt like crying, yet she wasn't sure exactly why. It wasn't as if she'd even liked him over much – he was too pushy and opinionated by far for her. All the same, it had felt nice to hear how he liked her and wanted to be close friends.

Yet it wasn't only that. Somehow she felt as if she'd closed the door on an even more important new experience – as if she'd turned her back on something she'd been searching for all her life. There was such a mixture of emotions whirling around inside her, she realised, as she reached home and slowly climbed the front steps. Sadness, frustration, even anger – both at herself and at the world in general.

Her spirits sank even lower when she discovered her father stretched out on the lounge in front of a blaring TV, snoring loudly and reeking of beer. Her mother was in bed already, exhausted after a long week of teaching. She was tired a lot lately – Laura tried not to bother her these days with her assignments. Ian was staying over at a mate's house that weekend, she remembered then, so they could study together and prepare for an important prac exam at uni. And Elisabeth had apparently gone out for the evening with her latest boyfriend. Laura knew this greatly worried her mother – Elisabeth was only fifteen, after all, and supposedly hoping to go on to uni, but Laura could tell her heart was not in it. These days there were often disagreements between Elisabeth and her mother – about how late she could stay out or whom she could go out with or how many new clothes she wanted. Her current boyfriend was several years older – Laura had not been over-impressed herself when Elisabeth finally introduced him to her. She heaved a sigh, as she made her way to her room and slowly prepared for bed. Some days she wished she could leave home and live in one of the university colleges, or even perhaps share the old house some of her musician friends rented, within walking distance of uni.

As she huddled under the warm covers, Laura found herself thinking of the safe, firm rock she and Miss Burns had talked about and of the peace and protection Anne always prayed for her. I want all of that, she thought wearily – I just hope it's not too late. 'Oh God, I don't know how to pray – but I'm sure they do. Please listen to their prayers!'

laura

chapter ten

Laura worked hard at her studies the rest of that year, but she was also determined to have fun and take part in as many campus activities as possible. Such an opportunity might never come her way again to experience the easy camaraderie of student life and truly be a part of it all. Besides, her cousins' words still niggled. She wanted to show them how wrong they were – to prove, even if only to herself, that she could indeed have many friends who enjoyed her company.

In the main, things unfolded in a way that exceeded even her high expectations that year and showed that her cousins had been decidedly wrong. She continued to do well at debating, taking part in increasingly higher level competition and often being selected by Steve to join his team, despite their differences. But when both entered a fun 'mock' debate at the group's final meeting for the year, with the outcome decided by audience applause, Laura beat him convincingly. In fact, to her embarrassment, she thought the clapping and stomping of feet would never end. Initially, she wondered if everyone had felt sorry for her, being a mere first year student and also blind, but at the same time, she knew she had put her case well, with plenty of humour along the way. In the end, Steve himself confirmed she had won it fair and square.

'Congratulations, Laura! I have to say you're one of the feistiest girls I've ever

Laura

come across! You sure pack a punch with your words – *and* you have a good sense of humour to boot. Don't go telling yourself you won it because people felt sorry for you either – that wasn't the case at all. Anyway, judging by how you went today, it's obvious you can look after yourself quite well, thank you very much! I can just imagine you as a fiery little lady preacher, pounding the pulpit and converting even the most hardened sceptic. I hope I'm around to see it.'

Laura thanked him, but did not deign to respond to his final comments. She did not want to reignite any conversation about God at that point. Besides, what he had said was too preposterous even to imagine, she decided, as they all headed off to the refectory for one final coffee together.

They talked and laughed together late into the evening. Laura realised, when she finally headed home, how much she would miss all her uni friends over the long Christmas break. She did not have a holiday job, as many of them did – only the occasional gig with her Dad's band, while one of his mates was on holidays. At least she had some projects to work on – songs she had never had time to finish, plus other bits and pieces of writing she had had to put aside. Early in the new academic year, the Music Society was finally staging its festival on campus – she had promised to come up with some new material for that. Perhaps Jamie would help her. He had holidays owing to him, she knew – maybe he could spend a day or two at home with her. He was good at coming up with innovative ideas.

At first she could not settle to anything much. She was definitely tired, she realised, after all the effort she had put in throughout the year. And while she knew she had done well in her assignments, she was unsure how she would rate in her final exams. It was no easy task to think out loud and dictate essays, or even short answer responses, for her faithful Barbara to write down, especially at tertiary level. She wished her results were available before Christmas – that way she could have relaxed and joined in the festivities more fully.

Margaret collected the mail the day Laura's results finally came. She immediately noticed the university's crest emblazoned on one of the envelopes and her heart skipped a beat. Laura was on the veranda, trying out a new song on her guitar. Something in the way Margaret walked up the steps and along to where she was sitting told her that her results had come, even before anything was said.

'They've come, haven't they, Mum.'

'Looks like it. At least, there's an envelope from the uni here – want me to open it?'

'Yes, please.'

There was a silence – and then the words tumbled out.

'Laura! A high distinction in History – and distinctions in English, Psychology and Journalism! Can you believe that? Congratulations! Oh, Laura – I'm so proud of you!'

Then they were hugging each other, crying with a mixture of joy and relief.

'I can't wait to tell the rest of the family!' Margaret said eventually. 'Or rather, I'd better let you do it – you did all the hard work.'

When Laura managed to speak again, she knew what she had to say.

'Don't forget you helped me a lot. … But next year, Mum, I'll have to learn to stand on my own two feet more. Maybe even move closer to uni – I could share a house with some of my friends. How would you feel about that?'

Laura heard her mother's sharp intake of breath, so without waiting for a response, hurriedly went on to outline what she was thinking.

'It'd be a big step, I know – but I have to try it some time. Some friends of mine, Brian and Kerry, share a house with two other girls from the Music Society, but one of them has finished her degree and is moving to Melbourne. I said I'd think about it over Christmas and let them know by the end of the month. That way they'll have time to advertise for someone else, if I don't want to take up their offer. I think I could afford it on my student benefit – but would you be okay, Mum, without my board money? The advantage for you would be that I wouldn't be here asking you to do stuff for me so much. I'd have to organise my time better, that's for sure, and get Barbara to help me more – her kids are more independent now, so she's free to work a few extra hours, which is good. I think if I record more of my lecture notes I can save her some time and I know she prefers to help with my research for assignments than sit in on lectures. Anyway, I can look into all that, if I decide to go ahead.'

It had all come out in a rush, but at least it was out in the open now. Laura had known she had to seize the moment, rather than put it off any longer.

Eventually Margaret managed to put her arm around her shoulders and squeeze her gently.

'I knew the day would come when you'd want to spread your wings, Laura – but I guess I've felt too protective of you even to want to think about it. I'd miss you for sure – you're the one I talk to, now Jamie's not here. Ian's so focused on his studies, so that leaves Elisabeth – and you know the story there. I wish your father could be at home more. I wish it had *all* worked out better, Laura, but I don't want to hold you back just to prop me up. I'll be fine – truly. I enjoy teaching and I like the school I'm at. And we'll certainly manage without your board, Laura. After all, you won't be around to raid the fridge or the biscuit tin at all hours of the night then!'

Laura turned and hugged her mother, relieved she had taken it so well.

'I love you, Mum! You've supported me so much – I wouldn't have got nearly

laura

as far as I have without you. But I need to try being more independent – and this is a good opportunity to do it with people I like who have much the same interests as I do.'

Laura phoned her friends a few days later. Soon it was decided that she would move in at the beginning of February, when Brian and Kerry came back from holidays. Brian was a music lecturer, while Kerry was completing her Masters', as well as tutoring part-time. Laura knew they had been together for three or four years – she was really drawn to their laidback approach to life and their friendly, accepting attitude to people. She had warned them she would need help to settle in and find where everything was, but this did not seem to faze them.

'No worries!' Brian assured her. 'Actually, we're thinking of having someone else join the household as well as you. Tim works as a muso – he could have the room at the end of the veranda that we use for storing junk at the moment. That way, the rent will be lower for all of us. Kerry and I are trying to save up to go overseas and maybe even get married one day – you never know! So with you two, plus Viv, who wants to stay for another year, we'll all be one big, happy family.'

And it did work out well, once all of them adjusted to keeping things at least minimally tidy in the kitchen and lounge in particular, so Laura did not trip over anything and knew where to find what she needed to make tea or coffee, or get her own breakfast. In fact, after some weeks of disarray as far as meals were concerned, Laura herself finally took things in hand and suggested a roster system.

'It's obvious we need you around here, Laura,' Kerry laughed. 'We're a disorganised bunch, but what you've suggested should work well. Even Tim can manage to go out and buy Chinese, or a couple of pizzas – can't you, Tim?'

Laura warmed to Tim from the beginning. His happy-go-lucky manner and his obvious belief that life was meant for living to the full brought an added sense of fun to the household. He had plenty of friends, many of whom he brought home for late night suppers that went on into the early hours of the morning – and, as the year progressed, a succession of girlfriends as well. These affairs were passionate while they lasted, Tim sometimes disappearing for nights at a time to be with this one or that, but he always came home in the end, philosophical, if things had not turned out as he hoped.

And he was kind to Laura, as was the whole household, when in the middle of that year her father suffered a heart attack while at work in the pub. He lingered only a few days, passing away late one evening, when Margaret, Laura and Ian were still with him. He was only fifty-two.

At first, Margaret was filled with guilt, wondering if her constant pushing for

Ken to build up the lawn mowing business prior to his starting working at the pub might have contributed to his heart problem. But Ian, with what medical knowledge he had already acquired, was adamant this was not the case.

'Mum, there's no way you should feel guilty about this. Dad was overweight – and all his drinking certainly didn't help. You've covered for him for a long time and looked after just about everything for us. Now it's time you took care of yourself for a bit.'

Yet she grieved deeply for Ken, taking a month off from school to try to recover. Laura moved back home for a while too, despite a busy schedule of lectures and a mountain of assignments to complete.

'Your father really tried,' Margaret often repeated during those weeks, as Laura spent time with her, 'but somehow he couldn't seem to find his place and discover what he was really good at. He loved the band – that was when he was happiest. And he loved playing with you, Laura, when you were little. It was such a blow to him when you lost your eyes – you were the light of his life. He was quite different after that. He hated it if other kids were hurtful to you and was always very angry with his own family for not making you feel more accepted. I thought he was a bit hard on you first off, when he insisted you grow up doing everything the same as the boys. But he was right, wasn't he? He was so proud of you.'

Laura tried to comfort her mother, but found it hard to respond without bursting into tears herself. She swallowed the big lump in her throat and sighed heavily. Even now, so many years later, she could remember that special feeling of sitting on her Dad's lap as he held her close and tried to describe the pictures in her storybooks. She was his Laura, his princess, he would whisper to her – but she knew even then that his heart was broken for her. She remembered how she would put her arms around his tummy, in an effort to comfort him.

'Yes, Mum, he *was* right,' she managed to say eventually. 'Dad always believed I could do everything the boys and Elisabeth did. And he loved it when I'd sit on the veranda and sing his favourite songs with him. He was so proud that I knew all the words. And remember the little ukulele he bought me? I used to love playing that. You're right, Mum – he did try to be a good Dad.'

'He never wanted me to go back to teaching, remember? I think it made him feel insecure – that he'd failed as a provider. But I'm so glad I did now. Where would we be otherwise?'

'You did the right thing, Mum – but you need to look after yourself, like Ian said. Surely Elisabeth can do more? I know Ian will take care of the yard and stuff like that, at least while he's still at home. Next year, if he has to live in at a hospital somewhere, maybe you and Elisabeth can find a smaller house – perhaps a unit that's a bit easier to keep clean than this old place.'

Laura

Eventually, Laura was able to move back to the house nearer uni and pick up where she had left off. Yet she soon discovered that, while she was constantly busy with study and the various activities on campus, things were somehow not quite the same. On one level, life was fulfilling and challenging, but on another deeper, more intrinsic level, it was like something essential to her wellbeing was missing. She knew she was still grieving her father's death – only time would lessen the pain of such a sudden loss. True, they had not been as close in recent years, but they had always enjoyed a special relationship that had been made all the stronger by their mutual love of music. And she knew her father had truly loved her as best he knew how.

Yet it was something more that was troubling her, she realised, as she sat up late one night strumming his precious guitar that Margaret had wanted her to have – something that perhaps her father's favourite old country ballads seemed to grope for in their sad lyrics and melodies. Often they spoke of the pain of a broken relationship, of a hopeless love, of loneliness. Perhaps that was as close as she could define it at that point – a kind of lonely yearning or longing for something truly satisfying, for a love that would provide real understanding and security. She continued strumming softly for some time, lost in thought, her melancholy mood wrapping her around like a cloak.

She was glad of the support of her housemates – Brian and Kerry, with their kindness and thoughtfulness, Viv, creative and studious, always there to help her if needed, and even free-spirited, easygoing Tim, who, out of respect for her, had tried not to bring so many of his rowdy friends home of late. But after a while, at Laura's insistence, the household returned to normal – or at least to the same crazy state it had been before. Life had to go on, however heavy her heart was. And for all of them, the year was certainly passing at breakneck speed, with only a few weeks remaining to complete assignments and prepare for exams.

Yet somewhere in the middle of those busy weeks, Tim became more than just a friend. Laura was never quite sure exactly how it happened, except that it had something to do with the melancholy, bereft feelings that had threatened to overwhelm her at times since her father's death. One night, as she sat playing her guitar and singing softly in the lounge, Tim had joined her, signalling her to keep going. But it was unusual for him to sit quiet for long, Laura knew, so she put down her guitar at the end of the song and they began chatting, the conversation flowing easily from one topic to another. Tim was in a particularly mellow mood – and Laura liked that. He listened carefully, asked intelligent questions and laughed at funny little comments she made along the way. Then he had taken her hand and held it tight, before leaning over and kissing her gently on the lips.

Her first kiss.

'You're really sweet, Laura – sweet and funny and intelligent. I know I've been a bit wild and had quite a few girlfriends since you've known me, but lately I've been watching you and noticing all the nice things about you. I really like you, Laura – I'd like to get to know you even better in the next little while.'

He had kissed her again then and she had wanted him to – so much. They sat together into the early hours, until Brian and Kerry arrived home from a party and interrupted them.

The next night, he had come to find her, as she studied in her room.

'Let's go and have coffee somewhere, Laura. You need a break – and so do I.'

They had stayed talking in the café until closing time. Then, after driving home, had sat outside in the car for even longer.

'At least no one will interrupt us here,' Tim had laughed, as he kissed her again.

Laura was busy the following two nights, but that weekend Tim had invited her out for dinner. She was still sometimes a little self-conscious eating a meal in a public place, but Tim was totally relaxed. He was used to sitting with her at meal times at home, she realised – and, apart from that, he was the sort of person who was oblivious to what other people thought. And that was so freeing and refreshing for someone still driven by the need to be fully accepted and a dread of appearing different in any way.

Brian and Kerry watched the blossoming relationship with some misgiving, but knew they had no real right to intervene. Laura and Tim were both adults after all. It was Viv who eventually risked broaching the subject with Laura, when they were alone in the house studying one afternoon.

'It's probably none of my business, Laura, so please tell me to shut up if you want to – but I can't help noticing how close you and Tim are becoming. I just don't want to see you get hurt at all, given Tim's past history. If you need any of us to warn him off or anything, I'll be the first to volunteer!'

It was said as kindly and as lightly as possible. Laura took it well, on the surface at least.

'Thanks, Viv – I know you mean well and I appreciate your concern for me. I'm okay – really! I think Tim's changed quite a bit recently – but I'll take care. Besides, I've got too much work to do to be wasting a lot of time.'

Laura did discipline herself, studying late most nights, while Tim was out playing at whatever venue his band had managed to find work. Usually he arrived home after the others had gone to bed, so that he and Laura were often able to have the lounge to themselves. It was heaven, she had to admit, relaxing with him after an exhausting day over a cup of their favourite coffee.

Laura

Then one night late in October, when Laura was feeling particularly tired and vulnerable, their relationship moved beyond what she had ever expected it to.

'What's up, kiddo?' Tim had asked, as she laid her head on his shoulder and curled up beside him on the old divan.

'Oh, I'm just tired – and a bit blue. I heard some upsetting news today.'

'Want to tell me about it?'

'You know I have a sister Elisabeth – she's three years younger than I am and still at high school. She's had lots of fights with Mum about staying out late and not studying. I met her current boyfriend Paul a little while back and wasn't overly impressed – he's quite a few years older than she is and didn't have a job. Anyway, now she's pregnant. Elisabeth's asked if Paul can move in with her at home when school finishes, so they can save up to rent a place after the baby's born. She plans to keep the baby, of course. It's all she's ever really wanted, to get married and have kids. Poor Mum – it's the last thing she needs right now. She was just beginning to pick up after Dad's death – and now *this*! I guess she'll say yes though. After all, my brother Ian won't be home next year, so there'd be room for them, even after they have the baby.'

Tim listened sympathetically, but did not say much. He never did comment very often about what other people did, Laura realised – his was a 'live and let live' mindset, which included not worrying about others' opinions, so long as they did not impose their values on him. He held her close, soothing her and kissing her gently, and then more forcefully.

That night in particular, Laura needed that comfort and closeness – that sense of being thought of as special and desirable. She was angry and disappointed with Elisabeth, but, although she hated to admit it, also a teeny bit jealous of her little sister's success with the opposite sex. She had yearned for a male presence in her own life – especially since her hero Jamie had moved out of home and even more so, since her father had died. Almost involuntarily, she curled up closer to Tim, longing for him to fill the emptiness inside her, to provide whatever it was that seemed to be lacking in her life.

Tim needed little encouragement.

'Laura, come to my room!' he whispered in her ear eventually. 'It'll be okay – I'll take precautions. There's no need to worry. *Please!*'

Laura had no defences against his gentle but urgent invitation. It was wonderful to be wanted in that way, to hear the endearments he whispered to her, as they lay close together. And he was careful not to rush her, despite his own strong desire, aware that she was in very new territory. Afterwards, as she lay quietly in his arms, he stroked her hair, patting her like a baby and kissing her softly on the forehead.

'You're beautiful, Laura – I love you! Stay here, close to me – sleep tight!'

Amazingly, she did. It was wonderful to feel the protection of his arms around her, to hold him close and feel his heart beating, to know he truly wanted to be with her. Early the next morning, she woke with a start, overwhelmed with mixed emotions, as she remembered what had happened. Quietly, so as not to disturb Tim or the others either, she slipped out of bed and returned to her own room. She was unsure why she wanted to keep this more intimate aspect of their relationship a secret from the rest of the household. It was as if she needed to hug it close to herself – as if she could not risk a negative response from anyone, in case the bubble might burst.

Despite her deepening relationship, Laura managed to finish all her assignments on time and then threw herself into her last precious days of study before the exams. When Tim came home late from playing in the band, it was wonderful to rest her head, crammed to overflowing with information, on his shoulder and relax in his arms. Often the minutes would stretch into hours, as they spent the whole night together. For Laura, their romance was not a distraction. In fact, it energised her, spurring her on to give of her best in this final sprint to the line. Viv, and also Brian and Kerry, noticed the change in her, but did not comment. Better to let things take their course, they decided. Anyway, Viv at least had the distinct feeling she would not be thanked for interfering any further.

Then exams were over at last, with celebrations all round, including many late nights for Laura, partying with friends from the Debating Club and Music Society. Tim accompanied her to some of these, when he was not playing with the band, and in general, Laura's friends were pleased to see her so happy. Only a few, knowing Tim a little better, held their breath, wondering if he really had changed, or whether Laura too was merely a passing phase.

On her twentieth birthday, just after exams had finished, Laura finally introduced Tim to the family. Margaret had worked hard after school to prepare one of Laura's favourite meals and even Greg managed to turn up, for a short while at least, before disappearing to join his mates. Yet things were not the same – nor could they ever be – with Ken gone. Also the added factor of Elisabeth's pregnancy and the presence of her boyfriend complicated matters for them all. Laura's opinion of Paul had not changed, but she tried hard to relate normally to him for her sister's sake and also her mother's. Besides, she so much wanted them all to like Tim.

Jamie looked strained, she felt.

'I'm pretty tired,' he explained. 'It's been a big year and the work in our Adolescent Unit's certainly not easy. I'm thinking I might change jobs next year – I'm not quite sure yet. Maybe a holiday over Christmas will make me see things

Laura

differently.'

In turn, Jamie could see how relaxed and happy Laura was. Yet he wondered about Tim. He seemed warm and friendly and easy to get along with. Obviously too he thought the world of Laura – but psychologist that Jamie was, he was not entirely convinced. Then again, he told himself he was probably being far too protective and 'big brother-ish' where Laura was concerned, as he always had been. She was his little sister – and she couldn't see.

Soon after that night, Tim headed home to his own family in North Queensland for a few weeks. Laura missed him, but moved back home herself, while all the others from her uni household were away over Christmas, and tried to keep busy. She and her mother even managed a few days away together at a beautiful little cottage in the mountains south of Brisbane, lent to them by one of Margaret's fellow teachers. In the past, Laura had come away from such experiences feeling a mixture of happiness and sadness – happiness, because of the natural beauty she could smell and feel and hear all around her, but sadness too, in that she could not see it all as well. Margaret's ecstatic comments about their surroundings were a little hard to bear at times, but Laura was glad her mother was enjoying herself. She would never have wanted to take away from her delight in any way. This was simply how it was and had to be – no point in moping. Besides, she'd discovered over the years how much sighted people missed out on as well, because they did not take the time to stop and appreciate their surroundings with their other senses before moving onto the next experience.

'You deserve this break, Mum,' she commented one afternoon, as they sat together in the little back garden of the cottage, the scent of the old-fashioned climbing roses nearby so strong. 'It's been a hard year for you. Hopefully the coming one will be better.'

'Yes, it's been very difficult,' Margaret agreed, 'but soon I'll have a grandchild – and who knows what else will happen? Perhaps Jamie will find a girlfriend and get married at last – or even Greg might surprise us. Then again, maybe you'll beat them all to it, Laura.'

'I doubt it – I'm not sure Tim's the marrying type. Anyway, I'll be too busy this year for anything like that,' Laura responded lightly.

Deep down, however, she was surprised by the longing she felt at the thought of marriage – and marriage to Tim in particular. Its strength caught her off guard, causing her to take a long hard look at herself and what she hoped to achieve in the near future. She had done extremely well in all her subjects again that year, as she had discovered only days earlier. She wanted to continue the same way and finish her degree with a flourish. Then too, she definitely aimed to make it into the top debating team. As well, she hoped to co-write more songs with her musician friends on campus, or even attempt a short musical. After graduation, she planned to train as a teacher and possibly help kids like Kevin with learning difficulties. She was unsure where Tim would fit in all of that – but she certainly knew she wanted him to.

Later, as the sun began to set, Margaret went inside to prepare something simple for dinner. Laura stayed where she was, still thinking about the year ahead. A gentle breeze was blowing, pleasantly cooling her skin after the hot summer afternoon. In the nearby trees she could hear leaves rustling and birds twittering, while in the distance, children were laughing and calling out to one another. Then suddenly, everything around her seemed to become still. And into the middle of that pool of silence, she heard a voice speak five simple words:

'And where do *I* fit?'

She sat up, startled, but everything seemed the same as before. Had she been dreaming? Yet she *had* heard those words – she was sure she hadn't imagined them. They had been firm and challenging, but the voice had not been condemning – not at all. She tried to dismiss them, to turn her mind to thinking about seeing Tim again, but the words refused to go away, seeming to demand a response from her.

That evening, they chatted idly for a while after dinner. Then Laura made her way to her bedroom, leaving her mother to watch TV. She did not want to mention anything about what she had heard – she needed time to reflect.

Yet, in her heart of hearts, she knew who had been speaking to her. She could not explain how she knew, but she was sure it was God. As she lay on her bed, she remembered the other times she had felt a deep longing to understand and experience God more, to find that secure rock on which to build her life – like when she and Anne had read about Aslan and Narnia, and when she had gone to the meeting to hear Anne's friend on her thirteenth birthday and had so much wanted to stay behind and find out more. Then there was the time she and Miss Burns had had coffee together, just before uni started, when Miss Burns had prayed for her and given her Luke's Gospel in Braille. She hadn't read much of it since then – life had been too busy for such things, as Miss Burns had suggested it might. Where *did* God fit in the scheme of things for her, she wondered? Was it *anywhere*? Or was it more a case of her needing to *make* room for God in her life – or maybe to hand over the controls entirely? Yet she hadn't even made up her mind for sure if God even existed!

But today the voice had been real. And those other times she'd just remembered, when God seemed so close – they'd been very real too.

'Oh God,' she whispered, as she lay there, 'somehow I feel you're not going to leave me alone until I do stop and take you seriously. This coming year, before I

Laura

finish uni, I *will* work out where you fit in my life – I promise!'

Laura moved back to Brian and Kerry's house not long after. It was wonderful to be with Tim again – but things had changed in their household, now that Viv had gone. Sharon, a second year Music student with a bubbly, outgoing personality, had taken over her room – and almost, Laura felt on occasions, the whole household. She had a beautiful, husky voice, ideally suited to jazz and blues, and could be heard singing loudly most of the time when she was around the house. She loved inviting friends over, often cooking delicious, exotic meals for them. But in the process, many of the things in the kitchen were moved, so that Laura had trouble finding what she needed. Worse still, often the furniture would be rearranged or objects left strewn around the lounge room floor where she could easily trip over them.

Sharon was extremely repentant when Laura finally confronted her.

'I'm *really* sorry, Laura! I wouldn't want anything to happen to you for the *world*! I've always been a bit scatterbrained – too spur of the moment, you know, and not thinking about the consequences. I'll try to clean up better – I really will.'

But nothing seemed to change greatly that Laura could discern. And, to her surprise, she did not find as strong an ally in Tim as she expected.

'I think you might be being a little too tough on Sharon, you know,' he commented, after Laura complained about it once again to him. 'She just doesn't see the mess, I'm sure – and she doesn't *mean* to make trouble for you or any of us. And you must admit, you do insist on keeping things super tidy, Laura.'

'But ... but you know I *need* to be sure things are put back in the same spot,' she wailed indignantly. 'Otherwise I have to ask for help all the time – and I hate that!'

'Of course I know how important it is for you, silly!' Tim responded, giving her a hug and a light kiss. 'I think you're wonderful how you manage – but Sharon has to feel at home here too.'

Laura did not say any more. She merely snuggled closer to him, wanting to be reassured of his love. Tim kissed her again and she relaxed. Eventually they moved to her room, but when she woke later, he was no longer there. She wondered when he had left – usually he stayed until early morning at least.

She sat up, aware she could hear soft voices and laughter from the direction of the lounge. She moved slowly to the door, but hesitated then, listening carefully. It was not a group of Sharon's friends, as she had first thought. There were only two voices – a male and a female – and then silence, followed by footsteps in the hallway. Laura quietly returned to bed, pulling the covers over her head. She did not actually know who it had been or what they were doing – she did not *want* to know.

The next few weeks were very busy, with lectures starting up and the Debating Club getting under way once again. Laura was also working hard co-writing songs for the musical to be staged on campus later in the year. She tried to be home before Tim on the nights he played with his band, or to study hard earlier in the evening, so as to be free later. She tried – but with limited success. Often he did not get home until the early hours of the morning, by which time she was fast asleep. Or otherwise Sharon was around, with or without her many friends, which made things a little awkward for all of them.

And while he was still the same happy-go-lucky, caring Tim when they were together, Laura nevertheless sensed a slight withdrawal in him, a kind of shift in their close relationship. She tried to tell herself she was imagining things, especially when he assured her nothing was the matter, but she had always been particularly sensitive to how those close to her were feeling. And she had rarely been wrong.

Finally, just before Easter, the blow fell. Brian and Kerry, always solicitous on Laura's behalf, although never interfering, had been watching and wondering, ever since the household had regrouped after the holidays. And recently they had not liked what they saw. Tim was a good friend – but that did not mean they were prepared to sit by and allow him to cause Laura grief. Eventually, Brian decided to challenge him about his behaviour.

'Tim … hey man, I don't want to interfere, but it seems to Kerry and me that you and Sharon have been getting pretty close lately. Does Laura know about this?'

Tim grinned sheepishly and had the grace to look a little embarrassed.

'Come off it, Brian – you know damn well I haven't said anything to Laura yet. I keep planning to tell her – but gosh, I don't want to hurt her feelings. She makes it so *hard*!'

'We suspect Laura knows more than she's letting on, Tim. Remember she's had plenty of practice at hearing things and sensing what's going on. She's going to be badly hurt, but better to tell her sooner rather than later. Unfortunate – damned unfortunate – but hey, these things happen, I guess, and we'll try to look after her. It's just not too cool to be two-timing her, man – especially when she can't see.'

Tim reddened even more, but did not try to justify himself.

'I'll tell her tonight,' he promised.

Laura had had a difficult day. Nothing had seemed to go right with the songs she and her friends were trying to finish writing – all their efforts had sounded clichéd and uninspired. Added to that, she had attended the first team meeting

laura

for a big inter-campus debate coming up, but could not manage to get her team mates to agree on a unified approach to their subject. To top it off, at the end of that week she had a major History essay due. With a sigh, she took out her notes after dinner and tried to make some headway with the jumble of facts and quotes she and Barbara had collected.

Suddenly she heard Tim's footsteps in the hallway, and his quick tap-tap on her door. She sprang up, a welcoming smile on her face.

'Hi, Tim – how come you're home? I thought the band was playing somewhere tonight.'

'Oh, it got cancelled at the last minute,' he muttered, before rushing on. 'Laura, there's something I need to tell you – can we talk?'

Laura sat down heavily on the bed, sensing what was coming. Tim hesitated, before joining her and taking her hands in his.

'Laura … I promised Brian and Kerry I'd talk to you tonight. I …'

He paused, unsure how to continue. Eventually Laura broke the silence.

'Tim, I think I know what you're going to say – I've sensed something hasn't been quite right between us for a while. I can't pretend I'm not upset, but these things happen – and it's better to be honest if it's not working. But … Tim, please tell me honestly – is it Sharon?'

Laura's voice was decidedly fierce by this stage and Tim knew he had no alternative but to give her a straight answer.

'Yep, I'm afraid you've hit the nail on the head – I knew you would. But Laura, I honestly do love and respect you – I didn't meant it to happen this way.'

'Tim, I have to know this – have you been sleeping with her this last little while, under the same roof as me? When you knew I trusted you?'

Tim was silent. Laura had removed her hands from his and was holding them tightly together to try to stop them shaking.

'Laura, I …' but no words would come.

And then Laura's scorn spilled out.

'Tim, just go! Leave me alone! Get out!'

Laura could not move for some time. She felt as if all life had been sucked out of her – as if the future she had dreamt about had come crashing down on top of her. After what seemed like ages, she stood up, holding onto her desk for support. She felt physically ill and made it to the bathroom just in time, returning a few minutes later to lie curled up on the bed like a little lost child.

A short while later, Kerry came to check on her.

'Laura, are you okay? I'm coming in,' she said, after quietly knocking. 'Look, I'll get straight to the point – Tim's our friend, but Brian and I are so sorry this has happened to you. If it's any consolation, we've asked them both to move out as soon as they can arrange it – we feel it'll be better all round that way. A couple of overseas students Brian knows are still looking for accommodation. I'm sure they'll be delighted to move in here. Laura ... would you like to go home for a few days? I could take you, if you'd rather be there.'

Laura had sat up by now, looking so woebegone that Kerry's heart went out to her.

'No ... no, Kerry, I don't want to bother Mum with my troubles – not when my sister is due to have her baby soon. Besides, I don't want to let them see what a fool I've been. I might have known it wouldn't last long. Not when he had the choice between someone who could see and someone who couldn't,' she ended bitterly.

She had wept then and Kerry had tried to comfort her as best she could. But after she had gone, Laura was sure she had never felt so desperately sad and lonely – ever. Not even when the other kids hadn't wanted to sit with her at primary school or when she'd had to find her way by herself around the hall at the school concert.

'Oh God', her heart cried out, 'please help me! I don't know what to do – I need you so much'.

Laura

chapter eleven

Somehow Laura managed to survive that week and even complete her History assignment on time. In fact, she was glad she had to discipline her mind to focus on it, rather than mope about feeling sorry for herself. It was anger she could feel more than anything deep inside, which in reality fuelled her energy and enabled her to get things done. That week and the next, until Tim and Sharon moved out, she stayed at uni as much as possible, working in the library or curled up in a corner of the common room. And when she did come home, she usually went straight to her room. On the surface, she functioned normally, with many of her friends unaware anything was wrong, but underneath the protective shell she managed to form around herself, lay great hurt and rejection.

Fortunately, the debating team came together well in the end. Laura was able to collect her thoughts enough to help the others with their preparation, as well as present a brilliant argument herself when her turn came to speak. They beat their archrivals hands down, much to the delight of their many supporters present. The celebrations lasted long into the evening, but Laura could not seem to force herself to enter into the spirit of things at all. For her, it was a hollow victory, the delicious meal their supporters shouted them tasting like ashes in her mouth.

laura

At nights, she would lie awake for hours, tossing and turning restlessly, all sorts of questions running through her head. And almost always she would hear a mocking, accusing voice, sometimes loud and incessant, at other times softly whispering, planting the seeds of so many unsettling thoughts in her mind.

'How stupid were *you* to think he could ever have really loved you? Everyone was laughing at you – they didn't even have to do it behind your back, because you're blind and couldn't see them anyway. She's a lot prettier than you too. There's no way you'll ever find someone who really loves you, you know. After all, who wants to be saddled with someone who's blind?'

On and on the tape played in her brain, over and over.

As Easter approached, Laura felt as if she were dragging herself around campus, barely making it through each day. What disturbed her most was the lack of any spark of creativity as far as her song writing was concerned. She would sit for hours, trying hard to work out lyrics by herself or with her musician friends, but nothing seemed to gel. She knew she was letting them down too, since they often looked to her for fresh ideas. Eventually her frustration with herself boiled over one day, leaving her friends in no doubt how she felt.

'I'm so sorry, guys! I guess I'm going through one of those "writers' block" phases. I can't seem to think of anything original – everything sounds so corny! I'm pretty tired – I'm not sleeping much at the moment. Maybe I should give it a break for a bit.'

Her voice wobbled slightly, as she finished speaking, but she tried to cover it up quickly by pretending to cough. Her two friends were not fooled, however.

'Laura, we know things aren't going so well for you right now. We heard Tim had moved out – and the two of you haven't been together at anything lately. Don't worry, kiddo – you're worth ten times more than anyone else he could ever find! Why don't we all call it a day and go drown our sorrows with some strong coffee and hot chips? We could sit outside on the grass – maybe getting closer to nature will give us some creative energy.'

Laura was grateful for their understanding. They composed silly songs all the way to the refectory, trying to make her laugh, and she played along with it, even though it was an effort to do so. She felt as if she were falling into a dark, bottomless pit inside herself – and that she would never be able to climb out. And she felt so angry – angry with Tim for betraying her and not having the guts to be honest with her, but also angry with herself for being such a fool and for not knowing how to keep him loyal to her. It was irrational, she knew, but she was past thinking clearly.

'How about we leave our writing sessions for a couple of weeks?' she heard herself ask after a while. 'I know we have to come up with stuff for the musical, but I think I really need a break. Maybe my creative juices will begin flowing again then. I know you have to go now, but I think I'll sit here in the sun a bit longer. It's so relaxing.'

A short while later, she lay down on the grass and dozed off. After about ten minutes, she came to with a start, feeling a little disoriented. She listened intently, eventually realising she was near a pathway that led to the cloisters – but which direction did she need to take to get to the library? She quickly gathered her things together and stood up, but in the process of finding her way, almost ran into a stone pillar. Fortunately, she was saved by the quick action of someone walking nearby.

'Whoa, watch out! Gosh – are you okay? Oh hi – I think I've seen you in the debating team. Would you like some help? I'm heading for the Main Lecture Theatre – is that where you want to go too?'

Laura's replies to anyone offering help were still sometimes distinctly terse, but that day she did not have the energy to respond in any confrontational way. Besides, this girl's voice was quite friendly – and after all, she really did need help.

'Thanks, but I'm not heading there – I wanted to go to the library, actually.'

'That's on the way to the lecture theatre, if we take this shortcut here. I'll walk with you – I'm a bit early anyway.'

Laura was unsure why she asked the next question, but it was out before she realised.

'Is there something special on at the Main Lecture Theatre?'

'Yes – the university chaplain's leading something called an Easter Focus time, since Easter's only a week away. Have you heard him? He's an excellent speaker. Would you like to come – or do you have lots of work to do?'

'Well ... I guess I could spare an hour or so. Why not?'

Again, Laura could not work out why she was taking up such an invitation. They chatted idly as they walked, but all she had time to discover about her rescuer was that her name was Helen and that she was a Science student. When they arrived at the Theatre, Helen found her a seat right up the back corner near one of the exits.

'Sorry I have to leave you now, but it looks like I'm needed to help out here with a few things. Nice meeting you, Laura – God bless!'

Laura realised the meeting must be put on by the main Christian group on campus. She vaguely remembered such events being advertised in previous years around Easter, but had never really been interested enough to attend. She was glad she was sitting up the back – that way, no one much would see her there.

Soon Laura was even happier to be at the back with empty seats on either

Laura

side of her. The chaplain began addressing the audience in a gentle, relaxed way, but with passion and fervour, as he retraced Jesus' journey to the cross. His content was deeply thoughtful and well chosen for his university audience, which impressed Laura. Yet it was not so much what he *said* that affected her, but something else – something indefinable. Strangely, she found herself experiencing the same feeling she had had when she heard Anne's Uncle Brian speak – the feeling that everything she had heard about God and Jesus in the past suddenly fitted together and made sense. And once again, it seemed God was speaking just to her. More than that, it was as if God really knew her and cared about her – even to the extent of knowing the depth of the pain and hurt she was currently experiencing.

And then it was that the tears began to spill over and run down her cheeks. She surreptitiously groped for a tissue to wipe them away, but they kept coming. Soon the speaker was concluding his message and she could hear others in the rows nearby quietly leaving, but she remained where she was, unwilling to move. Gradually, the tears slowed – but then she thought she heard a voice, just as she had at the cottage during their holiday.

'Laura – I did this for you!'

How could she be hearing her own name, apart from anything else? Why would God address her personally like that? Surely she was imagining it? Yet the words sounded so loving and touched her so deeply – there was no denying it. As she stayed where she was, trying to collect herself, someone came and sat next to her.

'It's me again,' Helen said brightly. 'Are you okay – or would you like to talk?'

'No ... no, I don't think so – but thanks anyway! I think I'd better get back to the library. I'm glad I came though.'

'That's fine,' was all Helen said. 'I'll let you go then – see you round!'

Laura was relieved she did not press her any further. She liked the way she did not fuss over her either and left her to do her own thing.

Back in the safety of the library, Laura's mind was far from the topic she was supposed to be researching. She sat with her chin cupped in her hand, all sorts of emotions tumbling around inside her. Above all, she realised, she felt a strong sense of anticipation – as if something wonderful were about to happen. Maybe it already had even – she was at a loss to understand it all. It was as if a lifeline had been thrown to her where she lay curled up in her deep, dark pit. She knew it was there, but she was still groping for it, unsure, even if she did grasp it fully, exactly how it would draw her to the top, or what it would be like once she reached the surface. Yet she wanted so very much to get out, to find her feet again and move on.

That Easter, Laura moved home to spend some time with her mother and catch up with all the family. Elisabeth was still there, with only a few weeks to go until the baby's birth. Paul had managed to find work at last, so they hoped to move out in June, if they could find a suitable place. Laura could sense, however, that there were issues in their relationship. It showed in the way they talked to each other and in the general feeling of tension in the air, especially when her mother was around.

'I can't pretend I won't be glad when they move out,' she told Laura on more than one occasion. 'I have trouble making myself trust Paul completely – I'm not sure why. Perhaps I feel he took advantage of Elisabeth, considering how young she was, but I know it was as much her choice as his. Anyway, Ian will be moving back home for a while before his final exams, so that's an added reason for them to move out.'

Laura wished many times over these days that she could be back in her room at Brian and Kerry's place. She needed space to think through her recent experience and to try to make sense of it somehow. But she knew Tim would be in and out, moving more of his and Sharon's things and she could not face the prospect of dealing with them at this point. Besides, she was concerned for her family. Her mother had told her that Jamie would be coming to see them over Easter and that he was unhappy where he was. But they would not be seeing Greg – he had managed to get into more trouble with the law and was apparently lying low somewhere.

When Jamie dropped in on Good Friday, Laura could tell immediately that something was wrong. He was very quiet and seemed exhausted. She was glad when he suggested a walk to the nearby park, where they could talk uninterrupted.

'I feel I need a bit of fresh air and exercise – you don't mind, do you, Mum? It'll be a good chance for you to rest anyway, while Elisabeth and Paul are out too. With Ian coming later, Laura and I won't get a chance to catch up on things otherwise.'

Margaret did not mind at all. She was pleased to see that the close bond that had always existed between the two of them was still as strong as ever. Jamie had always been Laura's champion and protector. And right now, Margaret sensed Laura needed someone like him around.

They walked and talked – but to Laura's great disappointment, things were not the same. Jamie was obviously preoccupied with his own problems, so she felt unwilling to lay any more burdens on him. And eventually, he told her what was troubling him.

laura

'I love the counselling I do, but it's quite draining, especially with the kids who are in our Adolescent Unit right now. As well as that … well, Alan and I are really good friends and always have been, but for a while now he's wanted us to be more than that. He's a great guy and we get on well living together – but I've always drawn the line when it came to any sort of ongoing sexual relationship. I don't have any real issues with the idea of same sex couples, but I'm not completely sure yet if that's the path I want to go down – if it's where I really belong. I've thought about it a lot, but can't seem to make up my mind. I've had one or two great girlfriends, but somehow it never came to anything. So … I'm planning to take time off and get right away, not only from Alan, but from counselling in general. And Alan agrees I need to think things through and be absolutely certain before we commit to anything. I'm heading north first off – I'm sure I'll be able to get work easily enough as a waiter, or even a chef. I've got one job lined up in Cairns for a couple of months already. But Laura, I'm not going to tell Mum about the whole issue with Alan – and I don't want you to either. It'd worry her too much – and I reckon she's had enough to deal with in her life already. I'll keep in touch and let you both know where I am – and I'll still be there for you, Laura, if you ever need any help. Can't ruin my reputation as the best big brother ever, you know!'

Laura detected a disturbing note in his voice as he finished talking – kind of sad, she felt, and somewhat cynical. Her heart went out to him in his tiredness and confusion, but at the same time, she could not help feeling angry and a little ripped off. Despite what he said, her knight in shining armour would *not* be there to help her, she realised – he had enough issues of his own to sort out. She had suspected there was something more to his relationship with Alan than mere friendship, so was not overly surprised or shocked. Yet she struggled to find the right words to say in response, so stayed silent for some time. Finally, she patted his arm gently, as he lay beside her on the grass.

'Jamie, I wish I could help you more, but I'm only your kid sister and I'm in a bit of a mess myself at the moment. I don't want to bore you with the details – you've got enough on your plate already. But it has to do with Tim, obviously. I'll get over it – I'm determined to. And you'll probably laugh at this, but something I'm seriously trying to work out right now is where God fits in my life. I've been thinking about it for a long time actually – remember that meeting we went to together on my birthday years ago, where you and Mum got angry and dragged me off? And I always did like the way Anne and her family talked about God, remember. Miss Burns tried to explain things to me a bit too, not long after I finished school. I don't understand much yet, but this time I want to find some answers – and I've got a feeling God will give them to me. I think there *is* a God,

Jamie, whether we like it or not, and I'm wondering if this God knows more about what's happening for us than we realise.'

Jamie sighed and turned over.

'Well, you may be right, Laura – but I doubt it. I guess I still have the same questions as Dad had. Where was God when you lost your eyes? Or when the Thomas's little boy was killed? And why has life been so hard for Mum? I could go on, but you know what I mean. ... All the same, I have to admit it'd be great, in some ways at least, if God really *were* there and *could* show me which way to head in my life – and what it all adds up to, if anything. Life sure can be difficult at times, can't it?'

'I know what you mean,' Laura was quick to agree. 'Some days it all gets a bit much for me when I can't see and have to struggle on – let alone when things have gone really wrong, like now. But there's *got* to be more, Jamie – that's all I can say. You'll probably think I'm *totally* weird when I tell you this, but I believe God's spoken to me a couple of times lately and tried to get my attention. You're the psychologist – you could probably explain it away as my subconscious thoughts or my mind playing tricks or whatever – but it was more than that, I'm sure.'

Despite his morose mood, Jamie was trying not to laugh at her now, Laura knew.

'Oh, Laura – all wishful thinking, I reckon. But let me know if you decide God's really there. After all, I wouldn't want to find out when it's too late to do anything about it!'

That night, Laura lay awake for ages thinking over everything Jamie had said. There were so many emotions swirling around inside her, but more than anything, she simply felt very sad for him – sad that such an intelligent, understanding human being as her Jamie could be so confused and unsure about who he was and what he wanted out of life. She cried for him then – for the pain she had heard in his voice and felt in him, as he lay near her on the grass. And she cried for herself too, that her hero, who she believed would always conquer everything on her behalf, was himself in difficulties.

Yet it was Jamie's last words in particular that stayed with her, echoing round and round in her head. They were very like something Steve had said to her over two years earlier. His words had challenged her then and now they came back with renewed force.

'Don't put it off too long, will you, Laura – don't leave it until it's too late!'

She sat up in bed then, surprising even herself by suddenly speaking out loud.

'No, I *won't* leave it until it's too late – I'm going to believe in you, God, and

Laura

listen to you and do what you say!'

As soon as the words were out of her mouth, it was as if a weight lifted off her. She wriggled her shoulders and sat up straighter. At first, she wondered if she had imagined it, but the feeling continued. For some reason, she wanted to sing – it was as if she needed to express in some outward way the beautiful, refreshing feeling that was still surging right through her. But no suitable song came to mind, except for a simple little chorus she had often heard at Anne's place years ago. It was on the tape Anne had given her as a parting gift – but she hadn't listened to it for so long. Now she could remember only the first two lines, but she sang them anyway, over and over, humming the rest of the tune softly when she ran out of words.

> *Jesus, Name above all names,*
> *Beautiful Saviour, glorious Lord…*

Eventually she lay down again, conscious as she did of feeling so warmed and comforted. And soon after, she fell into a deep sleep.

The next morning she woke late, remembering immediately what had happened. She had slept soundly – the best she had since her break-up with Tim. She soon realised too that, while the dull ache of her own unhappiness and the sadness about Jamie were still there, she was feeling something more positive. Was it hope – or perhaps some degree at least of acceptance? She was unsure – but then there were so many things she was unsure about at present.

As she lay there, she knew clearly what she had to do next. She would try to contact Miss Burns. They had spoken briefly by phone at Christmas and had tried to arrange to meet for coffee, but Laura had not been free at the time. Anyway, at that point she'd been unsure whether they'd have enough to talk about, given the different directions they were taking in life. But now it was different. Now, however, she urgently wanted to get in touch with her.

They spent almost all of Easter Monday together. Miss Burns picked Laura up and the two of them drove to a nearby park on the banks of the Brisbane River. At first, Laura had not known where to begin, but Miss Burns knew exactly how to encourage her to share what was on her mind.

'Laura, before we go any further, please call me Carolyn! I know it'll probably feel strange at first, but I haven't been your teacher for over two years now, so it's about time we were on first name terms. Otherwise I'll start calling you 'Miss Harding'!'

'Well, I do want to become a teacher like you, Miss … oops, sorry, Carolyn, but I don't want to be called 'Miss Harding' *quite* yet. Makes me sound so old!'

'Exactly. Why do you think I want you to call me Carolyn?' she laughed.

'Besides, I've got used to the other students at Bible college calling me that – or worse! Like Kero, or Carrots – an obvious one with my red mop. The guys are pretty good at teasing us girls, but we give as good as we get.'

Laura began to relax and soon the whole story came tumbling out – the sorry details about Tim's treatment of her and the anger and rejection she was feeling as a result, and also her grief over Jamie and his decision to go away for a while. Yet, important as all of that was, Laura had so much more she wanted to share – the question she believed God put to her while she was on holidays at the cottage, the meeting at uni where the chaplain talked about the crucifixion, the experience afterwards of hearing Jesus speak to her by name, and finally the sense she had had that very week of something heavy being lifted off her, as she spoke out loud to God.

'It's funny,' she concluded eventually, 'but I remember promising after that first experience of thinking I heard God, that before I finished uni this year, I'd decide where God might fit in my life, if at all. I remember too feeling that God probably wouldn't leave me alone until I did. Well, I was right, wasn't I? But I didn't figure it'd take losing Tim to make me think about it all again – or hearing about Jamie's issues. I guess all of that teaches me a few things about God already.'

'What sort of things?' Carolyn prompted.

Laura thought for a moment before responding.

'Well, for starters, I think God's incredibly patient and doesn't seem to give up easily! And I also suspect that when God speaks, it's very important to listen – that if I ignore these times when God's tried to get my attention and continue putting things off until I'm good and ready, then I may end up leaving it too late, as Steve told me once.'

'I don't know about that, actually,' Carolyn said then. 'I think God gives us many, many more chances than we deserve. Laura, all your experiences remind me of an old poem called 'The Hound of Heaven'. It talks about how God keeps on looking for us and doesn't give up until we're found – it's like God's on the scent of our trail and won't be put off! We can tell our 'pursuer' to get lost, or we can turn around and hand ourselves over – and that's when we find the most incredible security and love. It reminds me too of the story Jesus told about the lost sheep – how the shepherd goes out and searches for this one sheep until he finds it, even though he already has ninety-nine others. Then after he's found it, he throws a huge party because he's so happy!'

'I'm not so sure whether God would want to throw a party for me – although I do believe now that when Jesus died on the cross, he did it for me, as well as everyone else. But it still absolutely blows my mind that God actually knows my name!'

Laura

The tears began to fall again then, for about the third time since they had begun talking. But this time Laura was crying more out of gratitude and amazement that God truly did love her and care about her.

'It makes me feel so humble,' she managed to get out eventually. 'God knows everything I've done – not only recently with Tim and all that, but right through my life – but forgives it all! That includes when I was so horrible to other people because they didn't accept me, as well as all the times when I was so critical and judgmental and impatient, like I was at school, remember? You tried to help me even then – I must have been such a trial!'

'We all are in our own way,' Carolyn laughed. 'But, you know, Laura, I'm not surprised at all that you heard Jesus call you by your name, because that's exactly what the Bible says he does. It says in one of the gospels that he calls his own sheep by name and leads them out – and that his sheep listen to his voice and follow him. From what you've said today, you've already promised him you'll listen and be obedient, so it sounds to me like you've come to a point where you truly want to follow Jesus with all your heart and hand over control of your life to him. Am I right?'

Laura was quiet for some time. As she sat there, she could hear the leaves moving in the trees and feel the breeze on her face and the warmth of the sun on her skin. A horn sounded on a boat as it made its way down the river, the shrieks of laughter from the passengers on board floating across the water. For a moment, it seemed that time was suspended – as if heaven was somehow waiting for her response. Eventually, she sighed and smiled at Carolyn.

'Yes, I do,' she admitted at last. 'It feels a bit like crossing a river, doesn't it – like changing sides and entering new territory. I'm glad we're sitting right here – it'll help me remember what we've talked about today. And every time I cross this river in the ferry to uni, I'll remember too. 'I think I made my decision the other night, when I spoke out loud to God, because I distinctly felt that weight lifting off my shoulders like I tried to describe to you before.'

'I understand that – I honestly believe you were experiencing God's Holy Spirit filling you with new life and light, lifting the heaviness off you and truly renewing you from the inside out,' Carolyn explained. 'Amazing, isn't it?'

'It's kind of unbelievable – and yet I *do* believe it,' Laura slowly replied. 'That's exactly what it felt like the other night. Then the next morning, I was still sad and disappointed about everything, but a bit more hopeful too that things would work out somehow. I know there'll be plenty of ups and downs ahead – I'm still the same impatient and intolerant Laura. And yet I know I'm different as well – something's definitely changed inside me. I've finally found that safe place we talked about once – remember? I belong to God now, Carolyn.'

Carolyn leant over and hugged her warmly. She was crying herself.

'I feel so privileged to be able to share this whole experience with you, Laura. I'm so glad you phoned. Can I pray for you now?'

They held hands as they prayed – heartfelt words that made Laura cry again.

'Father, you are *so* great – you know exactly how and when to speak to us and you are so patient and faithful! Thank you so much that Laura truly belongs to you now – and forever. Please help her in the days ahead to know and love you more, and strengthen her to be able to live as you would want her to. Comfort and heal the hurt and disappointment in her, Father, from the way Tim treated her – and help her to forgive him and Sharon. And Lord, please watch over Jamie! Speak to him, just like you did to Laura – help him to realise you love him and know his name too. And please give Laura friends around her at uni who will help her grow as a Christian. We trust you to keep your hand on her and guide in the months and years ahead, wherever you might lead her. Amen.'

'And God,' Laura added, 'I want to say I love you and that I'm really sorry for being so stubborn – and for all the times I've done things that weren't right. You know I don't know how to pray yet really – but thanks for listening anyway. And thank you so much for looking for me until you found me. Amen.'

They ate the picnic lunch then that Carolyn had brought. Afterwards, they walked along the riverbank, talking and laughing together about so many things. Carolyn told her about Bible college and the subjects she was studying that term. Also, she talked about what she hoped to do in Africa.

'I'm impatient to get started out there, but right now I know I have to focus on my studies and on working with the young people in our church. But I was thinking, Laura – I could probably meet with you every two or three weeks say, to see how you're going. Maybe whenever you come home to see your family, we could catch up. Do you think you'll have much trouble finding other Christians on campus? I guess it's just a matter of asking around, isn't it? Too bad you don't know who the girl Helen was who took you to the lecture at Easter time.'

'I know I'll need plenty of support and encouragement,' Laura admitted, 'so it'd be great to meet with you, Carolyn – as long as you can spare the time. I do have lots of friends on campus, of course, but not too many of them are what you'd call religious. Far from it, in fact!'

Laura was very much on Carolyn's mind in the days ahead, but she knew she had to trust her to God and pray for her to stand firm in her faith. Laura had promised to read the Braille copy of Luke's Gospel she had given her and to write down any questions she had for when they met next time. Besides, hopefully she'd meet others at uni who could answer any questions she had and help her understand things.

Laura

The assignments came thick and fast for Laura that term, along with important debates with other unis and colleges. She was busier than ever – and what spare time she did have was quickly taken up helping her friends write songs for the new musical. But she was determined not to go back on her promise to God, or to let Carolyn down. Each night she set time aside to read a chapter of Luke before she went to bed. That way, when she found it hard to sleep, at least she was able to mull over what she had read and reflect on any lessons or challenges it contained for her.

Then in the fourth week of term, as she was sitting having coffee in a quiet corner of the refectory and gathering her thoughts for an upcoming debate, she overheard snatches of conversation from a nearby table. One of the male voices sounded vaguely familiar, but Laura was frustrated that she could not pinpoint it exactly. Soon two younger people joined the group and the noise level rose markedly, as the discussion became more and more lively. Eventually, Laura realised they were talking about God. She gave up trying to prepare for her debate and listened more closely.

'Oh, sorry – are we disturbing you? Or would you like to join us? These two have lots of questions about God – perhaps you do too?' she heard the man whose voice she half recognised say.

A silence followed – then Laura realised he must be speaking to her.

'Oh, were you talking to me? I'm sorry – I'm blind, so I couldn't tell if you were speaking to me or someone else. No, you're not disturbing me – I had run out of ideas anyway. Perhaps I *will* join you for a while, until I finish my coffee.'

She listened, fascinated, as the discussion continued. The man who had invited her to join them was very good at explaining things and getting below the surface of any questions asked. She finished her coffee, but stayed on, until the two younger students finally left. As she got ready to go too, the man spoke to her again.

'Sorry I didn't introduce myself before. My name's John – I'm the university chaplain. I'm sure I've seen you around campus – are you in the Debating Club?'

Laura chided herself that she had not recognised his voice earlier, given his talk at Easter time had meant so much to her.

'Yes, I'm in the Debating Club. My name's Laura Harding – I'm very pleased to meet you!' she responded eagerly. 'I heard you speak in the Main Lecture Theatre the week before Easter. I really enjoyed it – and actually found it quite challenging as well.'

'I'm glad,' he said. 'Would you care to elaborate on that at all?'

Soon Laura found herself giving him a brief account of what had happened to her that day and in the weeks since then.

'So you see, I'm a very new Christian, with lots still to learn,' she concluded. 'That's why I was interested to listen in on the discussion you were having. Since term started, I've been meaning to find out about the Christian groups on campus, but haven't had time. Perhaps you could help me?'

'Well, you have a few choices, but the group who invited me to speak that day would probably be the most helpful for you at this stage, I think,' John told her. 'That's the Christian Union. The President's a girl called Helen Browning – in fact, I think I have her number here. Would you like it?'

Laura was delighted.

'Yes I would, thanks! I wonder if she's the girl who invited me to come with her to your meeting? Her name was Helen. I hope it is – I'd like to catch up with her.'

She phoned Helen that evening – and immediately there was a bond.

'Yes, I remember you – I'm the same Helen. How excellent!' was the immediate response. 'Let's meet tomorrow for lunch. I'm sure you must be very busy, but you have to eat *some* time.'

Over the next few weeks, Helen introduced Laura to various Christian friends on campus and also told her about their main weekly meeting in one of the lecture rooms. After that, Laura attended when she could, but also sometimes met informally with Helen and a few other girls over lunch. Usually they would sit outside on the grass, while one of them shared some thoughts from the Bible. Laura was often the centre of the lively discussion that followed, since she always seemed to have a myriad of questions, which the others tried valiantly to answer. But it was their friendship that she valued, even more than any answers they might give. Like her friends in the Music Society, the girls in this group accepted her for who she was, respecting her for wanting to find out things for herself and never forcing their ideas on her. Yet despite this, she was a little wary of spending too much time with them, thereby losing her many old friends. Surely, if her newfound faith was worth anything, she concluded, it ought to make her an even better friend to them, as well as withstand any onslaughts from those who might disagree.

Soon Laura began to feel more settled than she had in a long while, despite her busyness. The ache of missing Tim was still there – but slowly, she felt she was gaining a clearer perspective on things. It was as if she were functioning from a different centre, her feet planted on the firm rock for which she had so long been searching – and that made all the difference. She knew she had lots to learn about this Christian journey she had embarked upon, but she was determined not to stay quiet about her faith, whenever an opportunity presented itself. As it

Laura

turned out, that happened quite regularly – especially among her debating team-mates, who always delighted in discussing thorny issues.

'What? You've done *what*, Laura? How could you swallow all that sentimental rubbish? I thought you were a bit brighter than that.'

'They're brainwashing you, Laura. You're usually so independent and have always wanted to make up your own mind about things!'

'I can't see how *you*, of all people, could believe in a loving, omnipotent God. Where's the evidence for that?'

Other friends did not comment openly, but Laura guessed what they were thinking, piecing things together from whispers she overheard.

It won't last – it's only because her boyfriend's left her. When she gets over that, she'll realise she doesn't need a crutch like religion.

She did not respond on these occasions. She had no arguments anyway. All she could do was let them see it truly would last – that for her there would be no going back.

As for her family, she was aware Jamie fell into the same category as her more incredulous friends. Greg she had very little contact with now, but she knew that, just as he hated to be questioned about his own actions, so he would never question hers. Ian was away, working at a regional hospital out west, and Elisabeth was otherwise occupied, caring for little Jonathan Paul, who had made his entrance into the world a couple of weeks earlier than expected. As for her mother, even she, somewhat to Laura's disappointment, did not comment much. Admittedly she was distracted, not only by the arrival of her first grandchild, but also by the fact that Elisabeth and Paul, jobless once again, were having difficulty finding somewhere else to live.

'I always felt you'd make up your own mind about such things,' Margaret had responded rather absently to Laura's news. 'You know what your father thought though, Laura – and it would take quite a bit to change my mind too. Still, if you think there's something in it for you, I guess I can't stop you.'

As the months went by, Laura increasingly found there was in fact 'something in it' for her. She also began to think more seriously about where her future lay and what God might want her to do with her life. Her commitment was very real, deepening even more as she discussed things with Carolyn, as well as her uni friends, and listened to various Christian speakers on and off campus.

'I'd love to do what you're going to do in Africa,' she said enviously to Carolyn one day. 'I'm sure I could help somehow, but I guess there'd be lots of difficulties, with a new language and everything.'

Carolyn thought for a while before responding.

'I've found it's usually what you want to do deep inside that turns out to be the very thing God's calling you to do – what's really 'you', in other words,' she said in the end. 'After all, I don't think God gives us gifts and talents for no reason! So how can you be fully 'Laura' for him is the question, isn't it?'

'I know I could help blind kids overcome so many obstacles in life – or what they or others *think* might be obstacles. But I want to do more than that. I want to help sighted kids too – like Kevin, the boy who used to live next door to us. I know his life turned around after he learnt to read and so did his Mum's. And I want to keep writing – articles and short stories and of course songs. But I know how hard it is to earn a living that way – and I have to support myself. I certainly don't want to have to depend on a pension, as if I don't have the brains or the ability to look after myself.'

'Well, you've got a little while to decide what your next step should be and I'm sure it will all become clear, as we pray about it. But I know this, Laura – you're uniquely gifted by God and so determined and committed that I believe you'll make an impact wherever you are and whatever you do.'

Laura

chapter twelve

Laura was not looking forward to the end of the year. It was not so much the prospect of her final exams or the assignments yet to be completed that bothered her, but rather the severing of the many friendships she had formed at uni. Each one had been significant, but none more than her relationship with her housemates Brian and Kerry. They, of all people, had seen her through so much – it was hard to accept that soon they would be offloading most of their possessions and moving to other side of the world, at least for the foreseeable future. Soon too the Debating Club would be holding its last important competition for the year and already the Music Society was winding down, after staging its highly successful home-grown musical, in which she had played a vital role. Soon she would be concluding a key chapter in her life and moving on to the next stage of her journey.

At first she had hoped to continue on at the same university, training as a primary teacher in the area of Special Education. She remembered her experience with Kevin so vividly and the thrill it had been to listen and support him, as the written word came alive, and the door to the world of books, and education in general, opened for him. She knew, if given the chance, she could teach other

Laura

sighted children with similar reading and general learning difficulties. As it turned out, however, she was unable to persuade the powers-that-be on campus to see it that way.

'I'm afraid you're asking the impossible,' the head of the relevant department in the Education faculty had pronounced in what Laura felt was a rather patronising manner, when she finally succeeded in getting an interview. 'We need to be able to give you experience in classroom situations, as well as small learning groups and one-on-one sessions. I have no doubt that many of the students you'd encounter would have great fun playing tricks on a teacher who couldn't see them. Besides, how could you write on the board or check their work? Anyway, I'm sure no school would employ you, even if we were to train you. It would be too much of a risk and too difficult by far – for them and for you. Take my advice, my dear, and go and train to teach visually impaired students. We're sorry to lose you from this campus, but really there's no other option.'

Laura knew she was beaten, but did not want to go down without a fight.

'Well, that may be your opinion, but it sounds to me awfully like blatant discrimination! One day sighted people in education faculties like this one will realise how much blind teachers could contribute to the wellbeing of students who have difficulty learning under the current system. I don't intend to force myself into any place I'm not wanted, however – I believe God will open a door for me at another time and in another place.'

Before uni finished, Brian and Kerry insisted on giving Laura a special twenty-first birthday party. On the night, an amazingly eclectic mix of friends turned up – some intense and serious, others extremely laidback, some fervently Christian, others decidedly anti-Christian. Laura revelled in it all, loving the buzz of interesting conversation around her, the genuine warmth and support she felt from everyone, and the spontaneous entertainment that surfaced during the evening among some of her talented musician friends. It was like a microcosm of the past three years of her life, she reflected later – it would be etched in her memory forever.

Then at last exams were over and assignments completed. Soon Laura was farewelling not only her uni friends, but also Carolyn, who was finally heading to Africa, after two years of fulltime study, and impatient to begin her work there.

'I'm going to miss you so much!' Laura wailed, the last time they met. 'You've been like a lifesaver to me this year, Carolyn. It's been wonderful to be able to talk about anything and anyone and know you'd listen and not repeat a word of it. You've given me so many wise insights into things and believed in me all the way along – from ages ago, even before I decided to become a Christian.'

'I'm glad I could be here for you, particularly this year – it's been a privilege.

Now I believe even more wholeheartedly in you, Laura – I'm sure you'll do amazing things. I'd love to see you finish your training to teach visually impaired children, but don't give up your dream of helping other kids as well – and don't give up your writing either! One day I believe God will use your writing to open doors you never ever thought would open.'

Laura moved home that same week, feeling rather lonely and bereft – and, for the first time, a little unwelcome. Elisabeth and Paul and baby Jonathan had still not found a place of their own, nor were they likely to, until Paul was able to find another job. Laura could sense her mother was worried and tried to talk to her about it all.

'Mum, I'm sure I can get accommodation with some other students once uni starts, if that would be any use. And you need a break too. Could we go away somewhere together again for a few days?'

'I don't think so – not right now,' Margaret had sighed. 'Elisabeth needs help with the baby, and your grandmother's never really recovered from her stroke. I try to get over to see her as often as I can, but it's hard – she's so particular, as you know. I think she'll have to go into a nursing home soon. I'm the only real family she has – I wish I'd had *one* brother or sister at least. Still, who knows? We might have been scattered far and wide like our own family is right now.'

Christmas that year was shaping up to be quieter than normal, with Jamie unable to be there and Ian also unsure he could make it back. But it was special for Laura, in that she could now celebrate the real meaning of the season with a full heart. Margaret walked with her to the nearby church Laura and Elisabeth had attended three years earlier, but did not stay for the service. Christmas dinner was the excuse, but Laura knew her mother's reasons for not wanting to stay went deeper than that. She was disappointed, yet at the same time it was good to be able to sit quietly by herself and take in the music and Scripture readings, as well as the words of the service itself, including the minister's message. One or two people offered her a prayer book, but she politely refused, without explanation. It was only at the end, when she asked if someone could walk with her to the nearby street corner that they realised she was blind.

'Of course we can,' the minister had responded immediately. 'Stay right here – I'll get my wife Joan. She'd love to meet you anyway.'

Joan turned out to be a friendly, chatty person, who quickly introduced her to several other women, before taking her arm and walking with her the whole way home.

'It's no trouble at all!' she explained, laughing. 'My husband will be ages yet anyway. We'll get Christmas lunch some time. Actually, we're going on holidays for three weeks, but when we come back, you must meet my daughter Catherine.

Laura

She wasn't here this morning, because she's on duty – she's a nurse. I'll phone you when we come back – okay? I've got a pen and paper here somewhere, if you could give me your number. I'm sure Catherine would love to meet you. You might even want to go with her to one of our Sunday evening services – they start up again at the end of January. Have a lovely Christmas – wonderful to meet you. Bye!'

In the end, Ian arrived in time for Christmas lunch, but he was very tired and reasonably uncommunicative, after a week of long night shifts. Elisabeth was on edge, since Paul had drunk too much the night before and little Jonathan was windy, crying throughout the meal. In the afternoon, Ian and Laura went with Margaret to visit their grandmother, now in a nursing home across town. She recognised them and seemed pleased they had come, but after a short conversation, nodded off to sleep again.

'She doesn't look too good to me, Mum,' Ian said gently on the way home, trying to prepare his mother. 'It's hard to tell with old people. She might rally, but I don't think I'd be too hopeful. You've done all you can for her – she's in good hands.'

He was soon proved right. A few days later, Margaret's mother passed away in her sleep in the early hours of the morning. The funeral was held over until after New Year's Day, when Jamie would be able to fly down and join them for a couple of days at least.

'Lucky I could get away at all,' he told them when he arrived. 'It's our busy time, of course, but the boss managed to find a couple of casuals who could cover for me.'

Jamie seemed to be enjoying his current work as a chef.

'The complete change from counselling's been good for me, I think. I like having a job where I can work with my hands and don't have to worry about solving other people's problems. Not that I'm doing all that well with my own, come to think of it,' he laughed ruefully, as he and Laura sat on the veranda late one night talking. 'One thing's settled though – Alan phoned just before Christmas and told me he's now in a relationship with a guy who was friends with both of us. I'm glad he's happy, but it still leaves me unsure exactly where I fit in the scheme of things. Anyway, I'll stay where I am a bit longer and see what happens.'

Laura could tell he was feeling a little stronger, but also heard some loneliness and uncertainty in his voice. Taking a deep breath, she decided to say what she thought.

'I'm glad the change has been good for you – but Jamie, are you sure you're not just running away from things? Wouldn't it be better to deal with it all somehow?'

'Hey – *I'm* the counsellor, kiddo,' he laughed, touched by her concern nevertheless. 'You're not meant to be *that* insightful!'

'I guess all I want is for you to be happy and know where you're heading in life,' Laura risked responding. 'I'm sure you don't want to hear about Christian stuff and the Bible and all that – and there's no way I want to force you to listen either. But as far as I'm concerned, being a Christian's made all the difference in the world for me. I know I've got a long way to go yet and I certainly don't have all the answers, but it's so good to know that God's there and is actually *for* me, whatever happens and whatever stupid things I do.'

'Well ... I'm glad you're happy, Laura, but I'm not sure it's my bag. Too many question marks for me still, I'm afraid,' Jamie grunted. 'Let's change the subject, eh?'

'Sure – but before we do ...' Laura said hesitantly, very unsure of her ground now, as she felt for a small parcel beside her, '... don't be mad at me, but I bought you another little Christmas present. It's a modern version of the New Testament – I thought you might like to look at it some time. Please take it, Jamie, just to humour your kid sister, if nothing else. My favourite's Luke's Gospel – maybe you could start with that.'

'That's a very, very big 'maybe'! I'd have to be totally bored, I reckon – but thanks anyway,' he said lightly, stuffing it in his back pocket.

Laura had to be content with that. The conversation drifted onto other matters, notably her uni results, which had arrived in the mail that day. She had done better than she had expected, excelling once again in History. But above all, it was a relief to know she had actually made it through the three years of her degree. She had always been hard on herself, but just for a moment she decided she'd relax a little and enjoy the sense of achievement she was experiencing, which Jamie was obviously determined to add to.

'You're amazing, you know – and I'm not saying this simply because I'm your big brother. For someone who can't see, you've done fantastically well – and I'm sure it's been damned difficult for you at times. Congrats again, Laura – I really mean it!'

They had headed for bed then, since Jamie's plane left early the next day. At the airport, however, Laura took even more comfort from his final words to her, as he hugged her goodbye.

'Not sure when I'll see you next, but hopefully I'll make it to your graduation. Keep praying for me, kiddo – I reckon I need it.'

It seemed obvious in the days ahead, as decisions were being made about Laura's grandmother's possessions, that Margaret should move across town to her

laura

mother's unit. Laura could hear the longing in her voice, as she talked about it.

'Nan's place is in such a nice, quiet area – and she's always kept it spotlessly clean. Oh, it'd be wonderful to live in a tidy little place like that! This old house is terrible – the landlord's hardly done a thing in the eight years we've been here. Even when I do get time to clean, it's hard to see any results from my efforts. Still, I can't see how it would be possible to live in Mum's place – not unless I applied for a transfer to a school that side of town. Besides, there's Elisabeth and Paul and the baby to think of. And I know you said you'd find somewhere else to live, Laura, but I'd hate to do that to you, I really would.'

But Laura was firm.

'Mum, I think it'd be absolutely wonderful if you could move to Nan's unit! You've looked after us for so long, it's time you did the same for yourself. I certainly know I wouldn't be where I am now, with a degree and everything, if you hadn't helped me so much all through my school years and in my first year at uni. I know it wasn't easy with Dad either – especially towards the end. Please don't worry about me! I'll start looking tomorrow, but if I can't find a place before uni starts, then I can stay with you and commute from Nan's until I do. I know it's right across town from uni, but it'd only be for a while. And Mum, I also think this might be the impetus Elisabeth and Paul need to put a bit more effort into finding a place of their own. You'll probably have them staying with you forever otherwise.'

After a little more persuasion, Margaret finally gave in. Having decided to make the move, however, she was determined not let the grass grow under her feet. The next day, she gave a month's notice to the landlord and also phoned the Education Department, formally requesting a transfer in time for the beginning of the school year. She left the job she dreaded most until last – that of informing Elisabeth and Paul – but to her surprise, they took it in their stride, promising to begin looking for a place the next day.

'If we can't find anything, we might move up the coast for a while or out west,' Elisabeth told her. 'Paul doesn't like his job – and anyway, they were probably going to be putting him off soon. Don't worry, Mum – it might help things if we move away from the city. Perhaps Paul won't go to the pub so often, if his mates aren't around.'

Laura made enquiries at the student accommodation section of her new uni, but soon realised things would be a lot more difficult than she had imagined. Flats near the uni were in very short supply, while the houses still available for shared accommodation were hardly exciting prospects, to say the least. Besides, the more she thought about it, the less she liked the idea of throwing in her lot with virtual strangers. She remembered with longing the warm invitation she had received from Brian and Kerry to join their household and wished with all her heart something similar would happen now. Well, it was still early days, she tried to encourage herself – orientation week was more than a month away yet. She would put her name down to be notified if anything suitable came up and, in the meantime, enquire around among some of her musician friends. Then the thought occurred to her that perhaps the church nearby might know of someone willing to take in a boarder. The minister and his wife were still away, she remembered, but maybe there was someone else who could help.

The next Sunday, she went to the morning service, but discovered most of the people were away on holidays. Those she did ask could not think of anyone who might help, but the retired minister filling in for the day promised to leave a note about her request in the church office.

'I'm sure something will work out for you,' he said in his kindly old voice. 'I'll pray it will and that God will bring just the right people across your path.'

Despite his words of encouragement, Laura walked home feeling quite disconsolate. She knew she was missing Carolyn and Helen and all the others from her small group at uni, as well as the stimulation that her debating and musician friends had provided. In the days that followed, she was plagued with a host of strongly negative thoughts. What if nothing turned up and she had to live across town for the whole year? How would she manage all the travelling? And how could she honestly expect anyone from the church to help? After all, they hardly knew her. Probably the old minister had forgotten to leave the note even – no doubt he'd forget to pray for her as well. And what difference would his prayers make, anyway? Okay for *him* to say it would all work out! Laura could feel the hopelessness and confusion taking hold, as these and other equally gloomy thoughts whirled round and round in her head.

Yet she knew she needed to keep her spirits up, for her mother's sake. Besides, God *did* answer prayer. God *did* care about her and watch over her, as Carolyn and Anne had often prayed for her. She knew she had to focus on those truths and choose to believe them. But it became harder and harder to do so as the days went by.

Still she had to start packing, whether she boarded nearby or moved across town. Her belongings were no great problem to pack, however, since she had always kept most things in a very orderly way, so that they could be located easily. Yet as she began to sort through everything, she still managed to unearth several long-lost treasures – a smooth pebble from the creek near their old farm, a bird's feather, the glass potpourri container Anne had given her when they moved to Brisbane, with its silver lattice lid, and the tape of Christian music that had come with it. Laura lay down to rest for a while and to listen to some of the old songs.

Laura

As she did, so many memories came flooding back. The lyrics moved her too – and slowly a peace began to come over her.

Lost in her own world, she did not hear the knock at the front door, or footsteps coming towards her room. She jumped, when her mother tapped her on the arm.

'Laura, there's a girl here to see you – a Catherine Bradshaw, but she says you've never met. She's waiting for you in the lounge.'

Curious, Laura quickly got up, tidied her hair and went to meet her. She opened her mouth to introduce herself, but before she could, her visitor began talking.

'Hi – you must be Laura. I'm *so* pleased to meet you! Mum told me about you on Christmas Day and I've been meaning to look you up ever since, but haven't had time, with my shifts and all. My name's Catherine – but most people call me Cate. I live with my parents at the rectory down the road – at least, that's when I'm not staying over with one of my friends. Yesterday, our office secretary at church gave me your note about wanting to find somewhere to live this year, while you're at uni. So I hightailed it here as soon as I could, because I wanted to meet you in person and because I think I might have just the right place for you.'

Laura tried to digest all the information she was hearing, but had difficulty keeping up with her guest, as the words continued to tumble from her mouth.

'Jackie gave me your note because she knows I'm mad keen to take over our old rectory when my parents move out in a few weeks. They've bought their own townhouse a couple of streets away – it'll be much more convenient for them, after living in so many big old places. The parish wants to see the rectory used for some good purpose – some sort of ministry or whatever – and I volunteered to head up the task force whose job it is to come up with ideas. In the meantime, I think I can fill it up quite easily with people looking for a place to live that's not too expensive and also where the atmosphere's fairly laidback and accepting – within reason at least! I don't even really know you, Laura, but as soon as I saw your note, I felt it was so right to ask you to come and join us. I've been a committed Christian for years – ever since I started high school. I really want this to be a place where people can ask lots of questions about God and not be howled down – where we can all discover a bit more about who we are and what it means to belong to God. So what do you think? Sorry if I've totally overwhelmed you – Mum and Dad say I do that all the time. I'll shut up now and let you speak.'

Already, Laura could feel the excitement welling up inside her. At first, she thought she might merely have been carried away by Catherine's enthusiasm, but then she realised she too had a strong sense of rightness about it all – as if something had clicked firmly into place inside her. At the same time, the words 'This is it! This is it!' kept ringing in her head, over and over. Yet she was still cautious, not wanting to jump in too quickly.

'It sounds wonderful and I definitely do need somewhere to live as soon as possible,' she said in the end, 'but you hardly know me! I've only been to your parents' church a couple of times. Maybe we should chat a bit more first, so you can find out something about me, before you offer to share a house for a whole year!'

'That makes sense – and of course you need to work out if you'd be comfortable sharing with me too,' Cate laughed. 'But even without knowing much about you, Laura, I truly believe God's hand is in this. I know already that you've just finished your degree, that you became a Christian last year and that you're now going to train to teach visually impaired kids. And I reckon anyone who could do what you've done without being able to see must have lots of courage and determination, as well as being pretty bright and a hard worker to boot. But I'm dying to know more about you and I'm happy to answer any questions about me – so fire away!'

They talked on and on, until Margaret came to offer them afternoon tea. Cate realised the time then and gasped.

'Thanks, that'd be lovely – but I'm afraid I'll race off. I'm on duty soon – sorry! So what do you think, Laura? Could you put up with me and a few of my friends for a while? There's room for about seven or eight, as I've explained, since it's such a big old place. At the moment, it looks like our curate and his wife, Andrew and Robyn, will be part of the household. My friend Emma, who'll definitely be moving in, has a cat, and Andrew and Robyn own a gorgeous old Labrador and a couple of birds, so it might end up being quite a menagerie. Of course, there's still lots to discuss, but I'm sure things will work out. Besides, it'd be great fun – *please* say yes! You could even invite one of your friends to join us, if you'd feel better having someone there you know already.'

To Laura's surprise, she heard her own voice agreeing to join them there and then. And as soon as she had, she knew without a doubt she had made the right decision. Cate hugged her warmly, promising to be in touch the next day.

And that was how 'The Menagerie' came into being.

Within two weeks, Laura's possessions had been moved down the road bit by bit by a band of willing helpers and set up in a large bedroom on the side of the house that caught the morning sun. From her window, she could hear the leaves of the huge old camphor laurel tree next to the church rustling in the breeze and smell the roses growing nearby. She loved it all from the very beginning. In an amazingly short space of time, she and Cate had 'clicked', finding they could

laura

speak their minds freely to each other and make decisions easily about a variety of household matters. Laura particularly loved the fact that Cate did not come to her rescue all the time, but allowed her to decide for herself what she could and could not manage. She felt truly wanted, even more than she had in Brian and Kerry's household – and that for her was healing in itself. Despite appearing confident, especially in her debating endeavours, Laura's insecurity and fear of rejection, lasting legacies from her childhood, were never far beneath the surface.

By the time lectures were due to begin, the household had slowly taken shape. Andrew and Robyn now occupied the main bedroom, with its little porch attached, giving them space for a desk, plus the many books they owned, as well as room for their new baby, expected in the middle of the year. Cate's artist friend Emma had also moved in, complete with easels and paints and other paraphernalia, which spilled over from her room onto the side veranda. Ben, a shy first year student at the Conservatorium, whose father was a minister, and Phil, a reformed alcoholic in his thirties still occasionally in need of support and rescuing, shared a large room, thus completing the quota of The Menagerie's first occupants. There was still the empty sleep-out at the end of the front veranda, but Cate suggested they leave it that way for the time being.

'I've got a feeling someone might need it in the next few months. Let's wait and see who turns up. I reckon God's done pretty well bringing all of us together and helping us agree on most things so far. After all, we're such a mixed bunch.'

It still took Laura two bus rides to get to her new uni, but at least they were much shorter than they would have been from her grandmother's place. She was so glad her mother had been able to move, especially when she noticed, each time she visited, how much more relaxed and happy she was.

Just before the school year began, Margaret received a transfer to a school with a good reputation in an adjoining suburb to where she now lived.

'You deserve it, Mum,' Laura commented, when she heard the news. 'And you deserve your own little place too. I prayed you'd get your transfer in time for the beginning of the year – and you did. God *does* hear our prayers and care about us, Mum, don't you reckon?'

'Well, things do seem to have worked out well for me – and I hope it will for you too, Laura,' Margaret responded, ever cautious. 'I'd still need a bit more convincing though that it was God's doing.'

'You sound just like Jamie!' Laura had laughed.

Yet inside she could not help feeling sad. She consoled herself, however, with the thought that time could change things and heal the hurts and disappointments in her Mum – and in Jamie, for that matter. Time … and that same 'Hound of Heaven' who had so lovingly pursued her.

Laura's teacher training course, while interesting and helpful, was not particularly challenging, she soon found. Being blind, she had thought about many ways to overcome all sorts of obstacles in the learning process and had put them into practice herself. Also, she had already studied some education subjects as part of her degree, so was familiar with most of the theory they covered. But there was no doubt she loved the prac teaching they eventually did at the School for the Blind, not far away. The principal who had let her sit in on classes and borrow their resources years earlier was still there, delighted to hear of her success at uni.

'You see,' she kept saying to her pupils, whenever Laura came, 'I *told* you all you could go on and do whatever you wanted. Look at what Miss Harding's achieved!'

When the time for Laura's graduation from her old uni finally arrived, Jamie, true to his word, flew down from Cairns to attend the ceremony.

'Nothing could stop me coming, Laura,' he had said, as he hugged her. 'I mightn't have a job right now, but there's no way I'd miss seeing you dressed up in a cap and gown and marching across that stage!'

After the ceremony, Margaret congratulated her rather shakily.

'I thought the Professor would have a heart attack when you walked down those steps from the stage by yourself, without a moment's hesitation. I think he forgot you were blind until then. Well done, Laura – I'm so proud of you! My only regret is that your Dad couldn't see you get your 'piece of paper', as he would have called it.'

Laura too felt pain as well as pride. It had been a long, hard road – not only her time at uni, but all her years of schooling. Her mother had been a huge part of it all – Laura was glad she at least could enjoy the very tangible public reminder of what she had helped her achieve. But Laura knew how much her Dad would have loved it too, despite turning his back on his own education.

'Well done, princess!' she imagined him saying. 'That's my Laura!'

She forced the tears away, determined to join in the celebrations back at The Menagerie with gusto. Jamie was staying with Laura, because Elisabeth and baby Jonathan were having a short break at Margaret's place, while Paul was away doing seasonal work. Laura was glad Jamie could be with her anyway – it gave her a chance to introduce him to her friends and have him experience the creative, accepting atmosphere of their household. As it turned out, he loved it so much, that when it came time to go, he found himself strangely reluctant to do so.

'I'll be back, kiddo,' he promised Laura, as he said goodbye. 'I've got one more job lined up starting soon and then I might head south. Great to know I can bunk down here for a bit if I need to. I like this place – it's warm and welcoming

laura

and has a real community feel about it that's kind of nice for loners like me.'

Laura's heart went out to him again, but she knew now was not the time to push any talk about God. Jamie would make his mind up in his own good time. At least, that's what she hoped and prayed for. And if The Menagerie were to have some part in it all, then she could only be thankful.

With her studies being a little less demanding, Laura soon found herself in the thick of other activities at uni – a writers' group, the debating club and meetings run by the main Christian group on campus. Music was still a favourite pastime too and soon Laura took up her guitar-playing again – something she had largely neglected in the past couple of years. As well, in collaboration with her musician friends, she began to produce a steady stream of song lyrics, the effort involved soon threatening to monopolise most of her free time. Yet she revelled in the creativity of it all more than she ever had before – in that special feeling of using her unique gifts in a way that for her honoured God best and produced such deeply satisfying results. The words and music did not always come together easily at all – sometimes it took them hours or even days to thrash out only a few lines. But Laura loved being part of bringing something new and beautiful into being, however painful it was. And despite the fact that most of her collaborators did not believe in God – or at least that God had any real part to play in their lives – she felt that she was, in some small and fumbling way, pointing them towards the true Creator, as she worked with them.

Soon their original songs were making an impact at 'open mike' nights held regularly on campus, as well as at other informal get-togethers. Often too, Laura would invite her musician friends home to The Menagerie for meals and for ad hoc jam sessions. On these occasions, any of her housemates who happened to be around were also welcome. Sometimes Andrew would join in with his guitar and Cate on keyboard – and then things would take an interesting turn, as some of the songs currently sung at the Sunday evening church service were added to the mix. These were new and exciting times for Laura all round, with amazing opportunities to talk openly about her journey to faith in God. Never one to hold back, she prayed each morning that she would be ready to seize the moment, whenever it presented itself, and speak with sensitivity and grace, respecting the other person, but also challenging in love where necessary.

More and more as the year progressed, Laura also found herself cast in the role of confidante with several uni friends, as they negotiated their way through difficult patches in their lives. She was unsure exactly why they shared their troubles with her, but knew it had something to do with the fact that her blindness had made her a careful listener, extremely aware of the tensions and anxieties in others and quick to pick up on different nuances in their voices. She was unaware of these qualities in herself at first, until her housemates confirmed them over and over to her.

'Laura,' Andrew and Robyn would often say, 'God has gifted you with an amazing ability to get to the heart of things with people and hear what they're really saying, including what they can't – or won't – put into words. We see it all the time in you, in and outside this household.'

She was grateful for their affirming feedback, especially because it highlighted at least one positive outcome from having lost her sight.

'Well, I still can't understand fully why I'm blind and I probably never will,' she would usually respond, 'but I'm at least beginning to see how God's bringing some good out of it all – and hopefully there'll be lots more.'

Soon more of that good definitely did unfold, when Phil's ten-year-old son, Michael, began staying with his father on weekends. At first, his visits had been sporadic, but after Phil became stronger in himself as the weeks and months went by, they began to spend more and more time together.

'Mikey's Mum and I married too young,' he told Laura one day. 'The break-up wasn't her fault – I honestly didn't know what I wanted in life and ended up really hurting her and trying to drown my confusion in drink, just like my father did. I know it's over between us, but I'd really like to earn her trust again and repair some of the damage Mikey's suffered.'

Laura felt for him. She knew something of what he was talking about – it was the path her own father had walked, at least to some extent. And her heart went out to Mikey, as she heard his Dad struggling to help him with his homework weekend after weekend. Eventually she tentatively offered her services.

'If you like, Phil, I can sit with Mikey for a bit when he's here and help him with his reading. I'm sure if he could read better, other issues with his schoolwork would disappear. He's a bright kid – I can tell by the way he talks and how quickly he catches onto other things. He just needs help to sort out in his mind what the letters stand for and how they're organised into words. He reminds me a lot of someone I helped years ago.'

She told him about Kevin then. After that, whenever Mikey visited his Dad, she would sit with him on his bed in the sleep-out, gradually earning his trust and building up his self-confidence. Phil marvelled at her patience and the way she knew exactly how to affirm someone Mikey's age. And when, towards the end of that year, Mikey began to arrive with 'Well done' stamps all through his exercise books and often wanted to read before he went to sleep, Phil's gratitude and relief were almost boundless.

'Oh Laura,' he said one evening, giving her a big hug, 'I'd marry you tomorrow – except I don't think I'm the marrying type! But thanks so much for everything.

Laura

You've changed Mikey's life forever – and his Mum's and mine too.'

It crossed Laura's mind even then to wonder how Cate would have felt if she had heard Phil's comment about marriage. She wondered it even more, as the weeks and months went by. One night, as she and Cate sat cuddling Andrew and Robyn's baby daughter Amy, she felt she caught a glimpse at least of her friend's true feelings.

'There's something gorgeous about the feel of new little babies, isn't there, Laura – the softness of their skin, their little fingers and everything. I wish you could see her eyes – huge and sort of grey-blue. I sure hope I get married some day and have kids,' she sighed.

They sat quietly playing with Amy for some time, each lost in their thoughts.

'Do you think Phil will ever want to get married again?' Cate asked idly in the end, unaware how much she was revealing of herself to her friend. 'It must be hard, if it hasn't worked for you once, to pluck up enough courage to risk it again. Still, he's a different person now – and really trying hard, although I don't think Mikey's Mum's making it all that easy for him.'

Laura could hear the longing in her voice, but said nothing. Better not to interfere – better just to trust God and pray for her, she decided.

Another night, again without realising, Cate made her feelings even clearer.

'I wonder if Mikey always got lots of cuddles like this little baby gets from all of us? He seems to love her – I thought it was kind of cute last weekend, to see a boy his age holding Amy so carefully. He looked so pleased with himself too. Probably do him good to have a younger brother or sister, don't you think?'

'Well, you'd better talk to Phil about that,' Laura risked saying lightly.

They chatted for a while longer about their own parents and marriage and related topics, as they cuddled little Amy, but Laura was careful not to make her own feelings too obvious. She'd been hurt once and was not ready to go down that road again yet. All the same, she'd become quite close to Phil herself over the past months, mainly through helping Mikey. Still, she had to be realistic – with Cate available and interested in him, there was no way he'd seriously look at herself in terms of marriage. Anyway, he'd already told he wasn't the marrying type. But did he really mean it? Did he honestly know *what* he wanted? Poor Phil – and poor Cate, she thought too. She sighed heavily, her thoughts in a whirl.

Cate heard her sigh and, thinking she understood, patted her on the shoulder.

'Don't worry, Laura! One day you'll find someone who'll love you for who you are and you'll get married and have kids of your own, just as cute as little Amy here. See if I'm not right!'

Laura

196

chapter thirteen

Laura could not remember when a year had passed so quickly for her. It was fulfilling in so many ways – on campus, with her debating and music interests, her involvement with the Christian group, as well as her uni course itself, and off campus, with her prac teaching at the School for the Blind and also whatever was happening at The Menagerie. On top of all that, she had become quite involved in the evening services at church – informal times attended by quite a large group of young people, as well as a number of marginalised folk who lived in the rundown boarding-houses nearby and who had no relatives to care for them. Laura would often play her guitar and sing for them all, sometimes writing new songs based on her own experience of God's love and care and acceptance – exactly what many of them so desperately needed to hear.

With her mind on so many other activities and commitments, for once in her life she somehow managed to lose track of the due date for one of her major uni assignments. It was a chance comment by a fellow student that saved the day for her in the end.

'What? You mean our assignment's due *this Friday*?' Laura gasped in horror when she heard. 'But I've hardly started it! Oh dear – and they said they definitely

laura

wouldn't accept any submissions after the due date, didn't they? Guess that'll mean lots of late nights for me this week. Just as well everything's going smoothly at The Menagerie right now.'

But things did not go smoothly at all that week at The Menagerie. Andrew and Robyn's baby ended up with bad croup, necessitating a stay in hospital for her and her mother. Phil chose then, of all times, to go off the rails a little, largely because of difficulties with Mikey's Mum, and Cate was on night duty all week and unavailable to help. Added to that, Emma was working hard to finish some artworks for her college course, while Ben was frantically trying to cram in extra hours of practice in preparation for an upcoming performance. Laura, knowing it was her own fault that she had left things too late, was reluctant to make life more difficult for any of them, so tried her best to keep the household running well.

She finally finished recording her assignment late Thursday afternoon. Her current helper at uni had been unable to commit to any extra hours of work for her at such short notice, but fortunately, Jackie, the office secretary at church, came to the rescue.

'No trouble – I'd love to help,' she had said, when Laura had phoned and told her about her predicament. 'I'll pick up your tape on Thursday night, when I come down to the church for a meeting. I could drop it back to you around seven on Friday night, if you like. Sorry I won't be able to take you to uni to hand it in, but I have to go out for dinner. Can you get there some other way?'

Laura, so thankful for her help, breathed a sigh of relief and quickly assured her she could.

True to her word, Jackie arrived on the dot of seven with the completed assignment and hurried off to her dinner engagement. Unwilling to trouble anyone in the household for a lift, Laura quietly left the house soon after, having decided to catch the bus to the uni. She knew she had until nine-thirty to hand in her essay – surely she could make it by then.

Fortunately, she did not have to wait long at the nearby stop before she heard a bus approaching and quickly hailed it. A short while later, they arrived at the main interchange where she usually caught another bus heading directly to the uni. By now it had begun to rain, but in her haste, Laura had not brought a raincoat or umbrella. Worried that her assignment might end up messy and blotchy, she quickly pushed it up the front of the light jumper she had pulled on before leaving home and climbed on board the next bus, settling back into her seat with a sigh. There did not seem to be as many students on the bus as usual – but it *was* Friday night after all, she reasoned. She was familiar with every inch of the route, so was surprised when, around ten minutes later, the driver made an unexpected sharp turn to the right. As he did so, he called out to her.

'Hey lady – you have to get out now! I head back to the depot from here.'

Laura got up and made her way to the front.

'You mean this bus doesn't go right to the uni?'

'I'm afraid not – didn't you see the sign 'Depot' on the front?'

'I could hardly have – I'm blind.'

The driver was momentarily flustered.

'Well ... I'm sorry lady, but how was I supposed to know that? Don't you use a white stick or have a guide dog? I can't take you all the way to the uni – I'll be too late if I do. You'd better come back with me and get another bus from the depot, or a taxi.'

'No ... no thanks. Perhaps if you could tell me which direction to take, I could walk to the uni from here – I think I know the road anyway.'

'You sure? Well ... cross over here and keep walking straight ahead along this road for about 500 metres. Then take the first turn right, stay on that road as it winds up the hill and you'll get to the uni okay. That's the best I can do for you – I'm running very late already.'

Laura got out, crossing the road while the driver watched, and plodded on, the light rain beginning to soak through her thin jumper. It was easy enough to follow the driver's directions at first, since it was the same route she had travelled by bus many times. She remembered where the road twisted and turned, as it wound up the hill. But walking it was different from driving, she quickly discovered – and apart from that, she was tired and finding it hard to concentrate. She folded her arms tightly across her chest, as much to keep warm as to make sure her assignment did not get any wetter. The minutes passed and she began to wonder how much further she would have to go before reaching the gates. Once or twice she stumbled, walking too close to the edge of the footpath and almost ending up in the gutter. She continued on for around half an hour, becoming more and more confused. *Surely* she must be there soon! For a moment, fear and panic almost overwhelmed her. She stood still, breathing hard. She had to find the uni. She *had* to get her assignment in – it was worth a large percentage of her marks for the year.

She began praying, at first under her breath and then out loud. She called out, in case someone was within earshot, but all she heard in response was the rustling of leaves in nearby bushes – and not one sound that would indicate the presence of a living soul. She thought she might be somewhere on the section of road that bordered a bushy area in the uni grounds – or had she veered off on a side road that the bus driver had perhaps forgotten to mention?

'Oh Lord,' she found herself praying out loud. 'I'm scared and I'm tired – *please* help me find the uni as quickly as possible!'

Laura

She squared her shoulders and started walking again, trusting God to show her the right direction. Not long after, she thought she heard someone coming towards her, so stood still, listening intently. Sure enough, a few seconds later a man's voice spoke to her from close by.

'Hello there! Are you lost? It's a bit late for you to be walking by yourself, especially in this rain. Can I help?'

Laura knew she had no choice but to trust him.

'Well, I hope you can. I'm trying to get to the uni – I have to hand an assignment in. I caught the wrong bus and decided to walk the rest of the way. Can you tell me if I'm on the right road?'

'Yes, you should get there in about fifteen minutes – but I'll walk with you to make sure you find it.'

'Won't that take you out of your way? You just came from there, didn't you?'

'It's fine – I'm happy to help.'

They walked on in silence – a silence Laura did not feel was necessary to break. Then at last her helper spoke again.

'Which part of the uni do you need to get to?'

'Education – I'm training to teach visually impaired children. But if you get me to the main gates, I can find my way from there.'

'It's no trouble – I'll walk with you the whole way.'

Laura could tell they had reached the gates when she heard voices and music coming from the nearby cafeteria. They continued on together, heading directly to the administration section of the education building. Laura knew where the opening was in the office wall for students to deposit their assignments after hours and pushed hers through with shaking hands. Then, with a great sigh of relief, she turned to thank the man who had helped her so much – but there was no response.

She stood still, listening hard, but knew immediately she was alone. Whoever he was, he had disappeared without a sound.

For a moment, she wondered what to do next. It was so disappointing not to be able to thank her helper or find out his name. Then she heard someone coming.

'Laura! What are *you* doing here at this unearthly hour? I thought it was only crazy people like me who stayed back – especially on Friday nights.'

It was her prac teaching supervisor, Terry, who she knew was working hard to finish his Ph D before heading overseas.

'I had to hand in my major assignment – but I was hoping to thank the man who helped me find my way here tonight. Can you see him anywhere?'

'There's no one here now, Laura, apart from you and me. I saw you at the main gates a few minutes ago, but there was no one with you then either.'

Laura stood stunned. Had she dreamt it all? But no – it truly had happened. Then she briefly told Terry the whole story, her mind still in turmoil.

'Well, whoever he was, he isn't here now,' he said in a matter-of-fact voice, when she had finished. 'So how about I drop you off home now? I'm calling it a day myself anyway. Where do you live again?'

Laura told him and they were soon on their way. They chatted idly, but Laura was quieter than usual, as she tried to come to terms with her experience. Eventually, as Terry pulled up outside The Menagerie, she risked telling him what she was thinking.

'Terry, I don't know what you believe about God and all that, but I'm sure you know I'm a committed Christian. This may sound quite bizarre, but I'm wondering if the man who showed me the way tonight could possibly have been an angel. He was definitely there – I even talked to him – but by the time you saw me, he'd disappeared. I know God did things like that for people in the Bible and I did pray and ask for help, but I'm so amazed it actually happened to me!'

Terry laughed, but his voice was gentle as he responded.

'Oh Laura – I'm afraid I don't even believe in God, let alone angels! Most likely it was just some guy who thought he'd be kind to you on such a lousy night. But don't let me knock what you believe – I reckon God owes you a bit of help. I'm glad you got your assignment in anyway. I'm sure you'll do brilliantly – as usual.'

Laura thanked him and made her way quietly inside. What she needed most of all was a hot shower and time to reflect on what had happened. Fortunately, no one was around, so she was able to do exactly that, but it was some time before she fell asleep. She kept trying to piece together in her mind the sequence of the night's events, from when her helper had spoken to her on the road up the hill to the uni, until Terry came along. It had certainly been a strange encounter – yet never an uncomfortable one. Whoever the man was, she had known she was in safe hands. Eventually, still somewhat incredulous, yet at the same time convinced that an angel truly had been sent to help her, she sat up in bed and poured out her heart to God.

'Dear God, how can I thank you enough for rescuing me tonight? How can I have ever doubted your love for me and that you would always watch over me? I honestly do believe you sent an angel to rescue me tonight – and I thank you from the bottom of my heart. You're amazing – I love you so much! Please show me how to tell others about tonight in a way that will help them know they can trust you, whatever happens. Amen.'

She fell into a deep sleep then, exhausted after her eventful evening. And that

Laura

weekend, as the occupants of The Menagerie surfaced from their various ordeals and heavy workloads, Laura told them what had happened. In the end, it was Mikey who summed up their responses best.

'Aunty Laura, I believe every word you said – and I sure hope that angel knows how lucky he was to meet you too!'

Not long after that, lectures finished for the year. On the expectation that she would in fact graduate, Laura applied for a teaching position at the School for the Blind and was duly appointed, much to the principal's delight. Laura could hardly believe she would at last be earning a wage and, in the process, contributing meaningfully to the lives of visually impaired children. Memories of her Dad came flooding back, when she discovered she would teach some children from country areas, who would board with other families while attending the school. He had definitely not wanted that for his little Laura – yet somehow she sensed he would be so proud of what she would soon be doing. At first, she wondered if she should move out of The Menagerie and make room for others who might not be able to afford to live elsewhere, but was howled down by her housemates.

'Don't you dare even *think* of leaving!' was Cate's emphatic response. 'I know part of the reason we set up this place was to help those who could use a little extra support, financially or otherwise – but we need you here, Laura.'

'Besides,' Andrew added, equally emphatically, 'Robyn and I aren't sure how much longer we'll be allowed to stay at this church – we're supposed to move on after we complete our first year out of college. If we go, you'll be needed here even more, so please stay, Laura – at least till we know exactly what we're doing. You help all sorts of people so much through talking and praying with them, not to mention the ministry you have with your music.'

So Laura stayed on over Christmas and into the new year, content in the knowledge that Jamie would be with her while most of the others took some well-earned holidays. Contrary to what he had planned, Jamie had continued working in the Cairns area, but had now finally decided it was time to think about working as a counsellor or psychologist again. He arrived at The Menagerie on Christmas Eve, happy to be back and to see Laura. On Christmas Day, they travelled across town to Margaret's unit to spend the day with her and Elisabeth and little Jonathan, now a very active eighteen month old. Things had not gone well for Elisabeth in her marriage and now she and her son were living more or less permanently with Margaret. Paul tended to become violent whenever he was drunk, which was apparently quite often these days, since he was out of work again and depressed.

While Laura felt for her sister and little Jonathan, she was equally concerned for her mother.

'It was good while it lasted, being alone here,' she admitted to Laura, 'but what can I do? Elisabeth isn't coping very well – I can't throw them out on the street. But I have to admit I'd love my little unit back. Jonathan's a good boy, but Elisabeth doesn't discipline him much, so quite a few of my nice things are getting wrecked.'

Laura sighed. She wondered what it would take for Elisabeth to consider moving out and making something of her life, not only for her own sake, but for Jonathan's too. She decided she would talk with the others at The Menagerie as soon as she could about the possibility of her moving in with them.

Again, Ian had been unable to join them for Christmas, since he was now working at the Mt Isa hospital. Besides, he had become engaged to a nurse from there, so planned to spend Christmas with her family. As for Greg – well, no one had heard from him for some time. He was just being Greg – but it worried everyone.

It turned out to be a pleasant day together. In the afternoon, Jamie took Jonathan to a nearby park and the two of them returned quite some time later laughing and happy. Margaret and Elisabeth both teased him, as he came in the front door with Jonathan perched high on his shoulders.

'Oh Jamie, you'd make such an excellent Dad! When are you going to find someone nice and get married? You're thirty now – almost over the hill!'

Jamie took it in good spirit, but Laura noticed he was a little quiet on the way home. She decided not to comment, however – better to wait and let him talk when he was ready. In the meantime, she'd keep praying for him.

He stayed on at The Menagerie with her until the others eventually returned one by one from their holidays. During those weeks, Laura made the most of having her 'knight in shining armour' to herself. They went on special outings together – concerts, dinners in different restaurants and one or two shopping trips. And they talked, often late into the night, sharing childhood memories and laughing over some of Jamie's experiences up north and the interesting people he had met. Laura told him about her year too – about the songs she had written and about Mikey and how his reading had improved so much. Then finally one night she told him about the angel.

To her surprise, Jamie had not laughed. After she had described what happened, he sat quietly, taking his time to respond.

'Laura, I honestly believe that could have happened to you,' he said in the end, with only a slight tinge of hesitancy. 'I never thought I'd ever say anything like that, but … well, I think I've begun to change a bit over the past few months, especially since staying here with you and the others. Something strange happened to me too a couple of months ago. I was sound asleep, after a long, hard day at

Laura

the restaurant, and dreamt I was hiking somewhere and had wandered off this narrow, beaten track into a marshy area. There were spots that were safe to stand on, where the ground was firm and grassy, but whenever I slipped off them, my feet kept sinking down into this horrible mud and slime. I was getting exhausted, trying to make some sort of headway, because it was foggy and I couldn't see which parts were safe to walk on and which weren't. Then suddenly, I heard a voice calling to me through the fog. Whoever it was actually knew my name and kept on yelling out to me, kind of like this:

'Jamie, don't worry, listen to me! Put your foot there – yes, that's right! Now move a bit further to the right – good. Keep walking straight ahead – you're safe there. Now go to your left and circle around the edge of the muddy area. Don't worry – I won't let you fall in!'

'I knew if I listened to that voice and did exactly what I was told, I'd be completely safe – and that's what happened. In my dream, I walked right out of the marsh – and then the fog lifted and I was safe on the little track again. I never saw who spoke to me – but it sure was a beautiful voice. And I felt certain afterwards that somehow it was more than a dream – that perhaps God or Jesus or an angel was trying to show me that, if I listened and obeyed in real life, like I did in the dream, then I'd move safely through all the difficulties and pitfalls around me. So what do you think about all that?'

Laura felt a weight lift off her shoulders. She had sensed Jamie was keeping something from her – perhaps it had been this. And as she listened, she realised God knew exactly how to get through to Jamie much better than she ever would. She wanted to say so much, but decided it would be wiser to keep it to a minimum.

'What a wonderful dream, Jamie! Scary – but very special. I like your explanation too as to what it was all about. I've had experiences when I've heard a voice like that but not seen anyone – and I don't think either of us is round the bend. Well, not yet anyway! So … where does that leave you as far as God's concerned?'

He did not seem to resent the question at all.

'Not sure yet, to be honest,' he replied thoughtfully after a while. 'I've been reading bits of the Bible you gave me, by the way – can't say I understand it all, but I'll persevere. I think I know one thing I should do as a result of the dream though and that is, move to Sydney – for this coming year at least. I didn't want to say anything until now – until I saw Alan again. He contacted me some time back and told me the relationship with his partner hadn't worked out, so he'd like to catch up with me again. I wasn't sure if I wanted to or not – and it was about then that I had the dream. Anyway, I finally caught up with him yesterday. He's a great guy – but I've decided I don't think we're meant to be together. So now I'll definitely do that postgraduate course in Sydney I was telling you about. I know I could do something similar here, but I'm thinking it's probably better to live further away from Alan right now. I'll come back from time to time – I like it here at The Menagerie, with all your friends. I feel they accept me for who I am, just like they do all the guys from the boarding houses who come to the evening service, however different or difficult they sometimes are. I'll be sorry to go – but my course starts very soon.'

Not long after Jamie left, school began for the year. Laura was soon kept busy preparing interesting lessons for her 'little people', as she called them. Around the same time, The Menagerie underwent some changes. Over the break, Emma had decided to postpone completing her art course and instead head overseas for a year. Ben, returning for his second year at the Conservatorium, happily moved into Emma's room, leaving Phil with a room to himself, except when Mikey stayed over. This then left the sleep-out free for occasional guests like Jamie. Andrew and Robyn were willing to let it stay that way, especially since Amy would soon be too big to sleep in the little porch area attached to their room, and Cate agreed.

Laura could not get the thought of her mother's overcrowded unit out of her mind, however. Eventually, she asked if she could offer the sleep-out area to Elisabeth and Jonathan.

'She probably won't accept,' she told the others, who seemed to be happy for her to go ahead. 'She's not interested in anything to do with God, so might choose to keep her distance from us all.'

In the end, that was exactly what Elisabeth decided to do. Yet despite her refusal to take up their offer, she was touched that Laura's friends were prepared to accept her into the household.

'I don't think so,' she had laughed rather self-consciously, when Laura told her about it, 'but thanks anyway. They sound like a great bunch of people. Actually, I might move back with Paul soon – he says he made a New Year's resolution not to drink too much and so far it's working. Besides, there's a job come up as a cook at the pub where he's been living – I reckon I could do that. Paul could mind Jonathan when I'm not around. I really want it to work, Laura ...' – and here her voice became a little softer and uncertain. 'I do love him, despite everything. I never have been very interested in religion and stuff – I guess I'm a bit like Mum and Dad and can't understand why you had to lose your eyes and all that. And I know I've done things God certainly wouldn't approve of. But maybe if you could pray for us now and then, that'd be good. I want Jonathan to have a good life – I really do.'

Laura was disappointed, but not unduly surprised. More than anything, she

Laura

felt sad – sad that Elisabeth seemed so directionless in life and so lacking in self-confidence.

'I know you do – and I hope it all works out for you,' she said gently in response. 'I'll certainly pray for you – but you can pray too, you know, Elisabeth. God's not some ferocious old man in the sky with a big stick, like you might think. God knows all about us anyway and still loves us, so you can talk to God just like you're talking to me right now. Anyway, I promise I'll pray. And Elisabeth, if you change your mind, or if you need any help, will you please let me know? You'd always be welcome at The Menagerie – we'd find space somehow.'

In the midst of her constant teaching preparation, Laura was determined to continue her involvement with some of the 'regulars' at the evening service each Sunday, as well as provide ongoing help for Mikey when he was with them. But she was equally determined to guard the whole creative aspect of her life carefully. She found it so releasing, especially after a day of focussing hard at school, to relax with her guitar, letting words and ideas for songs come to her as she strummed away. And she loved collaborating with her musician friends to create something special and original that helped them express what they wanted to convey to the world. Because this usually required a unique relationship of trust and a respect for each other that built up over time, some of her friends from the Music Society at her old uni still came to write with her. She was hardworking and patient, as well as extremely talented, and they valued her input greatly. On the other hand, she could also be very determined, intent on getting her own way with lyrics whenever possible, and occasionally a little scornful of their suggestions. But her colleagues took it all in their stride – after all, they often had to concede, when a song worked well, that she had in fact been right. And they knew too that she had their best interests at heart.

It was certainly true that Laura wanted them to succeed with their music, but she also wanted them to find their place in life, hopefully taking God into account in the process.

To that end, she continued to be up front about her faith, but never in an insensitive way. And that was what had appealed to Richard, a frequent contributor at the 'open mike' nights on campus, when he first met Laura the previous year. At the time, he would often sit for hours drinking coffee and talking to any friends who happened to come by. Of course, he was supposed to be finishing an Arts degree, but had ended up spreading it out over the maximum number of years allowed by the uni, preferring to expend his energies on composing, as well as talking about the big issues of life. Somehow he managed to survive on his student allowance, supplemented by his casual job in the coffee shop, as well as occasional stints busking in the city, but mostly it was his girlfriend who footed the bills, Laura suspected. Richard was a colourful character, with a large frame and a bushy, black beard. Laura loved him, but at the same time was well aware of his eccentricities. He was infuriating to write songs with, she soon discovered, since he would continually veer off at tangents and was often distinctly allergic to hard work, but he was also hugely gifted and intelligent, with a large reservoir of untapped potential. And while he strenuously maintained that religion was a load of rubbish, he gradually became a frequent visitor at The Menagerie, not only to work on songs with Laura, but also to engage in lengthy, thoughtful conversations about God and faith and related matters with them all.

Late one night in March, Richard appeared at the door of The Menagerie very depressed and upset, having quarrelled with his girlfriend. It was a reasonably common occurrence, Laura knew – but this time things did seem a little more serious.

'Thank God you guys are home!' he blurted out, when he found Laura and most of the others still up having coffee. 'Man, do I need a place to stay for a few days and someone to talk to! Tracey's kicked me out – for good this time, by the sound of it. She says she can't take another year of me bumming around, not getting anywhere, never finishing off my degree and all that. She's packing up and going overseas for a while to join her sister in England. She says that maybe when she comes back, if I've done anything with my life by then, she might see how things pan out – but I don't know. Anyway, where does that leave me now? It was her wage that paid most of our rent, so I'm in trouble, that's for sure.'

And that was how Richard came to join the household, eventually occupying the sleep-out on a semi-permanent basis. Later that same week, Andrew and Robyn received the news that they would be staying put for another year, resulting in sighs of relief all round. And when, not long after, Mikey came to share Phil's room during the week as well as on weekends, because his mother had found another partner and preferred not to have him around so much, it was finally declared 'full house' at The Menagerie.

That year, Laura was particularly looking forward to Easter, not only because it was a special time of remembrance and celebration for her, but also because Anne was getting married. They had kept in touch regularly while at uni and especially after Laura had become a committed Christian. Just after Christmas, Anne had phoned excitedly to tell her she was engaged.

'I've known Simon for ages – since we were kids really – but when we moved up north next door to you, our families lost touch. Then when I came back to Melbourne to study, I met up with him again through our church community, but I wasn't interested in any sort of relationship and neither was he. After he finished uni, he went overseas to do aid work for a couple of years – it wasn't until last year

Laura

when he came home that we connected on any serious level. Now we're very sure God wants us to be together – we're so happy, Laura! We plan to be married on the property back up home – we don't want a huge wedding and Simon's relatives are prepared to make the trip, as are some of our friends. But I have two special favours to ask of you. Would you consider being my bridesmaid – along with Sarah, of course – and would you also sing at the wedding?'

After Laura managed to catch her breath, she had been quick to respond.

'Of *course* I'd love to be a bridesmaid and to sing, if you want me to – but what wonderful news! Congratulations to you both – I can't wait to meet your Simon! Not that I'm totally surprised, you know. You *did* manage to mention him fairly frequently over the past year, whenever we talked. Imagine going back to the farm too! I haven't been there since we left – that'll be very interesting. What were you planning to do as far as dresses go? It might be a bit difficult, with Sarah and you both in Melbourne and me here in Brisbane.'

'Actually, I'm phoning from the farm right now, because we came up here for Christmas,' Anne told her. 'We're passing through Brisbane in a couple of weeks, so I was hoping you'd be around then and we could go shopping together and maybe buy all our outfits in one go. You could meet Simon too – not that he'd want to go clothes shopping with us.'

'Yes, I'll be here – and Jamie too. Perhaps he and Simon can entertain each other while we're out scouring the town,' Laura laughed. 'It should be sale time, so maybe we can bag some bargains. You're welcome to stay with us for as long as you need to – Andrew and Robyn and Amy are away on holidays. Cate will be too by then and Ben's gone home to his parents. Emma leaves for overseas tomorrow and I'm not sure what Phil's organised – but that's no problem. There'd still be plenty of room for you all, whatever he does. Just call us when you know what day you'll be arriving.'

It had been a wonderful two days together. Simon had got on well with Jamie and the two of them went to the movies and visited the art gallery, as well as making a quick trip down to the Gold Coast, which Simon had not seen since he was a child. This left Anne and Sarah and Laura free to wander the shops, taking as long as they needed to find their outfits.

At first, although very happy to spend time with her old friends, Laura was a little apprehensive about the shopping aspect of their visit. Buying clothes was a difficult task for her. In the past, she had tended to rely heavily on her mother's choice of style and material, particularly since she had always made Laura's dresses herself. After moving out of home, Laura had bought very few new clothes, so that when she had started teaching, she had had to ask her mother to go with her to choose some decent outfits to wear each day for school. Once or twice, she and Cate had bought things together, but Laura was never sure if Cate's taste was the same as hers, so had not felt confident enough to wear her new purchases too often. Now, she'd have to trust Anne and Sarah to help her decide – and she'd have to take Sarah's preferences into account too when choosing their bridesmaids' outfits. On the morning of their shopping expedition, Laura lay in bed thinking about what lay ahead and smiled wryly as she handed the day over to God.

'Lord, I'm not sure if you're into fashion much, but I do know you care about me. Please arrange things so that we find just the right outfit for each of us! And don't let me be too stubborn or difficult, when I don't need to be. Amen.'

The day began amazingly smoothly, as they searched first off for Sarah and Laura's bridesmaid dresses. Eventually, they settled on matching outfits of pretty powder blue satin, with long, full skirts and plain bodices with thin shoulder straps, adding a chiffon wrap of the same colour to their purchases, in case the day turned out to be cool.

'It makes me feel decidedly elegant,' Laura laughed. 'I've never worn anything like this – the material feels beautiful.'

'It looks lovely with your blonde hair, Laura – and matches your eyes too,' Sarah said happily, without thinking.

She broke off in confusion, with a quick apology, but Laura had not found the comment out of place at all.

'It's okay, Sarah – whether my eyes are real or not, I'm glad everything matches. I think I'll need to get the skirt put up a bit though – otherwise I'll be falling flat on my face!'

Anne remembered how important it was for Laura to be able to move with confidence, gently exploring the surface with her foot as she went. They quickly arranged for the dress to be shortened, before turning their attention to finding Anne's special dress.

And that was when things became a little more difficult. Laura remembered clearly a time years ago, not long after she had first met Anne, when she had asked her mother if her friend was pretty or not. She remembered her mother hesitating before finally mentioning Anne's friendly face and thick, long hair, adding that because she was so nice, it didn't really matter what she looked like. It was more what her mother had *not* said on that occasion that had conveyed so much to Laura. Since then too, she had discovered for herself that Anne was built on much sturdier lines than she and Sarah were. Now, as they began to look through the racks of beautiful dresses, with the shop assistant trying to help, Laura could sense Anne's frustration mounting and her confidence waning.

As Laura waited, she moved slowly along the racks, touching each dress in

Laura

turn. She could feel beautiful, smooth satin, then stiffer material, which she thought was probably called taffeta, and then an occasional softer, gossamer-light fabric. Eventually, her hands rested on a garment that seemed to have two parts – a dress of chiffon-type material, with a plain bodice and straps and a full, floating outer skirt over a satin underlay, together with a long-sleeved jacket that seemed to be shaped in at the waist. It was the material of the jacket that fascinated Laura most – the finishing touches on it felt so interesting and unusual. Parts of the jacket felt smooth and silky, while other slightly raised sections were more furry – probably flower-shaped patterns, she guessed. Around the edges there was a narrow ribbon of embossed lace, while a thin, silken-type braiding formed curves and loops over the front panels. And as Laura continued to examine the outfit gently, her fingers discovered little round beads dotted here and there too and three larger beads acting as buttons that fitted through loops attached to the opposite front panel of the jacket. Eventually she let her hands rest on the beautiful garment for a moment and breathed a silent prayer.

'Anne, do you think this one might be all right?' she asked quietly, showing it to her friend. 'I love the feel of the jacket, but do you like it?'

Laura knew by Anne's hesitation that she was not overly impressed.

'Well … it's not quite what I was looking for, but I'll take it and maybe try it on later.'

Time went by, with one outfit after another being discarded. Laura could tell her friend's embarrassment was increasing rapidly. A thoughtless comment by the shop assistant that Anne was rather a difficult shape to fit did not help either. Laura sat quietly, until finally Anne gave up, her voice sounding rather teary.

'Well, I knew this might be hard, but I didn't think it'd be *this* hard. We could go somewhere else, but I don't want to take all day. I've heard this shop has the best range anyway. Oh, I don't know *what* to do!'

Even Sarah, usually very placid and patient, was becoming a little tense.

Laura decided to risk it again.

'Anne, is the one I showed you still here somewhere? Have you tried it on?'

'No … but I guess I may as well.'

There was silence, as she did so. And silence again, as she stood in front of the mirror, straightening the jacket and smoothing out the skirt.

Laura could hardly contain her curiosity.

'What does it look like, Anne? Do you think it might be okay?'

'Okay?' Anne breathed eventually, her voice shaky. '*More* than okay! It's *lovely*, Laura – absolutely right! And it fits perfectly. Oh my goodness – I could have tried this on first and saved us all this trouble.'

'But you wouldn't have had anything to compare it with then,' Laura consoled her. 'Besides, you weren't to know it'd look so good, especially when it wasn't what you had in mind at all. What do you think, Sarah?'

'It looks so beautiful, Laura!' she said immediately. 'Everyone will love it.'

Laura sat quietly while the dresses were paid for, feeling very satisfied with herself. As they took themselves off to lunch before attempting any further shopping, Anne turned to her, still so excited about her purchase.

'Laura, how on earth did you know that dress would be so *right* for me? We could see them all and we still couldn't find what I wanted.'

'Well, I prayed as I came to each dress,' she responded, smiling, 'and I just knew it was right for you. What do the little beads on the front look like exactly, Anne?'

'They're tiny pearls – and the big 'buttons' are pearls as well. They're so beautiful!'

It was reward enough for Laura to hear the satisfaction in Anne's voice that day, let alone the many flattering comments that came her friend's way at the wedding itself.

'Great choice of outfit, Anne! Where did you find it?'

'You look so elegant, Anne – that's a stunning jacket!'

'You look perfectly beautiful!' was Simon's simple, heartfelt compliment to his new wife.

'I feel absolutely wonderful in my 'Laura dress',' Anne whispered to Laura, as they posed for photos. 'Thank you so much, dear friend – and thank you, God!'

laura

chapter fourteen

Laura returned from the wedding a little depressed, yet happy everything had gone so well. The service had taken place outside under a large poinciana tree, near what used to be the boundary between the Thomas's property and theirs. She had loved the simplicity and sincerity of it all – and she had certainly enjoyed performing the song she had written especially for the occasion. It had been almost a surreal experience, singing words she now believed with all her heart that asked God to bless and watch over Anne and Simon, as they began married life. So much had happened since those afternoons when she and Anne had read and studied and played together as young girls. Then, she could never have envisaged a day when she would be comfortable asking God to bless anyone. In fact, so much she could not have envisaged had happened since those years at the farm – both good and bad. She had always felt, even then, that she could succeed at school and university and go on to achieve whatever she wanted to in life – her parents had built that into her spirit. Yet she had not envisaged that the road would be so hard at times, or that she would have to overcome so much, including the deep rejection she had experienced from Tim. And she had never thought her family would go through so many crises – her father's difficulty

laura

in finding work, his alcohol problems and eventual death, her brother Greg's brushes with the law, Elisabeth's relationship issues that were still causing pain. Ian she was unsure about, since he was a little removed at present, and Jamie – each day she prayed for him, that he would listen to that voice which she believed was God's and choose the right path in life.

As Laura had visited their old home, now an integral part of the community Anne's parents and their friends had set up, so many things triggered vivid memories from her childhood. The unevenness of the floorboards, as she walked from the sleep-out she had shared with Elisabeth to the lounge room, where all the family had played so many games together. The feel of the veranda railing beneath her fingers, as she stood recalling the times she had curled up at her Dad's feet and sang his country ballads with him. The sound of hens clucking in what seemed to be the same old pen across the yard – she'd always loved feeding her own chickens there. The old mulberry tree, its trunk so gnarled now, and the rough ground nearby evoking a memory of the first time Jamie had hauled her along in their old cart, taking her way up above the paddocks to see their cubby. They had done so many wild, crazy things together, she and her brothers. Yet Jamie had been there to make sure she was safe – he had always taken his responsibilities seriously. And he had always been there for their mother as well, right through their growing up years. Had Margaret looked to him too much for support, in all those times when she'd been unable to depend on her own husband? Perhaps that's part of the reason Jamie's the way he is now, Laura thought with a pang.

She sighed as she sat cross-legged on her bed, trying to focus on preparing the next day's lessons. All she could do was pray for her family, trusting God to bring healing and renewal – and a change of heart for those who needed it. It had happened in her own life in such unexpected ways – God was certainly creative enough and loving enough to care for them as well.

Eventually she packed up her schoolwork and burrowed down under the covers, but sleep would not come. Her thoughts kept returning to the wedding – in particular to the happiness she had heard in Simon and Anne's voices, as they exchanged their vows, and later during the protracted farewells. Anne had given her an especially warm hug, as she stood at the gate to wave goodbye.

'Bye, Laura! Thank you for everything – you were wonderful! I'm *so-o-o-o* happy!'

She had returned her friend's hug, but could not help feeling wistful – and a little jealous. Now, as she tried to sleep, questions about her own future began tumbling through her mind. Would she ever find a life partner like Anne had – or did God mean her to remain single? She remembered Cate's words the night months earlier, when they had been sitting playing with little Amy – she had been so sure Laura would have a family of her own one day. Tears began to slide down her cheeks, but she brushed them away hastily. She was tired, she realised – and a little lonely, despite the friends who surrounded her. As she turned over in bed, a picture of Simon and Anne lying close together, their arms around each other, flashed through her mind. 'Oh God', she prayed, 'I want that warmth and closeness too – I want to know that someone treasures me more than anyone else in the world!'

Some time later, she heard footsteps in the hallway outside and Phil and Cate whispering together, as they tiptoed past her door. Nothing unusual about that – after all, Phil was now working as a nurse assistant at the same hospital as Cate. They'd probably been on the same shift. Both Phil and Mikey had certainly come a long way since moving into The Menagerie, she reflected, as she eventually drifted off to sleep. It had been wonderful to be part of their journey – she was proud of them both. Very proud – and very fond of them too.

Over the following weeks, Laura noticed that Cate and Phil seemed to be rostered on the same shifts more and more – convenient for them, since they could share a car ride to and from the hospital. But she knew there was more to it than that. She only had to listen to the happiness and excitement in Cate's voice and hear Phil's laugh, which had become much more frequent of late, to know something was happening between them. She hoped there was, for Cate's sake – she remembered the longing in her friend's voice, as she had talked about Phil that night they had nursed Amy together. But she hoped Phil would follow both his head and his heart and consider Mikey's happiness and wellbeing, as well as his own. She loved Cate – they had clicked from the very beginning. But she knew Cate did not have the patience with Mikey that she herself had – patience which had no doubt come from her own struggle to overcome obstacles and lead an independent life.

Finally, one Saturday night, when the whole household met together over dinner – something they tried to do regularly to discuss any issues and share one another's journeys – Phil and Cate announced their engagement.

'My divorce came through a couple of months ago, so since then I've felt free to get to know Cate a bit more,' Phil explained a little sheepishly. 'I know I used to say I wasn't the marrying kind' – and here Laura could tell he had turned in her direction – 'but I think I was trying to talk myself out of what I knew was happening between Cate and me. I guess I felt too scared to jump in and try to make a go of it again. But I'm a different person now from when Mikey's mum and I got married. And I have to trust God to help me stay strong and not go back to my old ways. I think Cate's a brave woman to take me and Mikey on, but she

Laura

says she's made up her mind.'

Laura joined in the chorus of congratulations that followed, but deep inside, she could not deny she felt disappointed. Yet she steeled herself, determined to rejoice with those who were rejoicing, and rose to her feet to make a witty speech, which soon had everyone in stitches.

'So when's the wedding?' they all wanted to know. 'And do you plan to stay on here?'

'We'd like to get married as soon as possible,' Cate told them. 'After all, why wait? We know each other pretty well, since we've lived under the same roof for over a year. I could move into Phil's room and Mikey can have mine for the time being – if that's okay with you all.'

No one objected and soon it was all arranged. Andrew would marry them at the end of June in the church. Then they'd have a special celebration lunch in the park near the river where Laura and Carolyn had first picnicked and talked about God together.

'That way,' Phil explained, 'all my mates from the AA group, plus the folk who come to the evening service from around here won't feel too embarrassed to front up. They don't have any spare money to buy good clothes, so that way they can wear whatever they like.'

It turned out to be a truly special wedding. Only a couple of Phil's relatives attended, but Cate's family, wheat farmers from the Darling Downs, all came to support her. Mikey proudly stood beside his dad as best man, while Laura again acted as bridesmaid and Ben provided the music. Richard, still a semi-permanent part of The Menagerie, was in his element at the reception in the park, organising the tea and coffee and cold drinks, while others dispensed homemade cakes, slices and delicious desserts to all the guests. Laura loved the whole feel of community celebration, despite being unable to ignore a twinge of jealousy inside her from time to time. This is the sort of reception I'd like to have when I get married, she decided. Or is it 'if'?

More likely 'if', she concluded rather morosely that night, as she sat by herself in the lounge, her tired legs stretched out on a footstool in front of her.

Richard found her there asleep some time later, almost stumbling over her in the dark.

'What the hell? Jes …, oh sorry, Laura! I didn't know you were here. Only wanted to get a CD of mine. Sorry!'

Laura, trying to surface quickly, was unsure whether he was apologising for his language, which still needed a bit of cleaning up, or the fact that he had disturbed her.

'It's okay, Richard,' she managed to respond. 'I must have dozed off. Doesn't make any difference to me, after all, whether the light's on or not.'

'Sorry I woke you up, anyway. Hey, now that I *have*, would you like a coffee? I was just about to make myself one.'

Laura, knowing she would be unable to fall asleep again for a while, took up his offer. It was pleasant to sit together, reminiscing about the day and munching on a few leftovers.

'Great day, wasn't it?' Richard said, sipping his coffee with a satisfied sigh. 'I must say, you Christian folk know how to look after one another – as well as outsiders like me.'

'Still an outsider, Richard?' Laura decided to risk asking.

'Well ... perhaps not *such* an outsider, I have to admit, as I was before I became an inhabitant of this here Menagerie! This whole experience sure has enabled me to see how you folk function up close and personal. And I must say I really am grateful you all risked having me here. I certainly was in a pretty desperate predicament, although I can see now it was of my own making. The eternal procrastinator – that's me.'

'I hope you don't stay that way, Richard. Eternity's an awful long time – you might end up leaving it too late. I once had someone at my old uni challenge me along those lines. He told me to make sure I didn't leave it too late to decide where I stood with God. I know you like *talking* about religion and stuff, but don't you think it's time to *do* something – like seeing where God really fits in your life? I was challenged about that too in a pretty amazing way once.'

Laura told him the story of how she had heard a voice in the garden, when she was on holidays with her mother.

'I heard the words, as clearly as if you were speaking them to me now: 'And where do *I* fit?' I didn't act on them immediately – there were too many things going on in my life then – but I believe God didn't leave me alone until I really *did* answer that question. Probably the same thing will happen to you, you know.'

'So I may as well give in now, eh? That's what I like about you, Laura – or one of the things, anyway. You're nothing if not direct. But I know you honestly do care what happens to me – it's not as if you're only wanting to talk me into believing the same as you or anything. I'd call it integrity – I really admire that. Tracey was a bit like you, I reckon. She wanted me to decide where I was heading in life, but I never would. Funny – now that I'm closer than I ever have been to doing that, she's not here any more.'

'Ever hear from her?' Laura asked gently, picking up on the sadness in his voice.

'No way! She said she wouldn't keep in touch when she left – and she meant it. She wanted to get right away. But I know her sister's address in England, so I

Laura

could contact her if I wanted to.'

'And do you?'

He was quiet for a while.

'Not sure ... no, I don't think so. At least, not quite yet. I want to see if I can get a few songs published or recorded or *something*, before I even think of contacting her. And I'm planning to finish my degree this year too. Now *that* will be a real miracle!'

He laughed his raucous laugh, but quickly quietened down when Laura reminded him the rest of the household was no doubt asleep.

'Tell you what, Laura. Why don't you come with me to the coffee shop tomorrow night? There's a few interesting artists around campus this year and some of them are writing good stuff. You'd enjoy it, I reckon.'

Sometimes Laura took him up on such offers, but at other times she declined. He kept asking, however, and she knew by his persistence, as well as by the way he took every opportunity to sit talking with her when both of them were home, that their relationship could no doubt have blossomed into something more than friendship. Yet whether he admitted it or not, she was well aware she was only a fill-in for his Tracey. In all likelihood, she'd never be more than second best. She cautioned herself not to let the relationship get too deep, whatever her feelings were for him. Besides, as she knew Andrew and Robyn and the others would remind her, it was better not to get too serious with someone who was unsure what they believed about God. It only complicated matters.

She was very busy at school all through the next term, but also spent many hours co-writing songs with Richard and others. On top of that, she had become even more involved with some of the people from the boarding houses around the area who attended the Sunday evening service. She had started teaching guitar to one or two and was even managing to help a few of them read at last. She was always delighted when her 'star pupils', as she called them, were able to decipher the words of the simple songs the church sang on Sunday evenings, or when they volunteered to read the Bible out loud during a service and managed to get through all the verses. She could hear the sense of achievement in their voices – and it always moved her to tears.

'I'm so proud of you!' she would say to them later, as she hugged them. 'I think you made God smile tonight.'

Finally, at the end of September, one of Richard and Laura's original songs made it onto a CD of contemporary ballads recorded by a young female artist beginning to make a name in the industry. Sheree had first heard Richard sing the song at an 'open mike' night and had liked it immediately, she told them. Laura loved Sheree's rich, velvety voice and her sensitive rendition of the song.

But she knew too, from artists she had met when singing with her Dad's band, how difficult it was, both for the singer and the songwriter, to break into such a competitive field and to stay there. Richard was over the moon, however.

'Wow – this is so wonderful, Laura! We've finally made it! I knew I'd get lucky one day.'

'Richard, it *is* great – but it's only a beginning. There's a long way to go yet,' Laura tried to caution him.

'Come on, Laura, let's celebrate! Wow – wait till Tracey hears about this!'

Laura was quiet for a moment.

'So ... you *are* going to contact her then.'

'Well ... I know I said I wasn't going to, but ... hang it all, I really do want her to know and be proud of what I've done – or at least, what *we've* done. Laura ... would you mind?' he asked, his voice suddenly serious.

Laura knew immediately what he was trying to say. And she found she did not have the heart to spoil his excitement, or discourage him from doing what his heart was clearly telling him to do.

'It's okay, Richard,' she eventually responded. 'I understand. Truly it's fine ... as long as you tell her you love her at the same time!'

'You're a good friend, Laura,' he laughed rather sheepishly, giving her a hug and a brotherly kiss, 'and a great girl all round. Thanks so much – for everything! I owe you a lot.'

By the end of October, Tracey had returned home from England. Not long after, she came to The Menagerie to help Richard move out. Laura heard that same note in their voices that she had heard in Simon and Anne's and also Phil and Cate's – and she knew there would be no going back for them. One night, the household put on a farewell party for Richard, which touched him deeply, Laura could tell.

'You know I love you guys,' he said, his voice full of emotion. 'I'll be back to see you all – and to work with Laura, of course. You've made me think a lot about this whole Christian business – as much by the way you treat people, including weirdos like me, as by what you say in whatever arguments you can muster against mine. Keep doing what you're doing! One day we might even join you – and hopefully we won't leave it too late, Laura.'

Laura dragged herself through the last few weeks of school. Not that she hated her job, or her 'little people' – but she knew she was quite worn out. It had been a huge year, with lots of changes and challenges – Jamie's move to Sydney, adjusting to teaching, so many opportunities to counsel and care for people, the emotional ups and downs of two weddings of close friends – and now the whole thing with Richard and Tracey. Most nights she went to bed not long after dinner

laura

and lay listening to the radio, or CDs, or some of her old tapes. She did not seem to have enough energy for anything more – certainly not the creativity required for song writing. Yet often when she listened to the more contemporary Christian songs, she thought they were sub-standard and repetitive – and that annoyed her. Some nights she would turn her CD player off in disgust, preferring her own thoughts and imagination to what she contemptuously labelled 'rubbish'.

'I know I'm tired and irritable and over-critical,' she said to them all one night at dinner, 'but I wish I could find some new Christian songs I really like.'

The conversation flowed on then, but afterwards, Ben, never one to talk much, came and sat beside her.

'Laura, there's a radio program you might enjoy,' he began rather hesitantly. 'It's only on at the weekends quite late at night and it features lots of the old hymns we don't sing very often now – at least not at our evening service. Quite a few of them have beautiful melody lines, but I think you might appreciate the words in particular. Sometimes they just play orchestral versions, but if you can record the program, maybe I could find the words for you, if you don't know them already.'

Laura was touched by his kindness. Ben was very shy and not one to put himself forward too often.

'Thanks, Ben,' she found herself saying. 'I'll listen to it tonight. I wasn't brought up in church circles, like you were, so I might not know many of them, but if you think it's good, I'd like to listen. What station is it on?'

Thus began a new journey of discovery for Laura, when she so much needed something to refresh her spirit. Hearing for the first time the well-known old hymns that had lasted down through the years was for her like opening a wonderful treasure trove of precious jewels. As Ben had suggested, she usually taped the programs. That way, she could ask him for any words she wanted, as well as listen to them again during the week. Cate and Phil, however, made it clear they thought little of her strange musical preferences.

'What on earth could you possibly like about those boring programs, Laura? It's mostly a heap of old-fashioned stuff that went out ages ago,' Phil laughed incredulously.

'I'm surprised *you'd* like them, Laura. You write new songs yourself all the time – why go back to the old hymns my parents used to sing?' Cate added.

But Laura was not deterred.

'They might not be everyone's cup of tea, but they're what I need right now,' she told them. 'Besides, many of them are excellent – full of good, strong statements about God that encourage me a lot. And they might be old, but they're new to me – I'm glad of the opportunity to catch up on what I missed out on all these years.'

They left her alone then. Cate at least could see she needed space.

Then one night at the beginning of December, Laura received a phone call. She was listening to a tape in her room and did not hear the phone ring. Robyn came to find her.

'Laura – phone for you! From a Carolyn, I think she said her name was.'

Laura picked up the phone, her heart in her mouth, hoping beyond hope it would turn out to be Carolyn Burns. Yet she knew it couldn't be – she was in Africa!

'Hello – Laura Harding here.'

'Laura, it's Carolyn – Carolyn Burns. How *are* you? It's so wonderful to hear your voice again!'

'Oh, Carolyn, it's wonderful to hear *yours*! But where *are* you? What are you doing?'

'I'm right here in Brisbane. I'm home on leave for a few weeks – I was hoping you'd be around, because I'm dying to catch up! That's if *you* want to.'

Laura could feel a lump in her throat, but she tried to keep her voice steady as she responded.

'Of *course* I want to! I'd love to. When could we meet – and where?'

It was soon arranged. That weekend, they spent most of Saturday together. Then on the Sunday, Carolyn came to the evening service and met some of the ones Laura had taught to read. Afterwards, Laura invited her home to have supper with the other current occupants of The Menagerie.

'This is so refreshing for me,' Carolyn commented. 'Having been in such a different cultural environment for so long and almost completely isolated from other western workers, it's wonderful to sit here like this with you. Also, it's so good to see how you're trying to make a difference in your own community here. But I'm sure, if you weren't careful, you could get very exhausted, pouring yourself into the lives of all the needy people in this area, just like I could where I am.'

'Yes, I think we've all experienced that from time to time,' Andrew responded, 'but we do try to support one another and be aware when one of us needs extra encouragement. Laura's particularly good at sensing where we're all at – I only hope we look after her well enough in return. Of course, we do try to find ways to care for ourselves too and allow God to refresh us, in the midst of everything.'

'Even where I was, in the middle of an African village, I found it helpful to listen to music – any good music really,' Carolyn told them. 'Sometimes I used to choose Christian songs or gospel music – but not all the time. Here you can take yourselves off to a live performance somewhere, or watch TV, or listen to the

221

Laura

radio – but it's not so easy to do that where I've been living. I've had to rely on my CDs and tapes – they've really been my lifesavers.'

Laura had forgotten how much Carolyn loved music. Now she remembered how there had almost always been CDs playing in the Special Unit and how strongly Carolyn had supported the school's music program.

'I remember now how you loved music at school,' she commented, 'and how you used to try to get all of us into the school music productions. Do you remember the time they refused to let me be in that Gilbert and Sullivan operetta and you stood up for me? And how you encouraged me to write our new school song instead? It all seems so long ago.'

Later, the two of them went to Laura's room to hear a tape of some of the songs she and Richard had written together. It was late, but Carolyn did not have the heart to disappoint her friend. Yes, she was tired herself from all the adjustments she'd had to make to fit into a new culture, but she could see Laura was probably even more so. It was the emotional wear and tear and the disappointments experienced on a relational level during the past year that were a large part of this exhaustion, Carolyn was sure – and she wanted to be able to help her friend however she could.

They sat listening to the songs for some time, Laura commenting here and there about a particular choice of word, or pointing out a melody line she and Richard had disagreed about. Carolyn found it fascinating, but eventually Laura realised the time.

'I'd better let you get home, Carolyn,' she said apologetically, 'but I was wondering … would you have time next Saturday to help me with something? I love listening to music before I go to bed – it helps me relax. On the weekends, there's a good radio program Ben told me about that features lots of old hymns I'm sure you'd know well. Would you be able to sit with me while I go through the programs I taped and tell me the names of the hymns? Some nights they play just music and no words – I guess they think everybody listening would know which hymns they are, but *I* don't. If you could, then perhaps Ben could see if they're in the old hymnbooks at church, when he gets time, and I could get Mikey or someone to read the words out, while I type them up on my Brailler. I'd ask Cate or Phil, but I know they hate the old hymns.'

Carolyn did not have to think about it for long.

'I'd love to. That's the sort of job I really enjoy – and I can imagine how helpful it would be for you to have all the words. Don't worry about asking Ben or Mikey or anyone else, by the way – we've got lots of old hymnbooks at our place. I'll bring some along – hopefully I'll recognise the ones you particularly want at least.'

But when she arrived the following Saturday, Laura was lying down with a migraine and at first could not even get up to greet her.

'I'm so sorry – I'll be right in a little while. I've been getting a few bad headaches lately – it *would* have to be today! The doctor thinks it's something to do with the operation to remove my eyes when I was little, but I suspect stress and tiredness don't help either. Sit here on the bed. My medication should take effect soon and then we can start listening to my tapes.'

Carolyn sat down, trying to keep as still as possible.

'It's been a long week,' Laura managed to say eventually. 'My 'little people' are getting restless, now that school holidays are almost here. I've been trying to make up my mind about next year too – whether I'll teach for another year, or whether I should think about enrolling in a Master's program. I've already made enquiries here and in Sydney. I could live with Jamie – he wants to find a bigger place next year. I love it here at The Menagerie, but Andrew and Robyn will have to go somewhere else next year for sure – and I know Ben's thinking of moving out. Cate and Phil haven't decided yet what they'll do, but if they leave, then I'd be the only one left. I'd have to start all over again with a whole new lot of housemates – and that's a bit much to think about right now. Besides, it has to be what God wants – I don't want to rush off and do my own thing, only to have it end in disaster. Sometimes I find it so hard to keep on believing God will guide me and watch over me. Yet I should know by now that's exactly what *will* happen, because look how God's cared for me and led me in the past! I guess I'm just tired and a bit discouraged – as you can no doubt tell.'

They were quiet again then. Laura lay trying to relax both her mind and body, while Carolyn sat thinking over what she had just been told. Eventually, she reached out and took Laura's hand.

'Let's pray, shall we? I'm going to ask that God will show you're not forgotten and that you'll know clearly the next step to take. Is that okay?'

Of course it was. There was something about the way Carolyn prayed that Laura loved. In the next few moments, it seemed to her that Jesus came so close and stood right near her bed, reaching out to her. And there was such a sweet presence in the room and a peace filling her whole body. At one stage, she was sure she felt a hand on her forehead, but knew both of Carolyn's hands were holding hers. Then she heard Carolyn asking God to take away the migraine and heal her completely. Was it Jesus' hand on her head? It felt so good she didn't want to move.

Eventually Carolyn finished praying. Laura lay there a few moments longer, then sat up, a relieved smile on her face.

'Thank you so much!' she said with feeling, holding her friend close. 'This

laura

might sound crazy, but while you were praying, I felt that Jesus was actually here with his hand on my forehead. I'm *sure* I didn't imagine it – I don't know why I ever doubt his love.'

After they had chatted for a while, Laura began putting a tape in the player and setting up her Brailler, ready for her to type the words she was certain Carolyn would be able to find.

'Fortunately I remembered to use the counter, so I know where each hymn starts. Otherwise we'd be here all day. Here's one I really like – what's this one?'

Carolyn listened to a few bars, soon realising she knew it well. She told Laura its name, while she hunted in one of her music books for all the words.

'I know the first couple of verses by heart, but I'm not sure of the rest. Yes, here it is – will I start reading it out? Tell me if I go too fast!'

To Carolyn's relief, she managed to recognise most of the tunes Laura had recorded. The afternoon wore on, Laura inserting sheet after sheet of paper into her Brailler, as she chatted with her friend.

'Just as well I've learnt to be very organised, otherwise I'd never find these again when I wanted them. See, I put a little code up the top here, so I can keep track of each one. Then I have a master list here like a catalogue. Now which one is this? Oh yes – "Thine Be The Glory" – I remember now.'

'Laura, I still can't work out how you manage to read so quickly,' Carolyn commented in amazement after a while. 'I thought I was quite good at my Braille, but I'm so slow compared to you.'

'I've had plenty of practice – and a good mum who started teaching me when I was really young,' Laura quickly explained. '… Well, I think that might be the lot at last. … No – wait! There's one more I wanted to find the words to – I almost forgot. I put the tape right on top here especially – I heard it for the first time a few weeks ago and as soon as I did, I felt it was important, for some reason. I hope you know it, Carolyn. I love the music – it has a sort of Celtic feel to it. Anyway, here it is.'

Soon the beautiful sound of harps and pipes filled the room. They both sat very still, listening intently. Then Carolyn gave a cry of delight.

'Oh Laura, this is one of my favourites. And you're right – I'm sure it has Irish origins. It's 'Be Thou My Vi …'.'

Half way through the title, she stopped short and gasped, stumbling over the final word she had been about to say. In her excitement, she had rushed on without thinking, but suddenly it had hit her – and she could not bring herself to finish. How would someone who was blind react to the idea of asking God to be her Vision? Yet she had committed herself now – she *had* to go on.

She opened her mouth, but no words came at first. Instinctively, she reached out and took hold of Laura's hand, realising as she did, that both of them were shaking. Had Laura guessed what she had been about to say? Carolyn was unsure – yet somehow, both of them were aware of the significance of the moment.

'What is it, Carolyn?' she whispered.

'Oh Laura … it's 'Be Thou My Vision'!'

They sat stunned, each overwhelmed and unable to hold back the tears. Eventually, when Carolyn could see clearly enough, she hurriedly began turning the pages of one of her hymnbooks with hands that still shook.

'Here it is – I've found the words. This is so amazing! … Oh Laura, this makes it pretty clear that God knew how much you needed to be encouraged right now, don't you think?'

But Laura was still too stunned to speak. She tried hard to stop her hands from shaking by pressing them together in her lap. Eventually she took a deep breath, squared her shoulders and began to get ready to type the words Carolyn was about to read out. All around them in the room, she was aware of that same sweet presence of God she had sensed earlier – only this time it was even stronger. Her hands still felt weak and she bowed her head, allowing herself a few more moments of quietness to collect herself.

Carolyn did not want to break the silence either. She sat still, marvelling at the grace of God that would give Laura exactly what she needed in such an incredible way. Then, slowly and softly, her voice quivering a little, she began to read the words of the hymn aloud.

Be Thou my Vision, O Lord of my heart;
Naught be all else to me, save that Thou art
Thou my best Thought, by day or by night,
Waking or sleeping, Thy presence my light.

Be Thou my Wisdom, and Thou my true Word;
I ever with Thee and Thou with me, Lord;
Thou my great Father, I Thy true son;
Thou in me dwelling, and I with Thee one.

Be Thou my battle Shield, Sword for the fight;
Be Thou my Dignity, Thou my Delight;
Thou my soul's Shelter, Thou my high Tower:
Raise Thou me heavenward, O Power of my power.

Laura

Riches I heed not, nor man's empty praise,
Thou mine Inheritance, now and always:
Thou and Thou only, first in my heart,
High King of heaven, my Treasure Thou art.

High King of heaven, my victory won,
May I reach heaven's joys, O bright heaven's Sun!
Heart of my own heart, whatever befall,
Still be my Vision, O Ruler of all.

Although she faltered at times, she did not stop reading, sensing this truly was Laura's prayer at that moment, straight from her heart to the heart of God. When she had finished, silence fell again, until Laura finally said one simple, clear word.

'Amen!'

It was all she needed to say. That one fervent word spoke volumes.

'Tell me when you're ready and I'll read the words line by line,' Carolyn told her gently.

'I'm ready,' Laura said eventually, wiping the remains of tears from her face and very deliberately putting her hands on the keys.

Carolyn read slowly, stopping from time to time, not only to make sure Laura could keep up, but also to respond to her frequent exclamations.

'Wow – what a great prayer! What beautiful words! *'Waking or sleeping, Thy presence my light'* – can you imagine what *that* means to someone who can't see at all? ... *'I Thy true son'* – I'm sure that includes daughters too. ... Oh Carolyn, I love this line – *'Be Thou my Dignity, Thou my Delight'*. I've always struggled with feeling rejected, but I know I don't need to, because God gives me such dignity. ... Oh, I really love the idea in this line too – *'Thou my soul's Shelter'*. Don't you think that's a fantastic phrase – *'soul's Shelter'*? ... That's so true, that man's praise is pretty empty at times. ... Oh, this fourth verse is really a declaration, isn't it? I certainly want God to be *'first in my heart'*, like it says.'

Laura was so moved by it all that her friend's responses hardly registered. Carolyn was not in the least offended, however. She could only continue to marvel, as they read slowly through each line again, how applicable almost every phrase was to Laura's life, particularly just then, when she so much needed reassurance that God would show her the way forward.

'One day the battle will be over, Laura, and you'll be there in heaven, just like this last verse talks about,' Carolyn said, when they had finally finished.

Laura turned then and reached out for her friend's hand.

'I believe I will, Carolyn, if I keep letting God be my Vision,' she said softly. 'I truly believe I will, whatever happens.'

chapter fifteen

From that point on, things seemed to take shape with amazing swiftness as far as the following year was concerned for them all. During the second last week of school, Andrew received the news of his appointment to a country parish west of Toowoomba.

'It'll certainly be a change from an inner city church, but, you know, I'm kind of looking forward to it,' he admitted, as they gathered for their group meal that weekend. 'Of course, it'll be a wrench to leave here, but we knew it had to happen some time. And we believe God must have a purpose in putting us in such a different environment for a period.'

'We'll miss you all so much,' Robyn added. 'Amy's going to be lost without Aunty Cate and Aunty Laura to spoil her rotten. Still, she'll have a new little brother or sister in a few months, so that should help.'

After the congratulations had died down, it was Cate and Phil's turn.

'Actually ...' Cate began, before Phil butted in, unable to contain himself any longer.

'What she's trying to say is – Mikey's going to have baby brother or sister soon too.'

laura

It was a while then before things quietened down enough for Cate to share the rest of their news.

'As you know, Mum and Dad are retiring in a couple of weeks. They've asked us if we'd like to mind their townhouse for them while they're overseas. They'll probably be away most of the year – they plan to spend a few months in England with my sister and also help out some missionary friends in Africa, if they can. So we'll be moving just before Christmas, if that's okay with you all.'

'What about you, Ben?' Andrew asked then. 'Have you decided what you want to do next year?'

'Well, I'm not exactly sure yet. Of course, I'll still be at the Conservatorium, but I'm thinking I might move back home for a while,' he said hesitantly. 'Mum hasn't been too well lately and Dad's asked to be appointed as a hospital chaplain here in Brisbane, which should make things easier for her. She really needs someone in the house with her as much as possible, so ...'

Laura's heart went out to him as she heard the resigned note in his voice. Ben was too easily imposed upon in her opinion, with his gentle, sensitive nature. She had watched him come out of his shell so much in the past year and grow in confidence as a person and as a musician, living away from home. Still, he had to make up his own mind – she couldn't fight his battles for him.

'That leaves you, Laura,' Cate said, after a brief silence. 'What are your thoughts about next year? I think we all feel bad that you might be the only one left here out of the lot of us.'

For a moment, as Laura felt their real pain and concern for her, her resolve almost crumbled. How would she manage without them all? She loved each one of them – they had all played a significant part in her life in different ways over the two years they had been together. She knew the time had come, however, to move on herself and take the next step into what God had for her. Yes, the months had been hard since Anne and Simon's wedding and then Cate and Phil's. She had come very close to being overwhelmed with self-pity and worry about her own future – particularly after Richard had finally sorted matters out with his Tracey. The tiredness she felt from a long first year of teaching hadn't helped either – but God had brought her through it all. Carolyn had phoned at just the right time and was even here to walk beside her in this difficult period of closing doors and saying goodbyes. As well, God had clearly strengthened and encouraged her through the words of the hymn Carolyn had found for her. Whatever the future held, she would never, ever be without her 'soul's Shelter' and her 'high Tower'. God would always be there for her – she knew that with certainty. And it was out of that well of God's grace and strength deep inside her that she found herself able now to face them all and explain her next step.

'Please don't worry about me – I'll be fine,' she reassured them, smiling. 'You all know how I've been tossing up whether to do further study or keep on teaching for another year or so. Well, in the last few days I've decided I'm definitely going back to study – I feel it really is what God wants me to do next. Remember how I applied to a couple of unis to be enrolled in a Master's program? Just this week I heard I've been accepted at Macquarie Uni in Sydney, so I'm taking up their offer and moving in with Jamie. I think I'll probably be accepted here as well, but the Sydney course looks more interesting. Anyway, I'd like to be with Jamie for a while.'

'Laura, you're not just doing this because we're all leaving here, are you?' Cate asked carefully. 'There'd be other options for you – we could help you work out something.'

'Thanks, Cate – but no, I believe God's in this,' Laura responded. 'I know I probably could've stayed on here and had others join me, if that was okay with the church – or maybe moved in with Mum for a while. Elisabeth's back with Paul again now – they both have jobs at a pub up north and seem to be doing a bit better. But ever since I spent time with Carolyn last weekend, it's become much clearer to me this is what I should do next.'

She went on then to tell them all about how Carolyn had found the words of 'Be Thou My Vision' for her and how much they had touched her. When she finished, she could sense the emotion in Ben, as he sat beside her at the table.

'Wow, Laura – I'm so glad I told you about that radio program,' he commented in an awed voice.

'So am I, Ben – Carolyn and I were totally blown away by what happened,' Laura admitted. 'It's still hard for me to take in the fact that God knew how important that hymn would be to me and made sure I found the words.'

'Remind me never to rubbish you about those old hymns you like ever again, Laura!' Phil laughed – but Laura could tell he too was moved.

'You won't have much chance to anyway,' Cate added, bringing them all back down to earth. 'We only have another few days together before we head off in different directions. I hope we don't lose contact altogether.'

'I'm sure Jamie would be happy to have any of you visit us in Sydney – already Carolyn's staying with us on her way back to Africa in April,' Laura said, trying again to keep her emotions at bay. 'He loved being here at The Menagerie – you all made a big impact on him. I don't think he's far away from knowing God for himself – I'm hoping and praying we can have some more good talks once we're sharing a house again.'

'Let's pray about that right now, eh?' Andrew suggested. 'I think we all need prayer really – it's not easy saying goodbye, is it?'

Laura

It was nowhere near easy, Laura discovered, as she said goodbye to her young charges at the School for the Blind and to the teachers, knowing she would not be back in the New Year.

'You'll always be welcome here, Laura,' the Principal told her. 'You've only been on staff for a year, but you've truly inspired the students, my dear – and all of us, in fact. Don't let those Southerners take you away from us forever!'

Some of her students were inconsolable when they realised she was leaving the school altogether. Laura found their pleas to stay difficult to handle and was glad when her final day with them was over.

'I'll come back,' she promised them, 'but you'll be so grown up I won't recognise you, I bet. Just make sure you do your very best for your teacher next year, do you hear? And remember, you can do anything you set your mind to – I expect to see many of you become really famous one day.'

Saying goodbye to all her friends who usually came to the Sunday evening service was just as difficult. In many ways some of them were more childlike than the children in her class at school – it was heart wrenching for Laura to hear them cry and difficult too to extricate herself from their warm hugs on her final night with them. Two of those she had helped learn to read proudly took part in the special farewell service for Andrew and Robyn and her, determined to get through the passages they had been given to read. Thankfully, Phil and Cate would still be involved with them, which eased Laura's mind a little.

'I'm sure God will send some other people along to join you all,' she told them. 'I'll pray that will happen. You take good care of Phil and Cate, won't you? You're all wonderful – I'm so proud of you! I'll come back and visit.'

By Christmas, all the occupants of The Menagerie had moved out. It had been a hectic time, yet Laura marvelled once again at how God orchestrated things so that everyone had somewhere to go and each one was able to assist the other pack and move. It touched Laura in those last days that, apart from Carolyn, Ben was the one who offered most frequently to help her sort things out and decide what to take to Sydney and what could be left with her mother. Always sensitive, somehow he seemed to understand her need to know what was packed where and to be able to make her way around her room and elsewhere in the house, even in the midst of the chaos that reigned. On the last night, when just the two of them were left in the old house, Ben insisted on taking her out for dinner. They chose a quiet little restaurant nearby, where Laura could curl up on one of the large, soft cushions placed around their low table and relax, now everything was under control. Phil and Cate were coming back the next day to take her and her possessions to her mother's place – there was nothing more she could do now.

'Thanks for being such a good friend these past few days, Ben,' Laura said sincerely, as they finished off their meal by ordering the hot, strong coffee and Middle Eastern sweets that were the restaurant's specialties.

To her surprise, Ben did not answer immediately. Then as she waited, his hand suddenly closed over hers in one convulsive move and his words came out in a rush.

'Laura ... I don't know how to say this properly or anything, but I wish I could be more than just a friend to you. I mean ... look, I know I'm younger than you and still studying ... and I have to keep an eye on Mum this year and all that – but would you ... Laura, I really do like you a lot and I'd hate to lose touch with you. Could we phone each other sometimes? Maybe I could even come and visit you. It's just that ... Laura, I think I love you – I could take care of you and just be there for you whenever you needed me. This probably sounds silly to you, but ...'

Laura knew she had to cut in at that point. Again, her heart went out to him – but it was better she speak her mind and not let him hold onto any false hopes.

'Ben, you're a very special guy – but let's just stay as good friends. You've got enough on your plate this year, without trying to pursue a relationship with someone in another city – and I know I'll be very busy with my studies, as well as trying to settle in and find my way around a new university and everything. You're really kind and sweet – just don't let your parents take too much advantage of you this year, will you? You have to lead your own life, Ben – God has so much ahead for you in the music world, I believe. Hold onto your dreams – and I'll pray God will bring someone alongside you in the next little while who's just right for you.'

Ben took it well – Laura wondered if he were even slightly relieved. As she lay in bed that night trying to sleep, she found she could smile about it, yet she had no desire to make fun of him. Ben was not for her, she knew that – but on this her last night at The Menagerie, she could not deny she felt quite alone and bereft. What would the next year in Sydney hold for her? And what about after that? Would she find anyone to share her life with, as Anne and Cate and even Tracey had? She stopped herself then, however – she had been down this path before. Deliberately, she focussed her thoughts on God. Whatever happened, God would be beside her forever, her 'Dignity' and her 'Delight'. God would be her Vision, always watching over her, always showing her where to put her feet, perfectly aware of what lay ahead. And as she closed one chapter in her life and began another, she knew she had to rest in that knowledge and trust God completely, undaunted by the challenges ahead.

Jamie arrived at his mother's place late on Christmas Eve, having driven almost non-stop from Sydney.

'Sure good to be here,' he sighed, stretching out his long frame on Margaret's

laura

lounge, while she heated up a late dinner for him. 'The car behaved perfectly – looks like it was a good buy, even though it's quite a few years old.'

'I hope you remember I'm not a good traveller,' Laura quickly reminded him. 'Your car could end up the worse for wear after our trip, I warn you.'

They laughed about it then, but in truth, Laura was dreading the long hours of driving, despite having Jamie all to herself. Being unable to see just where the road ahead lay had always resulted in severe motion sickness for her. She put it from her mind, however, determined to enjoy the last few days with her mother. She was glad for her mother's sake that Jamie had been able to join them for Christmas – Ian had had to cancel out yet again, although he promised to be with her for New Year's Day, along with his fiancée Megan. Elisabeth and Paul too were unable to make the trip from North Queensland – not only did distance and lack of funds pose a problem for them, but Elisabeth was expecting their second child and quite unwell as a result. As for Greg – well, again they were unsure of his whereabouts.

'At least he phoned for my birthday this year,' Margaret told them. 'He wouldn't say where he was, but he wanted me to know he's okay. That's something, I guess.'

They spent an enjoyable few days together, relaxing and reminiscing about so many things. But when it came time for Laura and Jamie to leave, Margaret clung to them, reluctant to let them go.

'I don't know – the older I get, the more sentimental I become,' she wept. 'I enjoy my teaching and I have some good friends on the staff at school – but I do get lonely and a bit depressed at times, I have to admit. I miss your father, despite our difficulties. I never thought I'd say this, but sometimes I wish I had your faith, Laura. You must get lonely too, but you always seem to stay so positive and hopeful.'

Laura could not pass up this opportunity to say something in those last few moments with her mother.

'Why don't you give God a go again, Mum?' she whispered, as she held her close. 'Just take some time to read the Gospels for yourself and ask God to speak to you. And I'll pray for you too – I really will.'

She was crying too now, suddenly overwhelmed with how much she wanted her mother to find the same peace and security she had found in God. She held her close again for a moment, before turning to get into Jamie's car.

'I love you, Mum – thanks so much for everything.'

It was a very quiet, exhausted Laura who drove into Sydney with Jamie the following evening, after taking the inland route and staying overnight at Tamworth. Jamie had done all he could to make the trip bearable for his sister, only talking when she wanted him to and driving as gently as he could, with as many stops as Laura needed. As she emerged shakily from the car and walked with him to the front door, she breathed a sigh of relief.

'Welcome to our place!' Jamie announced, as he opened the door with a flourish. 'The others aren't around at present, so we have the whole place to ourselves. Of course, we can't compare with The Menagerie, but I hope you'll be happy here – I really do.'

Laura stood still, thanking God for this house and for Jamie's welcome – and almost immediately, she sensed a rightness about everything. She was safe. She was exactly where God wanted her. And God would ensure that good would come to her in this place.

Jamie took pains to familiarise Laura with the layout of the house as soon as possible the next morning and then to help her settle in and organise herself.

'Have to make sure you don't wreck the place while I'm at work tomorrow or mess things up too much,' he joked, but Laura was touched as much by the way he tried to cover up his concern for her welfare as by the concern itself. 'Chris should get back later today and I think Scotty's due in on Saturday. Hope you don't mind being the only girl around – at least for the moment. We might take on someone else – just not sure yet. Better to wait until the right person comes along, like you guys did at The Menagerie, from what I can make out.'

Chris did not take long to make his presence felt after he arrived back, with his friendly personality and infectious laugh, not to mention the music that constantly emanated from his room in some shape or form. Laura took to him immediately. In some ways, he reminded her of Richard, yet it soon became clear he was much more focussed and determined to do well at his studies than Richard had ever been.

Scott was another matter, she realised, as soon as she met him. He was more reserved and softly spoken, but even as they sat around on his first night back, getting to know each other, she could sense the depth in him and appreciated his considered approach to any questions put to him. Laura knew he and Jamie had met at a counselling course, although he was now studying at theological college.

'I'm pretty passionate about injustice and inequality in the world at large,' he warned her, 'so while I don't always say that much, I can get pretty stirred up at times. I just reckon Jesus would've cared about such things if he were here on earth today – I want to do what he'd do and make a difference, wherever I end up ministering.'

He was fascinated when Laura told him about The Menagerie and also her involvement with the marginalised people who were regulars at the Sunday

Laura

evening service.

'Jamie did say you're a committed Christian, but I didn't know *how* committed,' he told her. 'I wonder ... do you have connections already with a church down here? If you don't, you're more than welcome to try out the church we're involved with. My girlfriend and I go to the evening service – she's a youth leader and part of the worship team – and one of my mates from college is the youth minister. He's actually preaching tomorrow night – would you like to come?'

'I'd like that – thanks,' Laura responded. 'When my friend Carolyn visits here soon on her way back to Africa, she promised to put me in touch with people she knows at various churches, but in the meantime, I'm happy to explore other places.'

As soon as they arrived at the church the next evening, they were warmly welcomed. Laura could hear the babble of young people's voices all around her and feel the expectancy in the air.

'Good things have been happening here in the past few months,' Scott's girlfriend Wendy told her. 'I can't wait to see what God has for us tonight.'

Laura found it wonderfully refreshing to be part of the vibrant, meaningful worship that began a few moments later. She loved other aspects of the service too – the times of prayer, the careful reading of Scripture, even the upbeat announcements segment. But the moment that eclipsed all others for her was when the youth minister began to preach. From his very first words, she listened intently, absorbing the lessons he was emphasising from the Bible reading and ready for God's challenge to her personally. But gradually a further realisation dawned that banished any other thoughts from her mind. She had heard the speaker's voice before – she was sure of it. The urgent, persuasive tone was so familiar – yet she could not place it. Her mind raced through a range of possibilities, but none seemed to fit. It sounded like someone from her uni days. Was it a guest speaker she had perhaps heard at one of the Student Christian group's meetings? All through the sermon she puzzled over it, wishing she could turn to Wendy and ask who the minister was. She had not even been told his first name, she recollected – all she knew was that he was Scott's friend from theological college. But wait ... had she heard someone announce, just before the sermon, that it was time to hear from Steve? It *couldn't* be – the Steve she'd known at uni had been studying law. Yet it sounded awfully like him – she'd sat beside him on enough debating teams to be able to recognise his voice. But there was something different as well – she couldn't make it out.

He stopped speaking a few moments later and soon the music started for the final song. Afterwards, various young people came crowding around Scott and Wendy, so that Laura had no chance to ask anything. It was not until some time later, when they were moving out of their seats, that Laura was able to catch Scott's attention.

'Scott, this sounds crazy, but I'm sure I've heard the speaker's voice before – what's his name?'

'Oh, I'm sorry – I should've filled you in more,' he responded, immediately contrite. 'Actually, here he comes now – I'll introduce you. Or maybe you've met before? Hi, Steve, this is Laura, our new housemate from Brisbane. She's Jamie's sister – you remember meeting him at my place? Laura, this is Steve – Steve Sherwood. Actually ...'

His voice died away, however, as he realised there was nothing more he needed to explain to either of them. Steve had grasped Laura's hands in both of his, a dumbfounded look on his face.

'Laura ... I can't believe this! How amazing! How *are* you? What ... oh, there are so many questions I want to ask you.'

'Not as many as I want to ask *you*, I bet,' Laura responded. 'I was sure you'd be ensconced in the office of some well-known law firm by now, arguing your way to fame and changing the world in the process. Yet here you are a youth minister – I can't believe it either!'

'Well, there's quite a story behind all that,' Steve told her quietly then, still holding her hands. 'But look, can I catch up with you some time? I'd love to hear what you've been up to in the last couple of years. I knew you became a Christian eventually at uni, of course, which totally amazed me, considering how I tried to harangue you into believing when we first met in the Debating Club and how much you hated it. I wanted to talk to you about all that way back then, but somehow it never happened.'

'There's quite a story behind that too,' Laura admitted, smiling at the memories of their clashes at uni. 'But I think you've changed, Steve – I can hear it in your voice. I can't wait either to find out what you've been up to.'

Soon it was arranged that Steve would come around for dinner the following evening.

'Not sure what we'll eat – probably takeaway, since we're all still getting settled in,' Scott told them, 'but sounds like you both have some catching up to do, so you're more than welcome. Jamie and Chris won't mind – there are always people dropping in at our place.'

The following evening, everyone seemed to enjoy it when Steve and Laura regaled them with their own versions of how they had met at uni.

'You don't have to tell *me* how fiery and determined our Laura can be,' Jamie told Steve at one point. 'I grew up with her, remember? She's always been a fighter – but she's had to be at times. And I'm proud of her – aren't I, sis? You're

Laura

a champion in my books.'

'Jamie's always been my 'knight in shining armour',' Laura explained then. 'He's rescued me from more scrapes than I care to remember and helped me out with assignments and the like over the years. I owe him a lot. Lately though, I think I've made the mistake myself of pestering him a bit too much about God and the Bible and so on – which is ironic, given that's what I couldn't take from you, Steve, when we first met. Now he's stuck with me here in Sydney!'

'I think I can handle you, miss,' Jamie responded, giving her a gentle shove from where he sat next to her. 'Remember, I invited you.'

'Hopefully I've learnt to shut my mouth a bit more since then and respect the fact that people might not want to talk about such things,' Steve commented. 'I was a bit of an insensitive bully back then and pretty full of my own importance – but I'm still passionate about God, as I hope you heard last night, Laura. And I still enjoy a good debate – my favourite subjects at college are apologetics and evangelism, which kind of fits, I think.'

For a moment, Laura wondered what Jamie might be making of such open talk about God and whether he might be feeling a little threatened. Yet she sensed no great discomfort in him, as he leant back in his chair beside her – in fact, quite the opposite. Chris too seemed interested, from the occasional comments he dropped into the conversation. Just then, however, he stood up and began to clear away their plates.

'Sorry to break up the party, but I've got a band practice to go to. See you again, Steve, I hope. Maybe we can engage in one of your God debates then, eh?' he said, smiling.

'I have to push off too,' Jamie announced then. 'My shift at work starts in an hour or so. See you around, Steve – good to meet you.'

And Laura could tell he meant it.

Scott made coffee for himself, Laura and Steve and sat talking with them a little longer, before he too had to leave.

'Wendy's having dinner tonight with a couple of the youth leaders, but I promised I'd pick her up from that and go out for supper somewhere. Sounds like you guys have plenty to catch up about anyway – you don't need *me* to keep the conversation going. See you later, Laura – see you at college tomorrow, Steve.'

'I still can't get over all this,' Laura said again, after an initial brief silence. 'It's weird too to look back and realise that even after I became a Christian at uni, I didn't talk about it with you at all. I guess whenever I saw you at Debating Club, we had other things on our minds.'

'It was also my final year of law,' Steve reminded her. 'I had to push myself so much with my studies – plus, to be honest, I think I was still a bit wary of bringing up the subject of God with you, despite seeing you on occasions at the Christian group. After all, you'd warned me off in no uncertain terms. And you'd beaten me quite a few times by then in debating challenges and the like as well – I remember you were a mere fresher the first time that happened! So I think my ego had taken a bit of a battering at your hands – and I couldn't handle that back then.'

'I was probably too proud to eat my words on the subject of God with you anyway, if the truth were known,' Laura admitted. 'It's funny – I hated it when you kept pushing me to read the Bible and all that, but I always remembered what you said about not leaving it too late to make up my mind about God. I'm sure your words did have an effect, Steve – and you meant everything you said.'

'You might not believe it, Laura, but you taught me a lot about how to talk to people about God and how not to,' Steve said slowly. 'It was unfortunate I didn't realise that until it was too late to recover any ground I'd lost with you. Still, it seems God's given me an amazing opportunity to redeem myself now. Hopefully I've picked up a little more grace and sensitivity in the meantime.'

He told her then some of the things that had happened for him in the past two years – big things that Laura guessed were still a little hard to talk about.

'I actually failed my final year of law,' he said with difficulty, feeling the familiar stab of pain inside him even as he did. 'I couldn't believe it at first – but now, looking back, I reckon it was one of the best things that ever happened to me. I wouldn't say God wanted me to fail, but I know for sure God's certainly used this experience to pull me up short and make me take a good, hard look at myself. I needed my pride dealt with – and what happened probably saved me from making worse mistakes later on in my life, especially in ministry. My parents had a hard time dealing with the fact that I'd failed though – and even more of a hard time accepting I wanted to study theology instead and become a minister. They're both solicitors, you see – it runs in the family. They refused point blank to support me in any further studies and wanted little to do with me after that – so I decided to move interstate and make my own way through college. It's been hard going – I've had various jobs along the way, like Jamie, by the sound of it, but currently I can get by on my part-time youth minister's wage, with a few odd jobs occasionally, which is great. ... But how about you, Laura? I've talked enough about myself.'

Laura had not missed the pain in his voice as he shared his journey with her. She felt sorry for him – yet she could pick up already how much he had changed as a result.

'I knew there was something different about you when I heard you last night,' she said softly, before embarking on her own story. 'I couldn't place your voice at first, but then I remembered someone had called you Steve – and it dawned on

Laura

me just who you might be. Obviously I've only heard you preach this once, but I felt you spoke with greater depth and sincerity than I ever remembered from our debating years or our conversations together – and that's wonderful, Steve. Thanks for filling me in so honestly – I appreciate it.'

Steve sat in awestruck silence, as Laura shared her own journey of the previous three years with him – the way God had broken through in her life, the need for her to change universities, her experiences at The Menagerie and in teaching her 'little people', the importance of Carolyn's ongoing influence in her life.

'I remember you knew her, didn't you, Steve? She'll be visiting me soon – perhaps you can catch up with her too. She's taught me so much and prayed for me ever since high school. I'll never forget the day she found the words of the hymn 'Be Thou My Vision' for me.'

Laura went on to tell him what had happened. And even as she did, she knew with deep certainty that the fact she was sitting talking with him at that very moment was all part of God's watching over her, being her Vision, lighting the way ahead for her. She remembered how sad and bereft she had felt at uni when she had rebuffed Steve and refused to talk with him, except in connection with debating. He had wanted to get to know her better even then – he had told her she was a special girl, but she had thrown his words back in his face. Well, they had both changed so much – and the walls that divided them had crumbled significantly. Could it be that God was giving them both another chance at a deeper relationship?

That first night, they talked until the early hours. And when he finally left, Steve kissed her gently, holding her close for a moment.

'I feel so honoured to know you, Laura. I used to think you were one of the feistiest girls I'd ever come across and I'd still say that – but I mean it in the nicest possible way. You've had to battle all your life – I'm so thankful you have God with you now to give you the strength to keep fighting, apart from anything else. Laura … I remember telling you once I thought you were a special girl and that I'd like to get to know you better. That's still how I feel – only even more so now. Is there any chance you might have changed your mind and would like to get to know me more?'

Steve could feel Laura trembling as he held her.

'I'd like that, Steve,' she whispered eventually. 'I'd like that a lot.'

The following weeks passed in a blur of activity and excitement for Laura. All at once, she found herself having to adapt to living in a new home with different people, while at the same time, having to find her way around a new university and settle into her Master's program. On top of that, she and Steve tried to spend time together whenever they could. Their relationship blossomed quickly – it was as if God had prepared both of them ahead of time, giving them each a certainty about it all and a trust in each other from the very beginning.

Jamie watched it all unfold from the sidelines, as it were, vigilant as ever on his sister's behalf. Yet even he found himself strangely at peace over it all. He liked Steve, sensing an integrity about him that impressed him. And his heart lifted to see the happiness on Laura's face and feel her joy whenever Steve was with her. Had God really brought the two of them together in such an amazing way – or was it merely coincidence? Well, he wasn't quite there yet with all this faith stuff – but he had to admit that if God could do that for his Laura, then it certainly would go a long way towards overcoming his own doubts. Yet, if he were being honest, he realised those doubts had been diminishing for some time. Laura had definitely been part of it, with her insistence that he read the Bible and her belief that God cared about people enough to speak to them personally, even in dreams. The guys at The Menagerie had also impressed him greatly – and even Scott in his own household had taught him a lot. He'd wanted to hear Steve preach for quite a while now – perhaps he should go to church on Sunday and do just that.

When Carolyn arrived just before Easter, on her way back to her work in Africa, it seemed obvious to her that Laura and Steve were very much in love and that the relationship was serious. She had never seen Laura so happy. For a moment her own heart skipped a beat and she stifled a rather envious sigh. That was not what God had for her, as far as she knew – but oh, it would be so wonderful for Laura! Please God, let it happen! Watch over the pair of them – and please keep Laura from any hurt and pain in all this.

Neither she nor Jamie needed to worry, as it turned out. On the last night Carolyn was with them, the household put on a special celebration dinner in her honour.

'After all, we don't get to farewell a real live missionary every day of the week!' Chris joked.

Carolyn sensed there was something more in the air, however, than her own farewell. Yet even she did not guess the extent of what would occur that night. They had just finished devouring her favourite dessert – a delicious pavlova, piled high with strawberries and cream – when Laura cleared her throat and demanded their attention.

'Okay, all of you – it's been great to celebrate together tonight and farewell my dear friend Carolyn in fitting style. But there's actually something more to celebrate tonight as well ...'

And here she hesitated and turned to Steve.

'We'd like to announce our engagement,' he said simply.

With that he reached into his pocket, took out a small box and opened the lid.

Laura

With great care, he held Laura's left hand steady and slid a pretty diamond ring onto her finger.

Amidst the general chorus of congratulations that followed, Laura explored the shape of her new ring and twirled it around, loving the feel of it. She wished she could see it for herself – but Steve had described it several times over to her already and she was sure it must be as beautiful as she imagined it to be.

'We haven't decided when we'll get married yet – but we don't want to wait too long. Around September would be the most likely time,' Laura told them.

'I wish I could say I'll be here for the wedding,' Carolyn said a little shakily, overwhelmed with the emotion of the moment, 'but at least I was here for the engagement. What a privilege – I'm so delighted for you both! Remember, Laura, how God promised to be your Vision and watch over you? Well, all I can say is, how could anyone doubt God after seeing how you two have been brought together like this?'

At that point, Jamie knew he needed to speak up.

'Actually … I wasn't going to say anything tonight, since I suspected my little sister here might have something to announce – and it's really Carolyn's night as well. But I think both of you will be delighted to know that last Sunday night I finally handed over the reins of my life to God. It's been a long journey – and I know I've got so much more of it to travel yet, as well as lots of questions that need answering. But I've made my decision and I plan to stick to it. I want to live my life God's way. I don't want to stray off that path I told you I dreamt about once, Laura, and sink into some sort of mess of my own making, as I almost did not so long ago. And if you can do it, kiddo, then I can too, with God's help.'

His eyes were moist as he finished speaking and became even more moist as Laura threw her arms around him and held him close.

'Oh Jamie, oh Jamie – that's even better news than our engagement! Well … you know what I mean! I've prayed and prayed for this to happen – and now it has, I can't believe it.'

'That's so great!' Steve added, hugging him as well. 'Wow – what a night!'

All of them felt that, Laura could tell – even Chris, who was still a little sceptical when it came to faith in God. But she would pray – and God would move. She had no doubt about that.

'I couldn't have imagined a more perfect last night in Australia,' Carolyn said then. 'It's been such a privilege to be around to see you take this step, Jamie, and to be part of Laura's happiness tonight.'

Fittingly, Laura had the last word – and fittingly, it was a prayer from her heart.

'Well, God, you've brought me through so much – from a little kid with no eyes, pretty much against you and the whole world and always trying to prove herself, right to where I am tonight. Only you could do it. Only you could see the way ahead and smooth the path for me. *Heart of my own heart, whatever befall – still be my Vision, O Ruler of all.'*

'Amen!' Carolyn said softly.

the end

laura

Other books by Jo-Anne Berthelsen...

HELÉNA

Twenty-year-old Czech music student, Heléna, meets and marries Stefan only months before the outbreak of World War Two, while preparing for a career as a concert pianist.

In the ensuing years, Heléna's faith and courage are challenged to the utmost, as she faces great personal tragedy and danger, and suffers loss of family, friends, wealth and career.

ALL THE DAYS OF MY LIFE

Heléna arrives in Australia where she is told there is no chance of pursuing her music career in her new country. In the years that follow, Heléna experiences great joy but also deep trials.

Inspired by the real experiences of a post-war Czech immigrant to Australia.

For more information about Jo-Anne or to contact her, please visit
www.jo-anneberthelsen.com